REDEMPTION'S LIST

JEANA R LAWRENCE

Redemption's List is a work of fiction. Names, characters, business places, events, and incidents are a byproduct of the author's imagination. Any resemblance to people, living or dead, places, or true events is coincidental and nothing more.

Dedication

This story has lived in my imagination for twenty years. I came up with the character of Jack when I was eighteen and had big dreams of becoming an author. That dream wouldn't have been possible without the love and support of my sweet husband. If he wasn't doing dishes, he was folding clothes, while I was in another land speaking to people who didn't really exist. Thank you for your sacrifice, my love. You will always be the color in my world.

Trigger Warning

Dearest Readers,

I care about what you have been through, so I'm including this page to help you make an informed decision. This book contains details scenes and discussions about the death of a sibling, a night of drunken sex (he is drunk, not her), the death of a parent from breast cancer, and the threat of a miscarriage. If you choose to read no further, I 100% support your self-care. If not, feel free to jump right in.

-JRL

REDEMPTION'S LIST

Jeana R. Lawrence

Prologue

Rylen

I was slowly dying. My heart could stop at any moment. Was it possible to die from backstabbing? If what I'd heard was true, I'd be gone soon. I felt like such an idiot.

"So, that's what this is?" I said, my voice wavering. "The two of you decided to punish me? I can't be here!" I swung the door open.

"Rylen, wait!" My boyfriend, Andon, unbuckled and stood beside his blue pickup as I turned away. "Where are you going?"

"Wherever you're not," I called over my shoulder.

The car door closed, and his footsteps hurried after me.

"Rylen, stop! You're being irrational."

I spun around, stabbing my finger into his chest. "Don't you dare turn this around on me, you slimy, backstabbing son of a bitch! How could you betray me?"

"I'm sorry, okay? I never meant to hurt you."

"Sorry?" I spat. "What did you think would happen, Andon?"

I stormed into the gas station, his voice fading behind me. I wanted to cry, but the tears wouldn't come. I felt more embarrassed than anything. I'd been a stupid girl.

I pushed open the door, nearly barreling over a homeless man. He smelled of dirty socks and wood smoke, and leaves were tangled in his matted, graying beard.

"Watch where you're going, kid!" It was Old Man Reynolds. He frequented these places, always spending his money on tobacco and shooters.

"Sorry," I mumbled, stepping past him.

Distracted by my anger, I walked to the back of the store. I snatched a Coke from the cooler, wishing for something more potent to make me forget.

When I rounded the corner, a man in a black ski mask held the clerk at gunpoint.

"Take it easy, man," the clerk said, hands raised. "My wife's pregnant."

Ski mask threw a backpack on the counter. "Empty the register! Nobody move! Touch that phone, and I'll blow the place to hell."

His hands shook, the revolver quivering like a rattlesnake's tail. In a blink, gunshots rang out, ricocheting off the walls. Glass shattered, and someone screamed. The clerk ducked behind the counter, clutching his bloody shoulder.

I dove for the floor, covering my head, but something bit my knee. I eased onto my back. Blood oozed beneath me, staining my jeans. I tried to apply pressure but felt dizzy. I lay back, readying myself for death. This was what dying felt like, but I wasn't ready to die. All my regrets flashed before me.

I should have been kinder to Old Man Reynolds, told my mom I was sorry, laughed more, and eaten more pancakes for dinner.

I never should have fallen in love. If I survived, I'd never love again.

The fluorescent lights above glared at me. Sirens blared in the distance, or maybe they were trumpets played by angels. Angel Soft fabric softener lay by my head. How appropriate. I'd never given much thought to how I would die, but I didn't think it would be like this.

Chapter One

JACK

Jack,
I just want you to know I hate you. I will live the rest of my days
hating you. There's a special place in hell for people like you, and I
will never forgive you for what you did. Stay gone! You owe me that
much.
> *-Cora*

I lost track of how many times I had read the letter. At this point, I could recite it, feeling every ounce of hatred replay in my brain. Driving was good therapy; who knew oldies on the radio and speeding past monotonous farm country could soothe a hated soul?

My headlights needed cleaning. The dirtied yellow beams barely pierced the impending dark as the sun lowered on the horizon. I should've stopped at the last rest stop; I needed food. My dog, Bam

5

Bam, was starting to get that bulgy-eyed look which meant if we didn't stop soon, we'd have problems.

The last rest stop was ten miles back, but the more I stopped, the more tempted I was to stay gone forever, just as the letter demanded. I wasn't sure if I'd meant to drive this far, but the letter had been in my hands mere minutes before I chose to leave. The next thing I knew, I was at the Minnesota and North Dakota border.

Bam Bam nuzzled my arm and whined, breaking the silence. The Rottweiler hopped into the front seat, grumbling until I acknowledged him.

"What do you want, boy?" I said, staring into his chocolate-brown eyes. "You gettin' hungry?" It was 6:17. My old boy always knew when it was mealtime.

"Okay. Hold on," I said, gesturing to a rest stop sign. I pulled into a gas station, a large red neon sign flashing "Al's Place" above the pumps. I parked under a flickering streetlight.

When I opened the door, Bam Bam jumped over my arm, searching for a place to relieve himself. He settled on a small patch of grass as I donned my cowboy hat and approached the gas station door.

It was a warm fall night the sky painted a pale pink as the sun dipped below the horizon. When I returned with a coffee and brown bag carrying our makeshift dinner, Bam Bam sat by the tailgate, his slobbery tongue hanging loosely out the side of his mouth. I opened the dog food and poured water into a plastic container I'd found in the trash by the snack bar.

"Here you go, boy," I said, placing his bowl on the ground. He lapped noisily while I opened my sandwich. I chewed slowly, considering. Maybe it was better to say to hell with it all? Nobody would know I was this close to home if I turned around now.

As if Bam Bam knew what I was thinking, he pulled his head up and stared at me as if to say, "Don't you dare!"

"What?" I grumbled. "She hates me." The dog licked his chops, perhaps considering my argument.

I sighed. "I'm an idiot," I said, though the dog never looked up to protest otherwise. He was now licking up the last remnants of Canine Champion Beef while moving the bowl across the dirt floor with a somewhat maniacal determination.

I wrapped my sandwich and discarded it in the paper bag beside me. Why did everything have to be drenched in mustard? I opened my candy and popped a few M&Ms into my mouth, savoring the coating. Bam Bam, now abandoning his task, sat in the dirt, wagging his tail and giving me a longing look.
"Sorry, boy, no frisbee," I said, hopping off the tailgate.

We loaded into the Bronco, and I switched the music to something more upbeat. I needed to stay awake. I placed my coffee on the dash, in the center of a roll of duct tape I used as a makeshift cup holder.

I paused in the driveway, finding myself at a crossroads. If I turned right, I could stay away from home; if I turned left, I could face everything I ran from.

It was dusk now, the sun behind the horizon, the flickering streetlight in the parking lot now knowing its purpose. Then, watching the light in my rearview mirror fully illuminate the parking lot below, I made my choice.

I was going home.

ଓ୦ଓ ଓ୦ଓ ଓ୦ଓ

Davenport, North Dakota, was my home, but I'd grown up twenty miles outside of town on my grandparents' farm. I drove by

Sally's Diner which I used to frequent. Through the window, Ned and Pete sat at their usual spots; I made a note to stop by soon and order a stack of pancakes.

At half past ten, I pulled into the driveway. When I killed the engine and opened the door, I thought I smelled fresh paint. The small farmhouse was just as I remembered. Someone from town was likely helping with the upkeep since my disappearance.

A light was on in the kitchen, meaning she was awake, likely finishing her tea and engrossed in Harlequin. I stepped, careful not to let my boots tap her wooden porch. The dog padded beside me, and I hoped the singing crickets would drown out his paws. I approached the screen door, seeing the tidy kitchen empty. Then, a figure appeared from the shadows, and there was the unmistakable sound of a pump-action shotgun.

"Hold it! Right there!" Margaret Young's voice commanded.

"It's me!" I said, showing my hands. "Don't shoot."

"Jacky?" she said, lowering the shotgun.

"Hi, Gran."

"Jacky!" She threw her frail arms around me, the shotgun clunking against my back. I wasn't tall for a man; I barely hit 5'9, but Gran's tiny frame felt frail against me. She buried her face in my shirt, murmuring something about missing me. Then she pulled back and slugged me in the shoulder.

"Where have you been?" she demanded.

"Ow, I'm sorry," I said, rubbing where the blow struck.

"You should be! You don't call or write." She took my face in her hands. "Let me look at you, my boy." She examined my face, turning it from side to side, and I tried to remember when I last showered.

"You look like hell!"

"It was a long drive," I said defensively.

"A year, Jack."

"I know. I'm sorry."

She slugged my shoulder again. "You damn near put me in the grave! Don't ever do that again. Understand?"

I nodded.

"I suppose…you have your reasons."

"I do," I said.

"We'll talk about it later. I made chicken and dumplings for supper. Sit, I'll make you a plate." She gestured to the patio table and flipped a nearby switch, so a light pierced the darkness above it.

"I already ate, Gran," I said, but she eyed me over her glasses.

"Food or candy?"

I sheepishly stared at her. It was no secret that I had a deep and passionate love for candy. "That's what I thought. Sit."

As she disappeared into the kitchen, I collapsed into a chair, suddenly aware of how tired I was. Bam Bam crawled under the table and began to snore noisily. A few minutes later, Gran appeared with a plate and a glass of iced tea.

"Eat," she commanded. "Let me know if it's warm enough."

I sliced a bite of chicken, chewed, and nodded. "It's perfect." I became ravenous, and as much as I tried to pace myself, I finished the plate in under ten minutes.

"You haven't been taking care of yourself," she said. "You're too skinny."

"I eat three meals a day, Gran," I said, wiping my mouth. Although I had noticed I'd tightened my belt a notch.

"Tomorrow, I'll lend you some money. You can go buy what you need."

"I don't—"

"It's settled, Jacky. Now, I suppose you'll want your old room back, but you have to help me move out my sewing machine."

"My old room is now your sewing room?"

9

Her eyes narrowed. "You left, remember? I claimed the territory."

I lifted my hands in defeat. "Keep it. I'll stay above the barn."

"This is your home. You don't need to stay in the loft."

"I know, but I was hoping to be your employee."

"She was silent momentarily, considering my request, and then she nodded. "All right, but I'll have to pay you starting wages." She winked at me. "I can't do you any favors."

"You're the boss, boss."

She paused again, thoughtful, before she spoke. "Does…" she trailed off. "Does Cora know you're here?"

"No," I said, pushing my plate away. "I didn't tell anyone I was coming back."

"Are you planning on telling her?"

"I can't avoid her forever."

She eyed me over her glasses again, interlaced her fingers, and placed them on the tabletop.

"Jack, I know why you left, but you didn't need to. You belong here. But tell me, what made you come back?"

I was silent. Gran knew the whole story, the ugly truth I tried to insulate her from, yet she welcomed me home. But I couldn't show her the letter buried deep in my pocket that now blazed a hole right through me.

"I realized leaving was a mistake," I stated.

"It took you a year to see that?"

I nodded, and a sigh drew from her.

"Okay," she said, standing to gather my dirty plate. "I'll leave you with this. You're allowed to make mistakes, Jacky. It's a side effect of the human race, and you'll never meet another soul that hasn't made one."

"I know that."

"Then why did you leave?"

"It was better that way," I said with more conviction than I felt.

"For whom? All your absence did was drive a wedge further between you and Cora."

I hung my head a little lower, and she continued.

"You have to find a way to make it right. In the morning, I want you to call Scott."

I opened my mouth to protest, but she spoke again. "He'll know what to do. What happened is in the past; it's what you do now that counts, Jacky."

I nodded again as she bid me goodnight. Then she reached for the screen door, and the springs groaned when she opened it. It banged closed as she entered the kitchen and put my dirty plate into the sink. She ran water over it and dried her hands on a kitchen towel.

As she disappeared down the hallway, her last words swam around in my head. I had to find a way to fix it, or Cora would always hate me. If everyone else knew the truth, they'd hate me too, but Cora's hate hurt the worst. I'd expect nothing less from my sister.

Chapter Two

JACK

"Hey. It's Scott. Wait for it."

BEEP.

I redialed. No answer.

The following day, I awoke to find Gran making breakfast in the kitchen. I ate quickly while she told me everything that had happened in my absence. She told me about Cora and how her life circumstances had worsened over the last year.

Now, I sat in my Bronco outside Scott's trailer house, repeatedly calling his number. After his indifferent voicemail, I said, "Scott, it's Jack. I'm back in town. Call me, please?" I ended the call, and Bam Bam nuzzled my arm.

"What?" I asked him. "You think he's home?" I patted his head, glancing at the porch, hoping Scott would appear. He'd parked his rusty old Chevy in the driveway. He had to be there.

"Okay," I said. "Stay here." I opened the door, put on my hat to block the sun, and climbed the steps to knock on his door.

"Scott," I called, waiting. I knocked harder.

Then, as if of its own accord, the door creaked open. I peeked inside.

"Scott?" The TV was on, the screen gray and snowy. A wadded brown blanket lay atop a burnt orange sofa, his deputy's coat discarded next to it. His boots looked as if they'd been kicked off from across the room. The coffee table was littered with Sports Illustrated magazines, beer bottles, and chip bags.

The kitchen table was much the same. More beer. More chips. More magazines. The sink held a mountain of dirty dishes, and the stench of sour milk assaulted my senses. Down the hallway, barricaded by piles of laundry, was Scott's bedroom. The reverberation of snoring told me I was about to find him.

The bedroom was simple, with a double bed, a closet, and a nightstand filled with beer bottles. The bed, surprisingly made with a blue and green quilt, was empty, but on the floor next to it lay a snoring Scott Wylder—deputy of police in Davenport, North Dakota, and my cousin.

"Scott," I said, nudging his bare foot with my boot. Luckily, he wore tan uniform pants and a white tank. On another occasion, he'd been naked.

"Scott!" I tried again, but he didn't respond. Finally, I took the toe of my boot and kicked him in the side.

"What!" he bellowed. "Who the hell?" He rolled to his side, eyes wide open, staring at me.

"Hi, Scott," I said, sitting on the bed.

"Jack?" he asked, rubbing the sleep from his eyes.

I nodded.

"Well, looky what the cat dragged in," he grinned. "How the hell are you?"

"I'm good. It's good to see you."

"Yeah, you too. I didn't think I'd see you again." He pulled himself into a sitting position and wrapped the blanket around his neck like a cape.

"That was the plan," I admitted.

"Where the hell have you been?"

I shrugged. "Everywhere. Drove until I got tired, slept in my Bronco."

"Sounds nice. Does Gran know you're here?" He scratched at his whiskery jaw and ruffled his hair.

"Yeah, once I got her to put the shotgun down, she gave me a job at the farm."

"You?" he said, a voice mixed with laughter and disbelief.

"People change, Scott." I watched him grab a beer bottle off the nightstand and bring it to his mouth. It was empty, and he tossed it aside, grabbing another one. It took him three tries before he found one with something in it. "Or at least some of us do," I amended.

"Look, I get why you left. Just didn't think you'd be stupid enough to come back." He tipped back the bottle again and offered it to me.

I declined.

"I can't change the past. What matters is that I'm here now."

"You sound like a fortune cookie," he said, a slight smile on his lips. He padded his pockets for a cigarette, pulled one out, and put it in his mouth. He eyed me as he flicked the lighter until the end burned orange.

"Does Cora know you're home?" he asked, exhaling his plume.

My eyes narrowed. "No, and don't tell her either."

"I value my head in its current position," he said slyly. "She's all yours, but she's gonna murder you."

"That's what I got you for, right? Deputy of police."

14

His mouth widened into a smug smile. "You gotta fight your own battles, Jack. Be nice, though. Cora's been through hell."

"Yeah, Gran filled me in. If I'd known what happened, I'd have come home sooner."

"She'd have just killed you sooner."

"That's why I'm here. I need your help. I need to fix it."

"Jackson Wylder is asking me for help? Maybe people do change."

"Save the smug douchebaggery, okay? I need a list of names."

"I ain't tellin' you shit. I could lose my job," he retorted, the cigarette bouncing on his lips.

"I just need a list of everyone who was affected by that night."

He was quiet, amusement in his eyes. "Ned, Pete, Sally—"

"I know all that," I interjected. "I need names I don't know."

"And what are you going to do? Invite them to spank you?"

My lips tightened, but I decided not to take the bait. "I'll find some way to make it right, Scott."

He tipped back his beer, thought for a moment, and then got to his feet, swaying slightly.

"Stop by the station. I'll see what I can do. Now leave; I have to go to work."

He set the beer on the nightstand and removed his shirt, his flabby belly hanging over his pants. He scratched at his skin and belched, then began to remove his pants.

"As much as I'm enjoying your strip tease, I was hoping you had something for me now."

"Nope." He dropped his pants, and I was grateful he wore boxers. "I'll see you at the station." He strode to the bathroom, and a few seconds later, the shower turned on.

Defeated, I flung myself across the bed and bolted to my feet as thoughts of Scott's active sex life made my stomach churn.

The bathroom door creaked open, and I shifted my gaze to see Scott eyeing me. A towel hung low on his hips. He rested one arm on the door frame above his head, and steam began to roll into the hallway.

"I might know of one person."

Chapter Three

Rylen

"Miss Clark," said the exasperated voice of Dr. Sullivan. "You do realize that not speaking during our sessions does nothing to help you."

It was incredible what staring out a window could do to a therapist's nerves. She must've thought I couldn't sense her frustration because I wasn't facing her. She tapped her pen, shifted her weight in her green leather-backed chair, crossed and uncrossed her legs, and sighed like it might snap me out of my windowpane-induced euphoria.

"Miss Clark," she said again. "If you don't participate in sessions, I can't help you."

I rested my hands on the arms of my wheelchair. My last knee surgery had landed me in a chair for part of my recovery.

"You're getting paid regardless, right?" I said, not taking my eyes off the window.

She sighed. "Yes, but…"

"So, what difference does it make then?" I met her eyes from across the room. There was a slight smile on her lips.

"Well, for one, there would be a big difference in your well-being if you talked to me."

I shook my head. "Not a chance."

I was dragged to this office because my mother, Diana Clark, playing the role of the concerned parent, decided to give a damn about my well-being. It'd been a year since the robbery, but she thought seeing a shrink and talking about things would benefit me. That was what therapy was all about, right? How childhood affects your day-to-day existence, and nobody gets out unscathed? No thanks, my windowpane was better company.

"At least tell me why?" Dr. Sullivan asked. "Why won't you talk to me?"

I eyed her suspiciously.

"You're not going to offend me. I've been in this line of work long enough, I've likely heard it before. Say exactly what you want."

I crossed my arms. "Talking is a waste of time. It changes nothing. So, what the hell's the point?"

For the first time that afternoon, I looked at her long enough to notice her attire. She wore a navy-blue pinstriped suit and a white blouse; her brown hair was tied back in a tight bun.

She looked up from her notepad and removed the small, black-framed glasses from the middle of her nose. "Talking isn't meant to change things, Miss Clark. It's meant to give you perspective and perhaps tools to help you heal from your loss. Talking is a tool."

"Please, don't call me Miss Clark. And unless you got a time machine to transport me back before everything happened…"

"I'm afraid not, Rylen," she said apologetically, "But I do happen to be pretty good at helping people…if they choose to speak to me."

I shook my head again. No way.

"You know trauma victims have to tell their story twenty-seven times before they begin to heal?" the doctor offered.

"That seems monotonous."

"Not at all. Talking has a way of creating a bond between people. People need to know they're not alone and safe to express their feelings without judgment."

"And I can talk about anything? You won't report back to my mother?"

"Unless you're plotting to inflict harm upon yourself or others, I am legally obligated to keep everything we discuss strictly confidential." She put her glasses back on her nose. "We went over that in the first session."

I was quiet. So, legally, she couldn't tell another soul, but would unpacking everything that happened over the last year be helpful? Or would it leave me feeling hollow and empty? I already had enough baggage to carry around without unpacking it all.

"What do you have to lose?" Dr. Sullivan asked as if she could sense my crumbling resolve.

If I were honest, a suffocating pressure had begun growing inside my chest. I felt like I would burst if I didn't let it out. Tears pooled under my eyelashes, and I quickly wiped at them, hoping she hadn't noticed, but she smiled weakly. She didn't miss a thing.

"I don't believe you can help me," I said.

Dr. Sullivan smiled again. "Well, nobody believed Noah when he built the ark either."

I glanced back out my window, hoping for some kind of release. It started to rain, and droplets began dotting the glass. A large drop started at the top and made a swerving trail to the bottom, picking up smaller ones in its wake.

Noah must've looked like a fool.

ౖౖ౦ⴲౖ౦ ౖ౦ⴲౖ౦ ౖ౦ⴲౖ౦

Our meeting ended, and I wheeled down the hallway. I pushed the elevator button and rubbed my sore knee. The bullet had shattered my patella. Three surgeries later, it was still unclear if I'd ever be able to walk without a limp. I was trying to push the thoughts away when my phone pinged with a text.

Sent Tuesday 4:32 PM
Mom: Sorry, hon. Got caught up at the office. I can't pick you up after therapy. Maybe call Andon? Love ya. P.S. Don't forget to take my pictures!

Typical. Diana Clark had two great loves, herself and her work, in that order, and anything that happened to be in the way became collateral.

I replied to her message.

Sent 4:33 PM
Rylen: I told you, I'm not speaking to Andon. Can't you get me and go back to work?

Sent 4:33 PM

Mom: Nope. Call Andon.

Resistance was pointless. I rolled my eyes and pocketed my phone. When I reached the lobby, large puddles had made the parking lot an obstacle course. A bus stop was on the other side, if I could only get there. I wheeled myself out the door, down the ramp, and into the parking lot as quickly as possible. I was halfway there when the bus pulled up.

I wheeled around a large, oceanic puddle when the chair abruptly stopped. My purse strap had tangled itself in the spokes of my wheel and wrapped around the axle. I pulled on the leather strap, but it didn't budge. I readjusted myself and sat on the edge of my seat, preparing to give another hard yank, when a black Bronco passed me. A tidal wave of brown water whooshed above my head. Simultaneously, the purse strap gave way, and the sudden recoil sent me backward, tipping me over the side of my chair. I landed in the middle of the swampy puddle like a drenched duckling.

The black Bronco stopped, the driver's door opened, and a man in a black cowboy hat rushed to my side.

You're supposed to count to ten before unleashing your temper.

I got to three.

I sat up, ready to deliver the best ass-chewing speech of the century, but then I got a good look at him. He wore blue jeans and a plaid shirt. He rested his hands on his hips, and a large round belt buckle sat between his shirt and jeans. His black Carhartt jacket hung open, and he'd submerged his feet in the puddle's depths.

He stood there watching me, and under any other circumstances, I might've admitted he was attractive. He was shorter than I preferred, but he was broad-shouldered with a spackling of dark stubble on his jaw. But the mirth in his eyes that said he found

21

my puddle excursion amusing could only mean he was a complete and utter asshole.

"You look like you need a hand," he said

"I need legs, you idiot!" I snapped, but he only smirked again.

He reached for my chair and set it upright, then pulled a red handkerchief from his back pocket and wiped off the seat.

"Please, just go, okay? You've done enough," I said, scooting myself up.

"I'm not leaving you like this," he countered.

Up ahead, I could see the bus close its doors and pull away from the curb.

"Great," I grumbled, and he looked over his shoulder to see the bus turn and disappear around the corner.

"Was that your ride?" he asked.

"No," I deadpanned, "I'm always upset when the bus leaves."

I tried to pull myself into my chair, but from the ground, and with only the use of one of my legs, I had no leverage.

He knelt beside me, one knee drowning in muddy waters.

"Put your arms around my neck?" he said, his face too close to mine.

"If you're asking me to strangle you, I'd be more than happy to."

He smirked again, and his blue eyes showed a bit of amusement. "Duly noted, but no. I was going to carry you to my truck."

"Oh, hell no!" I said, my eyes wide.

"You wanna stay here?"

"I can manage, okay?" I said, trying to pull myself up again and failing.

"Clearly."

I looked at him, my eyes narrowing. If looks could kill, he would've been holding his head.

"I don't even know you. You could drive me into the woods and sacrifice me."

"How do I know you won't sacrifice me?" he asked pointedly.

His answer surprised me, forcing me to bite back a smile.

"Stranger danger goes both ways, sweetheart," he finished.

"Don't call me sweetheart. My name is Rylen," I said, exasperated.

"Look, Rylen, I'm all for being cautious, but you've got two choices here. Either quit being a stubborn ass and let me give you a ride or die of hypothermia."

I opened my mouth to protest, but nothing came out. All sacrifices aside, riding in trucks with handsome strangers was preferable to dying alone in the ugly mud. I sighed, embracing defeat. Securing my bag, I wrapped my arms around his neck, locking my hands together.

I wasn't a big person, but I was suddenly aware of every greasy burger I'd ever eaten. I was barely 5'4 "and just shy of one hundred twenty pounds. It didn't matter because he placed one arm under my legs and lifted me easily. The water sloshing under his steps, he carried me the way a husband carries his bride into their new life. I palmed his shoulders through his jacket, and he was impressively rock solid.

I opened the passenger door for him, and he sat me in the front seat. At that moment, I realized my shirt was soaked, likely transparent, and right at his eye level. It was a blessing and a curse, but all the women in the Clark family were big-busted. I was no exception, and I pulled my jacket closed, hoping the noticeable parts of me weren't so...noticeable.

I warmed my frozen hands against the blazing heater while he loaded my chair into the tailgate. The interior of the Bronco was blue, with leather bucket seats and a bench in the back. The radio played a local soft rock station, and an iPod sat on the dash next to a roll of duct tape holding a coffee cup.

A deep rumble came from the backseat, and I looked to see a snarling Rottweiler baring his teeth and growling at me.

The driver's door opened.

"Bam Bam, no!"

The dog lay his head between his front paws but kept his eyes glued to me.

"Sorry, he's a bit territorial," he said, climbing in. "He's friendly once he gets to know you. I'm sure you two have much in common," he added.

I darted my eyes up from my bag. "What's that supposed to mean?"

He grinned mischievously. "Nothing," he said unconvincingly. "I'm Jack, by the way."

"Rylen," I repeated.

"Where to, Rylen?" he asked, closing his door.

"Do you know where Clairvoyance Estates is?" I asked, listing off the road to my mother's house.

"Is it over there?" he asked, gesturing with a hitchhiker's thumb to the left.

"Just go that way," I said, pointing right. "I'll tell you when to turn."

He nodded and shifted the Bronco into gear.

Chapter Four

JACK

Okay, I admit. I drove through that giant puddle on purpose. I hadn't meant to make her fall out of her chair. That part was an accident. As we left the parking lot, I selected a playlist of various artists on my iPod. An upbeat country song filled the truck cab, and she instantly made a face implying that I should change the song or die.

"Okay," I said, offering her the iPod. "You choose."

She hesitated, confused, like I'd asked her to paw through my underwear drawer. Then, she took the iPod from my fingers and scrolled through my playlists.

"You have good taste," she said. "Except the country."

"My Pop liked it. It makes me nostalgic."

"It makes me barf," she said, making her choice.

I laughed and tipped an open package of M&M's into my mouth and chomped on the candy.

"Want some?" I asked, extending the package.

"No, thanks."

"You don't like them?"

"I don't want them."

"How could you not want them?" I asked in mock horror.

"What is this, *Green Eggs and Ham?* I said no, okay?"

I shrugged and tipped back another mouthful, purposefully chomping like a cow on cud. It seemed to annoy her. I chomped louder.

"Why do you use an iPod?" she asked, turning it around in her fingers. "Don't most people use their phones?"

"I don't have an iPhone."

"Oh, okay," she said, her brows arching with surprise. She placed the iPod on the dashboard.

"So, are you from here?" I asked as I made the turn.

"Yep," she said curtly.

I popped a few more M&Ms into my mouth to hide my smirk. Her short, one-word answers conveyed more than complete sentences—no small talk. I didn't need her to like me. I was a stranger, doing her a favor, but she could at least be cordial.

Her phone buzzed, and she pulled the latest iPhone out of her pocket. A picture of a guy wearing a white baseball cap backward filled the screen. He had perfectly white teeth and a cut-squared jawline. I'd guess most of the female species would have referred to him as "hot."

I thought he looked like a tool.

She scoffed, ignored the call, and returned the phone to her pocket.

"I always felt like phones were electronic leashes," I said. "I'd rather not be found."

"You don't have one?"

"No, I have a phone," I said, pulling my flip phone out of my pocket and tossing it to her. She caught it easily and turned it around in her hands, scrutinizing it. "They have their practical purposes," I added.

"Oh," she said, underwhelmed. "I think I had one like this when I was fourteen."

I chuckled. "Don't judge."

"I'm not." She tossed the phone back.

"They're expensive, and I don't like owing people things. Besides, an iPhone is just a status symbol anyway."

She lifted a brow. "Now, who's judging?"

I shrugged. "I'm not saying everyone's that way."

"That's good," she deadpanned. "Otherwise, I might assume you're judging me."

I smirked. "I'm not."

Her phone rang again, and she dug into her pocket. It was the pretty boy again, and she swore as she hit the ignore button.

"Somebody *really* wants to find you," I said.

"You have no idea."

"You know, we're looking for a new sacrifice for the next full moon. You could volunteer him."

She turned to look at me, her face breaking into a delighted grin that made her brown eyes twinkle.

"I knew it," she said, chuckling.

I beamed at her, but as if she'd caught herself doing something she'd not meant to do, the smile faded, and she turned to the window.

An elderly couple in a red Mustang convertible with the top down rolled up to the light next to us. His white mustache was well-groomed, and he wore a baseball cap and black sunglasses. The woman next to him also wore sunglasses, and a white visor framed her permed curls. Both of them wore a white sweater tied around their necks. A set of golf clubs sat in the back seat.

"So, what's their story?" I asked, gesturing to the couple next to us.

She looked out her window and then at me.

"I don't know them," she said, confused.

"So, make it up."

She looked at me, dumbfounded.

"You've never looked at two people and wondered what their story was? What were their names, or where are they going?" I asked.

"Can't say that I have."

"Okay, watch. Here to our right, we have...Paul and Donna Jefferson. Paul is retired military; see that perfect mustache? And Donna taught school for forty years."

She chuckled, so I continued.

"They're currently in town because Paul's daughter from his first marriage is getting married this weekend at the country club, and they're here to talk her out of it."

"Interesting," she said thoughtfully. "Paul must've found out her fiancé owned an iPhone. There's no way in hell he'll let her marry someone with such pretentious snobbery."

I turned to meet her eyes. She gave me a knowing look, then grinned like she'd bluffed at poker and won the jackpot. I held eye contact until it was uncomfortable, but I couldn't take my eyes off her.

"Why are you staring at me?" she asked.

"You were staring first."

"Was not."

"I can't figure you out."

"Don't try."

A horn blared, breaking the spell, and I hit the gas. We were about to pass Sally's Diner when she spoke again.

"Can you pull over for a minute?" she asked. "I need a picture."

I pulled into the parking lot as she dug a black camera out of her bag.

"Oh no," she groaned, punching the power button. "Don't tell me."

"What's wrong?"

She sighed. "It won't turn on. The bag is soaked."

"Oh, sorry, that was probably my fault."

"It was *definitely* your fault! You soaked me," she grumbled, shoving the camera back in her bag. She snapped a photo of the front of the diner with her phone and stashed it in her pocket.

"I'm really sorry. I owe you one," I said.

"It's fine." She said in a voice that clearly meant the opposite. "Don't worry about it."

"I told you. I don't like owing people things."

"And I told *you*, it's fine. Now drive."

When we pulled into the Clairvoyance Estates subdivision, I knew instantly that Rylen came from wealth. The largest house on the block belonged to her. It was painted blue with white trim and consisted of three stories, a three-car garage, and a white wrap-around porch. A Jeep was parked next to the house under a black vehicle canopy. Another building, separate from the house yet painted the same color, sat behind it.

"Nice place," I observed.

"It's my mom's house. I stay over there," she said, pointing to the smaller building on the right. "It's a studio my dad built. I live above it, or I did until this happened," she said, gesturing to her knee. "For now, I sleep on the couch because my mom converted my bedroom into a home gym."

29

I smiled. I could relate to feelings of replacement. "Yeah, mine got turned into a sewing room. So, what happened to your knee?"

She blew out her breath and adjusted her weight in the seat. "I had surgery."

"Surgery put you in a chair?"

"No, I sprained my ankle trying to climb the stairs, okay. It's temporary."

"Why did you have surgery?" I asked, but I already knew.

"It's a long story."

I shrugged. "I got time."

"I don't."

Before I could answer, she opened her door and turned to slide out.

I killed the engine and hurried around to help her. There wasn't a wheelchair ramp, so I put her chair on the porch. When I went back to collect her, she wrapped her arms around my neck, and I lifted her out of the seat and carried her across the paved driveway, up the four stairs.

"Thank you," she said, settling into her chair. "For everything."

"Anytime."

She lifted a hand to shield the shining sun. "She looked more like a Susan."

"What?" I asked.

"The woman in the red car. You said her name was Donna. She definitely looked more like Susan."

I grinned and nodded my head, a small laugh escaping me. "Now you're getting the hang of it."

I couldn't take my eyes off her again. She had perfect cheekbones, round brown eyes, and dark curly hair that smelled like cherry vanilla. Immediately, I knew Rylen possessed the most unique kind of stop-you-dead-in-your-tracks beautiful I'd ever seen.

She stared back, confusion over her eyebrows.

"You're staring again," she said, not breaking eye contact.

"Definitely."

"Still tryin' to figure me out?"

I smiled. "I like a challenge."

I tipped my hat and bid her farewell but felt her eyes on my back as I walked to my Bronco.

"Jack," she called; I turned to face her. "I left my purse in your truck."

I retrieved her bag and brought it to her.

"Thanks," she murmured, balancing it on her lap. "Let me pay you."

She began to unzip the top, but I shook my head. "Wouldn't dream of it, sweetheart."

She didn't protest and watched me climb into my truck and drive away.

I was halfway down her road when my eyes traveled to the seat next to me. Sitting with the strap coiled beneath it was her camera. I'd taken it out of her bag. I didn't condone stealing, but she never would've given it to me had I asked. It was my fault it got ruined, so I would fix it for her and return it.

I'd fix everything.

Chapter Five

Rylen

Hey kiddo,
I'm still in LA. Life is busy. Working sunup to
sundown. Let me know what the doctor says about
your knee. Take it easy. Love ya lots.
-Dad

The following day, I lay on my back in my mom's study, staring at my phone screen. I was nineteen, but my dad still started his emails to me with "Hey, kiddo." We'd email roughly once a week, keeping the conversation light, and I'd fill him in on my healing process. Maybe being called 'kiddo' by a loving father was something you never outgrew.

"Rylen, are you up?" My mother called from the hallway. "I need to speak with you before I leave." I rolled my eyes. She didn't wait for me to answer her question before shouting the next order of business.

"I'm in the study," I said to the open door. I sat up on the couch and leaned against the armrest. If there had been one massive oversight in creating this monstrosity of a house, it was that it didn't have a bedroom on the main floor.

Behind me sat an enormous mahogany desk with a high-back leather chair. Oak bookshelves filled with novels, manuals, and encyclopedias sat behind the desk. In front of me, a gas fireplace was set into the wall on the other side of a glass-top coffee table. My mom had been pretty cool about letting me invade her office, opting to take her laptop elsewhere, so I had to give her some credit. But the second I could walk unassisted, I was moving back into the space above the studio, where an encounter with Diana Clark would be strictly voluntary.

"Oh, there you are, darling," my mother said from the doorway like she had solved a grand mystery. She wore a gray suit, a pink collared blouse, and diamond-studded earrings. It was barely eight a.m., but her flawless makeup already accentuated her high cheekbones and full lips. She'd spun her chestnut hair into a delicate French twist, a few strands loosely framing her face. Diana Clark turned heads wherever she went.

She walked to the desk, her high heels clicking in her wake.

"What time is your doctor's appointment today?" she asked, pulling open the desk drawer and rummaging through it.

"It's at two," I answered.

"You're seeing Doctor…"

"Dr. Allen, Mom."

"Right, which one is he?" she asked, pulling items from the drawer.

"She was the surgeon who operated on my knee…again."

"Oh yes, right," she said, stacking items from the drawer on the desk.

"Mom, I was thinking that I should move into the studio as soon as I can put weight on my ankle."

The drawer slammed shut.

"Let's not worry about that right now," she said, meeting my eyes.

"I'm in your space, and it's not like Michael is coming back to claim it and..."

"Rylen!" she snapped. "Not now."

I sighed. I should've known that mentioning my late brother's name would set her off.

"What time is your appointment over?" she asked, pulling out another drawer.

"I don't know. It's just a follow-up."

"Alright," she said, sighing. "I'll take a late lunch and drop you off, but you'll need to call Andon for a ride home."

Frustration sparked inside of me. "I'm not speaking to Andon, Mom," I said. "We broke up a year ago."

"You two haven't patched things up yet?" she asked, lifting a stack of books and searching the table beneath.

"He slept with Ali, Mom. We're done."

"People make mistakes, Rylen. You have a lot of history just to throw it away."

I hated the way she brushed off his infidelity as if he'd only accidentally stomped on my heart and, therefore, was acquitted of any consequences.

"What are you looking for?" I asked, changing the subject.

"A phone number," she said, dropping to her knees. "I wrote it on a pink sticky note and can't find it anywhere."

My mother would never remember anything if it weren't for sticky notes and calendar chimes from her electronic planner. She'd

34

even write me sticky notes in the morning and put them on the coffee pot.

"Do you mean that sticky note?" I asked, pointing to the neon pink square attached to the file cabinet. The name ADAM was written in all capital letters in bold Sharpie like she'd traced the word repeatedly, etching him into perfect existence.

Her head popped above the desk's surface, like she was coming up for air, and the chair swiveled beside her. She followed my gaze to the file cabinet and stood.

"Yes! Thank you, dear," she said, plucking the paper from the face of the drawer.

"Who's Adam?" I asked, though I already had a pretty good idea why ADAM was significant. There was a reason my father had extended his business trip, and I was reasonably sure it had nothing to do with work. My parents' long, yet rocky, marriage was volatile at best. And it didn't help that my father, Gregory Clark, constantly made excuses for not returning home, and my mother had mystery men written on sticky notes.

"No one, honey." She folded the pink paper and stuck it in her pocket. "So, how's therapy going?"

"Fine," I said with a shrug.

"That's good. Any progress? We need to get your problem nipped in the bud."

"Not really." Did she have any idea how patronizing she sounded? If it were as easy as nipping it in the bud, it wouldn't be a problem.

"Hmm, well, Sarah Sullivan came very highly recommended. I'd better be getting what I paid for."

My mom, insisting I see the most expensive therapist in Davenport, made my weekly appointments and charged the expenses to her credit card. And it was all in the name of aiding my recovery.

"Did Andon give you a ride home?" she asked.

Yet her efforts seemed futile because it was another thing to set herself aside and give a damn about whether or not I got home.

"No, I figured something else out."

I wasn't going to mention Jack, and the one good thing about having a mother who was too wrapped up in herself to care was that she wouldn't press me for details.

"Listen, I've been meaning to mention the fundraiser to you. I've been thinking about ways you could contribute and..."

"Mom," I interrupted. "I am contributing. I'm taking pictures, remember?"

"I know, but you should be there, Rylen. You're Michael's sister. How will it look if my own daughter doesn't attend?"

"I can't even walk. Can't you please find someone else?"

"That's what I wanted to mention to you. I've got the perfect thing, and you don't have to walk. We'll discuss this tonight. Keep the pictures coming. Be ready when I pick you up at one thirty."

She walked to me, leaned in, and kissed my forehead before she was out the door.

I let out a heavy sigh and flopped on the couch.

§oc∾og §oc∾og §oc∾og

I must've fallen asleep because I woke up to my phone vibrating with an incoming text. I opened the screen.

Sent Wednesday 10:30 AM
Andon: Hey, your mom asked me to pick up some chairs for the fundraiser. I'm bringing them over.

She was unbelievable! I sat up, texting him my reply.

Sent 10:30 AM

Rylen: Now's not a good time. Come back around 2?

I smirked—when I would conveniently not be home.

Sent 10:31 AM

Andon: Too late. Almost there. :)

The doorbell rang, and my eyes widened. How did he get here so fast? I'd managed to avoid Andon for the better part of a year, but now I had to at least speak to him.

I scooted off the couch, maneuvered into my chair, and wheeled to the entryway.

When I opened the door, the man standing outside wasn't Andon.

It was that annoying cowboy.

"Hey, Rylen," Jack said, casually tipping his hat.

He looked much the same as yesterday: the same boots, jacket, and hat, dirty blue jeans, shiny belt buckle, and annoying toothy smile.

"Uh, hi?" I said, doing nothing to conceal my surprise. "What are you doing here?"

"Sorry for dropping in, but I believe this is yours."

He pulled my camera from behind his back. I could've sworn it was in my bag. I'd meant to go through all the photos I had taken yesterday and organize them, but by the time I got home, I was too tired to move. Not to mention being frustrated with my mom which extinguished any motivation I may have otherwise mustered.

"Oh," I said, taking it from his outstretched hand. "I didn't realize I'd left it. Thanks."

"You didn't leave it. I took it," he said, as if admitting thievery was normal behavior.

My eyes narrowed. "You mean you *stole* it?"

No, I borrowed it. Thieves don't return things," he added. "I took it apart and cleaned it. It works now."

I picked it up and hit the power button. Sure enough, it chirped to life.

"Okay," I said, wheeling over the threshold so I faced him on the porch. "What is this?"

He shrugged. "What's what?"

"This." I pointed between the two of us. "What's your angle? You wouldn't let me pay you, so now I have two things I'm indebted to you for? You gonna show up one day and call in a favor for little Vinny?"

"No," he said, his voice laced with laughter. "I told you, I don't like owing people things. Besides, I only know a big Vinny."

There it was again—that same perfectly annoying toothy grin. I wanted to smack it off his face – his rather handsome face. Stop it, Rylen!

"Look, I broke your camera, so I fixed it. There's no repayment needed. You're a good photographer, by the way."

"You looked at my pictures?" I asked, feeling as if he'd snooped through my nightstand drawers.

"I had to." He dug into his jacket pocket and pulled out a thumb drive, but an M&M wrapper was stuck between his fingers. He plucked the wrapper out and crumpled it in his fist.

"Here." He held it out to me. "I copied everything onto this."

I took the thumb drive. "Thanks, I guess."

"You shouldn't act so annoyed. It's not like I read your diary."

"You would've if I'd left it," I said.

He smirked. "Maybe. I'd be interested in your secrets."

Heat flooded my cheeks and traveled down my neck. Goosebumps prickled on my skin, and I crossed my arms again to get a hold of myself. He was annoying, and he wasn't *that* good-looking, yet he could noticeably fluster me.

"Seriously, your pictures are great. I never knew an empty street could be so interesting. You really bring the town to life. Are you planning on becoming a professional photographer?" he asked.

I shrugged, looking at my feet. "I don't know. It's just a hobby. Maybe one day."

"*Why* are you taking pictures of things around town anyway?"

"It's for my mom," I said. "She asked me to do her a favor."

"Is she a real estate agent or something?"

I eyed him suspiciously. Why was he so interested?

"No, she's a lawyer."

"Oh," he said uneasily. "Got it. It's none of my business."

"No, it's nothing legal. She's in charge of the Davenport Fall Fundraiser in a couple of months. It's this big charity thing, and yeah…I'm taking photos for the auction. Anyways…"

I turned my chair to wheel through the door, hoping he would take the hint and get off my porch, but he still stood there when I swiveled around. I didn't know how much more obvious I could be.

"Thanks for fixing my camera," I said, reaching out to close the door when he spoke again.

"Do you have more photos you need to take?"

I stopped mid-close. "Yes, why?"

"I admit I shouldn't have *borrowed* it without asking, so let me give you a ride. I might know of a few places you could add to your portfolio. I'll take you there if you want. Then you never have to see me again."

"Don't you have something better to do?" I asked.

He smiled again, and it touched the corners of his blue eyes. Something ignited in my stomach, and I envisioned stomping on fluttering butterflies. I wouldn't admit that he had a perfect smile.

"Don't you?"

It was late morning on a Wednesday. Didn't this guy have a job? Yet, his offer was compelling. Especially if I'd never have to see him again, I could get the photos I needed, and I would've done my part. I wouldn't have to bother my mother or swallow my pride and ask Andon to pick me up.

Oh crap! Andon! He'd be here any minute, and the only thing worse than seeing Andon would be seeing Andon while Jack was standing on my porch.

"Well," Jack said, turning to leave. "The offer's open *if* you change your mind."

He headed down the stairs. Going with Jack would provide the escape I needed. I could tell Andon to leave the chairs on the porch, and I wouldn't have to see him. But could I tolerate Jack's company for an afternoon?

"Okay," I said a bit too eagerly.

He turned around, seeming surprised at my agreement.

"Let me get my jacket."

§౦౦౦§ §౦౦౦§ §౦౦౦§

Jack lifted me into his truck and loaded my chair into the back. His dog growled at me, and I was beginning to expect nothing less from his grumpy, temperamental canine.

Jack scolded him, and Bam Bam lumbered into the backseat, keeping his eyes on me like I was a juicy tenderloin suspended in the air.

"Here," Jack said, handing me his iPod. "You choose."

A small smile crept to my lips. I tried not to let his simple gesture please me, but I didn't have to ask, which meant I didn't have to listen to country.

We'd barely left my road when Jack's phone rang, and he dug it out of his pocket.

"It's Jack," he answered cheerfully. "Oh hey, Sally." There was a pause, and he clicked the blinker to turn right.

"Reynolds was in there again, huh? I appreciate you telling me. I'll drop in and take care of his bill." Another pause. "I know that, but I don't mind; it's good of you to feed him, Sally."

I tried not to be interested. Was he talking about Old Man Reynolds? And who was Sally? But I pushed all inquiries away. It was none of my business.

I didn't care. Jack was a means to an end, and after today, I'd never have to see him again.

My phone buzzed with a text from Andon. He'd dropped off the chairs on my porch but was disappointed I wasn't home.

I smirked – poor baby.

"No worries," Jack continued. "I'll find him and take care of it." Another pause. "Yep, see you soon."

He ended the call and put the phone in his pocket.

"That your girlfriend?" I asked. I'd only meant the question in jest, but I instantly regretted asking. If I didn't care, why would I ask?

He chuckled. "Definitely not. I'm too busy for a girlfriend."

"Doing what? Fishing strangers out of mud puddles?"

"No, I also get cats out of trees and help old ladies cross the street."

A small laugh escaped me. Maybe I *could* tolerate his company for one afternoon.

41

"Can you take me to the park?" I asked. "I need to get a few pictures of the fountain."

"Sure, I'm going there myself, but I need to make a stop," Jack replied. "Is that okay with you?"

"I guess," I said, scrolling through another playlist.

He pulled into a Burger Boy drive-thru. The thought of greasy food made my stomach churn.

"Do you want anything?" he asked, cranking down the window.

"No thanks," I said. "I don't eat greasy food."

"What? It's a gift from the gods," he said reverently.

"What is? Diarrhea?"

Jack laughed, and I felt like the sound danced around me. I pretended to be fascinated with my camera to keep myself from laughing.

"You are funny, Rylen Clark."

That caught me. When did I tell him my last name?

"Has anyone ever told you that?" he said.

It's on the mailbox by our driveway, but still...

"I've heard it once or twice," I admitted, not taking my eyes from the digital screen.

"I think I've got you figured out."

"I doubt it."

"I have a theory."

"Which is?" I asked, looking at him.

But he shook his head. "I can't give away all my secrets. What would I write in my diary?"

I glared at him.

"But you should be funny. It's a good look on you," he finished.

"You should try eating a vegetable," I gestured to the trash bag hooked to the glove compartment which was bursting with

42

M&M wrappers.

Jack grimaced as he pulled forward and spoke into the intercom. "Hi, can I get fifteen cheeseburgers and one small fry?"

I gaped at him. Holy crap! Someone was hungry.

He said thank you and pulled forward. He must've felt my stare weighing on him because he threw his eyes at me.

"What?" he shrugged.

"You're going to eat *fifteen* cheeseburgers?"

"No, the fries are for me."

I was silent, waiting for him to say something that made sense.

He shrugged. "Well, you said I needed more vegetables."

§୦ᴄ∽୦§ §୦ᴄ∽୦§ §୦ᴄ∽୦§

Davenport Community Park was located in the center of town. I needed a picture of the singing fountain, the town's most popular, yet corniest, tourist attraction. In the summer and fall, the fountain played one song every hour until noon. Then it would play for an hour straight and again at six. If you were in the park, dancing was customary. Couples would meet for dates; old people would take dance lessons and show off their skills. Moms would meet other moms and dance with their kids, and the sidewalks would become jammed with a plethora of strollers and squawking toddlers.

The fountain had its own following, with a Facebook page where people could pay a small fee to dedicate songs to loved ones. Warm summer evenings would draw in teens. Andon and I would often go on weekends to meet up with our friends for pizza and frisbee golf.

It was a time in my life that would no longer be mine, and I hoped to get my pictures and get out of there before my memories came back to torment me.

We arrived just before noon, and the warm sun shone brightly above our heads like a bright yellow beacon of happiness. Sometimes I felt like the sun was that overly peppy friend you just wanted to throat punch. The cottonwood trees swayed slightly in the fall breeze as the park filled with moms with their small children and older couples walking their dogs.

Jack offered to push me, but I declined. I hated relying on people for even the most minor things, and after I could walk again, there were still things I'd never get back. I'd always need other people to help me, and I hated how weak and alone I felt.

When the music started, couples began to dance. I sat in my chair, snapping pictures and watching as an old couple dipped and spun. Children laughed; a few dads stood nearby watching through their sunglasses, sipping fancy coffees with white lids.

Jack wandered off toward the food trucks with Bam Bam on his heels, then reappeared with a tall white cup in each hand.

"Milkshakes," he said. "Strawberry or chocolate?"

"Neither."

"Oh-kay, strawberry," he said. "It's real strawberry, too. Not that artificial crap."

He held the shake out to me, and reluctantly, I took it. He settled on the grass beside me, pulling his knees into his chest. He set down the bag of burgers he'd nestled under his arm and took off his hat.

"You could've asked me, you know," I said.

He didn't make eye contact and reached out to pat Bam Bam's head. "You would have said no."

"You don't know that."

"You said no the moment I brought it to you."

"I have a good reason."

"Being a pain in the ass is not a good reason."

"Oh, because being a contrarian is a hobby of mine," I deadpanned.

"Apparently."

He lifted his eyes to me and used his hand to shield the sun. "Are you lactose-intolerant?"

"No! It's that…"

"Because if you are and you drink that, I'm not driving you home."

I stifled a laugh. "No."

He had a point. There was nothing worse than being stuck in a vehicle with a non-compliant lactose-intolerant.

He shrugged. "Like I said, pain in the ass."

"If you must know…"

"Why do you have such a hard time accepting it when people are kind to you? You're like the poster child for paranoia."

My jaw fell open. Untrusting was different than paranoid. Wasn't it?

"Look, it's a warm day," Jack said. "And I thought you could use a drink. If you don't want it, you can throw it away – makes no difference to me."

He put his hat back on and lifted his shake. His cheeks sucked in as he drank from the straw. Then he popped the lid off and pulled the straw out to lick the bottom where most of the chocolate had settled.

I stared down at my own shake. The pink ice cream was swirled around the bottom of the lid. My only reason for saying no was that my physical activity had drastically decreased, and I was trying to cut sugar from my diet. But again, his actions spoke for themselves. He'd thought of me, and I didn't have to ask. And he expected nothing in return. I didn't have to pay him or return the favor. It was simply a genuine act of kindness.

And I was ruining it.

"Thanks," I said.

His gaze traveled over to me, seeming surprised at my gratitude. A small smile touched the edges of his lips.

"Anytime."

Across the park, Old Man Reynolds walked down the sidewalk. He wore a tattered camouflage jacket and dusty canvas pants. Even at a distance, I could see the toe of his red sock poking through a hole in his boot. A pink princess backpack, likely containing everything he owned, was slung across one shoulder.

"Right on time," Jack said. "I'll be right back."

He stood and gathered the bag of burgers in one hand. Bam Bam padded next to him as he walked to where Reynolds had stretched out on a bench in the shade.

When Jack approached, the old man sat up, and Jack handed him the food bag. Reynolds looked stunned, but he accepted it and nodded his thanks. They exchanged a few words, but I couldn't hear them.

I picked up the shake and took a big drink.

Maybe I *was* being a pain in the ass?

§oc∼ɔo§ §oc∼ɔo§ §oc∼ɔo§

I finished every last drop of my milkshake. Jack gave me an approving grin when I slurped up the last remains of creamy goodness. Then the frisbee came out and we took turns throwing for an exuberant Bam Bam. Jack was impressed with my technique. I told him about warm summer evenings and frisbee golf, but I stopped there. The memory had started to sting, and I didn't want to emotionally bleed in front of him.

Jack was wrestling a chewed frisbee from Bam Bam's slobbery chops when I asked, "Why do you call him Bam Bam?"

"Because of where I found him," he said, flicking the frisbee across the lawn. The dog yipped and bounded after the flying disc.

"Okay, I'll bite. Where did you find him?"

He sat back on the grass and crossed his ankles out in front of him.

"California. I worked for a while on the pier in San Diego."

"That's kind of cool. What did you do?"

"Anything I could find. When you're living in your truck, you can't be too picky."

Now I knew why a sleeping bag was rolled up in his backseat.

"Why were you living in your truck?"

And why was I asking? I wasn't supposed to care, but his lifestyle was obviously so different from mine. I was starting to believe he was unlike anyone I'd met before, and it piqued my interest.

He shrugged. "I was looking for someone, and I wanted to see the country. So, I drove until I ran out of money. I'd find odd jobs here and there and work until I had enough to get me to the next place I wanted to see."

"Sounds exciting."

"There were moments." He unbuttoned his shirt sleeves and rolled them up to his elbows. I thought I caught the smallest hint of a tattoo on the back of his left forearm, but unlike him, I didn't want to stare.

"Anyways, one night I was leaving this fish and chips joint on the pier when I heard this loud crashing. *Bam-bam Bam-bam.*"

The dog, who was content to chew the frisbee to shreds, settled himself on the grass beside Jack.

"I followed the sound, and behind the restaurant, stuck between two dumpsters, was this guy." He padded Bam Bam's head, who paused momentarily to give his master loving puppy eyes.

47

"Poor ol' boy."

"Yeah, he was caught in a fishing net and his paw was cut up real bad. Looked like he'd been out there for days. He tried to tear my arm off, but I cut him free."

"And the rest is history?" I asked.

"Nope," Jack said with a chuckle. "He ran off. He didn't trust me, but I came back the next day with a steak. Took me three steaks before he'd let me come near him." He ruffled Bam Bam's ears, who'd gone back to mangling the frisbee. "Then I bandaged up his paw, and he jumped into my truck."

"You're persistent. I'll give you that."

"Yeah," he said, his eyes locking with mine. "It gets me in trouble sometimes."

He was staring again. A warm wind ruffled my curls, and something slid between my breasts – a bead of sweat. Great, now I was keenly aware of my boobs while he was shamelessly staring at me. God, why did he do that? And why couldn't I look away? Was it more than him trying to figure me out?

My phone buzzed and broke the spell. He looked away, and I reached into my pocket, instantly realizing I'd lost track of time and had nearly forgotten about my doctor's appointment. I'd been enjoying myself, and I wasn't merely tolerating Jack. He was more pleasant than I'd given him credit for. If my mother hadn't been blowing up my phone with reminders, I would have gladly stayed right where I was.

We were in his truck, almost back to my house, when I broke the silence.

"Thanks for driving me," I said. "I had a lot of fun...surprisingly."

"Surprisingly?" he repeated. "What kind of a backhanded compliment is that?"

"I didn't mean it like that," I argued.

"You might as well have told me I look pretty in this light."

I chuckled, but anything further died on my lips when we turned into my driveway. Andon's blue Toyota pickup was parked in front of my garage.

"Oh no," I grumbled, burying my face in my hands.

"What's wrong?" Jack asked, putting the Bronco in park.

Andon got out of his truck and leaned against the door. He crossed his arms, waiting for me.

"You know that guy?" Jack asked.

A deep rumble came from the back seat as Bam Bam growled, like he was ready to dart out the window and tear Andon's leg off. I was beginning to like this moody canine.

"Easy, boy," Jack soothed.

"That's my ex," I said. "I didn't know he was going to be here."

"You want me to run him over?"

I smiled, shaking my head. "He'd just come back to haunt me."

Andon looked disgusted as Jack collected my chair from the back and opened my door. Jack tipped his hat to Andon as a way of greeting, but Andon ignored him, his scowl deepening when Jack lifted me out of the Bronco and put me in the chair.

"Thanks for everything," I told him, adjusting in my seat.

"Anytime," Jack said. "I'd say we could do it again, but I promised you wouldn't have to see me again, remember?"

"Oh, right."

"I keep my promises."

If I were honest with myself, I'd admit that I had a good time. Even though he was incredibly frustrating, I'd laughed more today than I had in months. But he'd promised we could part ways. At first, I would've welcomed it, but after today, after sitting in the sun, drinking milkshakes, and playing with the dog, I realized the only

49

thing that waited for me tomorrow was loneliness. That reality hadn't bothered me until now.

"Oh, before I forget..." He opened the passenger door and dug into the backseat. A small white plastic bag hung from his wrist, and he held it out to me. "This is for you."

"You got me a gift?" I said, surprised. "Why would you do that?"

He smirked. "Just take it, poster child."

I snatched the bag and nestled it on my lap. Oh God, what if it were something weird? Like a sign that congratulates you on having a good poop or a candle that smells like hotdogs? Why the hell would he buy a gift for someone he hardly knew?

He took a few steps back and tipped his hat. "I guess I'll see you around, Rylen Clark."

He'd done nothing but irritate me most of the day, so why did I feel disappointed at the thought of not seeing him again?

I watched the cowboy wave his final goodbye, and then he climbed into his truck and backed out of my driveway.

"Yeah, see ya," I said, but I knew I wouldn't.

Behind me, Andon cleared his throat, but my eyes stayed glued to that black Bronco. I wanted another milkshake. I wanted to play frisbee in the sun and watch couples dance by the fountain. I wanted to do it all again tomorrow, and I didn't want this to be the last time I saw him.

All I could hear as he sped away was a small voice in the back of my mind, revealing a great truth that I wasn't brave enough to say aloud.

Wait.

Chapter Six

JACK

It was dark when I parked in front of The Hiding Place. I hadn't been to a nightclub in over a year, not since I left Davenport. I was only here because it was Cora's last known whereabouts. I wasn't the bar scene type; the sweat and stale beer reeked of desperation.

Bam Bam looked at me skeptically. "Here goes."

The dog whined in return. I grabbed my hat and crossed the parking lot. No bouncer was present, so I walked in as if I belonged. Inside, pool tables occupied the front, and a few guys were racking balls. The after-work crowd sat on bar stools, sipping drinks from stout tumblers, staring at the nearby TVs blaring the football game. The dance floor gleamed under the dim lights, and the DJ was setting up for the late crowd that would arrive in the coming hours.

I ordered a Coke and waited for Cora in a booth with a package of M&Ms. I had rehearsed my speech, but I didn't know what to expect. When she appeared behind the bar, all words escaped me. We were the same age, twenty-two. She was older by three minutes and enjoyed taunting me about it, but the weariness in her eyes made her appear older. She'd colored her hair blonde again, and it curled on the ends, the sparkles from a rhinestone clip winking from the lights when she turned around. I watched her move easily between the tables, making small talk with regulars and fending off handsy men. She politely declined their offers and gestured to a simple gold band on her left ring finger when they would push for more.

A lump grew in my throat. My sister had remained faithful despite it all. No wonder she'd promised to hate me. Guilt ate at my stomach, like a parasite, and I wondered if I could slip out the back door without her noticing, because this was a bad idea.

A bouncer, a mountain of a man, kept watch. Cora often made eye contact with him, signaling she could handle herself if her male customers got a little too friendly. After three Cokes, it was time for her break. I put on my hat and slipped outside, hiding behind a dumpster. A rat nibbled on a French fry, and I plastered myself against the wall as Cora stepped out, lighting a cigarette. She dug into her purse and pulled out her phone. She hit a button and brought it to her ear.

"Hey, Tonya. It's Cora," she said. "How's he doing?" There was a pregnant pause, and she looked at her feet, exhaling. "Okay, no, I understand. I have to work in the evenings. So…" she trailed off, listening, taking another puff from her cigarette. "No, that's impossible," she spoke again, letting out her drag. "I could ask my Gran, but she doesn't drive and…there isn't anyone else. I've already cut my hours back, Tonya. I…" She stopped again, nodded, and clenched her teeth together. "Okay, I'll see if someone can cover for me, and I'll be there tomorrow."

She ended the call, and, even from my vantage point, I saw her knuckles turn white as she squeezed her phone in her fist.

"Son of a bitch!" she growled.

Then she looked up knowingly and spoke again.

"Sneaking up on a woman in the dark is a good way to get knifed." A cold chill slithered down my spine, and my ears burned as I revealed my hiding place.

"Hello, little brother," she said, her words oozing with disdain. She took another drag of her cigarette, the exhale coming out of her nostrils like a fire-breathing dragon.

"Hello, Cora," I replied. "How are you feeling?"

Her eyes flashed with fury, understanding that her secret was out. "Who told you?"

"Gran filled me in. I'm really sorry. How is he?"

But she shook her head. "You don't get the *privilege* of asking about him. This is *all* your fault."

"I know. How did you know I was back?"

"It's a small town," she said, lighting a second cigarette. She dropped the first one to the ground and stepped on it with the toe of her black heel. "Plus, I'd expect to find you among dumpster rats."

"Haven't lost your charm, I see."

She let out her drag, her eyes scanning me head to toe. "You look like hell. Haven't you ever heard of a razor?"

I ran a hand over my three-day stubble. "I've been a little busy."

"Yeah, I heard about you feeding Reynolds in the park the other day."

I'd forgotten that little detail. Cora was well-liked. She made good tips, especially from her male customers, and most of them swore unabashed loyalty to her, which meant she had spies everywhere.

"He was hungry, so I fed him."

"You mean you owed him."

I shrugged. "What difference does that make? He got fed, didn't he?"

"Little brother," she tutted. "What's everyone going to think when they find out it was all a big lie?"

"I don't know what you're talking about."

"Yes, you do!" she snapped. "You've been all over doin' good deeds. Helping Sally. Fixing Ned's truck. Tryin' to be everyone's superhero, Jack?"

"I don't look good in spandex."

She chuckled, but there was no humor in it. "Then there's the girl."

"Leave her out of this."

"*You* brought her into it. Is she aware that your chivalry is only meant to numb your guilt and soothe your tortured soul?"

I didn't answer, but I didn't have to. Her deep green eyes could see everything within me that I couldn't bring myself to admit.

"Of course not. It'd be a shame for her to find out the truth." She puffed her cigarette. "Wouldn't it?"

"Don't threaten me, Cora," I growled.

She lifted her hands in mock defense. "It's not a threat. It's a warning. You ruin everything you touch. Not that I give a damn about you. If you don't leave her alone, she's going to find out, and I don't want you to screw up her life."

"Wow, caring about someone other than yourself," I spat. "Tell me, how does it feel?"

"I'm a little nauseous, but that only started once I laid eyes on you." She stepped towards me and held the cigarette down by her thigh. "I'm not offering you one. I have three left and I'm broke. I had to cut my hours, but you know all that. You were eavesdropping."

"I don't smoke anymore."

She lifted a brow, scrutinizing me. "Interesting. So, Jack comes back; he's suddenly helpful. He doesn't smoke. I bet you quit drinking, too?"

"I did."

"I don't buy it," she said sharply. "You're not a *nice* guy, and when the rest of this town figures out, you're helping them to clear your conscience, they'll see…"

"I'm trying to make things right, Cora."

"Forgiveness can't be bought, *Jack*."

"I know that. I'm…"

"Do you know what you've done?" she snapped. "Do you have any idea what you took from me?"

"Yes! Why do you think I came back?"

"And you didn't think that maybe staying away was better? There isn't a world that exists where I won't hate you. It should be you rotting in that jail cell. Not Hudson."

"You made that clear. I got your letter." I was all in now. I could have claimed plausible deniability and pretended I never received it. I pulled the folded page from my jacket and held it out to her.

She crossed her arms. "I was wondering when you were going to bring that up."

"You were the only person who knew my exact location last year, and you sent me a hate letter."

Her eyes narrowed, and she flicked her cigarette, the gray ashes falling to the ground.

"I was hoping you'd take my subtle hints," she said evenly. "Next time, I'll be clearer."

There was another pregnant pause, and I realized that I hadn't been able to look her in the eye throughout our conversation.

"I don't blame you. I'd probably hate myself too," I admitted, finally meeting her eyes.

"Hudson'd been sober for six months, Jack."

Although she said my name, she gazed off into the night behind me like she was reminiscing about a life lost to the darkness.

"He was finally getting his life on track." She blinked back tears, but more gathered under her lashes. "We were going to get married and be a family. I've never had a real family before."

My eyes traveled to the simple band on her finger, and she followed my gaze and then hid her hand from view.

"Gran taught me to make a stew with beef and potatoes. Hudson would only eat it if I cut up the onions real fine so he couldn't see them. I was going to be a wife, and we were going to care about dinner, packing lunches for work, and falling asleep before the evening news. And now…." She trailed off, wiping tears streaming down her face. "Now I don't have anyone to eat my stew because you called the police and fucked it all up."

"No, I didn't. It wasn't me, and even if it had been, what were you going to do? Live the rest of your days hiding with a wanted criminal? Don't be ridiculous."

She smirked. "Took the police three months to find him in the bottom of that warehouse."

"I told him to turn himself in. Dumbass should've listened to me."

"He *did* listen to you," she hissed. "How do you think he got arrested in the first place?"

"I didn't know he would go through with it."

"And that releases you of all responsibility?"

"I didn't say that."

"You knew he was vulnerable," she snarled, anger now taking the place of sorrow. "You knew he was trying to make a better life for me, but you didn't care. You only cared about money and winning. Hudson was just collateral, and that makes you guilty as hell."

I took off my hat and wiped my brow with my sleeve. I couldn't argue with her.

She shook her head, fresh tears pooling in her eyes. "I will live the rest of my days hating you, and if there is an afterlife, I'll hate you then, too."

"I'm sorry, Cora."

"You're sorry?" she scoffed.

"It's all I can say. I don't deserve your forgiveness. Just tell me how to make it right, and I'll do it."

"You wanna make it right?" she spat. "Then you can go to hell, and you had better make sure I *never* see you again."

She flicked her cigarette into the darkness and reached for the door.

"Cora, wait," I said. "Cor-ah."

"My break's over," she said, an outstretched arm holding the open door, but she looked over her shoulder. "I hope you know what a piece of shit you are, Jack."

Only the rats heard my reply since the door was closed by the time I said, "Believe me. I do."

Chapter Seven

Rylen

It was Tuesday, and that meant I was back in Dr. Sullivan's office upholding my oath of stubborn silence. My appointment had fifty-three minutes left, and I was certain she'd fire me by the end of the hour if I continued my silent streak.

I faced the window again, staring out into the parking lot. I saw the doctor's reflection behind me, crossing and uncrossing her legs, tapping her pen. She was always a picture of poised perfection, but it looked like I might finally be trying her patience.

She wore one of her suits again— navy blue with a ruby red blouse. The suit had been recently pressed, the iron marks still crisp and peaked on the legs of her trousers. I saw no wedding ring, so I guessed she was the sort of person who filled her Saturday mornings with black coffee, cozy audiobook mysteries, and copious amounts of ironing.

Her face was heart-shaped, and she wore light makeup with brown and cream undertones.

"So, tell me how your week was."

I stayed silent. Fifty minutes to go.

"O-kay," The doctor said. She set her notebook on the mahogany coffee table before her and removed her glasses. "Rylen, I know you're being forced to come here, and I empathize. But payments have been made in advance. So, unfortunately, you're stuck with me until further notice."

I swiveled around, and words were out of my mouth before I could stop them.

"How long?"

"Three months."

"Three months! Look, Doc, you might as well put me out of my misery and fire me now."

"I don't fire clients."

I grinned mischievously. "So, *I* can fire you then?"

"You can try, but I happen to have a strict no-refund policy. I don't think your mother would be very pleased."

I felt myself deflate. If I'd done the math correctly, Dr. Sullivan made two hundred bucks an hour which meant my mom's bill for three months was upwards of two grand. Firing the doc would go over like a lead balloon.

Sullivan spoke again, placing her glasses back on the bridge of her nose. "Though I'd be curious to know what you'd write on Yelp as reasons for termination. I do happen to have four and a half stars."

"It's nothing personal, doc. I'm sure you're a fine therapist. I just don't like talking about myself."

She shrugged. "Then talk about something else." She lifted her sleeve and glanced at her watch. It was gold and shiny –

expensive to match her pristine suits. "You have forty-five minutes. Pretend we're two old friends catching up."

I shook my head. "I can't do that."

"Why not? Do you have another friend you can talk to?"

The truth was, I didn't. Ali had been my best friend since the first day of third grade, on the playground at Davenport Elementary. I had been swinging, and Billy Fleckenstein, later dubbed Bully Fuckenstein, had pushed me down and taken my swing. When I'd started to tear up, Fuckenstein called me a whiny little piglet.

Ali, who had been a head taller than any third grader around, tapped him on the shoulder, and when he turned around, she'd socked him so hard he staggered backward and bounced on his ass. His lip had bled, and at first, he'd been too stunned to move; but when he tried to get to his feet, she'd threatened to pound his nose in. Then she pulled me to my feet and dusted off my pants.

Ali got suspended, but she didn't care. We were best friends after that. I used to believe our bond was unbreakable. We had survived the dramatic ups and downs of Junior High, and nothing could be stronger than we were—until she did the one unforgivable thing that destroyed it all.

She slept with Andon.

Since the truth had come out last fall, our group of mutual friends had dwindled into nothing. Some had taken sides and refused to speak to me. And for the friends who were on my side, I was often too embarrassed to hang out with them. I'd stopped answering their texts, and, eventually, they stopped trying.

For a year, I'd been alone in a large, dark house with only the company of my own shadow stretched across the cathedral ceilings above me. And now, no matter what I did to try and stop it, I found my thoughts drifting back to Jack and my brief afternoon in the park.

In the webs of my mind, I relived everything, letting the memory rejuvenate me. The sunshine, the ice cream – the joys of simple pleasures had gone right into my bloodstream, and I was counting down the hours until I could have another hit.

Or maybe Jack had found a piece of me that'd been lying dormant. It was always there, this person I used to be; percolating under the surface, waiting to erupt.

Then I heard myself admit a great truth: "I don't have any friends."

I don't know why I admitted it to her, but the doctor had kind blue eyes and maybe saying it aloud would alleviate the pressure building within me.

"That must be difficult," she said.

I sniffled, the sting of tears behind my eyes.

"It's okay to be afraid, Rylen. Being vulnerable is scary, but you are safe here, and everyone needs a friend to talk to."

I scoffed. "That's just it. My ex cheated on me with my best friend, and everyone took sides. I've never felt more alone in my life." A tear slipped out, and I quickly swiped it away.

"That's painful," she said gently. "But being alone is a choice as much as it is a feeling."

"I didn't *choose* for my boyfriend to cheat on me, Doc."

"Of course not, but you *can* choose what you do with it. You can choose to begin new relationships, and sometimes, through those new friendships, we find peace. But you're not going to find peace hiding in your house."

A small smile touched her lips. The doctor was more perceptive than I'd given her credit for. I guess it wasn't too difficult to figure out my coping mechanism. But still, what else did she know that I hadn't told her?

She picked up her pen and the yellow legal pad. Then she folded her hands, readying herself for me to open up and expose what had shattered my soul.

"I think it's time to start living again, Rylen. What do you think?"

My God, I wanted that. She was the matador waving her red cape, and I was the bull charging forward, yet it seemed the only way to get there was to go backward. But I wasn't ready for that. She had said I didn't have to talk about myself. So, I told her about coming face to face with Andon and my unfortunate encounter in the driveway.

ୡୖ⌇୰ଽ ୡୖ⌇୰ଽ ୡୖ⌇୰ଽ

Andon cleared his throat again, and I pulled my eyes from where Jack's Bronco had disappeared, ignoring the twinge in my chest. I swiveled around to face him and closed the distance between us.

"What are you doing here?" I spat, stopping a few paces in front of him. I tried to control my anger, but in my mind, I was going for his jugular.

"Take it easy." He lifted his hands to show he was unarmed. "Your mom said you needed a lift to the doctor's office. She couldn't make it, so she called me."

My brows rose. Of course, she would blindside me like this. Of course, she'd bait and switch. Of course, she would meddle in my love life.

"She did what?" I asked coolly. "I'll skip it."

"Come on, Rylen," he said, stuffing his hands in his pockets. "It's important. Let me take you."

If dictionaries had pictures, all you'd have to do is look up the word dreamy. An image of Andon Martinez would appear under the word, and no further explanation would be needed. Standing at six feet two, with chocolate eyes, dark hair, and a cut and smooth

62

jawline, it was no mystery why he'd made a sixteen-year-old me weak in the knees.

"It's a follow-up. It can wait." I said, swiveling away from him. "You can go now."

"Rylen, wait. We need to talk."

He stepped in front of me, and I seriously considered running over his foot.

"Move!" I snapped. "There's nothing more to say."

"Please, give me five minutes, okay?"

I crossed my arms like a stubborn toddler. I wasn't in a position to run from him. I couldn't even get up the porch steps unless I asked him to help me. If I didn't at least hear him out, he'd further accost me. I agreed for the sake of my own sanity.

"Fine. But you have to help me inside."

He smiled victoriously. I envisioned pushing two sides of my cracked heart back together before the aching paralyzed me. I used to love that smile.

He helped me up the stairs, pushing me up a makeshift ramp, and I unlocked the front door. It swung open, and I wheeled inside.

"So," he started, closing the door. "Who was that guy?"

"He's a friend." However, it felt weird referring to Jack as a friend when I would never see him again. "It's none of your business."

"I know. I just…" He stared at his feet and stuffed his hands in his pockets again. "I miss you, and I want you to forgive me so we can go back to the way things were."

My eyes narrowed. He couldn't be serious.

"Look, I wanted to tell you so many times," he said huskily. "I didn't mean for it to happen."

"I suppose you're going to tell me it was an accident," I snapped.

"It sort of was." He pulled his white cap off and ran his hands through his dark locks. "I didn't *intend* to sleep with Ali. One thing led to another and..." he shrugged, then knelt and took my hand. "I'm really sorry."

"They all knew, didn't they?" I asked. "The night of the barbecue. Everyone knew except for me."

It was the night of the robbery, too. We had been driving home from an end-of-summer barbecue. Our mutual friend, Justin, was leaving for boot camp, and all our friends were there to say goodbye. As the evening continued, the booze started flowing, and tongues became looser. Then Ali had shown up, in her typical better-late-than-never fashion, wearing knee boots and a hot pink strapless dress. Then the snickering started. The comments that had been intended as jokes had planted the small seeds of my ever-blooming doubt.

I cornered Justin in the hallway and demanded he tell me what they were snickering about. Now I knew I had been the ass of every joke.

"Ignore them. They're assholes." Andon said, gazing into my eyes. "I'm sorry, Rylen. I've been wanting to tell you that for a year."

He let out a breath, but I wasn't ready for it to be okay. I wasn't okay, and I wasn't going to let him off that easily.

"When did it start?"

He pulled on his shirt collar. "Why is that important?"

I narrowed my eyes and bit off the end of each word. "Answer. The. Question.

He sighed, fiddling with a string on his sweatshirt. "The night of Sharon's funeral, okay? She was upset and..."

I ripped my hand away. "Oh, so it was pity sex, then?"

"No!" he countered.

"You couldn't help yourself, could you? Saw an opportunity to bang Ali Rowdenski and..."

64

"She came onto me," he said pointedly.

"Of course she did. She's been in love with you for years."

He opened his mouth to say something, but words escaped him. He hadn't known Ali's true feelings.

"Look, Rylen, you weren't at the funeral, okay? You didn't see how upset she was."

"So, the two of you decided to punish me for it?"

He stood. "Don't act like you're completely innocent in all this. You should have gone to the funeral. You should have been there for your friends. God, this little victim game you're playing is exhausting." His words sliced through me. I wouldn't even be in this chair if it hadn't been for him. He destroyed everything, and now he was trying to blame me?

"We had a future," I choked. "And you ruined it. I've never been more embarrassed in my life." I swallowed the lump in my throat. I thought the well had gone dry and that I couldn't cry over this anymore, but I felt the sting of tears behind my lashes.

"I know I ruined everything, and I'll never be more sorry. Ali and I are over. We broke up last month. But you and me," he knelt again, his hand found mine, and he interlaced our fingers. "We belong together. I miss driving you around while we blast Pink Floyd. The Mustang is almost done. I want to take my girl for a ride. And there's no one else I want on my team for frisbee golf. I miss watching crappy movies and throwing popcorn at the people in front of us. I stood beside you when they buried Michael. I've always been there for you, Rylen. It was always supposed to be me and you."

"Stop," I whispered.

Don't talk about the park, and when I felt alive. Don't talk about a life that got ripped away from me. Don't talk about the possibilities.

"We have been together since we were fifteen. You were my first love, and nothing, not even Ali, can change that. It kills me that we've been apart, that I haven't been there for you."

His other hand brushed the brace on my broken knee, his fingers sliding down the back of my calf.

"You must have been terrified," he said, a voice barely above a whisper.

"You have no idea," I said softly. A tear escaped, and he used his thumb to brush it away.

"How many surgeries?" he said, his hands now cupping my face.

"Three. I'm mostly titanium now."

"I'm so sorry, baby."

Then his lips drew closer to mine, and I found myself under his spell, tilting my head to one side.

"I should've been with you," he whispered, his mouth inches from mine.

"You drove off," I said bitterly.

"I know," he whispered. "I'm a dumbass."

Then he put his lips on mine, and we kissed, the sensations both familiar and foreign, bitter and sweet. At first, I was tentative and reserved, as there was something else, I'd kept buried deep inside, but with every touch, he slowly brought it to the surface, coaxing it out of me.

Hope.

My hands came up, and I grabbed his face, fingers caressing his neck because I could no longer deny that I desperately wanted him back in my life. The boy who stood next to me while they buried my brother.

The real Andon, who'd owned my heart since I was fifteen.

His hands stroked my sides, then my arms and shoulders. His lips were soft yet demanding, and I opened my mouth against him.

Then his phone rang, and he broke the kiss, reaching into his back pocket.

"Sorry. It might be work," he said, "I didn't tell my dad where I was going."

When the phone came into view, a picture of Ali in a black bikini lit up the screen, and he hesitated.

"Ignore it," I growled.

"She'll call again. Let me see what she wants." And before I could protest, he answered. He listened to her babble for a few seconds, and then he looked concerned. "Wait, hold on," he said, getting to his feet. "Just calm down, okay? Where are you right now?"

He paused. "Okay, I'll be there in a few minutes." He ended the call and pocketed his phone. "I have to go."

Now, I knew how chopped liver felt.

"You guys haven't broken up yet, have you?" I said flatly. Ali wouldn't call him so easily if she were angry at him.

"We're *breaking* up. She's having a hard time with it."

"You seem eager to comfort her."

"She has a flat. She doesn't have anyone else to call, okay?"

"So, she summons you, and you drop everything and go to her?"

"Rylen, she needs help," he said, exasperated. "What else am I supposed to do?"

He opened the door, and I wheeled out onto the landing, watching him saunter to his truck. I found it devastating how quickly his priorities changed. Ali would always be there, connected by a heartstring, and he'd run to her at every beck and call. Leaving me longing for what I'd lost, clinging to old memories and empty promises, with the taste of his lips still lingering on mine.

"I'll see you soon, okay?" he called as he opened the truck's door.

I nodded stiffly, not because I wanted to see him but because my throat was too tight to say otherwise.

He got into his truck and backed out of my driveway, and when he was gone, he took my last thread of hope with him. Then the floodgates opened, and a strangled cry escaped me, drowning me in a sea of tears.

"I'm an idiot," I said aloud. I crossed my arms over my heart, trying to keep whatever was in there safe, vowing to keep it protected.

I don't know how long I cried, but when I wiped my eyes, I still had the small bag Jack had given me nestled on my lap. I'd forgotten about it.

I used my sleeve to wipe my face and lifted the bag. Whatever was inside was hard and flat. I slid the bag down and inside was a book by Dr. Seuss: Green Eggs and Ham.

What the hell? Confusion clouded my mind. Was he trying to be funny? Trying to be cute? I cracked the spine, and there were two simple lines on the blank page in the front, written in blocked male handwriting.

IF IN FUTURE DAYS YOU FIND YOURSELF WITHOUT TRANSPORTATION

CALL ME, I'LL COME, NO MATTER MY LOCATION.

—JACK (701)-299-4567

Chapter Eight

JACK

It was almost midnight when I pulled into Gran's driveway. I killed the engine when my phone chirped with a text. It was Sally.

Sent Thursday 11:47 PM
Sally: Thank you so much for your help this afternoon. Come in next week for a meal. It's on the house. :)

Sent 11:48 PM
Jack: No problem. Call me if you need anything else.

There was a tiny piece of me that'd hoped the text had been from Rylen. Surely, she hadn't missed what I'd written on the front of the book? Or maybe she saw it and thought I was too pathetic to bother with. Maybe she thought my efforts were idiotic, and we'd part ways for good. My conscience wasn't clear yet. Other than Cora, I owed her the most, but it would have to be on her terms.

I pocketed my phone and opened the door; Bam Bam jumped out and scampered across the lawn.

"Not there! Come on, man." But it was too late; the dog had already assumed the position and defecated right in the middle of Gran's lily patch. He looked at me with large, puppy eyes, whining while he finished his squat. Then he yipped a few times, a newfound spring in his step as he trotted up the porch.

Dumb dog. I'd have to leave the pile until morning. I'd spent the whole afternoon fixing the fryer at Sally's Diner. I yawned deeply and was about to go to the barn loft, where I'd created my quarters, when the car in the driveway caught my eye. I'd been too distracted with the dog to notice it when I pulled in, but I'd recognize that burnt orange El Camino anywhere. It had belonged to Hudson before he'd been arrested.

I opened the screen door to find Cora and Gran sitting in the living room.

Gran was in her pink robe and slippers. Cora was dressed in black, her makeup smudged and greasy. Her hair was windblown, like she'd flown here on the back of a dragon. They were sipping tea from matching mugs, the strings dangling over the edges.

"I've really missed you, Gran." Cora beamed, then lifted her gaze to the door, where I cleared my throat.

Gran craned her neck. "Jack, honey, look who stopped by."

Cora eyed me over her mug. There was a fire in those dangerous eyes that suggested my life would be drastically shortened if I so much as twitched.

"Hi," I said, deflated. "Ah, Gran, I'm going to turn in."

Cora got to her feet. "I'd better be going too. Thank you for the tea." She took her mug to the sink and rinsed it out.

"Anytime. Come back soon, dearheart," Gran said as Cora plucked her jacket from a coat peg. "We'll make stew."

"I will. Goodnight, Gran."

She slipped out the door without so much as a breath in my direction. I followed her to the porch, but she was already down the steps. I went after her before her voice stopped me in my tracks.

"Don't," she snapped, turning on her heel.

I froze where I was.

She got into the El Camino and turned the key. The engine roared, the headlights blinding me as she backed up. The car rolled and bounced as she drove over small mounds and deep potholes. Then the tires squealed as she hit the gas and peeled out onto the highway.

When I turned around, Gran stood on the porch with her arms crossed. She'd been watching me.

"Jack, come in here, please." I knew better than to argue.

I followed her inside and stood in the doorway, but she pointed to the couch where she wanted me to sit. Reluctantly, I took off my hat and plopped on the cushion.

She pulled a manila envelope from her robe pocket. I recognized it as the one I'd left behind at the bar for Cora, stuffed with all the cash I could spare.

"Mind telling me what this is about?"

"Where did you get that?" I asked.

"Cora. It's the reason she knocked on my door at ten o'clock tonight. She told me to give it back to you. Of course, that's the polite version."

I sighed. "I'm sure she was sweet as pie."

"Jack." She set the money on the table beside her. "Why are you giving Cora an envelope full of cash?"

71

"She had to cut her hours at the bar."

"That's very generous of you. But it's an awful lot of money."

"It doesn't matter. She hates me."

"She doesn't hate you. She's just upset."

"She hates me, Gran," I insisted. "She's made it clear. She blames me for Hudson's arrest. She thinks I told the police where he was hiding."

Gran stiffened, and her lips thinned into a straight line. "Did you?"

"No! I was halfway to San Diego when Hudson called me, and I told the dumbass to turn himself in. But I didn't call the police."

She took a slow sip of her tea, nodding slowly.

"I believe you. I'm sorry she blames you. You were in her crosshairs long before that which makes you a convenient scapegoat."

I pointed to the envelope. "She needs it, Gran. Do you think you could try to convince her to take it?"

She scoffed. "Have you met your sister? Remember when you were kids and you told her mashed potatoes were mutilated monkey brains?"

I sheepishly stared at the ground. Gran had mashed purple potatoes with chunks of cooked carrots. The opportunity was too sweet to pass up.

"Yeah."

"And how long did it take me to convince her otherwise?"

"Point taken, Gran."

"Maybe Cora isn't where you should be putting your efforts." She placed her teacup on the coaster and folded her hands.

"What do you mean?"

"If you can't directly help Cora, then find a way to help her indirectly."

72

My brows crinkled. "I told you to quit using bleach to clean the bathrooms."

She chuckled. "Think about it, Jacky. If you can't air up the tires, then change the oil." She lifted her teacup and finished the last dregs of the tea.

"I value my life."

"You'll think of something. I want nothing more than to see my family back together. I'm not going to live forever."

"Don't talk like that, Gran."

She laughed softly and gathered her teacup. "Well, just know the past is all forgiven. I'm off to bed now. By the way, your faithful companion left me a little present in the lily patch. Be sure to pick it up before you turn in."

I nodded tightly. I'd forgotten that among Gran's many talents, she could smell crap a mile away.

She put her hands on the arms of her easy chair to boost herself up. Then I heard her take in a sharp breath, and she sank back down, putting a hand to her forehead.

"Gran?" I said, concerned. "Are you alright?" I got to my feet and walked to her, touching her shoulder.

Her eyes were tightly closed, and she took in slow, deep breaths.

"I tried to stand up too fast, that's all. I got a little dizzy."

Was that too fast? She moved slower than frozen molasses. "How often does that happen?" I asked, sitting on the coffee table across from her.

She shrugged. "I don't know. Off and on for a couple of weeks."

"Gran, you need to see a doctor."

She dropped her hand, her eyes zeroing in on me.

"I'm fine. The only thing a doctor will do is tell me I need to lose weight. Then he'll ask about my cholesterol and if I'm exercising.

And I'll tell him why, yes, I get exercise by bringing my piece of pecan pie right here." She made a motion like she was cutting a bite of pie and bringing it to her mouth.

I chuckled. "You need to take care of yourself, Gran."

"I'm fine," she said again. "Get me some water, will ya?" She pointed a nubby finger over her shoulder to the kitchen sink, and I rose to my feet. But as I passed, she grabbed my hand, running her clammy, wrinkled fingers over the back of my knuckles.

"I'm sorry, Jacky," she said again, looking up at me with large green eyes.

"Gran, you have nothing to be sorry for. I'm just worried about you."

She gave me a weak smile and nodded stiffly. I went to the sink and filled a glass, but my eyes drifted over to the back of her chair. I could see her reflection in the living room window.

She'd leaned forward, her elbows on her knees, and buried her face in her hands. I got the sneaking suspicion there was something she wasn't telling me. This wasn't only a dizzy spell. But getting Gran to open up was as hard as convincing nine-year-old Cora that mashed potatoes weren't monkey brains.

Chapter Nine

Rylen

It was official. Diana Clark's mission was to make my life a never-ending hellhole. It was Saturday, and at the ass crack of dawn, she barged in and announced we were meeting Andon's mom, Juanita, to pick out dresses. She continued to yak at me while I drowsily dragged myself off the couch and hobbled – my newest skill now that I had a crutch – to the bathroom, where I scrubbed my face until it was red and blotchy.

We sat outside in the late morning air. Perfect Cup coffee house was in a strip mall between my mother's office and Juanita's dress boutique. It was a decent place with a reasonably priced menu, but the scents wafting across the parking lot made me regret my recent vow of no carbs and sugar. Sally's Diner shared the parking lot, and hanging in the window was a banner picturing a steaming pile of golden pancakes slathered in butter and drenched in rich, warm syrup. My stomach rumbled, yet with every whiff, I could feel my butt inflating.

We'd just received our food when my mother purred, "Juanita, I have something for you."

"You do?" Juanita asked, pulling her glasses from the top of her head to her nose.

"I just couldn't help myself. I had to get it for you." She dug into her purse and retrieved a small black box with a bright red bow. "Happy birthday, dear friend."

"Diana, my birthday isn't for two more weeks."

"Oh, I know. I've just been *so* busy with this fundraiser, I didn't want to miss it."

Juanita delicately plucked the bow from the velvet box and opened the hinge. She gasped at what was inside.

"Diana! It's…it's…"

"Just like the one your mother had?" Diana finished.

Juanita lifted a brooch of an owl sitting on a silver tree branch. The owl's ruby eyes sparkled in the warm daylight.

"Oh, Diana, it's *just* like Mom's. Where did you find it?"

"I did some looking when I was in Milwaukee last week. There was the *cutest* shop downtown. It reminded me of your boutique. Anyway, isn't it wonderful? Now try it on and let me see."

"Thank you, Diana." Juanita pinned the owl to the front of her sweater, smiling adoringly at the replica of a family heirloom.

"Rylen isn't it fabulous?" my mother cooed, clasping her hands like she beheld Prince Charming.

"It's lovely, Juanita. Good find, Mom." I gave her an unenthusiastic thumbs up. Then I stabbed a bite of quiche so forcefully my fork squealed against the plate.

What or who exactly was supposed to be fabulous? Juanita's gift? Or the fact that my mother had given her a gift and made a big show of it?

Typical Diana Clarke.

"Ignore her, Juanita. Now let's find the perfect gown."

My mother scooted closer to her, and the two women disappeared into a magazine of retail dresses and pointy high heels.

I found my mind drifting back to the recent past, back to the cowboy and the odd gift I'd received.

In most cultures, it was customary to thank someone after receiving a gift. Even if the gift made no logical sense, it was still polite to at least acknowledge someone's kindness.

"Oh, I don't know, Juanita. Rylen needs something brighter. Yellow or maybe red."

The year I turned twelve, Great-Aunt Agnas gave me a case of Vienna sausages and a hamster ball. Some deranged gift-wrapper had plastered the paper with what looked like a convention of naked cat gremlins – the kind that make regular cats file restraining orders, and you're certain you've never seen anything as fucking ugly.

I didn't own a hamster. And I'd rather get a root canal and a colonoscopy simultaneously than eat a slimy sausage.

Agnas kept calling it a soccer ball and asked my mom how the team loved their snacks after practice. Thankfully, my mom lied her face off and Agnas was never the wiser.

But I was grateful. My mother, for all her faults, had raised me with proper manners, and Agnas got a homemade thank-you card with glitter and calligraphy. I even drew her a cat —with fur.

"Rylen!"

"What?" I said. My mom and Juanita looked at me with exasperated eyes.

"Pay attention! I only have a few more minutes before I need to be back in the office. Now, what do you think of this gown?" She pointed to an open page, and I felt my top lip curl back. Gown would've been the last word I'd used to describe the puffy yellow dress.

It looked like a giant banana.

"I-I don't think so, Mom."

"Rylen, you've got to pick something. We only have a few more weeks, and Juanita needs time to make alterations."

"How about this one?" Juanita pointed at a low cut, strapless black dress with a slit up the side.

"That's not bad," I agreed.

"Heavens no!" Diana declared. "Your ginormous *boobs* would fly out of it."

A loud crash turned our heads, and shards of dishes clattered to the ground. A scrawny, pimple-faced waiter boy, who'd been clearing the table next to us, was gawking at me with his mouth open.

I gave him a dirty look and pulled my jacket closed. Likely, his last encounter with boobs was when he was breastfeeding. His ears turned the same color as his pimples, and I wondered if they were all going to spontaneously combust. He tucked his chin to his chest and ran inside.

Juanita, having seen the whole show, stifled a laugh.

Unfazed, Diana thumbed through the pages of the catalog, shaking her head, occasionally making a *so-so* face at whatever she saw with potential.

"I love this one," Juanita said enthusiastically, pointing at a dress that looked more like lacy lingerie.

My mother giggled. "Maybe you should order that one for yourself. Harvey would love it."

"He'd have a heart attack!" she retorted, her words thick with a Spanish accent.

The woman chuckled, and across the table, Juanita lifted her coffee cup and winked at me over the brim.

A small smile tugged at my lips. One of the worst parts about losing Andon was also losing the bonus mom and friend I had in Juanita. As a teenager, dating her son, I'd spent many hours in her home. Despite the breakup, her kindness remained. Rumor has it that at a Fourth of July barbecue, she'd had too many wine coolers and said Andon had made an irreparable mistake.

A cell phone rang, and my mom dug into her black Coach purse. She tried to hide the screen, but I caught just enough of a glimpse that I could see the call was from Adam.

"Sorry, girls. I need to take this." She rose from her chair, taking her phone and purse. She chirped a cheerful greeting while walking into the coffee shop.

My stomach tied itself into a knot. If he was calling her on a Saturday, Adam had to be more than a nobody. She'd conveniently run off to Milwaukee last weekend for a work conference, but I'd called her office. There was no conference.

My Dad had better return soon.

"I'd better get going. I'm going to get a refill first," Jaunita said, rising. "Do you want one?"

"No thanks."

It was ten a.m., and I was dying for a milkshake.

My phone buzzed, and I opened a text from my mom saying she'd paid for our food, and she was off to the office.

"Great," I grumbled.

"What is it?" Juanita asked.

"My mom just abandoned me. I'm stuck here until at least six."

"I can give you a ride. I've got a few dress fittings, but I should be done by three."

"Really? You'd do that?"

She smiled sweetly. "Of course, my dear." She rounded the table and gave me a side hug. "I'll text you when I'm done."

"Thanks, Juanita."

As she gathered her purse and made her way inside, I was left with my own thoughts, and the lines of Jack's poem ran through my head.

It was pathetic. More than pathetic, it was corny and idiotic, yet I'd read it three times, and the tiniest hint of a smile had pricked at my lips. Okay, fine, like Grandpa taught me when I was five, I grinned like a skunk eating shit in the moonlight.

It was frustrating how much headspace this guy took up. Like I'd pulled the weeds up, but the roots only regrew, coming back to choke out all other thoughts.

Only Jack remained.

From the space behind me, there was the unmistakable sound of someone slurping the last remains of their drink up a skinny straw.

"Wow! You'd get arrested if you wore that in public."

I craned my neck to see Jack, hovering over my shoulder, staring at the open pages. The Harvey-heart-attack dress was front and center.

I slapped the catalog closed.

"What are you doing here?" I hissed.

He lifted his drink and slurped loudly. "Waiting for Pete." *Slurp*. "I'm meeting him here so I can fix his truck." *Slurp*.

"Oh," I said.

Why did I want him to say something else? Something like I saw you while flying down the freeway. I blasted across three lanes of traffic to say hello. "Seems like you're always fixing things for people," I observed.

"I kind of owe him, so I don't mind fixing it for him." Another big slurp.

He'd mentioned he didn't like owing people things. But why did he owe them?

"Looks like you lost your wheels," he said, seeing the crutches leaning against an outdoor pillar. "How's your knee?"

I shrugged. "It's okay. I could wheel faster than I can hobble."

"The parking is better, though." He popped the lid off his drink and drank from the edge.

It was a milkshake. The cup's logo said it was from Sally's Diner. If they had milkshakes *and* pancakes, I was done for.

"So, what brings you here?" He chucked his cup into a nearby trash can, and it landed with a resounding *thunk*.

I sighed and lifted the catalog, so the pages dripped down like slow raindrops.

He grinned all wide and toothy-like and leaned his elbows on the metal chair in front of him.

"Do I get a vote?"

"Absolutely not."

"What's the occasion?"

"The fundraiser," I said. "I was dragged here by force to pick out a gown I'm not going to wear."

"That's a shame. I would've liked to have seen that."

"Then you can wear it."

"I don't have the legs for it."

"That's a shame. I would've liked to have seen that."

He smirked, and I wondered why I hadn't noticed before how *steel* blue his eyes were.

"You're funny, Rylen Clark."

All week, he'd been in the webs of my mind. Maybe thanking him would be what it took to get him out; to pluck the weed up by its roots.

"Well," he said, tipping his hat. "I'll let you get back to *not* picking a gown."

"Um, hey listen. I wanted to say thank you for the book."

81

He smiled again. "I almost went with *Go, Dog. Go!* But I didn't want anything too difficult."

I chuckled. "Also, a strong contender. But I'm still trying to figure out why you gave it to me." Maybe I was being too honest, but I didn't care. After I'd thanked him, I'd be free of him and we'd never cross paths again.

He shrugged. "I heard you liked that book. So, why not? Making you smile was worth it."

I hadn't expected him to be so frank. Heat flooded my cheeks. He was blatantly flirting with me, and I was tempted to like it. "Thank you," I managed.

"Anytime."

He was doing that staring thing again. Gazing so intensely into my soul, I wondered if he could see between the fine cracks and small fissures what I'd been trying to protect.

Wow, he was good-looking. I could admit that I'd thought of his face all week.

He had a thin layer of dark stubble on his jaw, and the top few buttons on his plaid shirt were open. I could see a few wiry chest hairs poking out below the dips of his collarbones. A gold chain hung around his neck, the cross against sun-kissed skin. A package of M&Ms poked out of his shirt pocket.

I sucked in a breath, my heart thumping like war drums. If he kept looking at me like that, I'd...I'd...I couldn't take it any longer. I broke the spell and looked away.

A flash of platinum blonde hair caught my eye, and my stomach jumped. He stepped towards me, but I craned my neck to look around him. The blonde was lean, leggy, and someone I used to call my friend.

Ali was headed right towards us.

"Oh no!" I groaned, sinking into my chair.

He glanced over his shoulder, and before I could think, I grabbed his hand and yanked him forward. He looked stunned as I pushed him into the chair beside me. I squared his shoulders and ducked in front of his chest like a shield.

"Hide me!" I hissed.

"What? Why?"

He turned towards Ali, but I grabbed his face, keeping his eyes on me.

"Don't look! There's a tall blonde coming this way, okay? And I can't be seen by her."

He craned his neck again, but I squeezed tighter.

"Don't look, Jack."

"You mean Jumbo Barbie?" He pointed with a hitchhiker's thumb, and a laugh escaped me. She was wearing a strapless purple dress, and the bright blonde hair didn't help.

"Yes," I said in a hoarse whisper. "Can you please just…"

"Rylen?" inquired a voice.

Well, crap.

My eyes floated above Jack's head to see Ali, towering over us. She had three shopping bags hanging on one arm and her handbag on the other. She'd removed her sunglasses and held them in one hand. She had perplexed creases above her eyebrows, and I realized I looked like an idiot.

I was hunched over, still holding Jack's face tight enough for his lips to pucker out like an orangutan. My other hand rested on his thigh, and my knees were pushed against his legs.

I gave him an apologetic look and let him go. "Ali! What a surprise."

She smiled sweetly and, as always, everything about her was perfect. Hair, makeup, the works. Meanwhile, I couldn't remember if I'd brushed my teeth.

"Hey, I thought I heard your laugh," she said brightly. "How are you?"

"Yeah, I'm good." I gave her my best pseudo-smile, trying to sell the idea that I'd been more than perfect without her. "Ali, this is Jack. Jack, meet Ali."

He lifted a car-greased hand to shake hers, but she looked at it like he'd just peeled something dead off the sidewalk.

"Nice to meet you," she said.

"So, what are you doing here?" I asked.

"Shopping," she said. "I had a few errands. What about you?"

"I was..."

"Meeting me," Jack said, sliding his hand over mine, interlacing our fingers. "Saturday morning is kind of our thing. Right, sweetheart?"

I stared at him in disbelief. What the hell was he doing? His palm was rough and calloused, yet warm and strong. A tingle traveled down my spine.

Ali looked stunned, her eyes wide with skepticism.

I had to sell it, so I slowly nodded.

"Sweetie, I'm going to find Pete, but I'll see you later, okay?" Jack said.

Another nod. I'd forgotten how to form words.

He got to his feet, and I wanted to call after him to wait.

There's that word again...*wait*.

He tipped his hat to Ali. "Nice to meet you," he said, walking past her.

He was halfway across the parking lot before Ali found her voice. "Well, I didn't know you were seeing someone," she said, flustered.

Neither did I. My eyes narrowed. She didn't get to erase the past and talk to me like an old friend. "Why do you care?"

"Of course I care. He's kind of cute and he seems…"

"Ali," I said, cutting her off. "Just stop, okay? Please, I can't do this anymore."

Her throat bobbed, and her shoulders slumped.

"I know," she admitted. "I thought that we could…"

"We can't."

There wasn't any way. No matter how deeply I missed what had been, what she'd done was unforgivable.

She nodded tightly, her lips thinning into a straight line.

"I know what I did, Rylen, but you're not the only one that got hurt," she said, putting on her sunglasses.

My rebuttal was on my lips, but she didn't give me another second. She turned her back and walked away, the proverbial door slamming shut forever.

It was barely eleven, and already I could feel the unbearable sting of loneliness aching within. My jaw wobbled. Seeing Ali had ripped me open, reminding me of all I'd lost. Tears pricked at my eyes. I could feel the sting growing with every agonizing second.

I wasn't going to cry in public, and I wasn't going to allow her this power, but the more I tried to push the tears back, the more they flooded me.

I got to my feet and grabbed for the crutches. I hobbled down the sidewalk, trying to hide my face from mall-goers and pedestrians. But there was no stopping it. My tears fell uncontrollably.

If I could round the corner, I could cry in the alley between the buildings. I hobbled faster, turning a few heads. I was almost to the corner when my crutch hit a small pebble.

I was falling, the pavement rushing to my face, my crutches flying out to either side like wings, when I saw boots and felt a pair of strong arms grab me.

"Whoa!" Jack said, his arms around my waist. "I got you. Take it easy."

I'd involuntarily flung my arms around his neck, leaning all my weight on him, my crutches lying on the pavement. I looked up at him through my tears, and another round spilled down my cheeks.

"Rylen," he said, concerned.

He hadn't left. He'd waited.

I grabbed him tighter and buried my face in his chest, sobs now ripping through me. He ran his hands up and down my back, molding me against him.

"Hey," he said soothingly. "Tell me what's wrong."

I shook my head.

"I can't fix it if I don't know what's wrong. Whatever it is, it's going to be okay."

I didn't remember what being okay felt like, but that day in the park was the closest to okay I'd been in a long time. I wanted to believe him. More than that, I didn't want to be lonely anymore. I wanted more days in the park—more milkshakes in the sun. I wanted someone to call my friend.

I pulled back to look at him, clutching his shirt in my fists like he'd disappear if I let go.

He smiled tenderly. "You wanna get out of here?"

No, I couldn't leave. Yet what was waiting for me here? What did I have to lose?

I slowly nodded, and his smile broadened.

"Okay," he said, bending to get my crutches. "Let's go."

He could've driven me to Antarctica, and I wouldn't have cared. If I was getting far away from this place, maybe then I'd be okay.

Jack lifted me into his Bronco and stashed my crutches. He got into the driver's seat and took us out of town. I didn't know where we were going, but the further away we got, the more I felt myself breathe again.

I leaned my head against the window, dreading the flood of questions to come, but he didn't say anything. Eventually, my tears diminished into small hiccups. I caught a glimpse of myself in the side-view mirror. My mascara had streaked into black trails, and my eyes were red and puffy. I used my jacket sleeve to wipe them, but it was no use.

Bam Bam lumbered into the space between the seats. He nuzzled against Jack's leg, whimpering. Jack patted his head and took the next right, parking along the riverbank.

The tranquil sounds of rippling water washed over me. I took a deep breath, filling my lungs, breathing out everything I'd left behind.

He killed the engine and pulled a red handkerchief from his back pocket.

"Here," he said, offering it to me. "It's clean."

I must've looked like a drowned cat. I took it and I wiped my face, scrubbing at the smeared mascara.

"Thank you," I muttered. Now the questions would come. I'd broken down into a hot sobbing mess in front of him. I'd sobbed until I hiccupped like a lush with a case of wine. Surely, he expected an explanation.

"Are you alright?" he asked.

That wasn't the first thing I'd expected him to say.

"Yes," I murmured. "I'm sorry. I didn't mean to break down like that."

He shook his head. "You have nothing to be sorry for."

"I got snot on your shirt."

He looked at his chest, smiling at the crusty white smear. "I've endured worse, but if it makes you feel better, I was going to burn it later."

I sighed. "There's not much that's going to make me feel better."

He gave me a wistful look, like he was at a loss for words. This was already awkward enough without his silent pity. But the silence lingered, and the life that flowed between us began to slowly flatline. And the only thing more awkward than an awkward silence is pretending it's not awkward at all.

I said the first thing that popped into my head.

"I thought you were meeting someone?"

He shrugged. "Don't worry about it. I can do it later."

I felt my cheeks burn crimson. Not only had I broken down into hysterical tears and wiped my snot on his shirt, but I'd also made him miss his appointment.

"Sorry," I said again. "I'm usually better at controlling myself. She just got under my skin today."

"Ali did?" he asked.

I nodded and gave him mental bonus points for remembering her name. This guy paid attention.

"You gonna tell me what happened?" he asked, unbuckling his seatbelt. He leaned back in his chair like he was getting comfortable, preparing for my story.

I sighed. "I'd rather not get into it. It was a long time ago, and it's over now."

"Didn't look over to me."

I cut my eyes to him.

"If it were over, it wouldn't still bother you. Not like this."

"Fine," I said, turning in my seat to face him. "It bugs me, but there's nothing I can do about it. I wish I could travel back in time."

"And what good would that do?" he asked.

"Erase the past and stop everything from being so...so... *shitty.*"

"But then you'd erase your future, too."

I lifted a brow. "That's kind of the point."

The dog put his front paws on Jack's lap, and Jack patted his head. "Whatever happened in the past, it can't be bad enough that you'd erase your entire future."

"I don't know about that. The last year of my life's been pretty crappy."

"So, tell me what happened then."

I shook my head. "Nope."

"It might make you feel better."

"It won't."

"If I guess, will you tell me?"

"Nope."

He sighed deeply, and I bit back a laugh. He was persistent. My own personal Sam I Am. I loved and hated it at the same time.

"Well, if you're not going to tell me, we'll have to find another way to relieve your frustrations."

My eyes widened, and he gave me a slow, devilish grin. What a flirt.

He hadn't even bought me a drink yet. No guy had ever had this effect on me. High schoolers used to park along the riverbank to make out in the backseats. Was that why he brought me here? Did he think I was that sort of girl?

Although...

He lifted the door handle, and it swung open. The dog jumped out and scurried along the bank. Jack stepped out and turned to face me.

"You comin' or what?"

Okay, message received.

I opened my door as Jack appeared and helped me to the ground, placing his hands around my ribcage. I tried not to focus on his hands or the fact that butterflies sprang up in my stomach every time he touched me. I balanced precariously on one foot until he handed me my crutches.

He walked to the back of the Bronco and opened the tailgate. An unopened box of Huggies diapers caught my eye. It seemed out of place, but I didn't ask.

He took off his hat and then rolled up his sleeves to his elbows. His forearms were corded and covered with a light dusting of dark hair.

Protruding veins wrapped up his arms like rounded vines, and I could read the loopy cursive letters that stretched from his elbow to his wrist.

The Captain

I'd have to save my questions for later.

"It's time I introduced you to a little thing called Slugger Therapy," Jack said, retrieving a baseball bat from the floor.

"You just made that up."

He grinned. "Yes, I did."

He rested the bat on his shoulder and nodded in the direction he wanted me to follow. "Come on. I'll show you how it works."

I hobbled next to him as he led the way down the riverbank. I gave him more bonus points for keeping an arm outstretched, ready to catch me if I stumbled again.

We stopped walking in front of an abandoned, rusted Chevy. It had been there since my high school days, when Andon and I would meet our friends for Friday night bonfires and fireworks.

REDEMPTION'S LIST

The old Chevy had endured an endless, painful death. Long spider-webbed cracks were sprawled across the windshield. The remaining windows had been busted into tiny fragments, decorating the ground and the seats like glitter. The door panels, which had been sprayed with blue and yellow graffiti, were dented and drooping.

"What are we doing here?" I asked.

He didn't answer me. Instead, he swung the bat and landed a hit into the front fender, leaving a dent the size of a bowling ball.

My jaw hit the ground. "What the hell are you doing?"

"Your turn." He flipped the bat around so I could easily take it, but I shook my head.

"Come on," he pressed. "When are you ever gonna get another opportunity to let loose?"

"To let what loose?"

He shrugged, pointing from my head to my toes. "Whatever it is that's got you all tied up in there."

He offered me the bat again, but I refused. I couldn't let him see me let loose. He'd already seen too much.

"Fine, watch and learn."

He walked to the back of the car, resting the bat against his shoulder.

"Thanks for nothing, Frank," he said. "You drunken, lazy bastard!"

He slammed the bat into the trunk, pounding it over and over until it curved up like a taco.

"Who's Frank?" I asked.

"Who's Ali?"

Again, he swung the bat, taking out what was left of the taillight, and shards of red plastic sprang into the air around him.

"Ali was my best friend."

"Frank was my father."

The side view mirror came next, and once he knocked it free, he continued to beat it into the ground until it was in pieces.

"She slept with my boyfriend."

"Frank was a sadistic piece of shit."

He rounded to the front of the car, smacking the rusted bumper until it broke in two.

"I'll never forgive her."

"Frank had no remorse."

Smash smash smash.

The freedom he must've felt! The exhilaration of letting loose! I was getting high on it just by watching him.

Then my hand was outstretched, and I was wordlessly asking for the bat. Jack smiled and put it in my hand. He took a crutch from me, and I leaned all my weight on one, holding the bat in my other hand.

My throat bobbed. Maybe it wouldn't fix anything?

"Go for it," Jack said. "Let 'em have it. There's no judgment. It's just you and me, sweetheart."

I swung, hitting the hood so hard my teeth vibrated. I swung again, but I had too much momentum, and Jack caught me before I toppled over.

"Try again," he said, one hand steadying my hips. "Move your hand up the bat for better control." He put his other hand over mine, walking my fingers up the handle. "There, now get out of your head. Just be in the moment."

He stood behind me, his hands resting on my hips, his breath hot on the nape of my neck. I couldn't stop thinking about those hands and the bolts of electrical current surging through me.

I swung again, smashing the spider windshield.

"You're a cheating piece of shit, Andon!" I bellowed. "I trusted you. I thought we had a future."

Another swing. Another hit.

"You were my best friend, Ali. How could you betray me?"
I landed another and another.

"I lost everything. I miss my friends. Being alone sucks."

I smashed and smashed until there was nothing left of the windshield—until there was nothing left inside of me—until I'd admitted every last great and despicable truth and my arm was too tired to continue.

My chest heaved as I turned to find Jack smiling at me.

"Nicely done, Rylen Clark. Nicely done."

It was at that moment, next to the river, with sweat dripping off my chin, that I knew I was in too deep.

I'd tried to keep what was inside secure and protected, but it was too late. I'd tried not to like him. I'd fought with all the might I could muster, but just like the windshield I'd obliterated, all of my walls came crashing down into a million tiny pieces.

Chapter Ten

JACK

Rylen had been quiet for most of our drive back to the city. I was both pleased and surprised she'd admitted so much in front of me. I figured her silence was a side effect of all she'd said back at the riverbank, but she didn't need to worry. I had no room to judge her. We were stuck in traffic in front of the strip mall where I'd run into her earlier that day. Up ahead, police cars and ambulances worked quickly to clear an accident, but until then, we were lined up like ants at a picnic, waiting for traffic to move.

I heard Rylen sigh and turned to see her looking at her phone, her thumbs tapping quickly across the screen.

"Everything okay over there?" I asked.

"Yeah, just reading an email from my dad. He's headed to Texas this week."

"What's he doing there?"

She rolled her eyes. "A business trip, but he's been gone for six months."

"That's…odd."

She pocketed her phone. "I know, and it's like my mom doesn't even care. She works nonstop, and when she's not working, she's trying to control my life and talking to some dude named Adam."

I lifted a brow, saying without words what I was thinking, but I didn't want to jump to conclusions. She nodded, confirming what I thought.

"I'm pretty sure he's her boyfriend. She just hasn't told me yet."

"Why don't you ask her?"

"I can't ask her!" she said, appalled. "She can't know that I know."

"But *do* you know? Are you one hundred percent sure?"

She shifted in her seat, fully facing me. "She's lying and sneaking around. What more proof do I need?"

"It is suspicious, but give her the benefit of the doubt, okay? I'd be pissed if someone assumed I was a cheater."

She leaned back in her seat and crossed her arms. "That's just it. I don't think I want to know."

"Look, if it were me, I'd give anything to speak to my mom one more time, even if it were hard." My words had come out a little harsher than I'd intended, but I knew what it felt like to miss someone so deeply you would give anything for one more precious moment. Taking people for granted was a mistake I'd never make again.

She was quiet, my admission percolating in her brain. Her lips thinned, and her throat bobbed before she spoke.

"Your mom's gone?"

"She died when I was six. Frank had us for a while, then my Gran took me and my sister."

The truck in front of me inched forward, and I followed suit, lightly tapping on the pedal. When we stopped again, we settled into the quiet, and her gaze traveled to her window. Maybe I'd said too much? It wasn't any of my business. I should've kept my mouth shut.

I was about to retract all I had said when she spoke again.

"I'm sorry about your mom. If I'm honest, before things changed, my mom was pretty great. I miss those days."

I couldn't help the smile that spread across my face. "Thanks, my mom was great too."

Bam Bam crawled into the space between the seats and whimpered. Rylen reached to pet his head, but his lips curled back, and he growled, showing pointy canine teeth.

"Okay, I'm sorry," Rylen said, pulling her hand back. "Your dog hates me."

"Get back," I said, snapping my fingers. The dog whined and climbed into the back seat.

"Sorry, he just hasn't warmed up to you yet. He'll get there."

"In the meantime, I'd like to keep all of my limbs if you don't mind."

I shrugged. "Maybe you give off cat energy."

"I don't own a cat."

"Yeah, but do you own a dog?"

She blinked a few times, the crease between her eyebrows becoming more defined.

"No."

I laughed at her admission. "Exactly."

We inched forward again, and I tapped the gas before immediately braking.

"So, where's the first place you're going to go as soon as you can drive again?" I asked.

She stiffened like she was in finishing school, and someone had placed a book on her head.

"Um, I haven't given it much thought."

"It'll be nice to have your freedom back. I'd go crazy."

"Yeah," she said underwhelmed. "It'll be great. Where would you go?"

I smirked, and before I could think better of it, I cranked the wheel to the right and hit the gas. We bounced up the sidewalk, tearing up the grass, the tires squealing as I rolled into the parking lot.

"What are you doing?" she asked.

"Pancakes," I said, cutting the engine.

"What?"

I pointed out the window to Sally's Diner, and her eyes followed.

"Well, you asked where I'd go. The traffic's not moving, and I'm starving. So, I say we wait it out with a pile of pancakes."

I opened the door and hopped out, but when I turned around, she was still sitting there, staring at me like I had snakes coming out of my ears.

"You comin' or what?"

§∘↺∘§ §∘↺∘§ §∘↺∘§

I opened the door for Rylen as she made her way into Sally's Diner. The bells rang overhead, signaling our entrance. For me, walking into Sally's Diner was like returning to the comfort of an old slipper.

The carpet was a 1970s era burnt orange and likely the original when the place was called Milly's and belonged to Sally's mother, Mildred. Light fixtures hung on gold chains above our heads, with glass, umbrella-like skirts. The wallpaper was orange and pink, featuring white daisies. To my left was the cash register; next to it sat a cooler filled with slices of pie that slowly rotated. With chocolate

97

shavings, mounds of white whipped cream, and sugar crystals that caught the light and sparkled like diamonds, the pieces looked more like works of art than dessert.

Before I left, I used to be among the stool-sitting-bar crowd, discussing whether or not the rain would ruin crops and the current price of wheat. The same sorts of people, primarily farmers, came in almost every night for a late supper, a slice of pie, and a strong cup of coffee.

"Jack, how ya been, man?" Ned, a regular diner-goer, arose from his stool to greet me.

"Hiya, Ned," I said, putting my palm in his for a firm handshake. Ned's hair had gone from salt and pepper to all white, and the wrinkles around his mouth and eyes were more defined.

"What happened to your hair? You look like my grandpa." I teased.

"I'm twenty years younger than any grandparent of yours, kid."

I snickered, and beside me, Rylen stifled a laugh.

"Wake up, Pete," Ned said, slapping his hunched-over back. "Jack's here."

A sleepy-eyed Pete lifted his head from the counter, then blinked a few times like his brain was registering my face.

"Jack," Pete said, wiping sleep from his eyes. "How are ya, man?"

"Hello, Pete," I said, extending a handshake.

"When you canceled on me this afternoon, I was beginning to think you weren't really back."

"Sorry about that. I'll look at your truck tomorrow."

"It's no big deal. I'm just glad you're back. Pull up a stool," Pete brought his coffee cup to his lips but found it empty. "Wendy, will ya make a fresh pot?"

"Sure thing, Pete," said a voice.

Ned stepped towards me. He was long and lean and wore dusty overalls, lace-up boots, and a baseball hat that said, "Potato Farmers Do It Dirty." His face was thinner than I remembered, his jaw more pointed, his stubble more gray.

"So, ah, Margaret told me you were in town again. It's good to see ya," Ned said.

Pete turned on his stool to face me.

"Dolores mentioned that you stopped by and helped Miss Hillary have her calf. Then, when you canceled on me today, I told the old woman she was seeing things because nobody had heard from Jack in ages. Guess I'd better call her."

Where Ned was long and lean, Pete was stocky and thick. His face was perfectly round, like that of a chubby baby, and he had a small, turned-up nose supporting aviator-framed glasses with lenses as thick as Coke bottles.

"You're just upset, Petey, that your senile wife got it right," Ned said, slapping Pete on the shoulders.

"For the last time, Nedford Hampton, Dolores is not senile. In a way, she really *did* see Elvis."

"That's cause it was Halloween," Ned chortled.

I bit my cheek to keep from laughing, but Rylen released a small chuckle.

"Well, now, who might this be?" Ned cooed, his eyes landing on Rylen, who turned a shade of light pink.

"This is Rylen," I said.

"Nice to meet you, Miss Rylen," Ned said, offering his hand, which she shook with a tight smile. "What have you done to yourself, my dear?" he asked, gesturing to the crutches.

"Knee surgery," she said.

"Ah, gosh, I'm sorry to hear that, kid," he said. "What are you doing being seen around town with his ugly mug?"

Pete snorted as Ned elbowed me so hard in the ribs, I made a noise that sounded like a grunt and a squawk had a baby.

"Don't you listen to him," Pete cut in. "He's just jealous Jack's got you, because his Franny has no teeth."

"It was her veneer. It pops out sometimes," Ned grumbled, exasperated.

"Yeah, it popped out all right. Went flying across the room."

"Shush up, Pete," Ned growled, but Pete giggled when Ned wasn't looking.

Rylen, now beaming, stifled a laugh. "He's not too bad. It did take some getting used to, though," she said, winking at me.

"You're never going to heal if you have to look at that all day, kid," Ned added, pointing his thumb at me.

"Well, I think he's cute, but I guess it's debatable," she replied, laughing.

"I'll have to take your word for it. I'll tell you what," he began, "You ever need anything, anything at all, my dear, because this dumb rodeo clown decided to disappear on you…."

My feet were suddenly fascinating.

"…you give ol' Ned a call. Smart girl like you can find me in the phone book. Last name's Hampton."

"Thanks, but hopefully," she paused, and I lifted my eyes from my boots, "he's not going anywhere on me."

"Rylen," I groaned, rubbing the spot where Ned had prodded me. "I think we should sit in the back."

I was grateful that she nodded. I needed to get away from Ned's pointy elbows.

"Thanks for your help with Hillary, Jack," Pete said, giving a small salute as I walked away.

"Sure thing, Pete," I said.

"You two kids have a nice night now." Ned leaned on the bar beside Pete and crossed his legs. "It was nice to meet you, Miss Rylen."

"You too," she said over her shoulder.

I sat across from her and pulled in my chair as Wendy arrived with our menus.

"Here you guys go," she said, placing two glasses of water and two menus beside us. "I'll give you a few," she said, walking back into the kitchen.

I opened my menu and hid behind the list of specials.

"So," I said, keeping my face concealed. "You think I'm cute."

I laid the menu flat, meeting a pink-faced Rylen. I grinned at her and wiggled my eyebrows, and her face broke into a grin.

"Out of that whole exchange, that's what you're focused on?"

"Absolutely."

She rolled her eyes. "I said it was debatable. Even an ugly baby is kind of cute."

"Ouch," I said in mock offense. "My sister was the ugliest baby I'd ever seen."

Her brows rose. "How can you say that about your sister?"

"Because it's true. She was ugly. I mean, she's pretty now, but when she came out," I shook my head. "My mom said the nurse gasped."

She laughed again. "That's not a good sign."

"What about you?"

"Was I an ugly baby?"

"No. I highly doubt there was ever anything ugly about you."

"Good thing you didn't know me in seventh grade. Braces and headgear are killers to a girl's ego."

I shook my head. "Temporary discomfort wouldn't have changed my opinion."

She smiled shyly, casting those round brown eyes down to her menu. Her ears turned red, and she got all flustered. I liked the reaction I got when I flirted with her. It only encouraged me.

"I mean, do you have a sibling?" I asked.

She met my eyes, hesitated, opened her mouth to answer, and then closed it again.

"I *had* a sibling. A brother. He died three years ago."

"Oh God, I'm sorry to hear that."

"Don't be sorry. I'm over it now."

She lifted her menu, concealing her face. It was time to change the subject, but I pressed the matter.

"I can still be sorry that something terrible happened to your family."

The menu lowered, her eyes meeting mine across the table: large and searching, surprised at my frankness.

"It was terrible," she said quietly.

I should have broken eye contact, but she was staring at me, the way I often stared at her. The truth was I couldn't take my eyes off her. I didn't want to, and I found myself counting down the minutes until I could look at her again. But that would be it; looking is where it would stop. We could never be more.

"You're staring at me," I said.

"You stare at me."

"Guilty as charged, sweetheart."

"It makes me feel like I have spinach in my teeth."

I chuckled, holding eye contact. "If you did, I'd tell you."

"*And* it's what stalkers do. Are you a stalker?"

"Not today, but I am afraid you *are* stuck with me."

She scrunched up her face. "You're not going to follow me around like a lost puppy, are you?"

102

"Only if you rub my belly."

She chuckled. "Nope. You're on your own."

A tray of dishes fell, and I looked over my shoulder to see Wendy scurrying to the broom closet. Rylen lifted her menu again, saying her next words behind the pages.

"What's good here? I'm starved."

"Everything's good. Except for the salads. I never order them."

She peeked over the top. "Then how do you know they're no good?"

"Because it's salad," I said plainly. "Who wants to eat rabbit food when you can order pancakes?"

She folded up her menu and set it aside. "You must come in here a lot."

"I used to. Ned lives on the farm next to my grandma, and Pete is two miles down the road," I admitted. "I was in here a lot before I left."

"Why did you leave?" She brought her glass to her lips and munched an ice cube, her lips moist and pink.

"Ah," I paused, distracted, "Hmm, there were a lot of reasons."

"Like?" she pressed. "Come on. You made me spill my guts back at the car."

"I didn't like who I'd become. I thought people would be better off without me. So, I left."

"You mean, you disappeared?" she asked quizzically. "Like what Ned said?"

I made a mental note to bring her around fewer people who'd known me before I left. Rylen didn't miss even the most minor details.

"Sort of, I...."

"Jack!"

Sally appeared at the end of our table, a small notebook in her hand and a pencil behind her ear. She wore a blue dress with ruffled trim and a white apron. Her graying hair was pulled into a bun, and a black hair net was pulled over her head. Reading glasses hung on a gold chain around her neck, and a name tag was pinned to her apron.

"I didn't think I would see you again so soon," she cooed.

"How's it going, Sally?" I said, smiling.

"I'm doing alright. Hey, thanks again for fixing the fryer. She's purring like a kitten."

Rylen turned her head to look at me, but I didn't meet her eyes.

"It was no trouble."

Sally's eyes narrowed, and she waved her index finger in a "shame on you" motion. "That repairman was going to charge me seven hundred dollars plus parts plus labor." Then she turned to Rylen. "Jack stopped by last week and fixed it for me. She's practically good as new."

"I just replaced a wire," I cut in.

"You can't run a diner without a fryer. I would've had to close the place for a week. Gosh, I don't think Bill and I would've made it."

Rylen smiled. "That was nice of you, Jack."

"I was happy to help, Sally," I said.

"Well, just know Bill and I are very appreciative. Now, what can I get you, kids? Jack, you want your pancakes with M&M's?" Sally pulled her pencil from her ear and put her glasses on. The gold chain rattled against the plastic.

"Yes, please."

Rylen flashed a perplexed look, like I'd ordered alligator Pop-Tarts, but a smile was on the edge of her lips.

"All righty," Sally said, scratching my order in her notebook. "How about for you, dear?"

"Chicken Caesar salad," Rylen answered.

I shook my head, and Rylen winked at me.

"Sure thing, honey," Sally said, the top of her pencil moving vigorously across the page. "And this one is on the house, kids."

"Thanks, Sally," I said.

"Sure, it's the least I can do. I'll bring you some coffee. Wendy's got a fresh pot brewin'."

As Sally walked away, Rylen lifted her glass again and took a slow drink, eying me over the rim.

"What?" I shrugged.

"Pancakes with M&Ms?" she asked, the water glistening on her lips.

"Caesar salad? I believe I said they weren't very good."

"Well, you wouldn't really know, would you?"

"I know that I'd rather starve."

"Where does this deep-seated hatred of vegetables come from?"

"When I was a kid, my mom had a garden. Frank drank every dollar, so I ate a lot of vegetables. Then she died and…" I shrugged. "I haven't eaten one since."

Rylen was quiet, peering into me with those piercing brown eyes. She picked up her glass and took another drink, the ice cubes clinking together.

"I hate country music," she blurted. "My brother used to sing a lot, and he'd sing country songs, and every time I hear one…" She shook her head. "I can't stand to listen to it because it's like losing him all over again."

There was a lump in my throat. I hadn't felt it growing, but it was there. Rylen may be the one person on earth who truly understood what I'd lost.

I let out a deep breath. "Grief has this way of disguising itself within ordinary things."

She nodded slowly, and we sat in comfortable silence. We didn't need words to understand what the other had been through. Grief would always be universal and personal at the exact same time.

Sally returned with our orders and a fresh pot of coffee, and Rylen broke eye contact and looked out the window. Sally poured coffee into our mugs, the opaque steam rising into the air in thin wisps.

"You kids enjoy," Sally said, returning to the kitchen.

I nodded my thanks and had begun slathering butter over the golden surface of my pancakes when Rylen spoke again.

"What possessed you to put M&Ms in your pancakes?"

"What possessed you to order a salad?"

"Hmm, heart health. Cholesterol. Blood pressure. Need I say more?"

"You got enough dressing on that thing to choke a horse. That kind of defeats the purpose."

I generously dumped blueberry syrup until it flowed down the sides and swamped the hotcakes in a sea of purple.

"You got enough syrup on that to put me into a diabetic coma."

"Yes, but I'm not pretending to be healthy, am I?"

Her eyes narrowed, and she picked up her garlic toast and ripped it with her teeth.

I snickered, cutting a perfect triangle. "Haven't you had this before?"

"Sure, when I was four."

I chuckled. "You're funny, Rylen Clark. It's a culinary delicacy. The yellow M&Ms taste the best."

"They all taste the same."

"They do not!" I said indignantly, and her face broke into a grin.

I dragged my sleeve through a puddle of syrup and rolled it up to my elbow. Her eyes went to the ink on the inside of my forearm,

"What's your tattoo say?" she asked.

I laid my arm out on the table, the tattooed edges still fresh and swollen.

"That looks new," she said, wincing.

"I had it touched up," I said, pulling my arm back.

"Who's the Captain?"

I thought for a moment, leery of sharing this part of myself with her, but with those giant brown eyes peering into me and genuine interest painted on her face…. If this kept happening, I would give her anything she wanted.

"I'll take you to meet him sometime," I said.

Rylen looked like she wanted to press for more, and I wanted to trust her with this, but I feared I was already too involved.

I stabbed the bite, making sure there were at least four M&Ms, and held it out to her.

"First bite is yours," I said as a bead of syrup dripped onto my hand.

She smiled, considering, then took the fork from my fingertips. She put the pancake in her mouth and chewed slowly, then her eyes closed, and she sighed and nodded in contentment.

"You're right," she smiled, gesturing to my stack of pancakes. "You're in the presence of beauty."

And there, in a greasy diner with dirty farmers, with her pink lips, chocolate eyes, and dark curls, Rylen Clark had never been more right.

Chapter Eleven

Rylen

I couldn't sleep that night. The ibuprofen I'd taken before I went to bed hadn't touched my knee pain. The red numbers on my alarm clock taunted me with their glaring reminder. It was one thirty-two.

I sighed and reached for my phone. I was sure Jack was asleep, and I didn't want to bother him, but I couldn't help myself, so I opened a new message to text him.

Sent Monday 1:33 AM
Rylen: Hey, you awake?

Within seconds, my phone vibrated, and I couldn't help the idiotic grin that spread across my face.

Sent 1:33 AM

Jack: Nope. Texting in my sleep is among my many talents.

I smirked, typing back my reply, but the phone rang in my hand, and the name JACK danced across the bright screen.

"Hey," I answered, trying to hide the giddiness in my voice.

"Hey, isn't it way past your bedtime?" he asked playfully.

"Do you even know what time it is?"

"Nope, I don't wear a watch. I can let you go."

"No!" I blurted, sounding a bit too eager. "I mean, no. I texted you, remember?"

"You did. Are you okay?"

The small fact that he cared enough to ask made the butterflies within me dance. I threw the blankets back and pulled myself into a sitting position. "Yeah, just my knee hurts, and I can't sleep."

"Why? Run out of sheep?"

"No, my mind started spinning, and that never works anyway."

"I know." He added, "Sheep are far too distracting. Have you ever been around them?"

"No."

"Well, they're incredibly stupid. I once watched one get in a fight with his own shadow."

I chuckled. "Who won?"

"The shadow," Jack said, laughing. "I'm just saying that whoever came up with the idea that sheep are boring never spent any time around them."

I smirked. "What if you looked over and boom – two sheep doing the humpty dumpty – you'd completely lose count."

Jack laughed again, and I wondered if it would sound the same ten years from now. Would he still be my friend? Could we call each other at one in the morning to talk about nothing at all?

"What about you? Why are you awake?" I asked, twirling a thread from the blanket around my finger.

"My phone buzzed."

"Sorry."

"I'm kidding. I'm sitting on Sally's roof," he answered.

My brows crinkled. "No wonder you can't sleep. Is that a hobby of yours?"

He chuckled. "No, I hate heights. I told her I'd clean the gutters, and I wanted to keep my word."

I released the thread. "You mean you dropped me off and then you went back to Sally's?"

"Yep."

"Why are you cleaning gutters in the middle of the night?"

"This was the only time I could do it. I'm fixing Pete's truck tomorrow, and Sally didn't want me up here while she had customers. But anyway, I had to quit. The batteries in my headlamp died."

"You could've said you had things to do. I didn't mean to take up all your time."

"You didn't. I gave it to you." The rich, velvety timbre of his voice resonated within me, the warmth unleashing more fluttering butterflies. A camel in Timbuktu probably keeled over dead from all the chaos I was creating.

"I owe them both a favor," he added. "So, I wanted to be sure to repay them."

There was that word again. He *owed* them. But what had he done that'd put him in their debt? I wanted to ask more questions, but it was none of my business.

"You know what I do when I can't sleep?" Jack asked.

"Count goats?"

"You're funny, but no. I think about the most boring things on earth."

"Like what?"

"Watching golf. Ungodly amounts of it."

"Oh, God," I groaned. "That would suck."

"Not when compared to Catholic mass in Latin."

I giggled. "Transatlantic flight. No books or TV allowed."

"Traffic jam. Broken radio and a dead phone."

"In line for the ladies' room. No, wait – in line at the DMV."

"Nutcracker ballet," he said.

"Not so. All those men flitting around in tights can be very distracting."

"Yeah, true, they all look like they got squirrels stuffed down the front of their tights."

"That's why it's called the Nutcracker!" I chortled.

A laugh erupted from him, and I buried my face into a pillow to keep my own cackles from waking the house.

I wished we could spend more evenings like this, except he'd be on the sofa next to me, my legs resting in his lap, and we'd talk until the sky turned a pale pink with the ascending sun.

He yawned deeply, the sound of it like air flowing through a wind tunnel.

"Am I boring you?" I asked.

"Not at all. I'm glad you texted me. It gets lonely this time of night. I've been having trouble sleeping, too."

"Why?" I asked.

"Because I'll just lie there and think about everything I have to do. Everyone I owe who needs my help." He inhaled. "My mind spins, too."

"I can't help it," I admitted. "It's anxiety, and I don't know how to stop it."

"Neither do I but talking to you makes it better."

There was a pregnant pause, and I could hear my heart thundering in my ears. Was it possible that I'd met someone who knew exactly how I felt? And the best part was I didn't have to explain anything. He already knew.

"Sit on rooftops," I said, breaking the silence. "Add that to the boring list. Unless you're hunting Santa."

He laughed again, and the melodious sound wrapped around me like a soft, warm blanket. [OBJ]

"Nope. No red-suited fat men in sight. I sat down to watch the stars and now I can't look away."

I hobbled over to the windowsill and pulled back the curtains. The moon was round and full, like a perfect egg yolk, and the stars twinkled like small diamonds against black satin.

"Yeah," I said. "I'm looking at them too."

We were quiet for a moment, but I could hear the soothing cadence of Jack's breathing. I hoped he wasn't paying attention to my own breath because I realized I'd been holding mine.

"That's the worst part about being alone," I said. "You don't have anyone to look at the stars with."

I wanted more of this. I wanted to spend time with him, fill my days with laughter, and eat breakfast for dinner. I wanted to be dropped off after dark and do the same thing the next day.

"Will you pick me up tomorrow?" I asked.

He didn't answer right away, the silence indicating hesitation, and I feared my request had been too bold.

"I mean, I know you're busy and I don't need to be anywhere, so I understand if you can't, and…"

"Do you want me to?"

"Yes." I heard myself say.

"Then I'll be there. Good night, Rylen Clark." The sincerity in his voice was exhilarating, my fears dissipating like morning mist under a bright yellow sun.

"Goodnight, Jack."

I lay my head on the pillow as I ended the call, and I fell into peaceful sleep, dreaming about camels lined up in neat rows. Then I watched them tip over like dominoes, the chaos spreading like an epidemic, but I didn't care. A swarm of shimmering butterflies surrounded me, and I still had that idiotic grin plastered on my face.

§∞∽⌒∞§ §∞∽⌒∞§ §∞∽⌒∞§

The sun was slowly setting behind the hills, its rays streaking through the sky in orange, pink, and red. We were parked in front of the small strip mall again. Jack promised me Yo-Yo's had the best frozen yogurt in North Dakota.

Jack hoisted me onto the back of the tailgate, then hopped up next to me, letting our legs dangle over the edge. Bam Bam chewed a frisbee on the ground beneath us. A strawberry cheesecake frozen yogurt sat between us, and it would've been perfect, but Jack insisted we add M&Ms. He dipped the spoon into the yogurt and held it out to me.

"First bite is yours," he said.

I took the spoon and put it in my mouth, savoring the flavor of creamy strawberries.

"Okay," I said. "It's not bad."

"It's delicious," he countered, filling his spoon.

I dipped my spoon into it again, trying to scoop around the cold M&Ms.

"I'll never understand your M&M obsession."

113

"Many try and many fail." He scooped another bite and swung his legs, like a small child on a countertop, and chunks of mud flung off his boots into the air.

I turned my spoon, so the cream coated my tongue. "Hmm, okay; this is good."

"Told ya, best in the Dakotas," he said.

I detested cold M&Ms, but a yellow one coated in pink surfaced in the center of my spoon. I offered it to him, and he grinned and ate it, his front teeth scraping across the top of the plastic. There was something intimate about the act, like seeing a new friend's messy bedroom for the first time and not caring if the laundry was folded or if the bed was unmade and rumpled. I had a strong feeling I could show Jack all of my messes and he wouldn't care.

"Thanks for picking me up," I said.

"Anytime. Sorry, I was late. Pete's truck needs a new transmission."

"Are you going to fix it for him?"

He sighed. "If I can find a transmission, otherwise..." he shrugged. "I don't know what I'll do."

"Why are you helping all of these people? I mean, it's nice of you and all, but..."

"They need help, and I can help them. Simple as that."

He stuffed the spoon back in his mouth, and I decided I wouldn't press the issue for now, but he was my friend, and I didn't want him to be taken advantage of, even if he was willing to help.

"Actually, you showed up just in time. My mom is driving me crazy."

"Yeah? What's she doing?"

I took another bite, savoring the rich cream, hoping the cold sweetness would dull the ache that gnawed at my heart whenever thoughts of my mom drifted into my mind, like a dark cloud that hung over my head.

"The usual. It's just amplified by the fundraiser and wanting me to pick a gown and…" I sighed. "I did my part. I took her pictures, and I *loathe* dresses and fancy occasions, but I don't have the guts to tell her I don't want to go."

"What's the fundraiser for?"

I dipped my spoon back into the pink yogurt and shoved another bite in. I was stalling, trying to buy myself time, but I think I knew I'd end up telling him the whole story.

"The charity is for the families of those who've lost loved ones from driving under the influence." I paused, feeling my throat bob. I hadn't allowed myself to speak about this in a long time.

"My brother Michael…" My voice cracked as images from that night came rushing back, but Jack's unwavering gaze somehow made it possible to continue. "A drunk driver hit him. He was killed instantly."

"Oh God. That's terrible," he said quietly.

"The thing is, I think fundraisers are stupid, because all the charity in the world doesn't bring back what you've lost."

"No," he agreed. "Not even close."

"After that, everything changed. We weren't a family anymore. There were no movie nights, no more family trips to Florida, no more Christmases. Because I didn't just lose my brother that day. I lost my parents too, who they used to be. My dad's away on business. My mom works so much that I barely see her, and when I do see her, I always feel like she'd rather be somewhere else. I've never been so lonely, and I'm stuck inside that big house with an asshole cat that hates me."

A small laugh escaped him. "I knew you gave off cat energy."

"Madam Plunkett is not *my* cat."

He grinned, and I let myself laugh.

"My mom wasn't always like that, though," I admitted. "She used to make pancakes on Saturday mornings and tell the worst, most corny jokes you've ever heard. She used to sing in the shower, off-key, at the top of her lungs. I had to bang on the door and remind her we had neighbors."

He chuckled, and I realized I was being transported back to a place long ago, to a memory I had not visited in quite some time. Something in my chest started to ache.

"I'm so angry at her. Because now..." I shrugged. "It's like I'm living with this ghost of who she used to be, and..." I paused, swallowing the lump in my throat, "And I'm afraid she'll never make pancakes again."

It was a great truth that I'd never told anyone before, but I couldn't help myself. Jack's steel blue eyes burned a hole through me, unlocking everything I kept within, breaking down all my barriers and revealing what I'd found the most terrifying.

Exposer.

"At the diner, when you said sometimes grief hides within ordinary things?"

"Yeah?" he said, compassion illuminating his features.

"I think that's what happened to them. Everything reminded them of him, and it doesn't seem to matter that I'm still here. They let grief *suffocate* them, and I'm afraid they'll never come back. They'll never be who they used to be."

His gaze never wavered, those piercing steel pools causing my involuntary surrender. I had lied to him at the diner. When he looked at me that way, I didn't feel like I had spinach in my teeth. I felt like I could barely breathe.

His fingers traced gentle lines on the inside of my arm, and then he interlaced our fingers, locking us together. I stared at our hands, then lifted my eyes to meet his. He was staring again, but I didn't care.

I wanted him to see me.

The sun had begun to set, streaking the sky in pink and orange. I goosebumps pricked at my skin, and our breaths began to plume in the crisp air.

"Cold?" he asked softly.

I nodded, and he pulled off his jacket and wrapped it around my shoulders, cloaking me in his warmth; then his hand was back in mine.

His right arm stretched behind me, and he wrapped it around my shoulders, pulling me closer. I lay my head in the crook of his arm, catching hints of Ivory soap and car grease. He rested his cheek on the top of my head, his right hand gently gliding up and down my arm.

But this didn't make sense. This connection. This contact.

We were only friends, and friends didn't touch—not like this. If we crossed the line between friendship and lovers, and then it failed…there wouldn't be a way for me to survive. I'd already lost all my friends, and I couldn't bear to lose Jack too.

I tried to quiet the panic swirling inside my head when Bam Bam sprang up from under the tailgate and charged across the parking lot, barking like a maniac.

Jack jumped off the tailgate. "Bam Bam, no!"

He darted across the gravel lot after the barking dog, who appeared to be chasing nothing at all. I laughed when his hat flew off his head, rolling on the dusty ground behind him, but he didn't stop. He'd hardly gained any distance between himself and the idiot dog.

The rumble of an engine startled me, and a red Mustang rolled into the spot next to us. Instantly, I knew who it was, even before I saw the backwards white baseball hat. Before the door opened, chords of Pink Floyd rang out into the brisk evening. Before the blonde, who sat in the front seat next to him, locked eyes with me. My jaw dropped, but Ali was just as surprised to see me as I was to see her.

Chapter Twelve

JACK

I was proud. I'd managed to prove that man's best friend could quickly turn into man's best idiot. I'd finally grabbed hold of Bam Bam, and I held his collar as I walked him back to the truck. But as I approached, I noticed Rylen talking to a tall man in a white hat. It was the same guy who'd been waiting for her after she'd taken pictures of the fountain. The long-legged blonde, whom I'd met outside the coffee shop, stood next to him, and by the look on Rylen's face, she either wanted to disappear immediately or projectile vomit.

I loaded Bam Bam into the tailgate, and he sat beside Rylen like a faithful guard dog. I made a mental note to give him a few extra treats once we got home.

"Yeah, I just got her running a few hours ago," the tall man said, who I figured must be Andon.

My eyes traveled to the thin blonde. She wore heavy makeup and large hooped earrings. Her straight hair hung like a curtain past her hips. She wore tight jeans, high-heeled boots, and a white sweater that hung off one shoulder.

"It looks nice," Rylen said, gesturing to the classic Mustang parked beside them. "I'm sure Harvey is thrilled."

"He is," Andon said, stuffing his hands into his pockets. "My dad says to stop by the shop anytime. You know you're always welcome."

Rylen was about to answer when Ali cut in.

"I suggested we take Rosey for a test drive," she piped. "Then we ended up here." She slipped her hand into Andon's palm, but he looked uneasy, like he wasn't sure if they should touch.

She had guts. I had to give her that. When you'd stolen your best friend's boyfriend, it took a certain amount of temerity to act like you'd done nothing wrong.

Rylen, still wrapped in my jacket, turned her attention to me. "Jack, this is Andon and Ali."

"We've met," Ali said evenly, then she busied herself with her phone, tapping French-tipped nails on the screen.

Andon scowled, then cut his eyes to me. I could feel him sizing me up. Then he smirked, and I saw him tighten his grip on Ali.

"How have you been, Ry?" Andon asked, showing pearly white teeth, "You should join us."

Ali stiffened and shot him a what-the-hell look.

"We're just leaving, actually," I said, and Ali relaxed.

Rylen pulled my jacket off her shoulders, but when she did, her cell phone fell to the dirt.

Andon lunged for the phone, and Bam Bam pounced for Andon. The dog jumped at him, barking and baring his teeth. I was torn between stopping the dog and letting the pieces of Andon fall where they may. I grabbed his collar and yanked him back. Ali screamed, and Andon stumbled back, tripping on a rock and landing on his ass.

"Bam Bam, no!" I said. "Sorry, he thought you were lunging for Rylen."

"Control your damn dog!" Andon sneered, getting to his feet.

"Take it easy, *Andy*. He's protective."

Rylen snorted a laugh.

"It's Andon," Ali snarled.

Bam Bam lunged for him again, and it was all I could do to hold him back a second time.

"An-don, I can't hold him much longer, so if I were you…" I said.

Ali looped her arm into Andon's and pulled him away, the dust from the incident covering the butt of his jeans.

ଽ୦ୢ୰ଡ଼ୄ ଽ୦ୢ୰ଡ଼ୄ ଽ୦ୢ୰ଡ଼ୄ

It was past ten when I pulled into Rylen's driveway. It had started raining, and only the swish of the windshield wipers filled the silence between us. She'd been quiet since we left the parking lot, choosing to stare out the window into sheer darkness. Andon must've seen her before he parked. Why else would he choose to park next to us?

"Hey," I said gently. "You, okay?"

"He started restoring that car when we were sixteen," she said wistfully. She looked down at her hands, "I was supposed to take it for a test drive with him as soon as it was done."

"But he took her instead?" I said.

She nodded. "It's stupid. It's just a car," she said, frustrated. "I don't even care about him anymore."

"It's not the car that hurts. It's what it stands for," I said. "And that's not stupid."

121

She looked at me then, her brown eyes catching mine through the darkness.

"Ali and I met on the playground. She was my best friend. We were thick as thieves, and she could've had anyone she wanted, and she took him from me."

Silence struck me, and though I had already known she'd been cheated on, I saw red on the edges of my vision.

"All of our friends knew. It was going on behind my back for a year before I figured it out. I didn't want to believe it at first, but…" she trailed off. "It's so embarrassing."

"It's not *you* that should be embarrassed."

"I think Ali's punishing me. Or she slept with him out of spite. Or she wanted some sort of twisted revenge."

"Why would she do that?"

"Because she's Ali," she snapped, whipping her eyes to me. "And because I didn't go to her mom's funeral. Sharon died our junior year, barely a year after my brother, and I just couldn't handle it. It was…it was too raw." She stared at her hands again, picking at chipped purple nail polish. "Sometimes I regret it, though. I loved Sharon like a second mother, but other times like today…" she trailed off.

"I don't think it would've made a difference," I said.

"What do you mean?"

"Whether it was revenge or not doesn't matter. You could've gone to the funeral, and she still might've slept with Andon. She made her choice."

"I guess you're right."

"I should have let Bam Bam chew his face off when I had the chance," I said.

That earned me a light chuckle, and through the dark, I could see the slight smile that pulled at her mouth.

"It might be safe to say that Bam Bam tolerates me now," she said.

"If he's protecting you, you have his trust."

She lifted a hand and stroked Bam Bam's head; affectionately, the dog rubbed against her legs.

She smiled weakly, and I heard her take a breath.

"Do you…" she started. "Do you want to come in?" Her voice held a mixture of hope and worry. "My mom's gone, or if she's home, she OD'd on melatonin."

The question surprised me. We'd always said goodnight while I stood on the porch. Maintaining a friendship with her was easy as long as I never knew what was on the other side of that door and never crossed that line.

Still, as the last few hours replayed in my mind – how her hand felt, how she molded against me, the cherry vanilla scent of her hair, and how it intoxicated me – I was keenly aware that the line had become blurry.

It was undeniable; I wanted to know more.

But I had to tread carefully.

"Alright," I said, cutting the engine.

I helped her up the stairs, and she balanced on a crutch while she typed in a numbered code on a keyless entry. Then she opened the front doors, and I stepped onto a welcome mat in the entryway. I hadn't been inside her house since the morning I'd returned her camera, but this time, something felt different.

A large glass chandelier hung above my head. Crystal and shiny, the magnificent piece gave off enough light to completely illuminate our surroundings. The Clark home should have been featured in a House & Home magazine.

A staircase rose to my left. A burgundy carpet descended from the top to partially cover the wooden steps. Family photos in black frames climbed the wall on the opposite side, and a polished wooden railing with white rungs made the stairs seem like a pathway to heaven.

I removed my hat and set it on the bench near the door.

"Do you want something to drink?" Rylen asked, hanging her jacket in the closet.

"Sure. Should I take my boots off?"

She looked down at my feet, considering my suggestion.

"Yeah, that's a good idea. The cleaner doesn't return until next week – otherwise, I wouldn't care."

I toed them off but was reluctant to go much further for fear of dirtying or breaking something. Seeing my hesitation, she marched back to me, took my hand, and pulled me through the entryway like a kid through the toy aisle.

"Come on. It's a house, not the Colosseum," she said.

"It's nice," I said, noting how slippery socks were on ceramic flooring. "It's just…."

"It's a lot," she finished.

She released my hand and flipped on a light over the bar. The kitchen was impeccably clean, almost sterile. Every appliance was made of shiny stainless steel and featured the reflections of those walking around it. It had white marble countertops that reminded me of toasted marshmallows with crisp golden tops, and streaks of silver swirling around them. The cupboards were cherry mahogany, the cabinets as tall as the ceiling, and the bronze handles lined up in perfect paired arches.

"I bet this floor was fun in a wheelchair," I said, and she laughed.

"I almost took out a blender going around the corner. What are you thirsty for?"

"Whatever you're having."

She went to a double-doored refrigerator and opened it.

The ceramic flooring continued through the kitchen until it was stopped by cream-colored carpeting. The kitchen was next to the living room, and a giant big-screen TV was mounted on the wall above the fireplace. A black leather sectional sofa, with cup holders strategically placed between the seats, sat in a semicircle facing the TV, and large speakers sat on each end of the couch.

On the other side of the wall were double French doors and rows of windows with burgundy-colored curtains and cream-colored shades. The curtains were pulled back on each side with golden cords.

Outside, the small building I'd noticed when I first dropped her off was to the right, and a large deck featured an outdoor fireplace and a few wicker chairs around a glass table.

"Is an iced coffee, okay?"

"Sure," I said, returning to the kitchen.

"Okay." She placed two cans of coffee on the counter and walked over to the cupboard where the glasses were stored. "Unless you want white wine?"

"I don't drink," I said.

She looked over her shoulder at me.

"I *shouldn't* drink," I amended.

"Why not?" She opened each can and poured the brown liquid into the glasses.

"Because I can't stop."

She turned towards me and handed me a glass. She took a small sip, waiting for me to continue.

"Frank was a raging alcoholic, and I swore I'd never be like him. But when I drink…" I shrugged. "I can't just turn it off. So, I quit turning it on."

She took another drink, swallowing as she nodded. "Okay then, we won't drink."

125

Inwardly, I breathed a sigh of relief, but I should've known Rylen would've been supportive. She valued loyalty, and it ran deep.

A small smile tugged at my lips as I took a drink and gestured around the kitchen. "This is some place."

"My dad's an architect. He owns his own firm. He designed this place," she said, looking around our surroundings, "probably five years ago?"

"It's amazing."

"He wanted a place he could be proud of. Somewhere he could bring his work colleagues. Accept that he's never here."

There was a lamp arm without a shade mounted to the wall behind the stove, but a spigot was attached to it. I pulled it to myself, examining it, leaving fingerprints on the polished steel. I looked at her to see if she would bother satisfying my curiosity, but her eyebrows rose, and there was a trace of a smile on her face. I twisted the top of the fixture, and water sprung out the bottom, soaking my crotch.

"Oh shit!" I said, twisting it off. "Sorry."

Rylen exploded into laughter.

"You could've warned me!"

She continued to laugh. "But this was more fun. It's a pasta arm," she said, digging a towel out of a drawer.

My brows crinkled, perplexed.

"It's so you don't have to carry a pot full of water across the kitchen."

"Oh," I said, noting that the sink was less than three feet from the stove.

She wiped up the stove and then handed me the towel. I dabbed at my jeans and ran the towel over the floor with my foot. Then I tossed it onto the bar, hitting a file folder and knocking it to the floor.

"Oh shit," I said again. "Sorry, I didn't see that there."

"No, it's okay," she said.

She limped over to the scattered papers and bent over, wobbling on her crutch, but I stopped her and dropped to my knees. I was making neat stacks of stapled pages when I came across an X-ray from the local hospital. Before I realized I was snooping, I lifted it to the light.

"Is that you?" I asked, looking over my shoulder at her. Her bone was shattered into tiny fragments.

"Yeah, that's my knee," she said sullenly.

As I lifted the fanned-out pages back to the bar, I realized I had accidentally knocked a file holding her medical records and a police report to the floor. Silently, I straightened it, trying not to read certain highlighted words that filled me with guilt.

Gunshot victim. Hollow point. Bullet wound. Robbery. Left patella.

The words spun around my head, tormenting me, placing the blame, and demanding penance like mad maniacs chanting and dancing around a convict about to be burned at the stake.

Only I was the convict, and all the favors in the world could never make up for it.

My palms grew clammy, my fingers beginning to quiver. My throat tightened, making it difficult to draw a breath. A ringing echoed in my ears and the world around me spun.

I should never have crossed this threshold, but she was so damn beautiful, and I couldn't help myself. She needed me. No, I needed her. I needed her to be my friend, but now it wasn't only a balm for my wounds; it wasn't only a way to right my past mistakes.

Not anymore.

I feared if I didn't back away now, my closeness to her would expose the truth. If she knew the truth, she would hate me. That would destroy me.

Cora's hate was enough.

I had made neat stacks of the papers when her voice snapped me back to the present.

"I was at the wrong place at the wrong time. My mom was supposed to drop that folder off with the DA." She rolled her eyes. "It looks like she forgot."

She walked to where the towel had fallen and used the end of her crutch to pick it up. I decided to change the subject.

"So," I said, watching as she discarded it in a laundry hamper inside a closet. "Do I get to see your room?"

She cracked a small smile, but her cheeks turned a light pink. I inwardly scolded myself. The request was nothing more than curiosity, but if we were going to remain only friends, her room was the *last* place I should see.

"I'd show you if I had a room. My mom turned it into a home gym, remember?"

She closed the closet door and walked back to her drink.

"Then show me your favorite room. Best room in the house."

She thought for a minute, considering my request, and then she nodded. "Okay, but you have to help me on the stairs."

"Sure."

I followed her to the entryway and helped her climb the staircase; once we reached the top, I returned her crutch.

"Okay, real quick," she said, pointing to two closed double doors behind her, "That's my mom's room." I nodded, and she pointed to each door as she continued.

"That's my old room. These two are guest rooms, that's the bathroom, and this...." she said, hobbling to the last door at the end of the hallway. "This is my favorite room."

She opened the door, and when she turned the light on, I immediately knew this was the grief she'd spoken of.

"This is Michael's room," she said softly. I stepped through the door frame, posters of Jimi Hendrix, U2, and Kurt Cobain staring back at me. A bass and two electric guitars sat on stands, and a full drum set sat behind them. A keyboard was seated opposite them, pages of handwritten sheet music spilling over the side. A large stereo was resting on a table in the corner, and a record player with a crank was perched next to it. Bookshelves filled with records and textbooks on guitar theory lined the rest of the wall space. Rope lights swooped from the walls in upside-down waves, and a lava lamp, bouncing and bubbly, was on the table by the stereo.

The bed was made; a gray-haired cat was curled into a ball atop a single blue blanket that replaced a bedspread. A white pillow, crisp and plump, without creases, sat at the top of the bed.

She glanced at the bed, noticed the cat's curled condition, and swooped it off the bed with one swipe.

"Plunkett!" she bellowed. The cat hissed like a snake. "Buzz off." The cat scampered out the door, and Rylen gave me a satisfied look.

"You certainly have a way with animals," I deadpanned.

"Asshole cat," she retorted. "Anyways, this is my favorite room. I come in here a lot."

"You guys were close?"

"Yeah, we were."

I looked around the room, and a framed photograph of a young man with dark curly hair and round brown eyes caught my attention. A girl, a younger Rylen, stood under his arm.

"Is that you and him?" I asked.

"Yeah, I took that maybe a week before he died."

"It's incredible," I said. "It's a great photo."

"Thanks, I wanted to be a professional photographer before..." she gestured to her leg.

I tried not to wince.

129

"But details matter; it's what makes something go from good to great."

Knowing this about her, this detail about her personality, explained why I felt she didn't miss anything. And it would only get harder to keep secrets from her.

I ran my finger over the side of a cymbal, eliciting a slight "ting" sound.

"Your mom was okay with all the noise?" I asked.

She sat on the edge of the bed. "Not exactly. You know the little building that's in the backyard?"

I nodded.

"Well, upstairs is a small apartment, and downstairs is a studio. My dad built it for Michael, so he had more room. Sort of a bribe."

"A bribe?"

"Dad wanted him to stay here. Live in the apartment. Join the firm. But Michael didn't want anything to do with it. He found out he'd been accepted to Berkeley the night he died."

"Wow, he must've been amazing."

"Yeah, he was. Sit down. I'll play you a cover he did."

I sat on the bed as she plugged her phone into an AUX cord connected to the stereo. She grabbed the remote and pressed a few buttons. Then she hit a switch on the wall, and the lights turned out. A moment later, she hit a button, and the rope lights turned on all around us as the music started.

"This is Michael singing?" I asked, bringing a knee up onto the mattress.

She nodded.

"I'm impressed."

She lifted her legs onto the bed and lay back to look at the ceiling. Then she patted the spot beside her, and I lay back, staring at the posters above us. Even Calvin and Hobbes seemed to fit in with her brother's personality.

"This is a country song," I said, realizing too late that maybe it wasn't something I should've mentioned.

She turned her head and looked at me, and I noticed her eyes were wet.

"Yeah," she whispered. "It's the best one I've ever heard."

I rolled onto my side and lifted a hand to her face, feeling the moisture of her tears on my fingertips. Her eyes closed at the feel of my touch, but her lips moved, and I realized she was singing, her voice not so different from his.

I felt my throat bob, and alarms had started wailing in the back of my head. Touching her was dangerous, but it was too late. I was too far gone. I was utterly and voluntarily drowning.

God, I wanted to kiss her, but there'd be no going back after that.

Then as if I had no control over myself, my thumb traced the outline of her lips, and she opened her eyes to look up at me. Her hand fanned across my chest, gripping my collar, and she pulled me down to her, telling me she wanted this too.

Our foreheads touched, and her hand tangled in the back of my hair. I felt her chest expand beneath me, her mouth slightly open, and she whispered my name.

Our lips had just brushed, a whisper of a kiss, when a light flipped on over my head. Rylen and I shot up like meerkats, and I bonked my head on the wall behind me, the "thud" low and bass drum-like.

And there in the doorway was the astonished, perplexed, and furious face of Diana Clark.

Chapter Thirteen

Rylen

"Mom!" I shrieked.

I could count on one hand the times I'd been completely mortified. There was the third-grade playground butt-showing incident. Will Thomas had been chasing me. He'd slipped on the gravel and accidentally grabbed the back of my pants. I've been leery of elastic ever since. When I was sixteen, I'd barfed on Andon's dad, Harvey, moments after meeting him. My suspicions had been correct when I'd thought my cafeteria bologna sandwich had tasted funny. And when Ali and I had still been friends, she once bet me fifty bucks that I couldn't walk up to a group of cute guys at the park and ask one of them to pull my finger.

I lost any trace of dignity I had left when the guy I'd picked from a distance happened to be deaf, and his friend had to sign to him what "pull my finger" meant. Though humiliated, I'd been fifty bucks richer, and Ali bought lunch because, after that, she had to.

But out of all my nineteen years on planet Earth, this one would forever be written in the Chronicles of Embarrassment as the moment when Diana Clark burst through the door and caught her daughter in Michael's bed with a stranger.

I never wanted anything more than to sink through the mattress, plunge through the floorboards, and plummet into a deep, dark hole where I would hide until the end of my days.

Diana stood in the doorway, stupefied, as if she'd caught Santa lounging under the tree, wreathed in pipe smoke, wearing nothing but a smile. She wore one of her fine suits, pinstriped gray, and black high-heeled pumps. Her hair was tied behind her head; I could see the little blue vein on the side of her forehead begin to pulse.

Her lips were tight, her face morphing into anger as her eyes darted between Jack and me. A cell phone was to her ear like she'd been talking to someone, heard the music, and decided to investigate.

Madam Plunkett pranced through the door like she'd just found a stash of tuna. Her tail flicked in a haughty, triumphant rhythm, reminiscent of a child about to see a sibling get their ass beat. Revealing in the anticipation that promised to be better than pure catnip.

Jack, who'd smacked something into the wall, stood beside the bed, rubbing his head. One foot was bare, his shirt was ruffled, his collar flipped up, and one shirttail was untucked from his jeans.

How had he lost a sock?

And, oh my God, his crotch was still wet!

I wanted to die.

I caught a glimpse of myself in the dark window's reflection. My curls had poofed out big and afro-like. My cheeks looked pink and hot. My eye makeup was smudged and dramatic, the love child of Kiss and a mangy raccoon. There was no denying what had taken place between us, and in the shrine of Michael's room which only made matters worse. I was horrified. No, worse than horrified. There wasn't a word to describe this kind of humiliation. It hadn't been discovered yet.

Jack and I... We almost... And she saw us.

I could still feel the warmth from his body against me—the brush of his lips on mine.

Wait, did he kiss me?

"Adam," my mother said into her phone, "Let me call you back."

A chill slithered down my spine at the mention of that name.

She pressed a button on her phone screen and slowly brought her eyes up to us.

"Why are you two in here?" she said coolly.

"Mom," I said, getting to my feet, "I didn't know you were home."

"Why wouldn't I be, Rylen? It's midnight."

The clock on the nightstand read 12:02. I hadn't realized it was so late. I unplugged my phone and switched off the stereo, sensing her gaze scorching a hole into me like laser beams.

Jack straightened the blanket, fluffed the pillow, and found his missing sock by the foot of the bed.

Madam Plunkett glared at me indignantly; fully aware I was about to get what I deserved. With a huff, she coiled up on the end of the bed. It took every ounce of my willpower not to grab her by the scruff of the neck and feed her to Bam Bam.

"Out," my mother demanded, pointing to the door behind her.

I hobbled into the hallway, Jack right behind me, and she closed the door with a sharp slam.

"Now, why were you two in there?" she repeated.

"I was showing Jack a cover Michael recorded. We lost track of time," I replied.

Her eyes cut to Jack, and I thought he might throw up, but he recovered and smiled uneasily.

She met my eyes. "I saw what you were showing him," she said smoothly.

I began looking for that black hole again.

"Now, it's very late. Perhaps you should show him the door?"

She turned to leave, walked halfway down the hall, then turned back to look at us.

"And Rylen, this will never happen again. Have I made myself clear?"

"Yes," I said meekly. If I had a tail, it would've been between my legs.

She was partially down the stairs when she spoke again, "It was nice to meet you, Jack."

I winced when the office door slammed behind her.

"I better go," Jack said quietly, and I nodded as we walked down the hall.

Jack helped me down the steps, and I stood in the entryway, watching him pull on his boots and hat.

"Your mom hates me," he replied, the weight of his words visibly bothering him. "This was a bad idea."

"She doesn't hate you. We just surprised her. She never goes in there, so…." I trailed off. "I'll talk to her, okay? It'll be fine."

He nodded, but kept his eyes on the floor, and I reached for his shoulder.

"Hey," I said. "What's wrong?"

He brought his eyes to mine, and I found myself staring at his lips; under any other circumstances, I'd be tempted to take up where we'd left off.

"Nothing, I just feel like I got you in trouble," he admitted. "I was the one that……

"Don't worry about it. I'll take care of it. Okay?"

I squeezed his shoulder, and he pulled me into a hug.

"Can you be ready tomorrow at eight?" he asked into my shoulder.

"Eight at night?"

"Yeah," he said, pulling back to meet my eyes.

He locked his sturdy arms around my waist, and I didn't want him to let go.

"I have to work on Pete's transmission, then I told Ned I'd look at his tractor, but I can pick you up after."

There it was again. This *need* to help other people without expecting anything in return, but at what point did goodness turn altruistic? I pushed the thought away. I knew Jack wasn't like that.

"You still owe them?" I asked.

He shrugged. "They're my friends. We help each other."

"Why aren't they paying you?"

"They can't afford to, Rylen. Now, can you be ready at eight?"

I had to let it go. I didn't want to fight with him. "Okay," I agreed. "I'll be ready."

I wanted him to kiss me again, but he dropped his arms, and disappointment squashed any lingering hope. I'd only had a brush of a kiss, and already I craved more. If my mother hadn't barged in, the rest would've been easy, shrine or no shrine.

He opened the door and stood with the handle in his hand.

"Goodnight, Rylen Clark."

On every occasion before now, when we'd say goodnight, I'd be filled with the excitement of seeing him again. So, as the door latched and I heard his truck engine roar to life, I couldn't understand the uneasy feeling churning in my stomach.

REDEMPTION'S LIST

ℰℴ⌒ℴℰ ℰℴ⌒ℴℰ ℰℴ⌒ℴℰ

The light was on under the office door, and I let out a heavy sigh. I'd hoped my mom would sneak up the stairs and slip into her room while I said goodnight to Jack. Then in the morning, we could pretend nothing happened and return to our normal strained relationship.

No such luck.

If she was still up, that meant she was waiting for me, and if she was waiting for me, she wanted to talk, likely about what she'd seen. If she wanted to talk, I'd be expected to believe that she cared about me even when every message from the time I'd become an only child told me otherwise.

When I was seventeen, Juanita was the one to ensure we Andon and I were safe. My mom never asked. Maybe she was naive and assumed Andon and I weren't having sex, but what red-blooded seventeen-year-old wasn't hot to lose it the first chance they got? Or my mom assumed I knew how to avoid a pregnancy, which I did, so there was no need to bring it up. Or maybe she didn't want to know and had no interest in inquiring because she never cared in the first place?

Once I turned eighteen, I'd put myself on the pill, and even though the doctor's visit had shown up on my mother's insurance EOBs, she never breathed a word about it. Even anger or disappointment about my virginity status would've been better than silence because at least anger showed some level of concern.

"Rylen," my mom called through the door. "Come in here, please."

I sighed and bit my bottom lip. Here it goes.

When I stepped inside, she was sitting behind her desk, her hands folded in front, her elbows out like wings. Her cell phone lay face down on the desk in front of her, and I wondered if she'd finished her phone call with Adam, the one who'd monopolized all her attention.

"We need to talk about a few things," she said.

"Right now? I'm tired, and I want to go to bed."

"Sit. It won't take long."

I flopped on the couch and rested my leg on the coffee table.

"Sheriff Heisherman called. The police arrested someone who they believe was an accomplice in the robbery. They have two men in custody now."

"Why didn't I hear about this?"

"I don't know. You seem to be pretty busy these days."

I let out a breath. I couldn't argue that being with Jack had consumed all of my free time.

My eyes traveled to the file lying on her desk. The one Jack had knocked on the floor.

"You forgot my file on the counter this morning," I said, fighting the annoyance in my voice.

"I didn't forget it. I scanned the files and sent them electronically."

"You did?" I asked, astonished.

"Yes. Why is that so hard to believe?"

"It's not. I just…. I assumed."

"Well, you assumed wrong."

There were likely fifty typed stapled pages in that folder, and she'd tediously scanned them. One by one. Front and back.

She'd put effort into getting my files where they needed to be and kept the hard copies for herself, and all along, I'd assumed she'd shoved me aside.

"I came in here because the DA said he was missing a page," she said. "I was going to send it to him before bed. But the file's out of order. I can't find what I need."

"Oh," I said, burying my face in my hand. "Jack accidentally knocked it off the counter."

She rose from her chair and walked around the front of the desk.

"I guess it will have to wait until morning, Rylen," she started, leaning on the front of her desk and crossing her arms. "I'm not going to ask you about your personal life."

"That's a relief," I replied, resting my arm on the back of the sofa.

"Regardless of my feelings, just be safe, okay?" Her eyes narrowed, and her voice lowered, "But not in Michael's bedroom."

"Sorry. Jack asked to see my favorite room." I offered, "But nothing happened, Mom."

Not really, anyway

Despite the late hour, she straightened her blazer, because my mom would never look anything less than flawless at 12:42 in the morning.

"I don't think I would describe what I saw as *nothing*. I didn't realize you were dating somebody."

"I'm not. We're friends."

Truthfully, we were in that strange place between friendship and something more. But I didn't know what to call it.

She stopped and cocked her head to one side, like she hadn't heard me correctly.

"Friends? Didn't you run off with him the other day? Juanita said you disappeared without a word."

Oh crap! I'd forgotten to text Juanita and tell her I didn't need a ride home. It had been hours later when I saw that she'd sent a text looking for me. I was an idiot to hope she wouldn't have mentioned the incident to my mom.

"Yes. I ran into Jack at the Villa," I admitted.

"You seem to be spending an awful lot of time with him."

JEANA R LAWRENCE

"He picks me up after therapy." All the things she wasn't doing. "Why do I feel like I'm sixteen?"

"I don't know. Why do I feel you're not being honest with me?"

I shrugged. "What do you want me to say?"

She exhaled. "Rylen, did you even try to make amends with Andon before jumping into something with Jack?"

I scoffed and struggled to keep my voice even.

"Are you kidding me? I didn't jump into anything. I don't know how else to explain it to you. Andon is a cheat. He slept with Ali. We're done."

"People make mistakes, Rylen. That doesn't make them bad people."

I leaned forward, putting my elbows on my knees.

"Why are you defending him, Mom?"

"I'm not defending him!" she snapped. "I'm pointing out that you two have a lot of history to just part ways."

"Since when does having a lot of history make lying okay? Lying is never okay."

"Everyone deserves a second chance, Rylen, regardless of how badly they messed up."

I balled my hands into tight fists. I felt like a car teetering on the edge of a cliff, about to plummet over the edge and detonate into flames. The flames that I'd been holding back until now.

"Who are you saying that to? Me? Or yourself?"

Her eyes narrowed. "Excuse me?"

But the car was already falling, and once I'd started, I couldn't stop. The car had started rolling rapidly downhill, crushing everything in its path, taking no prisoners.

"Are you even listening to yourself? You're supposed to be on my side, and all you've done is defend that piece of shit."

Jack was right. Bam Bam should have mutilated him.

140

"Rylen, I am on your side. I…."

But I kept going. The car had hit the bottom of the ravine, exploding into an orange fiery ball of rage.

"No, you're not! And who are you to give me any sort of relationship advice when Dad can't even stand to be in the same house as you?"

That was a step too far, and the moment the words left my mouth, I wished I could push the car back uphill. Or that I had a giant lasso so I could rope every sentence and pull them all back. Then I'd swallow the words whole; every ash-covered syllable would never again see the light of day.

Her mouth thinned into a straight line. Her eyes were wide with shock as her gaze held mine. I felt my skin break into goosebumps as she blazed holes into me with her astonished stare. Her voice was quiet, smooth, and calm when she spoke, a testament to her remarkable self-control.

"What's that supposed to mean?" She asked, rocking on the edge of anger and rage.

I stared at the floor; my candidness now replaced with an overwhelming need to be silent.

"Don't be a coward," she said evenly. "You obviously have more to say. Now say it."

I needed to ask her the question that I'd continually shoved out of my mind, because knowing the truth could be much worse. I wanted to ask all of my questions.

Why did Dad leave?
What have you done?
Were you unfaithful?
Who the hell is Adam?

But forming the words seemed next to impossible. I'd already lost a part of myself in a car crash; I couldn't bear it if what remained was ripped further apart. If that happened, no number of music posters or recorded cover songs would be able to put me back together.

I crossed my arms and stared at the coffee table.

"Well, since you already know everything, I won't bother enlightening you."

She picked up her phone and walked to the door.

"Mom," I tried weakly, but she ignored me.

"Don't forget; the fundraiser is next Saturday. I still need your help. It's the least you can do." She turned to leave but glanced at me over her shoulder.

"Since you'll be off the crutch soon, I think it might be time for you to move back into the studio. It's awfully crowded in here, don't you think?"

Something inside my chest broke, and my eyes pooled with tears as she switched off the light and climbed the stairs. When darkness filled the space around me, I longed to call after her, limp up the stairs, and throw myself into her arms like a child with a skinned knee. I wanted to crawl under the quilted blankets on her king mattress and wrap myself in her scent. I'd bury my face in my dad's pillow, fill my lungs with the familiar trace of dandruff shampoo and Brut deodorant, and finally be able to breathe. Then I would tell Mom I had a nightmare where Michael died, Dad moved out, and I got shot.

She'd smooth my hair, kiss my forehead, and sing me a lullaby that lulled me into a deep sleep. And when I opened my eyes in the morning, all would be as it should be. The scents of percolating coffee and golden pancakes awakening me from my long slumber.

Chapter Fourteen

JACK

I tossed and turned that night, barely sleeping a wink, but as soon as the clock hit 7 a.m. I got up and drove into Davenport to find Scott. I pulled into the parking lot and saw Scott's police cruiser parked out front. I told Bam Bam to stay and slammed the truck door behind me so hard the ground vibrated. I swung the door open a little harder than I meant to, and it banged against the outside wall as I stepped inside.

Scott was behind his desk, the shiny brass of his deputy badge catching the sun from the open door behind me. A phone was to his ear, the coiled black cord stretching across the length of his desk. His eyes widened when he saw me, and he said something into the phone I couldn't understand and hung up. I slammed my fists on his desk, the black coffee from his mug teeter-tottering, slopping over the edges.

"I'm done!"

JEANA R LAWRENCE

"Jack," Scott grumbled, rushing to move papers away from the spilled coffee. "You can't come barging in here when I'm working." He grabbed a napkin from the trash and wiped up the spill.

"Talking on the phone to women you want to screw is not working," I muttered.

"Actually, that was the DA's office," he said, tossing the soiled napkin into the bin.

"What did the DA's office say?" I blurted.

He sighed with annoyance and placed his fingertips together like a tent. "What do you want, Jack?"

I flopped into a chair opposite his desk and said what had kept me up all night.

"I need you to find someone else."

"What are you talking about?" he asked.

"The list. I can't keep doing this."

Realization dawned on him, and he smirked, "Your redemption list? Being the town do-gooder getting to you, Jack?"

"No, asshole, it's…."

"You've made quite a reputation for yourself. Sally told me about the fryer. Saved her over three hundred bucks in repairs. If it suddenly stops, folks are going to wonder why."

I leaned forward and spoke quietly.

"That's not it, Scott. It's her."

"The girl?"

I nodded, hating the guilt gnawing at my stomach.

"All you had to do was give her a ride after her appointments. Why has that become so difficult?"

"It's hard to explain. I…." I trailed off. "You still hang out at Drake's, right?"

"Yeah so?"

"So, there's got to be someone who can help her," I said.

144

"Why doesn't she just drive herself?" Scott asked, lifting his half-empty coffee mug to his lips. The mug was white with black letters that said, "I'm Too Sexy for My Shirt." I wanted to warn everyone that I have seen this so-called sexy, and nobody should ever be subjected to its horror.

"She hasn't been cleared yet. Doc's orders."

I'd never asked Rylen when she could drive again, but it didn't matter. I had to end things and put some distance between us before things got worse.

"Honestly, Jack, I couldn't care less what you do, but you don't owe her anything else. The rest of it's not your problem."

The door opened behind me, and Sheriff Heisherman walked in carrying a crate of coffee and two bags of food from Sally's Diner. Heisherman, wearing his aviator sunglasses and tan sheriff's uniform, nodded at me while he set a coffee and a bag on the edge of Scott's desk.

"Thanks, Ed," Scott said to the Sheriff, who waved in reply. "Look, Jack, I've got a lot of work to do today. We can meet up later for a beer if you want."

"No, I'm not drinking."

"Still?" he asked, surprise perched over his eyebrows.

"Still."

"All right, then, you can order a Chamomile, and if you can't give the girl rides anymore, tell her."

"I can't leave her when she still needs help."

Scott grinned again, "It sounds like you have a bit of a crush on your Miss Daisy. Not that I blame you. She's smokin' hot."

"Her name is Rylen, and don't talk about her that way. We're just friends, so shut the hell up."

But as the words left my mouth, even I realized I protested too much.

He stood and reached for the food bag at the end of his desk. "So why don't you tell me why you can't give her rides anymore?"

"I need to work more. Gran's wages are shit."

He nodded and sat back in his chair, placing the diner bag on the desk before him. Then his eyes narrowed, his voice dropped, and he leaned forward as he spoke.

"If you start anything illegal again, I won't be able to look away. I'm a deputy now."

"No, I'm done with that," I said quietly, hoping that Heisherman was too enthralled with biscuits and gravy to listen. "I haven't gambled since I left," I whispered.

"You better not, or I'll kick your sorry ass."

"I'm not, Scott. I won't. I earned every dime I have."

He lifted his coffee to his lips again and took a slow drink, eying me over the brim like he was deciding whether or not to believe me.

He swallowed, then said, "Cora was in here the other day."

I sighed, "Oh, what did she want?"

"Details about the arrest."

He pulled in his chair and opened the bag. The smell of breakfast wafted into the air as he set a Styrofoam plate in front of him. He opened the lid, the steam rising in wispy white lines as he filled his fork with scrambled eggs.

"Just leave Cora be. It wasn't your fault."

His statement surprised me, and I did nothing to hide the astonishment on my face.

"At least. Not entirely."

He put the food in his mouth and chewed quickly, picking up a triangle of toast. Scott had said the one thing that I'd kept repeating to myself like a damaged record. Maybe one day, Cora would believe that too.

"When are you seeing her again?" he asked, building a small yellow mountain on top of the toast.

"Cora?" I asked.

"No, bonehead. Rylen."

"Oh, I'm picking her up tonight at eight. I'm taking her to see the Captain."

He eyed me apprehensively. "Do you really think that's a good idea?"

"Of course not, but I told her she could meet him before...."

Before I crossed that threshold. Before I climbed the stairs and entered Michael's room. Before I heard her sing, and before my hands stroked her damp cheeks. Before she grabbed my shirt, and my lips lightly touched hers, irrevocably blurring the line between friendship and more.

"I'm going to keep my word, Scott."

Scott shrugged, stabbing a home-fried potato. "All right, I'll see if I can find someone else to help her, at least until she can drive again. Now buzz off; I'm way behind."

I stood and pushed in my chair. I got halfway to the door when Scott spoke again.

"Jack, one more thing."

I paused at the doorway and glanced over my shoulder.

"Are you going to tell Rylen about your involvement?" he asked.

"No, and it's going to stay that way," I snapped.

He nodded, realization painted on his face. "So, that's what this is about."

§ⱺ◟◞ஐ §ⱺ◟◞ஐ §ⱺ◟◞ஐ

It was 7:59 p.m. when I pulled into Rylen's driveway. Through the window, I saw her sitting on the bench by the door, watching for me, and then her face broke into a grin as she rose from her seat and moved out of sight. I'd anticipated this moment all day, a mixture of dread and excitement flip-flopping in my stomach.

I went to the front door, and she opened it before I reached the top step. Her round brown eyes sparkled, and my intentions about keeping distance between us nearly evaporated. My breath showed in the night air, hovering above us like all the words I had to say. She invited me in, saying I could wait out of the cold while she put on her jacket, but I declined. I wasn't going any further; I couldn't cross that line again.

The entire day, all I'd done was replay what it felt like to touch her skin, smell her hair, and look into her eyes while she sang. I'd relived what the slightest kiss felt like in the webs of my memory, and though the images tormented me, it would always have to be enough because this was where we'd say goodbye.

I helped her into the Bronco and closed her door, giving myself a mental scolding as I walked around to my side of the truck. She'd only smiled at me, and already I was putty in her fingers.

I opened my door and climbed in, swearing I would get through the night without touching her. This was the last night we would spend together before someone else took over. Scott had texted me that afternoon with a few people willing to help until she could drive again. And somehow, before the night's end, I'd have to find the courage to tell her this was goodbye. She'd be blindsided, and I couldn't help the sinking feeling of guilt that threatened to pull me under. It'd become so familiar I could wrap myself in it like a warm blanket, yet it iced me to my core. I doubted she'd understand. I would disappear from her life, and she'd be better for it.

"Where's Bam Bam?" she asked, gesturing to the backseat where the dog normally sat.

"I didn't bring him tonight. It's not a dog-friendly location."

"Where are we going?" she asked, noticing as we passed our usual exit.

"It's a surprise," I said.

"I hate surprises," she grumbled. "Just tell me."

"You hate surprises? Why?"

I slowed as the light turned yellow and pulled into the turning lane.

"Because the anticipation kills me. I can think of *amazing* surprises, and when I find out what it is, I'm totally bummed."

"Don't do well with disappointment, do ya?" I asked, cranking the wheel to the right.

"Nope. Let's say your dad is like, 'I've got a surprise for you, honey. You're never going to guess what it is," she said, mimicking a male voice in a peppy tone. "And he gets you all pumped up, and you envision tropical vacations and piles of sunken treasure, and then," she paused, sighing. "Then you find out the big surprise was a brand new pogo stick, and you try not to be disappointed, but deep down, it kind of sucks."

I chuckled, "That sounds like a true story."

"I was twelve. I've hated surprises ever since."

I laughed again. "Well, you don't have much longer to wait."

She shifted in her seat to face me and gave me her best sad puppy eyes, "Tell me," she whimpered.

"No," I said, stifling a laugh.

"Pleaaaase."

"You're ridiculous."

She batted her eyes, "How about now?"

"Okay."

"Really?"

"No!"

"Jack, I don't think you understand the consequences of your actions."

"I understand them perfectly. You're just impatient."

"Impatient is a kid at Christmas. This is anxiety. People with anxiety don't do well without knowing. I mean, have my days come to an end? Are you taking me to be a ceremonial sacrifice?"

"Who told you?" I said, goading her.

Her eyes widened, but a smile was on the edges of her lips. I laughed at her reaction as she crossed her arms and threw her nose haughtily into the air.

I'd miss this—the banter between us. We never took the other too seriously. To any observer, the light back and forth between us would seem meaningless. After I walked away from her tonight, no matter how hard I looked, I knew I would never find it again with anyone.

"You could've fed me a last meal, ya know." She looked around the dashboard and between the bucket seats. "Where are the M&Ms?"

"What?"

"We usually share a bag of M&Ms when you pick me up. Where are they?"

I looked at the dashboard. My gas gauge hovered above empty. I'd forgotten to fill up before driving into town to get her. Normally, I would buy the M&Ms and the coffee while it was filling, but tonight, I showed up empty-handed.

"Oh," I said, my palms turning clammy. "I guess I forgot."

"The candy king forgets the candy?"

"Sorry."

She eyed me suspiciously, but didn't say anything more about it. There was a deafening silence in the truck as I took us further through town. My slip-up had thrown us off kilter, and I feared we wouldn't recover.

A man in a red Toyota pulled up to the light next to us, and she pointed out the window at him.

"What's his story? I bet he's a doctor….no…. photographer. His car's too crappy to be a doctor. He's definitely a starving artist."

I lifted myself in my seat to get a better view.

"Could be," I said, shrugging.

"What's with you?" she asked.

"What do you mean?"

"I don't know. You seem like your mind's elsewhere. What's wrong?"

"Nothing, I'm just tired."

She reached for my shoulder and rested her hand there. "We don't have to do this tonight. We can go back to my house and watch a movie or something."

"No!" I blurted, and her eyes widened. "I think it's best if I stay outside your house."

She lowered her hand and rested it on her leg, "Is that what this is about? You're being weird because of my mom?"

"No, Rylen. I just don't like seeing you in trouble."

I hit the left turn signal, and she stiffened.

"I'm not a kid. I don't get in trouble," she said coolly. "I told you I would take care of it, and I did."

"What did your mom say?" I said before I could think better of it.

She paused like she was deciding what to tell me. She bit her bottom lip and stared at the floor.

"We got into a big fight, but it wasn't about you. It was about my dad and some other things. She made me feel like shit; then she dared to ask for my help at the fundraiser."

"Are you going to help her?" I asked.

"No. Why should I? I called her on her crap, and she didn't like it. Now she's trying to make me feel bad to get what she wants."

151

I nodded and pursed my lips, but she looked at me quizzically.

"What are you not saying?" she asked.

"I don't think you should be so quick to assume she's trying to manipulate you."

"But that's what she's doing," she retorted.

"Not necessarily. She's been asking you to help for weeks, right?"

"Yeah, so?"

"So, she needed your help even before she had the *ammunition* to manipulate you."

"That's what I'm saying. I said no, and now she's using it to get what she wants."

"Or maybe she's not. Maybe you're wrong, and the two are unrelated, and she honestly needs your help."

"Whose side are you on, Jack?" she bellowed, her brow furrowed in anger.

I pulled into the parking lot, hitting the brake a little harsher than I'd meant and we lunged forward.

"Yours, Rylen!" I snapped. "I'm pointing out that it's better to assume the best in people rather than the worst. Trust me; you'll be a lot happier."

She was silent, her mouth slightly open, visibly taken aback by my outburst. She hadn't even noticed we'd arrived at our destination.

"I'm sorry," I said softly, turning off the engine. "I didn't mean to snap at you."

She moved her eyes to the windshield, her lips faintly quivering. I'd never seen her beyond mildly annoyed, and even then, minutes later, she was back to being herself. Seeing her clam up because she was hurt was new, and she was hurt because of me.

"I still want you to meet someone inside. He's really important to me, please, Rylen.

She nodded stiffly but kept her eyes out front like staring at the autumn leaves would make our disagreement disappear, and we'd be back to a place of our own with meaningless banter. Outside, I opened her door, but her gaze hadn't shifted, and she wiped a single tear from her cheek with her sleeve.

"Rylen."

But still, she didn't move.

"I don't want to fight with you, and I don't want anything to pull us apart. I'm sorry I upset you."

She turned her head to look into my eyes, and I moved into her, put my arms around her waist, and pulled her into my chest. She put her hands under my jacket against my shirt, welcoming my warmth.

If this was my last night, and I'd already made a mess of it, to hell with not touching her.

"Will you come with me?" I asked cautiously.

She nodded again, and I lifted her out of the seat, her hand moving from my shoulder down my bicep to my wrist. I handed her the crutch, took her hand in mine, and slowly we walked towards the entrance of Davenport Community Hospital.

Chapter Fifteen

Rylen

Hey Kiddo,
I'm sorry Mom's been difficult. You should stay in the studio if you can manage the stairs. The extra key is in my top drawer. I'm glad you're recovering. I'm in New York this week. Pitching my hotel design to stuffy businessmen. Wish me luck!
Love,
-Dad

I stood in the lobby and leaned on my crutch while Jack signed our names on the visitor's clipboard. My phone chimed, signaling an email from my dad. It usually took him a day or two to respond, so I was surprised he'd answered so quickly; perhaps putting an SOS in the subject line had gotten his attention. I'd emailed him this morning after waking to find the house cold and empty.

"You, okay?" Jack asked, pulling me from my thoughts. I pocketed my cell phone, taking the visitor's name tag from his hand.

"Yeah, I just got an email from my dad."

I stuck the tag to the outside of my jacket.

"Everything all right?"

"Yeah, fine," I said unconvincingly.

I was sure he didn't believe me, but he didn't press the matter; instead, he took my hand and led me to the elevators.

If Mom and I hadn't fought the previous night, she'd leave a sticky note stuck to the stainless-steel coffee pot explaining her whereabouts. It was usually brief and to the point, and she'd sign it with a simple, "Love, Mom." I'd started collecting them, stacking them together in no specific order. The bright neon squares, now tiny tokens of handwritten care, felt like the only bits of concern I received. And if the house caught fire, a messy pile of notes in a drawer in Michael's room is the first place I'd go. Michael's room was sacred, and everything was to be left in its original form. Diana never went in there; she avoided it like leprosy. So, I knew my hiding place was secure.

The usual sticky note perch was vacant when I'd limped into the kitchen this morning. I was sure she was still angry with me but seeing it empty was comparable to a giant middle finger–message received–I was unworthy of ten seconds of penmanship on a three-by-three square. There would be no concern for me today. Eventually, she'd decide I'd been punished enough, and we'd never speak of it again. It'd be swept under the carpet, next to the other issues we never acknowledged, and the rug would be pulled back into place – leaving a sea of rounded swells obvious to all except her.

The elevator dinged and the steel doors opened. Jack took my hand again and led me inside. He'd hardly let go of me, and when he did, moments later, he'd touch me again someplace else. Something had clearly been bothering him. It seemed to be gone now, yet there was still a stiffness about him, like his shields were up, but he was trying to knock them down. I'd never seen Jack bothered by anything, and I tried not to let it worry me.

"Are you going to tell me why we're here?" I asked as the large silver doors opened.

He shook his head, we moved inside, and he pressed number six as the doors closed.

"I told you. You're meeting someone."

The doors opened, and immediately I knew where he had taken me. I didn't even try to conceal the shock on my face as he reached for my hand yet again.

"Come on," he said. "They're waiting for us."

At the nurse's station, four nurses in pink scrubs sat behind computers. Another nurse was on the phone and hung up when she saw us.

"Hey, Jack. Back again, huh?" she said.

She was tall and slender with bags under her eyes that showed fatigue. Her purple glasses were cat-eyed and reminded me of something a librarian would wear.

"Hey, Sheila," Jack said, leaning his elbows on the counter. "How is he tonight?"

"He's doing all right. We're proud of his progress."

"Sheila, this is Rylen," Jack said, gesturing to me on his right.

She smiled brightly, "Hi Rylen. I'm the charge nurse on this floor."

I nodded back, too dumbstruck to speak.

"We'd like to see him," Jack said. "If he's up for company."

"That's probably alright. Let me make sure I have the proper paperwork on file."

She hunched over a computer, squinting at the white screen. The mouse clicked, and she typed something on the keyboard, then spoke over her shoulder.

"Tonya, can you take Jack and Rylen to see the Captain?"

"Sure thing, Sheila," said a voice, but I couldn't see who had spoken.

"We really appreciate you, Jack. You're so sweet," Sheila cooed.

"Anytime," he replied. "I'm happy to help."

A younger nurse, with a blonde ponytail approached us. She gestured for Jack to follow her, and he retook my hand. The white, fluorescent lights reflected on the flooring in front of us, leading like a path of breadcrumbs as our footsteps tapped down the hallway.

Tonya opened room 617 and pulled back the curtain. The first thing I saw was a tiny blue hat nestled on a head no bigger than an apple. And there, bundled in a white blanket, cuddled in a nurse's arms, was the tiniest baby I'd ever seen.

All words, all coherent thoughts disintegrated.

I expected the Captain to be an old, dying man – someone gray and wise. A baby was the last person I thought I'd see.

Tonya closed the curtain behind her as she left, and Jack hovered over the nurse holding the baby against her shoulder. She sat in a rocking chair and a grey sweater over her scrubs, her hair pulled up in a clip, and reading glasses perched on the top of her head. A book lay open on the table next to her as if she'd been knee-deep in a cozy mystery minutes before we arrived.

"How is he doing, Renee?" Jack said, in a hushed tone.

She smiled. "I just got him to sleep."

"Great. Rylen, come here."

I closed my mouth and shook my head. Nope, I wasn't going near that thing.

Babies were one thing, but tiny, fragile, sick babies that I could drop and break were another.

Jack approached me, taking my hands. "It's okay. Come on."

He pushed the small of my back, and I tiptoed closer. The nurse holding the child, Renee, gave me a warm smile and cradled him so I could fully see his face. His skin glowed with a soft pink, while his lips resembled delicate rosebuds. His perfect nose was dainty and slightly turned up. Dark eyelashes fanned gracefully against a sweet, peaceful face. Tiny grunts escaped him as he slept, surely dreaming of his own paradise, untouched by cords, machines, or monitors.

"What's his name?" I asked hoarsely.

"He hasn't been named yet," Renee said wistfully. "Jack started calling him the Captain. Rest of us started calling him that too."

A baby without a name? How could that happen?

The baby stirred, and she looked lovingly at him. "He sure gets a lot of attention. It seemed fitting."

"Where's his...." I started to ask the obvious, and I only got a word out before I thought better of it and kept the rest of the question locked in. But the nurse shook her head, and something inside me clenched. All of my own issues paled in comparison.

Where was his mother? Where was his family? Who did he have to rely on? Was he alive mere weeks, and already he was alone?

Jack appeared on my left, bare from the waist up. I hadn't noticed him undressing and my gaze lingered. Regardless of the temperature, he favored long-sleeved plaid, leaving me with only a fleeting glimpse of his forearms. His jeans hung low on his hips, the black band of his Joe boxers peeking just above a gleaming belt buckle. A light dusting of dark chest hair covered his rounded pectorals, tracing over his nipples, and trailing down his abdomen around his navel, vanishing below his underwear.

He naturally tapered from broad shoulders to narrow hips, forming a flawless V. His arms were sculpted, with veins protruding from his shoulders and wrapping around his toned forearms like creeping vines. A gold chain hung around his neck, the cross pendant resting just below the hollows of his collarbones. But the subtle dips between his ribs and the sharp contours of his abdominal muscles convinced me— I'd never seen another man as exquisitely beautiful as him.

I scolded myself for shamelessly gawking at him in the presence of a child, but let's be honest, I wasn't expecting that. I closed my mouth, feeling moisture pooling on my tongue.

Had I been drooling?

With no visible reaction to Jack's nudity, Renee stood and motioned for him to sit in the rocking chair. Perhaps nurses were used to bare bodies. I obviously wasn't cut out for it. She peeled the blanket off the Captain, leaving him in a tiny diaper, and he shuddered at the sudden cold. She gently placed him on Jack's chest and wrapped the blanket around the baby's back.

"Babies are warmest when they're against your skin," Jack said. "This little one's had a rough go of it, so I hold him occasionally."

Jack alternated between patting the baby's bottom and rubbing his back as he rocked, humming sweetly until the baby settled.

"Okay, you guys," Renee said. "When you guys are ready to call it a night, hit the call button. I'll be back to check on you in a bit. Thanks so much, Jack."

"Anytime," he said, smiling.

I plopped on the bed and watched as the nurse closed the door.

"So," I started, peeling off my jacket. "You do this a lot, then?"

159

"When I can."

I shook my head, "All the nurses know your name. It's more than that."

He shrugged, "A few days a week, I guess."

"Who-" I stopped. "I mean, how do you know the Captain?"

"He's…" he paused, choosing his words carefully. "He needs help, and I'm helping him."

"You said he was important to you."

"A child without support is very important," he said casually.

I didn't like his vague answer, but he would get away with it for now. I made a mental note to bring it up again at the next chance I got.

"He's not mine," Jack said, breaking my thoughts. "If that's what you're too embarrassed to ask."

I shook my head. "I didn't think so. Where are his parents?"

He sighed. "Social Services is working to find a foster placement, but the mother is trying to get her act together."

"And the father?"

Jack shook his head.

"So, he's alone?" I heard myself say, and something about those words spoken aloud drove the split in my heart further apart.

"I'm afraid so. So, holding him is the least I can do."

I nodded, "Why is he in here?"

"Lots of reasons. He was six weeks premature, and his lungs didn't fully develop. Do you want to hold him?" Jack asked.

"No!" I blurted.

But Jack stood, holding the baby against his chest. Then he lowered the bundle down to me, and I put my arms out on instinct.

"I'm going to drop him!" I exclaimed.

"No, you're not," Jack said soothingly. "You're a natural."

160

He adjusted the blanket so the baby's feet would stay warm, and he sat on the bed next to me, wrapping an arm around my shoulders and pulling me into him.

"He's beautiful," I cooed. "It's been a long time since I've held a baby."

"I can't tell," Jack said in a whisper.

Staring at the Captain's face, I heard my own heart thundering in my ears. I felt it slam against me, realizing that the greatest problem I faced was my mother, and her blatant disregard for me, while this baby, right from the beginning, had to fight for his place in the world.

Jack suggested that I'd misjudged my mother's intentions. But that was the thing about carelessness – it was hard to decide whether it was ignorance or if someone honestly didn't care about you. Maybe I was wrong about her intentions, and there was no intended malice, but wasn't it worse not to be considered at all? To not even be a blip on someone's radar because they inadvertently didn't think of you? At least with malice, someone purposely thinks of you.

Yet, there was still another vast difference between the Captain and me. I have always known that I was wanted from the day I was born. I had a place to belong for the first sixteen years of my life. I had a family, and we lived and operated as a unit. I had two loving parents and an older brother that I adored. I didn't need much more. I had them, and we were impenetrable.

Then it all changed, and I lost everything.

I felt a tear run down my cheek. I was a selfish human. And as I held a helpless infant in my arms, who in time would know the real meaning of alone, I realized it was better to have known what love was and have it taken away than to start living life never knowing any difference.

"Hey," Jack said. "Are you okay?"

"Yeah," I said, using a sleeve to wipe my eyes. "What's going to happen to him?"

"I'm not sure," he said.

He saw the moisture around my eyes and pulled me closer to him. I rested my head on his chest, basking in the warmth of his skin and the gentle scents of Ivory soap.

"Why do you call him the Captain?" I asked.

I felt him smile, and he ran a hand over the baby's delicate head.

"Well, he's my Captain," he said.

The baby's arm escaped the blanket, and I reached to grab his wrist, but he wrapped his hand around my finger and held on tight. Then, what Jack said made sense, and it didn't matter who the baby grew to be or what he was named. Whether we would see each other years from now, I would never forget this. I would always remember it as the moment when he became my Captain, too.

␝oɔ∫o␝ ␝oɔ∫o␝ ␝oɔ∫o␝

The sky turned pink as the sun rose over the hills. We'd spend the night taking turns holding the baby while the other slept. And when the baby fussed, Jack changed his diaper and walked the floor, humming a made-up tune. If that didn't work, I'd make a bottle, and we'd take turns feeding and burping him.

It was seven in the morning when Renee finished her shift. She shook us awake, thanked us for our help, and told us we should go home. She gathered the Captain into her arms as the day nurse entered to receive the report.

We drove home in silence, both of us too tired to converse, and I dozed with my head on the cool window. Jack pulled into my driveway and opened the door so I could slide out. He handed me the crutch, and I leaned on it as I walked to the front porch.

"So, was it a good surprise?" he asked, stopping a few steps in front of the porch.

"Yeah," I said, facing him on the bottom step. "It was amazing. I hope they find a good home for him."

"They will," he said reassuringly, but then he seemed saddened, and I feared that whatever had bothered him earlier had returned.

"Do you want to come in?" I asked, and he went rigid, as if someone had jabbed him with a pencil. "We could make some coffee."

"I don't think that's a good idea," he said.

"Jack, my mom's not here," I said pointedly. "She always parks in the driveway."

He averted his gaze to his feet, his hands, anywhere but my face, this throat bobbing before he spoke.

"I can't do this anymore, Rylen."

"Can't do what?" I asked.

"This." He pointed at me, then himself. "Us. I can't do it anymore."

"You can't… be my friend?"

He shook his head. "Are we friends, Rylen? Because I don't think we've been just friends in a long time."

His boldness surprised me, but if he got to call a spade a spade, then so did I.

"If that's true, why haven't you kissed me again?"

The top few snaps on his shirt were open, revealing the dip between his pectorals. A few tendrils of dark chest hair peeked out, and I resisted the urge to grab the two sides of his plaid and yank.

He exhaled, and I lifted his arm by the sleeve of his jacket and pulled him forward, closing the distance between us. I wrapped his arms around the small of my back and draped mine around his neck. His chest expanded, and his eyes closed, but I couldn't tell if it was from agony or ecstasy.

I cupped his face, his three-day stubble prickly against my hand, but I didn't care. It was his lips I wanted.

"Kiss me," I whispered, my lips hovering above his.

He opened his eyes, his mouth partially opened, and I felt him take another breath.

"It's all I think about. Jack…. please," I whispered.

"I can't," he breathed. His eyes closed again, like he was admitting a terrible truth, and saying it aloud made it worse. "I'm sorry."

Disappointment washed over me—from the top of my head to the bottom of my feet. I felt my ears turning pink at the sting of rejection. I hadn't asked him to kiss me. I'd told him to. Hell, I'd practically begged, and he'd pushed me away.

I released his neck. "Do you think I'm unattractive?"

"What?" he said, dropping his arms. "No!"

"It's okay if you do. I'd rather know now than go on feeling-"

"Rylen," he said, cutting me off. He lifted a dark curl off my forehead, his fingertips lingering in my hair. "You're breathtaking," he replied in a low whisper.

I opened my mouth to say something but closed it again, unsure if I heard him correctly; then I charged forward. Flattery could wait.

"There's someone else then?" I asked. "Are you with the Captain's mom?"

"No! I told you the baby isn't mine."

"That doesn't mean you're not with his mother."

"I'm not. There's no one else."

"Then what?" I demanded. "What the hell is it?"

He shook his head. "I can't explain it."

164

"Try," I snapped, my embarrassment morphing into annoyance.

He bit his lower lip, wrestling with whatever held him down.

"This has to be goodbye," he said quietly. "I can't pick you up anymore."

"What?" I asked, astonished.

"Look, both Ned and Pete said they could help out. Just until you start driving again." His eyes drifted to the vehicle under the cover at the driveway's edge. His assumption was that it was mine, but that car no longer had an owner.

Something inside me snapped like a cracking whip, fueling the simmering anger brewing within me.

"You're such a stupid ass!" I said, verging on tears. "I haven't driven in three years. It's not my knee that keeps me from driving. It's that I can't drive. Not anymore."

My revelation took him aback; his lips thinning; his brow furrowing. "Why didn't you tell me?" he snapped. "I asked you about driving again. You should've told me the truth."

"It's not something I tell many people. It's embarrassing."

"I'm not many people, Rylen," he said coolly.

"So, now I owe it to you?"

"No, I mean I'm not just a nobody. At least, I didn't think I was."

"I didn't think I was either, but…. newsflash," I said, dripping with sarcasm.

"Don't be an asshole! What the hell am I supposed to do now?" he snarled.

"Why are you the one that's mad? You're not being ditched."

"I'm *not* ditching you, Rylen. I'm no longer able to be your taxicab. I'm sorry if that greatly inconveniences you."

"I never asked you to, Jack! I never asked for a damn thing."

"You *did* ask me. The other night on the phone."

165

"Then why did you come? If picking me up was so troublesome for you, why bother?"

I'd cornered him, and he was silent. He put his hands on his hips.

"I don't understand you," I said. "You barge into my life, and we spend all this time together. You act like you like me, and you *flirt* with me like crazy. And sometimes when you look at me, I feel like…" I stopped. I wasn't going to tell him that I felt like my heart was going to explode. "But it's not supposed to mean anything? Are you just toying with me?"

"No," he said huskily, "I was never toying with you." I was surprised he'd admitted it. But then he scowled. "But I don't like being lied to, Rylen. You led me to believe something that wasn't true."

"You don't get to accuse me of dishonesty. Not when I know the baby is more than just someone you're helping."

"There are some things I can't explain," he said.

"Then you should understand perfectly why I didn't tell you! And if you leave me, then-" I stopped, unable to say it out loud. My voice quivered as I finished. "Then I'll be alone again."

Tears pooled in my eyes, the sting of reality slicing deep. Because the truth was without him, I had nothing.

"I don't want Ned, Pete, or anyone else," I explained. I felt my bravery building, and if he was going to walk away from me, he needed to know. "I just want you."

He stood with his hands on his hips, his feet shoulder-width apart, processing everything I'd told him.

"I've been nothing but honest with you. I expect the same in return, and if for whatever reason you can't do that…" I paused, despising what I had to say next. "Then go and don't come back."

166

I was certain he would rush me, and I'd throw myself into his arms. He'd confess whatever it was that tortured him, and we'd be together. He'd choose me.

But he didn't.

"Fine," he said under his breath. "If that's what you want."

I blinked a few times to clear my vision, realizing he was undoubtedly climbing into his Bronco. Tears streamed down my cheeks and dripped off the end of my jaw as the engine roared to life. I did nothing to stop them. I did nothing to stop him. The question "Why?" was on my lips, but I had no more fight left in me. The tires squealed as he sped out of the driveway, and I saw him beating the steering wheel with his fists, his mouth open in a wretched cry. I waited until he disappeared before I collapsed on the porch and let out a cry so unfamiliar to me, it was as if it'd come from the hidden places within my soul.

Chapter Sixteen

Rylen

It was Tuesday, and that meant I sat on Dr. Sullivan's sofa. She'd pulled her hair into a ponytail at the nape of her neck, and she crossed her legs at the knee. This time she wore blue jeans, a Led Zeppelin T-shirt and Converse sneakers in place of a suit and heels.

"How has your week been?" she asked.

I rolled my eyes. I didn't want to talk about it, but of course, she expected me to discuss something.

"I took your advice," I said evenly. "I tried to put more effort into getting out of my house. I tried to make a friend."

She smiled warmly. "How did it go?"

I wanted to crawl into a black hole and stay there forever.

"It blew up in my face. I don't want to talk about it. I just want to forget about him."

"Who?"

"Jack."

168

"Okay. Again, you don't have to talk about yourself. So, why don't you tell me about Jack?"

I shrugged. I had to sit there for another fifty-two minutes. I might as well do something to pass the time. I explained how I'd met him. How he kept showing up wherever I was. How we'd smashed the car and eaten pancakes and talked late into the night. And though I hadn't known him long, we'd become close. I told her I'd shown him Michael's bedroom and that my mother barged in just before we kissed. I said he'd shamelessly flirt with me and made me laugh every time we were together.

Then I told her about the Captain and Jack's vague explanations and odd behavior. I ended with the fight, how we'd quarreled, and how he drove off, leaving me sobbing on the porch.

"How did we go from sharing this beautiful moment to arguing and going separate ways? I cried for almost an hour."

"I'm so sorry," she said. "I can't believe he left after all that. It must've been gut-wrenching."

I nodded, "I'm torn between wanting to know why and wanting to forget it ever happened."

She used a finger to push up her glasses and opened her notebook. "I do have to take a minute to celebrate that you were brave enough to put yourself out there – to make a friend after what you've been through. It took a lot of courage."

"I must've done something wrong, though. He doesn't want to be my friend. I pushed him, and he ran, and it's all my fault."

"I wouldn't be so quick to place blame. What else can you tell me about him?"

I sighed. "I don't know. He doesn't care about social things. He doesn't drink or care about other people's opinions. He is who he is without apology, and I can be myself when I'm with him. It's refreshing."

"That's really great to hear, especially when your relationship with your ex was so different."

I nodded. "In the beginning, Andon was a great boyfriend. But meeting Jack was like realizing I'd been living in black and white." I shook my head, feeling idiotic. "That sounds stupid when I say it aloud."

"It's not stupid," she said gently. "Many women dream of finding someone like that."

My chin quivered under the threat of tears, but I was determined to hold it together. All I'd done for three days was cry.

"I've been so alone this last year, without my dad, without Andon. I don't think I knew who I was anymore. Then I met Jack, and I remembered what it's like to be happy, like my world finally has color."

Dr. Sullivan smiled again. "Sounds like he's a wonderful boyfriend."

"He's not my boyfriend. I mean, we kissed once, but it wasn't a real kiss, if you know what I mean?"

She nodded, still smiling. "I do."

"It doesn't matter, though. He made it abundantly clear he didn't want me."

"I'm sure that stings. Especially if you have strong feelings for him."

I nodded. "I do. I wanted more, and I thought he did too, but…" I trailed off. "I feel like such an idiot. I'm a hazard to my own relationships."

"That's not fair. You said yourself that he flirted with you and acted like he wanted more."

"He did, but he also thinks I lied to him."

"And did you?"

"No!" She peered over her glasses at me. "Okay, I guess I should've been more upfront about a few things. But our relationship

170

was so new, and I was going to tell him." I sighed. "I didn't intend to be dishonest."

"It sounds like Jack's mind was made up *before* he found out about you not driving."

"It was. I don't know what I did. I have so many questions, and he won't answer any of them."

"You mean the baby?" she asked, uncrossing her legs.

"Yeah, I mean, isn't it weird? You don't just go hold a stranger's baby. The baby has to be his, and he's just lying about it."

She thought for a moment, tapping her pen on pursed lips. "Not necessarily. Hospitals have programs where people volunteer to hold infants. There may not be a connection to the child, and Jack may just be helping out."

I lifted a brow, "That's a thing?"

She nodded, "And from what I've learned about Jack, it sounds like he's a helpful, caring person. Someone who would volunteer to hold a baby."

"He is," I agreed. "A friend of Jack's told me something though."

"What's that?" she asked.

"About a year ago, he ran away. Got in his truck and left without a word to anyone."

The doctor pursed her lips again. "It's hard to say why he would do something like that. Did you ever ask him about it?"

"I did. He didn't give me any details."

"Hmm, my best guess is he was avoiding something. A conflict perhaps. Tell me this," she crossed her legs again and scooted back in her chair. "Regardless of your suspicions, has Jack ever been dishonest with you?"

"Not that I know of."

"Okay, so that leaves you with two options. When he tells you that he can't give you a ride and that he can't have a relationship with you, you can either take him at his word or you can continue searching for a reason."

"But he didn't give me a reason," I retorted. "Can't is not a reason."

She shrugged, "It might be the only reason you receive. Your emotions are going to follow the truth you choose to believe. Taking him at his word is far less painful than believing there's something else."

"They're both painful," I grumbled, putting my elbows on my knees and burying my face in my hands.

"I'm afraid so but believing him is the better option."

She twisted her wrist and pulled back her sleeve to see her watch. There was no Rolex today.

"We only have a few minutes left. Just curious, how are you getting home from this session if Jack is no longer your ride?" she asked.

"My mom's picking me up. She took the afternoon off to get ready for the fundraiser this weekend."

"That's a kind gesture."

I scoffed, "Trust me, there's a price."

"What makes you say that?"

I shrugged. "I know her. Somehow, she'll use giving me a ride as a way to rope me into going."

"This is for the charity your brother's death started, right?"

I was slightly taken back. I'd never told her that. The Doc was thorough in her research.

"Yes, it's this whole black-tie thing. The last thing I want to do is put on a dress and make small talk with people. They ask me how I'm doing and tell me how great Michael was. Then they stare at me pitifully, and tiptoe around me because I'm the girl with the dead brother. I just want to be treated normally."

"Have you told your mom this?"

172

"She doesn't care how I feel. She parades around like a poodle with a clipboard, eating up the attention."

The doctor bit her bottom lip, hesitating.

"Okay, I'm going to be the devil's advocate for just a moment. I want you to consider your mother's perspective. Try and put yourself in her shoes."

"Why?" I scoffed. "She's a glory hound. She only wants me to go so she doesn't look bad."

"I'm sure that's not the only reason." She took off her glasses and folded them into her hand. "Honestly, Rylen, while you may be the girl with a dead brother, your mother is the woman with a dead son."

The argument on my lips evaporated. I'd never thought of it that way.

"I've counseled many couples who have lost children, and I can't think of any of them who wanted attention or glory after their tragedy. In fact, many of them feel the same way you do."

"So, what are you saying, Doc?" I asked, my voice quivering around the lump in my throat.

"I'm saying that before you decide your mother's intentions, it would be prudent to try and see things from her point of view. Something tells me the two of you aren't so different. And after that, if you still don't want to go, you don't have to."

"It's not that simple," I replied.

"Is she going to drag you out of the house by your hair?"

"No."

Dr. Sullivan nodded. "Do you know where resentment comes from? Have we talked about this before?"

"I don't think so."

"Okay. When other people take away your ability to make your own choices, it can breed feelings of resentment. If your mom is strong-arming you into attending and you give in for the sake of peace, there's potential for resentment, and that will further damage your relationship."

"Won't it further damage our relationship if I don't go? She'll freeze me out for weeks."

"She could freeze you out anyway. You could go, and she could still find reasons to freeze you out. And, quite frankly, you're not responsible for the bad choices she makes."

"So, you're saying I shouldn't go then?" I asked hopefully.

"I'm saying you shouldn't go *unless* you want to."

"But then she wins. She's manipulating me. It's like emotional blackmail."

She shrugged. "Whether she is or isn't doesn't matter anymore. Not if it's your choice. If you do go, go because you want to, not because you're trying to appease her. You'll be much happier with the outcome."

She put on her glasses and rose from her chair, walking to the cherry-toned desk where she gathered my paperwork. I watched her open a drawer and pull out a receipt book. She flipped it open and selected a pen from the cup on the desk.

To see her dressed in something other than her striking suit felt peculiar, but I knew I could get used to it.

§ocꙩog §ocꙩog §ocꙩog

My mom's sleek silver Mercedes stood out in a parking lot full of dusty pickups. She'd left the engine running while she sat behind the wheel, a cell phone held to her ear as she chattered. Her sunglasses were perched on her face, her hair in a French twist, and she wore her trademark business suit. It was navy blue; she'd paired it with a hot pink blouse and a pearl necklace. Just because she'd taken the afternoon off didn't mean she wouldn't dress to kill. I couldn't remember the last time I'd seen her in something comfortable.

I opened the door, balanced on my good knee, and slid my crutch in.

"Juanita, that's a wonderful idea," she cooed, as I climbed into the passenger seat. "That sounds great. I'm picking Rylen up now. We'll be there in twenty. Okay, see you soon."

She hung up and started speaking before I shut the door.

"Rylen, dear, I found the most beautiful gown at Juanita's Boutique. We're going to stop by so you can try it on."

"What," I asked, annoyed. "Right now? Can we get some food first? I'm starved."

"You're not trying on a dress with a belly full of food. It will only take a few minutes. Besides, Juanita needs time to make alterations before Saturday night."

"You'll have to try it on my corpse if you don't get me some food."

I thought I caught a hint of a smile, but she shook it away.

"Tell you what, try it on, then we'll get an early dinner at Luigi's. They have that kale salad you like."

Kale salad? Oh, barf. I had never and would never like kale.

"I don't like kale," I said.

"No?" She touched her chin thoughtfully. "What am I thinking of then?"

"Can we go to Sally's?" I asked, hopeful.

"Sally's?" She repeated as if I'd just asked her to go to outer space.

I nodded, "They have really good pancakes."

"Oh," she said, considering my request. "I'm not in the mood for pancakes. Maybe another time. Let's go." She fastened her buckle and put the car in gear.

What she really meant by saying "maybe another time" was "how about never."

I slouched in my chair, coming to grips with the reality that I was about to try on a dress for a fundraiser I wasn't going to. Yet something told me now wasn't the time to break that news to her.

"It will be so nice for you to have your freedom back. Have you talked to Dr. Sullivan about driving?"

She stopped at the stop sign and pulled onto the highway.

"Not yet." I didn't want to talk about this.

"Well, please do, dear. It will be easier on us all."

"I can't help it, you know," I said defensively.

She cut her eyes to me. "I do know. Why do you think I have you in therapy? Dr. Sullivan came very highly recommended."

It's funny how someone could sound so patronizing yet, almost convince you they were doing you a favor.

"She's a good listener. Maybe you should talk to her. I'd be okay with that if you wanted to."

She chuckled, and I felt myself deflating. Although I disliked talking about myself, I enjoyed talking to the doctor and felt better afterward. Now, after offering her my therapist, my mother not only laughed at the idea, but she'd also laughed at me.

"I don't need therapy, Rylen." She waved an index finger through the air, her manicured nail painted pink and glossy. "What I need is a dirty gin martini."

What she really meant was "that's not on my checklist, Rylen."

Fix daughter. Check.

Encourage said daughter to get back together with Andon. Check.

Ensure the daughter attends the fundraiser. Check.

Make the daughter miserable in the process. Check.

Sleep well at night because you've done your parental duty—Double Check.

"What's your dress size now?" Diana asked.

I hesitated, keenly aware that I'd gone a little soft in the middle. The lack of mobility and Jack's late-night pancake and candy feeds had caught up to me. To make matters worse, being a Clark woman meant I was shaped like a top-heavy hourglass. I was never able to comfortably wear dresses with zippers. It was either too tight, or the zipper stopped midway up my back. So, I avoided dresses and all functions that required me to wear one.

"I'm not sure, actually."

"Hmm, well, I had Juanita order a couple of different sizes, and she's agreed to make alterations if we need them."

"Great," I mumbled.

Of course, she'd found the dress and bought it before I ever agreed to attend. Of course, she'd ordered a few different sizes, dissipating all excuses. Of course, she'd tell me the dress was nonrefundable yet still return the sizes that weren't needed.

Of course, Diana Clark would never just take no for an answer.

I reached for the radio, adjusting the station so I could connect my phone to Bluetooth. If she was going to doll me up and starve me, I could at least die happy with Pearl Jam.

"Turn that down. I'm talking to you."

"What?" I grumbled, turning the volume lower, but she reached past my hand and turned it off. "Hey, come on."

"Rylen, I'm not done! And it's important, so pay attention. On Saturday afternoon at two o'clock, you have a hair appointment."

"I what?"

"Just a trim to clean up those straggly ends."

I pulled a curl over my shoulder, inspecting it. I guess it had been a while.

"You have a manicure at three and a wax at four," she finished.

"Um, what are they going to wax?"

She ignored me. "I'll give you my credit card. Be in the high school gym at six thirty sharp. You can help me set up the final touches," she ordered. "The fundraiser starts at seven. It's going to be wonderful."

My mom continued to talk as we made our way through town. I nodded at the appropriate times and occasionally offered an "uh huh" to keep up my listening facade.

As we drove, I couldn't help searching for Jack's Bronco as we passed various parking lots. Where was he when he wasn't with me? I pushed all thoughts of him away.

Whatever we had was gone, and it stung like vinegar on a paper cut.

I blew out a sigh of relief when we parked in front of Juanita's Boutique. The newest window display was a mannequin wearing a 1920s pink ruffled dress and holding a parasol above her head.

I closed the car door behind me and limped to the front entrance.

Bells chimed over our heads when we walked inside. Dresses hung on circular racks, and shoes lined the walls behind them. A display table of perfumes with pink and purple glass bottles and a tray with antique brushes, combs, and hand mirrors, caught my eyes. The polish brass reflected the gold light like a mirror.

"Hello, Juanita," my mother called, glancing around the shop, but the front was empty.

"Juanita?" she called again. I followed her down the hallway into the back of the boutique, where a large floral curtain hung, separating the store from the dressing rooms.

Abruptly, Juanita threw back the curtain; her glasses crooked on the end of her nose, her eyes as wide as frisbees. The alarm on her face was enough to make me stop in my tracks.

178

My eyes traveled over her shoulder to the girl standing in the center of the room. Her back was to me, but she stood facing three giant mirrors. Her eyes caught mine in the mirror, and she saw me watching her as I stood motionless in the doorway.

The edges of her veil sparkled with rhinestones—like a princess wearing a crown. White ruffles spilled over her hips into billows of pearled tulle and satin. A long sweeping train flowed behind her, and waves of lace wrapped around the ottoman as if floating on a cloud of white.

"Ali!" my mom declared. "What are…." But she didn't finish the sentence, as her eyes took in the sight before her. It was clear what Ali was doing.

"Hi, Mrs. Clark," she said shakily. "Hi, Rylen."

I nodded a greeting as Juanita stepped into the hallway and swiftly tugged the curtain closed behind her. She pulled at the end of her pencil skirt and straightened her glasses. A measuring tape hung around her neck, and her salt and pepper hair was pulled into a hasty bun held in place by a stubby pencil.

"I am so sorry, Diana," she murmured. "Ali barged in about ten minutes before you got here."

"We can come back," I offered quickly.

"No!" my mom blurted. "That's all right, we'll wait out here and let her finish. No rush."

And if getting dolled up and starved didn't kill me, then waiting to get dolled up while I starved would.

"It's a *gorgeous* wedding gown, Juanita," my mom said, placing a hand on her chest.

She smiled at that, "Isn't it, though? Andon asked her last weekend. We're so excited!"

"Yes, of course, congratulations."

"I don't know what I was afraid of. I should have known you'd understand. Be with you in a few minutes."

179

JEANA R LAWRENCE

She disappeared behind the curtain, and I busied myself with the perfume display, pretending to be fascinated so I wouldn't have to converse.

I picked up a bottle of cherry vanilla body spray. I knew Jack liked the fragrance. I'd caught him smelling my hair on more than one occasion.

I pushed the memory away. I wished they made pepper spray for the mind. I'd repel anything having to do with him.

My mother approached the table. "Are you alright?"

"Yeah," I answered nonchalantly. "Why wouldn't I be?"

Her eyes narrowed, all concern disappearing. "Well, it seems your ex is engaged, Rylen. I was just making sure."

"I don't care, Mom," I replied. I couldn't remember the last time I cared enough to think about either of them. Yet, there was something buried deep within that still ached, and I pushed it further down, away from my heart.

"You say that, but…." She stopped.

The door to the boutique opened, and a girl I'd never seen before stepped inside. She walked behind the counter and stashed her purse under the glass display cabinet.

"Juanita," she called. "I'm back."

She wore tight blue jeans, a T-shirt that said Juanita's Boutique, and large hoop earrings. She bent over and gathered her blonde hair into a ponytail.

The curtain opened, and Juanita emerged with Ali on her heels. She'd traded the wedding dress for gray yoga pants and a fitted pink T-shirt. She carried the veil under one arm and a pair of white heels in the other.

"Oh, Cora, I'm glad you're here," Juanita said. "Take Diana into the back and show her the gowns."

"Gowns?" I repeated.

"Of course. You're not the only one who needs to look exquisite," Diana said.

I rolled my eyes. It wasn't like my mother's closet didn't feature a plethora of exquisite gowns.

"Stay here, Rylen. I want it to be a surprise. It was nice to see you, Ali." My mother crooned, falling into step behind Cora.

Stay here? With her? Thanks a lot, Mom. I hate surprises. I pretended to be fascinated with a nearby shoe.

"You too, Mrs. Clark," Ali chimed.

"I'll give you a call in a couple of days," said Juanita, marching to the cash register. "You can come back and try the dress on after I've made alterations."

"Okay," Ali said. "Thanks, Juanita."

I could feel Ali's eyes travel to me. I was out of shoes, and my hands started to quiver. I hoped she'd remain silent because if she didn't, I wouldn't be able to push the hurt away any longer.

From behind the curtain, Cora's voice boomed. "Juanita! The delivery driver needs your signature."

Juanita sighed. "Hold on, Ali."

Wait! Don't leave me with her! But she was already gone.

I hobbled further into the shop. It was obvious that I was avoiding her, but I didn't care. But when I turned around, there she was, looking at me with a trace of hope in her eyes.

Jeez, read the room, Ali.

"So, how have you been?" she asked.

"Fine."

"I was surprised to see you the other night."

"It's a small town."

She was silent and we stared at each other like two cowboys in the wild west. Why was she bothering? I didn't know what she could've said that would've made our situation less awkward. When your ex-best friend gets engaged to your ex-boyfriend, there aren't enough words in existence to express the adequate level of remorse.

"Listen, Rylen, I'm willing to put all this behind us," she said. "Okay, it's been rough."

I tried to hide the shock that surged through me. And if she thought we could ever be friends again…

"That's noble of you," I scoffed.

"Rylen, this has affected more than just you and me. There are other things at stake."

"Like your reputation?" I snapped. The comment was bitchy, and I regretted it once I saw a glimmer of hurt in her eyes.

"That's not what I mean," she said evenly.

"I don't understand why you can't leave me alone, Ali. Unless you enjoy punishing me."

"Punishing you?"

"For not going to your mom's funeral. I was still grieving, but you didn't care."

She crossed her arms, and her eyes narrowed into tiny slits. "You think I slept with Andon to get back at you?"

"You're denying it?" I fired back.

She paused, shaking her head. "You think of yourself rather highly, don't you? To think that the choices I make have *anything* to do with you."

"I know how you are, Ali. You'd never miss an opportunity to go for the jugular."

Again, she was silent because she couldn't deny that I was right. I knew what she was capable of doing, but I never thought it would be aimed at me.

"Fine," she relented, dropping her arms. "The truth is I was pissed you didn't come. I thought you could set aside yourself for one evening and be there for me but…"

"I was grieving, Ali," I said, between gritted teeth.

She turned towards the door, but she left the veil and shoes sitting on the counter.

"Yeah, Rylen. We all *know* you were grieving. You made it abundantly clear that it was all about you, and nobody else mattered."

"That's not fair! You can't be pissed at me for something I have no control over."

She stopped just before the door and looked over her shoulder.

"No, Rylen. I'm not pissed at you for grieving. I'm pissed at you for being a *victim* of your grief."

There was that word again.

Victim.

Andon had said it in the driveway, but I'd ignored him. Hearing it again felt like a slap in the face. Maybe it was true? Maybe I'd become so wrapped up in my own guilt and sadness, I didn't remember how to be happy anymore? I didn't remember how to be a friend.

"You want me to leave you alone. Wish granted. I'm going to stop trying now."

I watched as the door slammed behind her, and she walked across the street to her car. But something I'd buried inside began to surface, and I found myself aching for what I'd lost. When we'd spend warm summer afternoons eating popsicles in my backyard, Michael and his best friend, Bryan, would pretend not to spy on us in our bikinis.

Then we'd lay on our backs on the trampoline and make animals out of the puffy white clouds rolling through the sky above us. But more than anything, I longed for the person I used to know, the one I'd called my friend. I would always wish that things had been different between us.

Chapter Seventeen

Rylen

Life is full of pros and cons, and once I was shoved into a dressing room, I found myself in a battle between the two.

Pro: My mom had picked a dress, so I didn't have to spend countless hours trying on rejects I could spot a mile away.

Con: My mom had picked a dress which meant I had no choice and I was stuck with whatever she saw fit.

I balanced on one foot and stripped to my underwear, unable to brave a peek at the wall where the dress hung on a hanger. I closed my eyes and slowly turned around. I could handle lime green; with my dark curls and round brown eyes, lime didn't look half bad. But I drew the line at putrid yellow or tangerine orange. There was no way in hell I was dressing up like a giant Oompa Loompa.

I peeked, and the color was the first thing I saw.

Black.

The second thing was style.

Strapless. Gathered on one side. Glittery.

The length.

Floor.

The last, and arguably the most surprising, thing was the slit that ran from the seam to mid-thigh.

I never would've imagined my business suit mother would've chosen something I liked, let alone a dress as stunning as this. It was the perfect combination of classy, yet sexy; ostentatious, yet modest, and I found myself eager to try it.

I pulled a size six off the hanger, wishing for a strapless bra, and stepped into it.

"Okay," I announced, "Can you zip me?"

I pulled back the curtain and took a step forward. My mom sat in a nearby chair against the wall. She glanced up from her phone once the curtain opened.

"Ry—len," Juanita murmured in her heavy Mexican accent. She clapped her hands together. "You're lovely."

"Thank you," I replied, turning so Juanita could zip the dress.

Surprisingly, the zipper easily slid up, yet it tightened the bust, and my breasts spilled over the top.

"My boobs are falling out," I grumbled, pulling it up.

My mother's eyes widened, and she stifled a laugh. "Sorry, Hun, it's the Clark woman curse."

"What is?" Juanita asked, cluelessly looking between us.

"Boobs!" we said in unison, and she laughed.

"Count your blessings, ladies," Juanita said, a giggle escaping her.

"This is why I hate dresses," I announced. "Zippers suck."

"I can let it out a few inches if you'd like?" Juanita offered.

"Really? That'd be great."

"Sure, and other than hemming it, you really look great, Rylen."

"Thanks, I'm taking it off now."

I was about to make a beeline for the changing room when my mother stood.

"Not so fast," she said, "Come here, so I can see you."

"Mom," I grumbled.

"Right now. Stand in front of the mirrors."

I hobbled forward, and Juanita lent me a hand while I climbed atop the ottoman.

My mother circled me, like an artist admiring every angle of their work.

"You'll need a strapless bra, of course. Do you think you'll be off the crutch then? So, you can dance if you want."

"Dance?" Who said anything about dancing?

She circled me again, approval sparkling in her eyes. "Yes, I think it'll do. Do you like it?"

"Yes," I told her truthfully. "It's *gorgeous*, Mom."

It was by far the most stunning piece I'd ever owned, but disappointment flooded me when I realized the one person, I wanted to see me wearing it wouldn't be there.

"Let's have her try it on with heels so I know where to hem it. Cora!" Juanita called.

There were footsteps then the girl from the front pulled open the curtain.

"Cora, please grab me three pairs of black heels, open-toed, size..." Juanita trailed off, her eyes floating to me.

"Eight," I finished.

"Sure, no problem." But when she left, she didn't close the curtain. Anyone on the street had a direct view of the girl in the black dress standing on the ottoman.

"I'm thrilled you like the dress, Rylen. It's nonrefundable," my mother added with a nervous chuckle. "You really do look magnificent." She raised her phone and snapped a few pictures, "I know formal occasions aren't your thing. I appreciate you doing this, dear."

"Thanks, Mom," I replied, genuinely meaning it.

"Michael would be so proud of you," she said wistfully. "I don't think I could face this without you."

My graze traveled to her as her eyes pooled with unshed tears. If my support was what she'd wanted, that's all she needed to say. Maybe the Doc was right? Maybe she wasn't seeking glory and like me, she couldn't stomach it? The event was in honor of her deceased child? I didn't like being identified as the girl with a dead brother, but how much more difficult would it have been as the mother with a dead son?

Maybe one evening in a lovely dress, in honor of someone I loved, making small talk with people who loved him too, wouldn't be so bad? And even if the dress was another form of manipulation, it didn't matter anymore.

This was my choice.

` "I think I have the perfect necklace," I said softly, touching the spot below my collarbone.

She smiled approvingly, dabbing her eyes with a crinkled tissue.

Cora entered the room, a stack of shoe boxes teetering in her hands.

"This is all I could find, Juanita," she announced, placing the shoes on the floor.

"Thank you, Cora."

Juanita knelt at my feet; held a measuring tape to the seam of the dress.

"I'm afraid we'll have to take it up a few inches, even with the heels."

She opened the first box; pulled out a black heel with thin straps and rhinestones. I lifted the dress, revealing my bare feet, and Juanita slipped the shoe on.

She did the same to the other side and returned the measuring tape.

"Can you have it hemmed by Saturday?" my mother asked, watching as Juanita jotted numbers on a yellow pad. "Saturday morning at the latest."

"I don't think I can wear heels and a knee brace," I said.

"You'll be fine," Diana replied, waving a hand like all my concerns would vanish. "You're beautiful. Let's not ruin it with sneakers."

Below me, Juanita caught my eye and winked, and that was all the reassurance I needed.

The bells over the door rang, and footsteps entered the shop.

"Mom?"

The voice was unmistakable.

Oh crap. Please, dear God, I could use a lightning bolt right about now.

The top half of my bra showed above the dress line. I wanted to dive into the dressing room and disappear before he knew I was there.

"Andon?" Juanita said, standing.

He stood in the doorway, gaping at me, dressed in blue jeans and his white baseball cap; his black t-shirt said Harvey's Automotive. I waved uneasily because what else do you do when your ex sees you in a stunning gown?

"Rylen," he breathed, "You…. you're…. wow."

"What are you doing here?" Juanita demanded.

"Ali forgot her bag," he replied, snapping out of his daze. "She asked me to get it on my way home."

Home?

She'd moved in with him? The hurt I desperately tried to push away began to rise again, strangling me like an elephant sitting on my throat. I slept in my mother's office on the most uncomfortable sofa known to mankind because what was mine was taken from me.

"Oh, um, Cora, please search the front," Juanita answered.

Cora, who'd busied herself collecting dresses, nodded and carried the gowns to the front.

"Let me finish, and I'll be right there," Juanita told him.

She was about to close the curtain, but the phone rang, and she groaned, exasperated.

"Oh, for heaven's sake! I'll be right back, ladies," Juanita answered, pushing past Andon.

"How have you been, Mrs. Clark?" Andon asked, leaning against the door frame.

"I'm well, Andon. It seems congratulations are in order."

"Oh, yeah, thanks," he said, nervously adjusting his hat, though his eyes traveled to me, gauging my reaction.

A phone rang, and my mother stood, digging in her bag. She looked at the screen and smiled.

"I need to take this," she told me.

She was further into the store when I heard her chirp, "Hi, Adam."

"What's that about?" Andon asked, nodding her direction.

"I'm not sure." Uncertainty was a better option than explaining copious infidelity theories.

I wobbled on my heels. If I were to do a face plant, of course it would be in a gorgeous dress in front of my ex-boyfriend.

"Do you want to get down from there?" he asked.

189

"Yeah. I just might fall on my face."

He walked to me and stood with his arms out. I grabbed his shoulders, and he put his hands on my hips. I stepped off the ledge, and he lowered me down. We stood like that momentarily, peering at each other, our unspoken words conveying more than we could say.

I cleared my throat; pushed a curl off my forehead.

"I'm so glad you're out of that chair," he said, dropping his hands.

"Thanks. I'll make a full recovery."

"That's great, Ry. I was really worried about you for a while. We both were."

"I doubt that." The words were out of my mouth before I could think better of it.

"Of course, Ali was worried. You guys were…."

He didn't finish the sentence, and I didn't need a reminder; I was currently in need of a new best friend. And now Jack was gone too.

"It was just surgery," I said casually.

"I know, but I'm the reason you were in that gas station," he added.

"It's no one's fault," I offered, patting his arm. "Besides, I twisted my ankle. That's how I ended up in the wheelchair."

He nodded stiffly, "I've thought a lot about this. I can't apologize enough."

"It doesn't matter anymore. I'm fine, really."

He gazed at me again, but it was so different from…don't think his name. But he possessed the ability to see through me, into my soul; no matter how hard I tried to hide what was in there, he still always saw me. But when Andon looked at me, I didn't feel anything.

Not anymore.

Andon took a step towards me, one hand lifting to touch my face, but I stepped back, out of his reach.

190

"Rylen, I...." he breathed.

"No," I replied, his brow furrowed in confusion. "Quit trying to fix it. It's done."

Understanding washed over him, only to be replaced by disappointment.

Jaunita entered the room, a brown Kate Spade bag in her hands.

"Is this it?" she asked.

He cut his eyes to her, "What? Oh yeah, that's it. Thanks."

Juanita's eyes jumped between us; her brow creased with confusion.

Yeah, no denying what she saw.

"I'm going to change," I blurted, escaping into the dressing room.

"Yeah, see ya," he said, walking to collect the purse.

I heard their voices becoming further away as they walked to the front.

"Next time, call before you arrive. I can't have you disrupting my appointments," Juanita replied, an edge to her tone. "And tell your fiancée the same thing. It's called common courtesy."

I was still hiding in the dressing room when I heard the shop door close and the unmistakable sound of Andon's Mustang roaring to life.

§oc∽o§ §oc∽o§ §oc∽o§

When I entered the hallway, Cora was waiting for me. She smiled and took the dress from my arm. I nodded thanks as I hobbled on my crutch down the hallway to the entrance. My knee had started to throb.

JEANA R LAWRENCE

I found my mother standing at the counter, frantically digging through her bag.

"They're perfect, Juanita!" she gushed. "Thank you *so* much." She pulled out a shiny American Express and placed it on the counter.

Behind the desk, Cora, glanced out the window, then looked again like she'd seen a convertible full of midgets. She shifted her weight, trying to see around parked vehicles. Irritated, she swore under her breath.

"I'll be right back, Juanita," Cora said, heading for the exit. And before Juanita could protest, the door swung closed behind her.

"That girl," Juanita grumbled.

In the parking lot, I walked to the front seat of the Mercedes. She fished the keys out of her purse, and the doors chirped as they unlocked. Voices drew our attention to the other side of the street, where Cora argued with a man in a black cowboy hat. The man's back was to me, but I knew who it was. I recognized the width of his shoulders, and how his ass filled out a pair of Levi's. I'd been tempted to grab that ass on more than one occasion.

I couldn't hear what they'd said, but she threw a white envelope at his chest. It hit the ground, and he bent to pick it up. He tried to give it to her again, pointing a finger the way a parent does with a child, but she threw her hands up and refused to take it, walking down an alley away from him.

Cora disappeared behind a building, but he was right behind her, his arm outstretched with the envelope.

"Isn't that your friend?" my mother asked, perplexed.

"Yeah," I admitted. "That's Jack."

Chapter Eighteen

Rylen

Wednesday Sent 3:48 AM
Rylen: Hi.

Sent 4:02 PM
Rylen: It feels weird not having you pick me up today. There's been a disturbance in the force.

Sent 7:56 PM
Rylen: Jack? Come on. Don't ghost me.

Sent Thursday 9:38 AM
Rylen: This is the only text I'm sending today.

Sent 6:35 PM
Rylen: Just kidding :) Please, answer me.

Friday Sent 2:32 AM
Rylen: Jack, I can't take this anymore.
Can we talk about this?

Sent 2:39 AM
Rylen: I hope your phone buzzes and wakes you up.
Buzz Buzz Buzz. 🐝

Sent 2:40 AM
Rylen: "All the Who's a snooze and warm in their beds." "All the Jacky's completely whacky for not texting backy." LOL, you see what I did there?

Sent 2:42 AM
Rylen: Be nice to know if at least you're reading these. Otherwise, I'm just texting into the abyss. The big black void.

Sent 2:45 AM
Rylen: OMG. You sleep like the dead! Fine, be that way!

Sent Friday 8:48 PM
Rylen: This is goodbye. You clearly don't want anything to do with me, so, I'll stop trying. I'll be at the Davenport Fall Fundraiser tomorrow night. If you're not there, you won't hear from me again. I'll leave you alone.

ဒိုင်္သို့ ဒိုင်္သို့ ဒိုင်္သို့

It was Saturday night, and I sat at the welcome table reading through the text messages I'd sent to Jack over the last week. It had been nothing, but ear-piercing, heart wrenching silence. Under other circumstances, I'd be embarrassed for sounding desperate, but I was out of options. If the silence continued tonight, it would be the end.

I'd find the strength to walk away.

My morning had started at six when my cell phone binged, and I sprang up, hoping it was Jack answering my desperate pleas.

It wasn't.

My mother had texted my phone to see if I was up rather than yelling across the house.

Within moments, the office door swung open. She ordered me to dress and demanded I do so. When I pleaded for coffee, she said she'd buy me an Americano on the way. We were due at Juanita's to pick up the dress by seven which meant we had to be there by a quarter 'til, or we were late.

Alterations had taken longer than expected, but Juanita had worked late into the night to ensure the gown would be ready in time. My mother, who was displeased with the delay, was reassured that we could pick up the gown on Saturday morning on our way to the salon.

The rest of the afternoon was filled with beauty appointments, so much so that I barely recognized myself with manicured nails, straightened, blown-out hair, and dramatic makeup. I could barely walk after they were done waxing.

I'd barely had time to eat. Every time I mentioned my increasing hunger, I was offered forms of kale or handfuls of almonds. Eating before putting on a lovely dress must have been frowned upon by the sadistic beauty gods. The act was considered as plumping instead of slimming. Ironically, if I died of hunger, it wouldn't matter my size.

Don't mind me, bitchy beauty gods. Just over here fantasizing about cheeseburgers.

Luckily, Juanita, who was my ride to the fundraiser since my mother needed to be there an hour early, found me in the pedicure chair and split her club sandwich with me.

I tried not to be obvious, but every few moments I'd sneak a peek at my phone, confident Jack had responded by now. But he hadn't. My heart plummeted a little more with every passing moment.

By 6:30, Juanita dropped me off by the high school door. I was supposed to find my mother as soon as I arrived, where she'd give me my assignment for the night. As Juanita parked the car, I limped inside without my crutch, grateful she'd hemmed the dress so I could wear flats.

Once my coat was checked, I scanned the growing crowd for my mother, but she found me first.

"Rylen, so glad you're here," she crooned.

I turned to see Diana Clark wearing a long red dress with a strap over one shoulder. A large silky white bow rested on the strap, and the middle was gathered at one hip. Her dark hair fell down her back in a waterfall; the ends were loosely curled. She wore a strand of pearls around her neck, with matching earrings and a bracelet which was a gift my dad had given her two Christmases ago. Her makeup was bold, flawlessly accenting her large brown eyes and pronounced cheekbones. Her lips were painted a rose red, an exact match to the color she wore. I've always considered my mother beautiful, but no other moment compared to this.

"Mom," I said, taking her in, and she smiled meekly. "You look amazing."

"Thank you, dear," she said. She stepped back and put a hand on her hip, scanning me from head to toe. "Not bad yourself."

I smiled, "Thanks. You picked a great dress."

"It's not the dress, dear."

I smiled again, and I felt a glimmer of hope. This was how we used to be.

"Come with me. I'll show you where you're sitting."

As I followed her into the gym, a mixture of shock and awe churned inside me. The lights, the decorations, and the tables with centerpieces all transformed a casual place into a magnificent banquet hall, and it was as unrecognizable as anything else.

As guests trickled in, they were escorted by men in white suit coats to their assigned seats. Circular tables were decorated with pearly white tablecloths, and puffs of silky burgundy fabric billowed in the center. Among the waves of burgundy, bouquets of red and white roses with sprinkles of baby's breath sat in crystal vases—napkins ringed with silver holders lay on delicate China plates framed by polished flatware. Goblets, set precisely above the knife tip, were filled with cucumber water, the hollow rounded ice cubes floating among thin slices of green. Servers in white-tailed coats held trays above their heads, filled with champagne flutes, the busy golden bubbles sparkling with excitement as they sailed to the top.

"Here." She gestured to a welcome table behind her and pulled out a chair. "This is where I need your help. When people walk

197

in, welcome them, answer any questions, and make sure they put their name in the box for a door prize. Think you can handle that?"

I nodded. "Seems easy enough."

I pulled out the chair and sat behind the table.

"Good. If people want to participate in the auction, they get a paddle." She pointed to a box behind me that held what looked like long-handled ping-pong paddles with large, bold numbers on their faces.

"Write down their name and what number they have," she added.

A clipboard lay next to me, and I picked it up to read the paper. There were two labeled columns: "Name" and "Paddle Number." She'd made this idiot-proof.

"On the second page, there's a list of items in the auction. Whoever wins, write the number next to the item. Put all payments in the cash box. Any questions?"

"No, I think I got it," I replied, flipping to the back page.

"Great, you'll take the first hour, then somebody will relieve you. Then you return for the last hour."

"That's it?" I asked.

"Yes." She smiled. "I told you it wasn't going to be difficult. Now I've got to go, Hun. Remember to enjoy yourself."

She flitted away, and I was left to greet people as they walked in, passing out paddles, jotting down names, but mostly keeping an eye out for a black cowboy hat. But I saw nothing even close. I thought I saw Jack a few times, eliciting a moment of hope, like I was suddenly levitating a few inches off the ground. But then the stranger turned around, and my heart pulled me down, sinking me back to reality.

I began preparing myself for a final goodbye, though I wouldn't say it to him. If I thought about it now, the sadness would consume me. Uncontrollably sobbing in the bathroom wasn't good for morale. So, I held on to the last threads of hope I could muster, refusing to say goodbye until the last second.

The lights lowered, and Diana climbed the stairs to the great stage at the front. The crowd erupted into applause as she stood in the spotlight, tapping the microphone to ensure it was on.

"Hello, Davenport!" she purred into it. The applause crescendoed, a few crowd members whistling before the sound gradually faded.

"Thank you so much for that warm welcome. My name is Diana Clark, and I'm the host for this evening's event. I wanted to thank you all so much for being here with us tonight. We have a fantastic evening planned for you, a delicious dinner prepared by our very own…"

"Mind if I sit here?" said a voice.

I looked up to see the girl from the shop, Cora, wearing a short blue dress and black heels. Her straightened hair hung over one shoulder. She wore dark makeup with lipstick the color of rubies.

"Sure," I said, gesturing to the empty chair beside me. She pulled it out and sat down, then scooted closer to the table.

"I'm supposed to take over when your hour's done," she said, glancing at the clipboard under my hand.

"Oh," I said. "Okay."

She sighed and buried her hands in her face. "How did I get myself into this crap? I really need to be someplace else. Do you ever wish you had superpowers? You could just jump time and be in two places at once?"

I smiled weakly. "All the time."

"Yeah, a little Superman speed would be great right now," she sighed, rubbing her temples. "Sorry, I'm a little stressed. My fiancé is in prison, and he's been getting his ass beat."

"Oh no."

"Yeah." She made a fist, cracking the knuckles on her right hand. "Sorry, again, I don't make a habit of dumping my issues on strangers."

"It's okay. And we're not strangers. We met at Juanita's."

She nodded. "I guess we did."

I wanted to ask her how she knew Jack. Why were they arguing outside the boutique? Maybe she was an ex? Did it end badly? I guess those details didn't matter. I no longer had a claim; if there had been one, he'd made it crystal clear it no longer existed.

My need for a friend triumphed over my curiosity, so all of my questions would have to wait.

"I can fill in for you. If you can't stay," I said.

Her eyes widened, like offering her a small token of kindness was the last thing she'd expected.

"I'd appreciate that," she replied. "But I promised your mom I'd help. Just don't tell her when I sneak out the back."

I smiled. "My lips are sealed."

She lifted a hand and snapped her fingers, and the nearby waiter brought over a tray of champagne, lowering it down to her. She took two and handed one to me.

"Thanks," I said.

"To better places?"

"And sneaking out the back," I added.

We clinked glasses, then she shot the golden drink back in one gulp.

I took a small sip, and she didn't seem to care that I hadn't followed her lead.

My mother was still on stage, soaking in the limelight, reading the evening's agenda like she was a duchess in the high courts, holding a scroll that unfurled into the audience and trailed into the courtyard. "And don't forget, ladies and gentlemen, fireworks start promptly at ten p.m."

"So," Cora began. "What happened to your knee?"

I glanced sidelong at her. If she was going to ask me personal questions, maybe I could ask her a few things.

"Ah, it's a long story. I don't usually dump on strangers either."

"We're not strangers, and you have to sit here for the next forty-three minutes; you might as well tell me. You gonna drink that?" she asked, pointing to my champagne.

I chuckled, handing it to her. "No."

This time, she sipped the liquid and sat back like a child preparing for story time.

"Tell me."

"Ah, okay, a little over a year ago, Andon and I were driving home." She rolled her eyes when I mentioned his name, and I bit back a laugh. "We got into an argument. I found out he was cheating on me with my friend." Her eyes widened, and she patted my shoulder. "Yeah, anyways, we pulled into a gas station; I was angry, so I ran inside. I'm not inside for two minutes when a man in a ski mask barges in the door and tries to rob the place."

She set her champagne on the table. "You don't have to finish this. I thought you slipped or something."

"It's okay, I've had enough therapy to actually talk about it now," I answered. "So, the robber points a gun in the clerk's face and tells him to empty the cash register. But the clerk had a gun under the counter, and he fired at him. I dove into an aisle to take cover. Andon drove off when the shooting started, and I don't remember anymore after that. I woke up in the hospital with a bullet hole in my knee. I've had three surgeries, and it's just now starting to feel normal."

Sometime in the middle of my story, Diana had disappeared from the stage, and dinner had begun as waiters held trays over their heads with plates of salad and baskets of bread.

Cora sank in her chair, her delighted child demeanor long gone. She stared at the table, slack jaw, the crease between her eyebrows deepening, as her eyes raced back and forth, lost in thought.

"Fucking Hudson," she hissed under her breath, her hand clenched into a fist.

"What?" I asked, unsure if I'd heard her correctly.

"Nothing," she said, quickly standing. "I'm going for a smoke. Be back in a bit."

And before I could say anything else, she'd evaporated, too.

ဥဝᐩᆳᲝ ဥဝᐩᆳᲝ ဥဝᐩᆳᲝ

My stomach grumbled, I was about to swipe a roll off a passing tray, when Diana issued a decree that eating at the welcome table was unrefined.

My hour was up, but Cora never returned. Luckily, Juanita found me, hauled me out of my chair, and told me she was taking over but to be back at nine.

I could've kissed her feet.

I headed for the kitchen as Diana approached the mic.

"Now, ladies and gentlemen, it is that time of night when we begin the auction."

I swiped a roll from the kitchen and leaned against the wall in the back of the room.

There was soft applause, and a screen lowered from the wall behind her. "I trust you all have your paddles ready. Our first item is...."

The picture of Sally's Diner filled the screen behind her, and I was both delighted and saddened at the sight.

"Dinner for two at Sally's Diner," she announced. "I have it from a reputable source, folks, that Sally's Diner has *excellent* pancakes."

A smile tugged at the corners of my lips. I had it from a good source, too.

"Ladies and gentlemen, I do have to mention that the *stunning* photography you'll see displayed up here tonight was taken by my exquisite daughter, Rylen Clark."

The crowd broke into applause again, and I plastered myself against the wall, hiding in the shadows. Did she have to do that? I appreciated the recognition, but not in that way.

"Let's start the bidding at...."

"Hello, Miss Rylen," I turned to see Ned and Pete both wearing suits with bolo ties and shiny boots. They smiled at me, and I pushed off the wall.

"Ned! Hi guys."

"You look wonderful, dear," Pete murmured.

"Thanks; you guys clean up well, too."

"Where's Jack?" Ned asked, scanning the area around me. "Wherever there is a Rylen, there is sure to be a Jack."

I shrugged. "I'm not sure. I think we're over."

"What do you mean *think*?" Ned asked.

Pete patted my shoulder. "He'll come to his senses, and if he doesn't, he's more of a dumbass than I gave him credit for."

I chuckled. "I hope you're right."

"Sold! To number twenty-four! Thank you so much, Harvey Martinez," my mother proclaimed.

I smiled as Andon's dad got up from his chair and dug out his checkbook from the inside of his jacket.

"Our next item up for bid is…." The picture behind her changed, and four Cooper tires sat in a stack in front of Harvey's garage.

"A set of brand-new tires from Harvey's Automotive. Let's start the bidding at…."

"Oh, excuse me, guys, I'm gonna bid on these," Ned said, "Call me if you need anything, honey."

"Thanks, I will."

He smiled softly, took a few steps into the room, and lifted his paddle into the air.

"I have five hundred in the back. Do I hear five-fifty," Diana paused, and Ned bounced on his heels in anticipation.

"Five hundred going once, twice. Sold to number thirty-five! Thank you so much to the gentlemen in the back."

Ned, pleased with his victory, patted the outside of his pants pockets.

"I bet he forgot his wallet," Pete grumbled as we watched Ned search the depths of his jacket. "Excuse me."

I chuckled, watching as Pete dug out his wallet, annoyed. Ned shrugged and followed him to the table where Juanita waited.

"Now, ladies and gentlemen," Diana announced. "We're going to take a short break. So, grab that special someone and make your way to the dance floor."

I leaned against the wall again, watching as my mother descended the steps. She was met at the bottom by a man I'd never seen before. He had honey-blond hair, a long torso, and broad shoulders. He was dressed in a navy-blue suit, and when he gripped her arm, she took a step back as if his presence surprised her.

I was about to run to her rescue when Sally blindsided me.

"Rylen, dear! Don't you look marvelous?"

"Thanks," I said, trying to see around her.

Sally wore a purple dress, her wild blonde curls tamed with copious amounts of hairspray. Her makeup was heavy; her glasses hanging around her neck on a jeweled chain.

"I meant to say hi earlier. I haven't seen you at the diner in a while. Everything okay?" she asked, sipping from the champagne in her hand.

"Yes, just been busy," I lied.

The stranger was now talking to my mother, her head nodding every few sentences. She scanned her surroundings, took his arm, and stepped into the far corner.

"Well, come back soon. We miss you. Now, Rylen," she took me by the elbow and walked me away from the crowd. I craned my neck to see my mother, but she was gone.

"Bill and I have decided to donate all of the money we've saved for the diner's renovation to your mother's charity in honor of Michael."

My eyes widened. "But what about your remodel?"

"Oh honey, it can wait. We've been saving for a while. It's just terrible what happened to your brother. And well, I lost my momma to a drunk driver too."

"You did?" I tried to conceal my shock.

She nodded. "I was seventeen. It was awful. The diner is all I have left of her."

"I don't know what to say," I said quietly.

"Nothing like this existed after I lost momma. Just know that I am so grateful that your mother started this charity. The support for the living is what it's all about – to rely on those who know your pain. We're stronger together."

My own words echoed in my ears. *Fundraisers are stupid. All the charity in the world doesn't bring back what you've lost.*

How wrong I'd been – how *stupidly* wrong.

"You're very kind, Sally."

She smiled warmly. "It's the least we can do, honey."

I felt a hand on my shoulder, and I turned to see Andon, his brown eyes peering into me.

"Excuse me, Rylen, I think your mom is looking for you."

"Oh, okay. Thanks so much, Sally."

"You're welcome. Come back to the diner soon."

As I walked away, I felt Andon's hand on the small of my back, leading me to the edge of the dance floor.

"Where is she?" I asked, scanning the back corner for a red dress.

"Sorry," he said. "I lied. I just said that to get you away from Sally. I know how you hate it when people start going on about Michael like that."

"Oh," I said. But I hadn't felt like the girl with the dead brother, and Sally's remarkable generosity had covered all pity I may have felt otherwise.

I turned to face him, but he extended his hand before I could break away.

"Will you dance with me?" he asked shyly.

"Where's Ali?" I asked, looking around us.

"She's...not feeling well."

"Oh," I said again.

"Come on," he said, "Just like old times."

I glanced at his hand and then back to his face, considering his offer.

"Okay," I said, "Just one, because I have to get back to the table."

"Sure," he said, smiling so big it touched his ears.

I put my arms around his neck, and his hands found my hips as we began to turn in slow circles. He was dressed in a black tuxedo, his dark hair gelled into perfect tips, and his face was freshly shaved.

He was taller than I remembered, or maybe I was used to being closer at eye level with someone else.

"I owe you an apology," I said, staring up at him.

"What could you have possibly done that you need to apologize for?"

"Well, that evening in the parking lot… I'm sorry Bam Bam attacked you. He's protective."

"He should be," he answered, smiling weakly. "Don't worry about it. Besides, I believe I'm the one that owes you an apology."

"What now?" I teased, rolling my eyes, and he chuckled at the jest.

"About a million things, but mostly I'm sorry I drove off that night at the gas station. I should've run inside after you."

"You could've been shot, too."

"I'd rather it'd been me. It's my fault we were there."

"You didn't know, Andon, and you already said you're sorry."

He sighed, twisting me around, and when I faced him again, he said, "Feels like all I do these days is apologize to someone. If not to you, then to Ali."

"Well, you owe me nothing."

He smiled, the sort of boyish grin that makes women weak in the knees.

"Yeah?"

"Yeah, I mean, it's taken a lot of smashing cars and expensive therapy to get me here, but…." I said with a laugh in my voice.

He chuckled. "Smashing cars?"

"Yeah, Slugger Therapy. I had to use something as your head."

He laughed again. "Okay, I deserve that. That's what I love about you, Ry; you're cool and easy to be with. I miss it."

I'd danced with him on so many other occasions. It was as if my body was on autopilot while inside my mind raced. Maybe it was naive, but there was a time when I'd believed we'd be together forever, and I would never long for anyone else. But circumstances change, people grow up, and the ones we believe we belong with transform into someone entirely different.

"You always were a good dancer," I said, and he smiled wistfully, pulling me against his broad chest.

The song ended, and couples pulled away to applaud.

"It's hot in here. You want to get some air?" he asked, nodding to the side door.

I followed him to the exit, slipping out the back doors to an area that overlooked the football fields and the running tracks. The dumpsters were down a few steps to the right. There was a heavy feeling in the air, a moisture that hung like a blanket covering us with the threat of snow.

"Do you want my jacket?" he asked, but the temperature difference felt good against my hot skin.

"No, thanks. I'm good."

He leaned his elbows on the railing in front of us. "Can I ask you something?"

"Sure," I answered, waiting as he found the words.

"Is Jack your boyfriend?"

"No, we're…." I trailed off. "I'm not sure we're anything, actually."

"You guys seemed like you were a couple in the parking lot that day."

"No." I said sadly. "We're not even friends."

He turned his body to me, so he looked into my eyes.

"Do you think we could ever be something again, Ry?"

"Andon, you can't think…."

"Ali's pregnant."

I stopped speaking; my throat instantly bone dry. "Wha?"

"Six weeks. We told our parents on Thursday."

And for the second time that night I was utterly speechless. "I don't know what to say," I whispered.

"Say you'll be with me anyways." He wrapped an arm around the small of my back and pulled me into him. "Tell me to break it off with her, and I will."

I pushed at his chest and took a step back.

"Why would you say that?" I growled. "You just told me Ali's pregnant! What the hell is wrong with you?"

"Rylen, I don't want to marry her," he said in a low voice. "I want you."

"You're having a child. It doesn't matter what you want anymore."

"Look, it was always supposed to be me and you; we both know that. I still love you, and I know you love me too. I don't have to marry her."

"Then why did you ask her?" I sneered, suppressing the rage in my voice.

He bit his lower lip, exasperated, "After she told me she was pregnant, it seemed like the right thing to do. But the closer we get to the wedding, the more I feel like..." he stopped, sighing deeply. "I couldn't go through with it without telling you how I feel."

"You and I are done, and if you don't want to marry Ali, then tell *her* the truth." I replied, keenly aware that I was sticking up for someone who'd betrayed me. "Own your choice, but don't you dare use me as your excuse."

I turned on my heel, and he said my name, trying to stop me, but I ignored him. I reached for the door and swung it open, satisfied that Andon was left with only the dumpsters to keep him company.

Chapter Nineteen

JACK

Sent Friday 8:48 PM

Rylen: This is goodbye. You clearly don't want anything to do with me, so, I'll stop trying. I'll be at the Davenport Fall Fundraiser tomorrow night. If you're not there, you won't hear from me again. I'll leave you alone.

My fingers hovered over the keypad. I didn't want her to leave.

I hoped she'd text again. She had to be kidding, but my phone remained silent. And even if she was, it made no difference. This had to be the end.

I wanted to tell her everything. But the thought of someone else hating me was more than I could stand.

Cora's endless disdain was one thing, but I wouldn't be able to take it if it were Rylen. The guilt suffocated me, and I only had myself to blame. It was my fault things had gone this far, and silence was the only choice I had left. She'd forget about me and live her life, even though I wouldn't forget about her.

It was early Saturday evening when Bam Bam barked in front of the screen door. I wiped the black grease off my hands. I'd spent most of the day under my Bronco, changing the oil. I climbed the steps to the front door.

"What is it, boy?" I asked, pocketing the handkerchief.

He licked his chops and whined at the door. I was surprised he was interacting with me. He'd barely looked at me over the last week. Even my dog punished me for leaving Rylen.

He barked again and scratched at the door. I opened it and he padded inside.

"Gran?" I asked, searching the tidy kitchen.

There was no reply.

"Gran?" I asked again, glancing down the hallway.

But then I saw her lying motionless by the coffee table. The tail of her bathrobe had flipped up, revealing her pink nightgown. One slipper lay beside her barefoot, and pieces of a shattered teacup littered the floor around her.

"Gran!" I went to her and got to my knees. When I put my hands on her, she stirred and opened her eyes. She blinked a few times, peering at me, then a small tear trickled from the corner of her eye.

"Jacky?" she said hoarsely. "Why am I on the floor?"

"I don't know," I replied. "Here, let's get you in the chair."

Slowly, I helped her sit up; she took a few deep breaths and got to her knees.

"Just go easy," I said, keeping my hands on her hips in case her knees gave out.

She let herself down into her recliner and touched her forehead with her fingertips.

"I'll get you some water," I said, walking into the kitchen.

"Thank you. I don't know what happened. I was bending over and suddenly felt dizzy."

I handed her the glass. She took a small sip and placed it on the lamp table beside her.

"Have you seen a doctor?" I asked, picking up her stray slipper.

"No, they all tell me the same thing. Your cholesterol is too high, Margaret. You need to walk more, Margaret. No more bacon, Margaret. I haven't been to the doctor in years."

I set my hat on the couch and pulled the ottoman over to sit down.

"They're just trying to look out for you. Put your foot up here." I tapped my knee, and she raised her bare foot.

"Jack, I'm old." She reached for my hand and interlaced our fingers. "I've lived my life and the only thing I want before I die is to see you and Cora reconciled."

"I know, Gran. She refuses."

"Keep trying," she said desperately.

"I did. What else am I supposed to do?"

I released her hand and got to my feet. I walked into the kitchen to retrieve the trash can.

She sighed, "Nothing, I suppose."

I got on my knees in the living room to gather the broken teacup pieces, disappointed to discover it was her lily cup.

"I liked that cup," she said. "It's a damn shame."

She pinched the spot between her eyes with her fingertips, closing them tightly.

"Gran," I started, watching her. "How often do these dizzy spells happen?"

She cracked one eye open to peek at me. "I don't know."

"How often, Gran?" I demanded.

"Every few days, okay?" She crossed her arms like a child in time out and stared at the wall.

I got to my feet and walked the trash back to the kitchen. "That's not normal."

"I'm dehydrated, that's all. Look," she took another drink from her water glass, but her hands shook as she set it on the coaster. "Good as new."

I went to the hall closet, opened the door, and wheeled out the vacuum cleaner.

"Don't be a stubborn ass. This is serious. You need to see a doctor."

She lowered her eyes and peered at me over the brim of her glasses.

"That's the worst case of pot and kettle I've ever heard."

I was quiet, and suddenly, we weren't talking about seeing a doctor anymore.

"Just because you can't fix it with Cora doesn't mean you should stop what you're doing altogether. People depend on you, Jacky."

"I don't know what…."

"Oh, stop it! Don't think I haven't noticed you sulking around this place the past week. The barn hasn't been this clean in years," she grumbled.

I sat on the couch arm and crossed my arms. "Being stubborn has nothing to do with it."

"Fine, then you're just being stupid."

I opened my mouth to say something, but she spoke again.

"Life is short, Jacky. Any of us could drop dead at any moment."

"Don't say that, Gran."

"It's true. I want you to be happy. I want to see you repair things with Cora and live a good life."

"Cora's not going to happen. She's made that clear."

"That doesn't mean you should be unhappy. I'm proud of you, Jack. You've helped so many people. And you haven't seemed as troubled." She stared down her nose at me. "Until this last week, when something clearly changed."

I couldn't meet her gaze, and my throat bobbed.

"I have a guess as to what it might be," she finished.

I fiddled with the button on my sleeve. "I can't keep doing what I was doing, Gran. It's not fair to Rylen."

"If you leave her, you're not being fair either. Not without telling her the way you feel. Or giving her a chance to think for herself. She might surprise you. Isn't there some sort of big party tonight?"

I rubbed my neck and pulled at my shirt collar. "It's a fundraiser for her brother's charity."

"Is Rylen going to be there?"

I paused, deciding not to tell her about Rylen's text message—the final goodbye.

"That's a safe assumption."

"Okay, then why are you still here?"

"It's complicated."

"You should be there. What's so complicated about that?" She locked her arms in front of her like she was on the dance floor. "Dance with her under the stars." She pulled her hands into her middle. "Hold her close." She puckered her lips. "Kiss her as the fireworks go off."

I stifled a laugh. "You read too many Harlequins."

"Maybe you should read one. Your lady skills need improvement."

I shook my head. "It's black tie; I don't have anything close…."

"Stop making excuses!" she cut in. "Go get her."

"And do what?" I said hoarsely. "Confess my undying affection?"

"Yes!"

"Gran," I started again, "It's not that easy."

"I know it's not, but when you find someone, you're brave enough to love you gotta fight for it." She leaned forward in her chair, gazing at me intently, gaining the reassurance I was listening. "And just so you know, if you don't dance with her, someone else will. Is that what you want?"

"No," I whispered. "What am I supposed to say?"

"Well, the truth is always a good place to start."

A chill slithered down my spine. "And what if she hates me?"

She smiled as if the answer were staring me in the face, and I was too stupid to see it.

"What if she doesn't?"

§০৫~০§ §০৫~০§ §০৫~০§

I changed my clothes as quickly as I could, jumped down the stairs, and climbed into my Bronco, watching as Gran waved on the porch. Bam Bam jumped inside, sitting on the front seat like I'd finally come to my senses, and I had one chance to make it right.

I drove so fast that I practically flew, and my heart thundered as I pulled into the parking lot. It was a few minutes after eight-thirty when I got there. Rylen'd be inside, knee-deep in festivities. What if she had forgotten about me already? What if she'd started seeing someone else? A lot could happen in a week. I'd thought about texting her the minute I'd made my choice, begging her to meet me, but there hadn't been time for thinking. I needed to look into her eyes when I apologized.

I killed the engine and opened the door. There was a chill in the air, the threat of snow lingering around me as I pulled on a sports coat Gran had found in the closet. The sleeves were too long. But with dark jeans, vest, and a bolo tie, I could blend in; I wouldn't stick out as the guy in plaid. And the moment I found Rylen, I was going to sweep her away, back into a world where only she and I existed.

As I walked to the front entrance, the doors opened, and Cora exited. I stopped dead in my tracks, still as a statue. I watched her as she took out a cigarette and dug in her bag for a light. Her hands shook as she flicked the lighter. It sparked, but there was no flame. She flicked it again, but it didn't light. She tried again and again; then she threw the lighter into the parking lot.

"Shit!" she screamed. "Damn it, Hudson!"

I pulled the Zippo from my pocket, and lit it, the yellow flame dancing across my face, revealing my hiding spot as I appeared out of the darkness. She saw the flame and looked to see me approaching her, offering her the light.

She hesitated, put the cigarette in her mouth, her red lipstick imprinted on the end of it, and she murmured thanks.

"Anytime," I said, pocketing the Zippo.

She let out her drag. "Aren't you pretty? But you're a little late to the ball, Cinderella." She replied, leaning up against the brick wall behind her.

"Yeah, Cinderella had nothing to wear."

"That looks like the work of Margaret Young," she said, gesturing to my jacket and shiny boots. "Your personal fairy godmother. But your jacket's too big."

I shrugged, "Pop had arms like an ape."

"It's not bad, though," she added, giving me a head-to-toe scan. "Who you tryin' to impress?"

216

"You got one of those for me?" I asked, nodding to the cigarette in her hand. She considered my request and dug one from the package in her purse.

"Thanks," I said, lighting the tip.

"Didn't you quit?"

"I did, but we can't all be saints, can we?" I said, letting out the smoke. "I hear they're bad for you, though."

"So is candy. That never stopped you."

I smiled at the jest, blowing a puff into the air above me. We stood like that in comfortable silence, smoking in the cold evening air as if we were old friends instead of enemies. I dared to think something had changed between us. Gran may see reconciliation before the end of her days.

"You're not going to try to give me any more money, are you?" she asked, breaking the silence.

"Nope. Ask if you want it."

"Your persistence is admirable," she replied, looking at me. "And annoying."

I took in another inhale, blowing the smoke into a gray cloud. "One of my better traits," I said, and there was a twinge of a smile on her lips, but she pushed it away.

"I met your girlfriend. She came into Juanita's to try on a dress."

"She's not my girlfriend."

"Don't bullshit me, Jack. I know you too well. It's insulting."

She took another puff, held the smoke in longer, and let it out of her nose like a dragon. "I tried not to like her," she continued. "I looked for reasons not to, but they didn't exist." She paused, taking another long draw. "But the thing I can't figure out is why is she in there and you're out here?"

"I told you why."

"That's not the real reason," she tutted, smoke escaping between her lips as she spoke.

I paused, chewing my bottom lip.

"I was afraid she'd find out about Hudson robbing the gas station, so I broke it off with her."

She shook her head. "Nope. That existed the moment you walked into her life." She flicked her cigarette, gray ashes falling to the ground. "Try again."

I exhaled, feeling the truth swell inside of me, and before I could think of something better, I heard myself say: "Because I feel guilty. No matter what I do to alleviate it I…" I stopped, and her face spread into a sly smile.

"And there it is. The real, the deep, the vulnerable, Jackson Timothy." She blew a cloud of smoke into my face, and I batted it away.

"You didn't tell her anything, did you?" I asked.

Her eyes flashed with amusement, and she smirked.

"I thought about telling her all the shit you've been doing around these parts was because of what Hudson did."

A chill crept down my spine. Did she know everything I've been doing? I prepared myself for her reaction, the blow-up of anger and hate.

"And?" I cautiously pressed.

"And I didn't say anything. Whether she's put things together on her own…." She shrugged and flicked what remained of her cigarette into the night. "You may not have been the one holding the gun, but you're just as guilty, Jack," she spat. "I like Rylen, and she deserves to know the truth. Either you tell her, or I will."

"Cora, you can't."

Her eyes narrowed. "Yes, I can, and don't think I won't."

"I came here to tell her. I need some time, okay?"

"You'd better. She deserves to know you have a habit of breaking everything you touch. I don't want her to be next."

My head turned when the door opened, and Scott greeted us. His brow furrowed at seeing us, and he shoved his hands into his blue dress pants pockets.

"Hey, guys, having a family reunion without me?"

We were silent, and Cora's eyes narrowed at him.

"Everything alright?" he asked, his eyes darting between us.

"Fine," Cora grumbled. "I gotta go. I got somewhere I need to be."

So, she never wanted reconciliation. It was blackmail she was after. I felt foolish for thinking we were anything more than two people who couldn't smoke inside.

Scott arched a brow, confused, as we watched until Cora disappeared into the black parking lot.

"What was that about?" he asked, rubbing the back of his neck.

"Nothing," I blurted.

I turned to walk through the doors, and Scott fell into step beside me.

"Cora's probably pissed, Hudson keeps running his mouth. He keeps ending up in the infirmary."

"I'm not surprised."

Inside, the lights were low; live music played as couples danced in slow circles. I scanned the crowd, hoping that my eyes would find Rylen's distinct curly hair in a sea of black ties and evening gowns, but there was no sign of her.

"It's really something in here, isn't it?" Scott said, taking two champagnes from a serving tray as the waiter walked by. He took a drink of the one in his right hand, then followed the same pattern with his left.

"Where is she?" I asked him, scanning the crowd.

"Who?" he asked, drinking from the right glass.

"Rylen."

Confusion perched over his eyebrows. "I thought you were done helping her."

"Scott," I said, grabbing two fistfuls of his jacket. "Where did you last see her?"

He thought for a moment and finished the drink in his left hand.

"What do I get if I tell you?" he smirked.

I grabbed his jacket tighter, "I won't beat the hell out of you."

"Okay, okay!" he relented. "She was on the dance floor with some tall Mexican dude. Then she went out the back door with him."

Red invaded my vision at the mention of Andon. The thought made my veins quiver with boiled blood. He'd touched her, taken her outside with him, and God knows what he tried to do once she was alone with him.

"When?" I said through gritted teeth.

He was about to answer when something caught his eye, and he looked above my head to the crowd behind me. I released his jacket and followed his gaze to see Rylen sitting at a table across the room by the stage.

And I was left breathless.

She wore the most incredible black gown, looking more stunning than I ever thought possible, and everything else around me evaporated. The music played; the lights were low; the servers bustled about; but it all fell away, and in my mind, it was only the two of us.

I wanted to run to her, and I envisioned jumping over tables and dodging servers, but I couldn't take my eyes off her. My hands shook, my palms becoming clammy as the shock wore off and anxiety took hold. I reminded myself not to think; tonight, it was about acting.

I watched her at a table near the corner of the stage, sitting with her chin on her knuckles and one elbow resting on the table. She fidgeted with something, her fingers busy on the tabletop in front of her. Her eyes were sad, forlorn even, her lips, painted a soft pink, were set in a pout.

I took two steps, but Diana approached the back of her chair. Rylen glanced over her shoulder at her mother. A man in a blue suit stood behind Diana. He was tall and blond with broad shoulders. I had never seen him before.

"What's takin' so long?" Scott chided. "Go."

I was about to move when Rylen abruptly stood, and her eyes widened. Flustered, Diana reached for her wrist, but Rylen pulled it away. The man in blue took a few steps toward them, and Rylen covered her mouth with her hand. Trying to explain, Diana reached for the man's arm and then tried to reach Rylen again. She said something, but Rylen pulled away again, and then she turned and ran out the side door, her face buried in her palms.

I swam through the crowd in the direction she'd gone. Her mother saw me, craning her neck to watch me chase after Rylen.

The hallway was dark, the lockers like cold statues, and I heard a door slam. I followed the noise, hoping the sound of my boots tapping against the linoleum wouldn't give me away. When I reached the door, I could see her outside through the window. She leaned against the railing, her head bowed, and her face buried in her hands.

I opened the door, and her shoulders slumped lower.

"Have you lost your mind? Why would you bring Adam here? Get away from me!"

"I can't," I answered.

Her head jerked up, and she turned to see me standing behind her. Her eyes glistened with tears, and she wiped them with the back of her hand. Her chest heaved as she took in measured

221

breaths. Her mouth was slightly open, dumbstruck like she couldn't believe her eyes, and I thought I'd never seen anyone more beautiful.

Yet her annoyance won out; I'd ghosted her for a week, and she closed her mouth, squaring her shoulders.

"What do you want?" she said indifferently.

The truth was always a good place to start. I knew it in my soul the day I pulled her out of that puddle.

"You."

And before she could react, I stepped forward, pulled her against me, and put my lips on hers.

Chapter Twenty

Rylen

I opened the door, and it slammed behind me as I entered the gym. Dinner was over, and servers carried trays of dessert over their heads as couples danced. But I had no appetite after meeting Andon.

I searched for a place to rest my knee and decided my mother's table was as good a place as any. I collapsed into a chair, leaning my elbow on the table and resting my chin on my knuckles. Did Andon believe I would do something like that? Did he think telling me his fiancée was pregnant would make me swoon, and I'd fall into his arms? Maybe he didn't know me at all? I'd never want anyone to abandon their child.

My thoughts floated to The Captain, and I wondered if there was hope for him. Would he end up as another kid abandoned at birth because someone like Andon got a better offer? I made a mental note to call the pediatric nurse and arrange a visit, even if I didn't have Jack.

Jack.

I wanted to dig out my phone to see if he'd responded. But his silence screamed at me all I needed to know. I guessed this was goodbye after all, and I was forced to accept it.

My stomach rumbled. I reached for the bowl of sugar cubes, and I popped one in my mouth, hoping it would keep me from fainting. I began stacking the sugar cubes in front of me, building a castle wall, much like the fortress around my heart, protecting it from all outward forces.

Two emotional beatings were good enough for me. At this rate, I was sure to die alone with fifty Madam Plunketts, and I was certain all of them would plot my accidental murder.

Too bad I'd run out of sugar cubes.

"Rylen, dear." I turned to see my mom approaching me; a man in a blue suit stood behind her. It was the same man I'd noticed before Sally had spoken to me and Andon had swept me onto the dance floor. The man was younger than I'd expected, barely older than me. My skin started to crawl.

"Rylen, there's someone I want you to meet," she declared, giving me a weak smile like she lacked confidence in what she was doing. "Rylen, this is Adam."

I stood, the chair scooting back like a plow. The dishes on the table rattled from my sudden movements, and my sugar cube wall came crashing down.

"Here?" I whimpered, covering my mouth with my hand.

She reached for me, but I pulled away. "Rylen, we have lots to talk about. Let's plan to go to breakfast tomorrow."

"I'm not going anywhere with you!" I bellowed.

Her eyes scanned around us; aware I could make a scene and ruin her perfect evening. She reached for his arm, and he stepped forward.

"Rylen, I can't explain it all here," she replied, dropping her voice. "Please, just do this for me."

"What about Dad?" I demanded.

"Dad?" she answered. "Honey, your father already knows."

She reached for my wrist again, but I couldn't stop the shock that poured out of me.

"And he's okay with it?" I sneered. "I can't believe you'd do this to me."

"Now, hold on a minute."

It was Adam who'd spoken, his voice a deep baritone, but I turned and ran away from her, out the door, down the hall to the back exit, hoping Andon had made his way inside already. I collapsed on the railing, relieved to be alone, and I buried my face into my hands as I cried.

Whatever rapport we'd built over the past week was gone. It had vanished the moment she'd brought her lover here, and we were back to being strangers who merely tolerated each other. If she picked him, I was confident our relationship would never survive.

The door opened behind me. I bit off the end of each word, "Get. Away. From me!"

"I can't," said a voice.

My head jerked up, and I turned around to see Jack standing behind me. His face was clean-shaven, and his boots were shiny and new. He wore a cowboy hat, the ends of his black hair hanging over his collar. His gray-blue eyes bored into me, past the castle wall I'd so carefully constructed, to the place I kept my secrets and desires.

I wanted to throw myself at him and rip his shirt open, filling my hands with his skin to ensure he was real. Then I was reminded of his frustrating silence, and I closed my mouth and straightened up, trying to appear indifferent.

"What do you want?"

A small smile teased his lips. He said a simple word, and I felt myself come alive again.

"You."

Then before I could say anything, he closed the space between us, pulled me against him, and brought his mouth to mine. He kissed me the way a man kisses a woman when he thinks she might break under the slightest touch. But what he didn't know was that I was already broken. And from the moment I'd met him in that miserable puddle, he'd slowly been putting me back together.

I wrapped my arms around his neck, meeting his reverent kisses with an urgency that had him wildly groaning against my lips, the sensations consuming me. It had never been like this with Andon, as each kiss was fueled with more passion, hunger, and desperation than I'd ever experienced. I knew nobody before Jack had ever made me feel alive.

I felt his tongue against the outside of my lips, and I opened my mouth against him, granting his request. He made a husky sound when my tongue found his, stroked it gently, then ran along his bottom lip.

I snaked my hands into the back of his hair, knocking his hat off his head. It tumbled to the ground as he wrapped his arms around my back, pressing me into his chest, turning me into liquid under his touch.

He slowed our pace, kissing me softly again, and I ran my hands over his shoulders as he brought one hand up to touch my skin. His fingertips drew tiny electric lines over my bare shoulders, my back, down my arms, and over the outline of my collarbone, and I clutched the lapel of his jacket to stay upright.

"That dress," he breathed against my mouth. "Oh, my God."

My lips curved into a smile at his approval, then he captured them in another full kiss, leaving me breathless.

"I missed you," I murmured, pulling away to see his face. "Never leave me again."

"Never," he promised, lowering his lips to my neck, but I took his face in my hands.

"Swear it," I pressed, peering into his eyes. "Swear, you stupid ass."

"I swear, I'm a stupid ass."

"Jack!" I pleaded, fighting a chuckle.

"I swear it, sweetheart," he said, cupping my face. His thumb traced the outline of my lips, then he said, "I'm yours, always."

Then I kissed his lips again with all the passion and desire I could muster, pouring every fiber of myself into him. I gave him everything I had and took what he offered, keeping it safe within me.

He broke the kiss and spoke again, "I'm sorry, I'm sorry, I'm sorry." He said it like a chant, speaking between each kiss while his mouth trailed from my forehead to my jaw.

"I'm sorry too, I should've told you everything. But I have so many questions," I managed. "You can't just kiss me and...." But I gasped as his lips lowered to my throat, inhibiting all thoughts.

"I know," he replied, his breath warm against my neck. "We'll get there, but right now, just this...."

I gripped the back of his arms as he kissed a path from my earlobe down my neck, and my breath caught when his teeth nicked the side of my throat. Then he kissed from my shoulder across my collarbone and further down between the tops of my breasts.

"We have to stop," he rasped, lifting his head. "Or that dress will end up on the ground."

He stepped back, and disappointment replaced anticipation as I immediately abhorred the loss of him.

"It would look better on the ground," I declared.

227

He chuckled, but shook his head, "Not here. You deserve so much better than that."

He bent to pick up his hat, then offered me his hand. "You comin' or what?"

Thunder crashed and Jack and I turned our faces to the sky as the threat of snow shifted into a rumbling thunderstorm. Dark clouds opened, releasing their sorrows upon us, soaking us within seconds. And then we were running, as fast as I could manage.

We ran around the building to the front parking lot. Jack's hand held tightly onto mine, the end of my dress swishing around my ankles, and I paused to lift it with my other hand. But Jack scooped me into his arms, and I let out a playful squeal as he kept running, the rain drenching us both.

I opened the door of his Bronco, and he set me in the front seat. He walked around the other side and got in, then pulled a blanket from the back seat.

"You must be freezing."

"Thanks." My teeth chattered as I slipped the blanket over my arms and held it closed in front.

He pulled at his tie and slipped it off his neck. Then he released the top two buttons on his shirt, opening it so I could see the chain on his neck.

The dog jumped between the seats, eagerly wagging his tail, and putting his slobbery chops into my lap.

"Bam Bam!" I rubbed his ears and grabbed his squishy face. "Good to see you, boy."

His tongue hung loosely while I petted him, his big brown eyes blinking with delight.

"Back. Lay down," Jack commanded, pulling him by his collar, and Bam Bam lumbered into the backseat.

"Your dog likes me now." I grinned.

"He *loves* you. He refused to look at me all week."

I reached a hand back and scratched under his chin, and Bam Bam raised his head, giving me better access.

"Just before I got in the truck, he started interacting with me again. I think he knew all along I was going to come get you."

"I didn't think you'd show up. I'd lost all hope."

He turned his head to look at me, his eyes simultaneously wistful and remorseful.

"I'm sorry it took me so long."

"This last week has been…"

"Horrible," he finished.

I nodded, and he gave me a sad smile.

"I think I can make it up to you," he said.

I creased a brow. "Really? What did you have in mind?" I crossed my arms and turned in my seat to face him. The playful part of me wanted to make him grovel; the other part wanted to forget about it altogether and never speak of it again.

He laughed, that toothy grin touching his ears, "Just wait and see, sweetheart."

He backed out of the parking spot and pulled the truck into the driveway. I took the iPod from the dash and scrolled through his albums.

"Are you ready?" he asked. "If we go left, we'll go into the city. If we go right, we go anywhere else. What'll it be?"

"Right," I said quickly. "Anywhere else, as long as I'm with you."

He smiled, delighted with my choice. "Okay then."

Then he sped onto the highway, taking us into our own world, where we had candy, inside jokes, endless music, and the promise of tomorrow. And I left everything else behind me, eating my dust.

ꕥ ꕥ ꕥ

The first stop we made was at a gas station where Jack bought every bag of M&M's available, pizza, and two giant cups of coffee. His eyebrows rose when I lifted a container of Caesar salad and put it on the counter next to his mountain of junk food.

Jack parked his Bronco on a hill that overlooked the high school football fields. Though I wanted to stay away, it dawned on me that I needed to return to the high school, sneak inside, and collect my jacket and purse. I'd been so wrapped up in my escape that I had completely forgotten about my belongings. But I wasn't going near that place until the fundraiser was over.

I opened the door and stepped onto the wet grass. We rolled the windows down and the music continued playing, filling the night with the sweet melodies of Eric Clapton. It had stopped raining while we were inside the gas station and the air had turned crisp and cool. Jack let down the tailgate and he lifted me onto the edge like he had on so many other occasions. He covered my lap with a blanket then hopped up next to me, our legs hanging over the side like children who were too short for grown-up chairs.

He unwrapped his pizza and offered it to me.

"First bite's yours."

And everything in my world went back to the way it was supposed to be. And decades from now, it would still be like this. I envisioned us sixty years in the future, old and gray, wrinkled and wise, and I knew he'd still give me the first bite of whatever we shared.

I chewed slowly, savoring the flavor of my first real food in almost twenty-four hours. I popped the lid on my salad and stirred the dressing into the lettuce with a plastic fork. I stabbed a bite and offered it to him; he made a face that was a cross between horror and disgust, then I thought he was going to throw up.

"Come on. It's not that bad," I chided.

"It's a vegetable. Of course it's bad."

"You can't taste that part. It's got enough dressing on it to choke a horse."

"Then you'd better watch out," he said, his voice laced with laughter.

My eyes flashed with amusement, and I slugged his shoulder. He let out a playful yelp and lifted a hand to rub the blow.

"Sorry, sweetheart, if it's green it's not for me."

I chewed slowly, blocking my lips with my hand as I spoke. "Some M&M's are green. That doesn't stop you."

"You can't compare candy to lettuce. They're on two separate planets."

I swallowed, watching as he took a bite of his pizza, and I filled my fork again.

"When's the last time you ate a veggie, anyways?"

He shrugged. "I don't know. Probably sometime before my mom died. Gran never made me eat them."

He chewed another bite of pizza and crumbled the tinfoil in his hands

"Yeah, my mom made me eat them. Sometime around middle school, though, I realized I didn't mind them as much."

"That never happened for me. I've tried liking them. I've prepared them in all sorts of ways. But every time I eat them all I do is think about my mom."

He paused, staring into the black night before us. I put a hand on his elbow, and he turned to look at me.

"I know it sounds stupid, but I think about it a lot," he admitted, but I shook my head.

"It's not stupid. It's what it stands for that hurts." I laid my head on his shoulder. "Grief hides itself within the most ordinary things. Music, vegetables, an asshole cat named Madam Plunkett."

I felt him laugh against me.

"She was Michael's cat. She worshiped him. I kind of worshiped him too."

He smiled against my forehead and kissed above my eyebrow. I lifted my head to meet his eyes. I could lose myself in the depths of that gray blue gaze.

"I think your mom would be proud of you, Jack. You're kind-hearted, and you expect nothing in return. You're annoyingly persistent..." He smirked. "...and you have this way of rescuing people. Even when they think they don't need it."

He sighed and closed his eyes like what I'd stated was too painful to hear. Then he released my hand and hopped to the ground.

He walked a few paces and put his hands on his hips, keeping his back to me. The lights from the football field cast his shadow behind him, his dark silhouette long and forlorn.

"Jack, come on. Don't shut me out. Tell me what's wrong."

Something in my tone must've reached him because slowly he turned to face me.

"I've done some things I regret," he murmured in a voice just above a whisper.

"We all have, Jack."

But he shook his head and walked back to the tailgate, standing in front of me. His eyes pleaded for understanding, and his hands straddled my hips.

"No, it's more than that. I hurt some people I care about, and they may never forgive me."

I took his face into my hands, my thumbs stroking his cheekbones.

"Tell me," I pressed, and he closed his eyes. "There's no judgment. It's just you and me, sweetheart."

He smiled weakly. "There's a good chance that after you know, you won't want anything to do with me."

"I doubt that," I whispered. "Because wherever there's a Jack, there will always be a Rylen."

Chapter Twenty-One

JACK

A long time ago, I saw a cartoonish poster of a mouse standing in front of a candle. The golden flame made the mouse's shadow appear as a large, magnificent beast with sharp claws and pointy teeth. The smirk on the mouse's lips showed that the rat bastard knew the joke was on you. The word FEAR was written in bold letters under the picture, reminding us all that monsters only existed in our imaginations.

I wanted nothing more than to believe that Rylen would still be there when I was done telling her everything, but the monsters inside my head told me otherwise.

What if she demanded to be taken home? What if she burst into angry tears, and never wanted to see me again? All those scenarios sent a sharp chill crawling down my spine.

"Do you want to know something about me?" she asked. "Something terrible?"

"If you want to tell me," I whispered.

"I do. I want you to know everything about me. Even the things I've never told another soul. Do you know why I started to see Dr. Sullivan?"

I shook my head, and she bit her lip like she was building the courage to say it aloud.

"The night Michael was killed; I was driving."

Everything around me disappeared, yet I heard a gasp. I didn't realize it came from me. I found her hands and held them in mine, interlacing our fingers again.

"He got into a fight with my dad," she continued. "They'd fought before, but this one was different. The kind of fight two people have when neither says what they actually mean."

I nodded. When all the words left unsaid are the reason you're fighting, but neither of you dares to acknowledge it.

"Michael got into Berkeley, and that night he told my dad he wasn't joining the family business. He never wanted to be an architect. My dad threw a coffee mug across the room."

My brows raised. "Jeez."

"Yeah. Finally, Michael left the house, and my dad screamed at him to never come back."

A tear escaped the corner of her eye, and she wiped at it with the back of her hand.

"You don't have to tell me this," I cut in, but she shook her head.

"Michael had a friend pick him up, and they went to a party by the river. Andon was there. I wasn't with him because I'd had a headache, but he texted me that Michael was there, and he was drunk, getting into fights with people. So, I went to get him before something else happened and he lost Berkley. By the time I got to the party, Michael was so drunk he couldn't even stand. He wouldn't leave with me either. He told me if he saw Dad again, he'd kill the bastard. I tried reasoning with him, but he pushed me down, then Andon punched him in the face and carried him to the car."

While she told her story, her eyes pooled with unshed tears; then she blinked, and they spilled down her cheeks and dripped off the edges of her jaw. She did nothing to stop them, allowing the tears to flow, as she stared into the night behind me. I wanted to hold her while she spoke, but she squeezed my hands.

"I started for home. Police cars were heading to the river, and Michael was underage, and I thought if we got pulled over...." She trailed off. "So, I went a different route home."

Her voice dropped to a whisper, quivering on every syllable. "We were T-boned, and he was killed on impact." She met my eyes, her lips quivering before she spoke. "That was the last time I drove."

I pulled her into my arms, her shoulders shaking as she wept, and she buried her face in my chest. Her hands balled up in front of me, gripping two fistfuls of my shirt, the white material bulging between her fingers as she squeezed.

"It's not your fault," I whispered in her ear. "Please, sweetheart. You were trying to help him."

She nodded against my chest, and I bent to kiss the top of her head. We stood like that for several moments, until her breathing evened, and she spoke again.

"Why didn't I buckle him up? Why did I take another route? Why did he have to fight with my dad and run off to that stupid party?"

"You can't think like that, sweetheart. You'll torture yourself." Take it from someone who knew what it was like to be tortured by the things he could not change.

"So, now you know why I can't drive. I have these panic attacks. My chest closes up, and I can't breathe. I don't know how to stop it."

I kissed the side of her head. "It's okay not to be okay, and even if you never drive again, I'm not going anywhere."

A few things were clearer now. Her father constantly traveling on business and her mother thrown into a soul-sucking career had left Rylen alone inside an empty house, battling paralyzing guilt. At one time the place had been called a home and had been filled with love, music, and laughter. The backyard was prepared for neighborhood barbecues. An entertainment center ready for movie marathons, yet all of it lay abandoned, untouched, and obsolete as the sting of Michael's death hung in the air like a ghost, leaving the place cold and hollow.

This left Rylen as collateral damage, unpermitted to speak his name yet expected to endure and come out the other side unscathed.

Grief comes in all shapes and sizes, but this was enough to swallow anyone whole, regardless of their strength.

"You're incredibly brave, Rylen Clark," I told her. "I've never met anyone more lionhearted than you."

Her head lifted from my chest, her eyes searching my face, and she gripped my shirt again and pulled my lips to hers. She kissed me deeply, moving her mouth over mine in worshipful kisses that made my mind cloudy, and I pulled her hips against me, overwhelmed with the need to be closer to her.

Her fingers moved to the front of my shirt, feeling for the buttons on my vest, and she slipped the top button open. But I broke the kiss to take her hands, holding them in front of us.

"We can't," I rasped, resting my forehead against hers.

"You're killing me," she breathed.

I grinned, shaking my head, "Not yet. I can't do that to you."

"It won't change anything. I'm not going anywhere."

"You don't know that."

"I do, and if you're unsure, just tell me, Jack."

My chest heaved, knowing I could no longer maintain my silence.

I wanted to know what was under that dress. What her body felt like under my hands, under my mouth. What every inch of her tasted like, and I would commit it all to memory.

But the shadow monsters inside my head didn't go away. They tortured me, tormented me, beating me to a damned bloody pulp.

"Okay," I answered. "I'll tell you. Are you familiar with Hercules?"

"Somewhat. Why?"

"There's a story in Greek mythology about the Twelve Labors of Hercules. In a blind rage, Hercules killed his wife and his children. When he came to his senses, he went to the Oracle Delphi to seek atonement and was told to serve King Eurystheus for ten years. While serving the king, he was told to accomplish twelve tasks, and only then would his sins be atoned."

I paused, watching as she processed my words, her eyes searching my face for more.

"I am Hercules," I clarified. "Something happened, and it was my fault. I've spent the last four months trying to help the people affected by it. Like the ripple effect."

"Did you kill somebody?" she whispered, her voice breaking.

"No! God, no."

"Then what?"

I made the mistake of looking into her eyes, and those deep brown circles offered me hope.

I sighed. Here it goes. "I ran an underground poker game. Everything was under the table – a thousand to buy in. I had players that played for me, and they got a percentage of the winnings. One night, I got word that one of my players was stealing from people."

"Ned," she blurted.

238

"That's one of them."

"Pete, Sally, Cora."

"Cora? When did you meet her?"

"She works at Juanita's, and she sat next to me at the fundraiser."

My palms grew clammy. What did Cora tell her?

"Why were you arguing with her outside Juanita's shop?" Rylen asked.

"I was trying to give her money. She had to quit her job. I didn't know Juanita had hired her."

"Why was she so angry?"

I shrugged. "Some women find chivalry insulting."

"They're idiots."

I chuckled, "So, long story short, I took care of the player who was stealing, and I've been working to replace the stolen money."

"Hold on, how does that make you responsible? You didn't know your player was stealing."

"These are people I care about, and every penny Sally earns makes the difference between feast or famine. I didn't know until it was too late, and after I found out, I got shit-faced drunk; I told him I'd beat the shit out of him if he didn't repay it. He was unable to. He'd lost it at the table, so it's up to me to repay it."

"I thought you said you didn't drink?"

And there it was again, that impeccable memory for details.

"I did then, but not anymore."

She nodded. "Okay, but how long do you intend to do this?"

"I'm not sure. I suppose until I've reached a comparable amount of free labor."

"You mean like fixing Sally's fryer?"

I nodded. "Sally's gutters. Ned's tractor. Pete's truck. Sheila's…." I stopped, and her face morphed into confusion. "I'll get to Sheila in a minute. I intend to help Sally remodel next spring too."

"Do these people know why you're helping them?"

"One of them does. The others were robbed, but they don't know who or how I'm connected to it."

"So, who knows?" she asked, her brown eyes wide with wonder.

I sighed, closing my eyes while I said her name.

"Cora."

"Cora," she repeated. "Is she your ex-girlfriend?"

"No," I said with a laugh. "She's my sister."

Her eyes widened, and I thought I saw a flash of relief.

"Your sister?"

"Yes. If I hadn't had a poker game to begin with, none of this would've happened. She blames me for causing so much harm to our friends and…" I sighed. "I can't say I blame her."

She thought for a moment, the crease over her eyebrows deepening while she drew the connections in her head.

"What about Old Man Reynolds?"

That caught me. "What about him?"

"That day in the park. I saw you give him a bag of food. Are you in debt to him too?"

"Rylen, I feed him because sometimes he'll go days without food. Even if he throws it away, I sleep better knowing he had the choice of eating it."

"So, you're feeding him to be kind?"

"I'm feeding him because nobody else does."

"Okay, but what about The Captain? How does he fit into all this?"

"It's not The Captain I'm in debt to. Not exactly. I'm only holding him because Sheila told me to."

"Sheila?"

"She's the charge nurse at the hospital. The Captain is her grandson."

Her eyes widened. "Sheila was stolen from too?"

I hesitated. This was a conclusion she drew on her own. An assumption I could let her believe without telling her otherwise. It wasn't exactly a lie.

"When I asked Sheila what I could do to help her, she told me to be there. Hold the baby because she couldn't. So, I did, and I called him The Captain because moments after I met him, I knew I would do anything for him."

She pursed her lips, nodding slowly.

"Have you thought about…." She stopped. "I mean, if his parents can't take him, and Sheila doesn't…."

"Am I going to adopt him?" I cut in.

She nodded, her eyes downcast like she was too embarrassed to say it aloud.

"I've thought about it, but my life isn't set up for it. I live at the top of a barn. I make eighteen bucks an hour, and he needs more than what I can give him." I paused, watching as she bit her lower lip. "Why do you ask?"

"Because I feel so badly for him." She shrugged. "I was going to call Sheila and ask if I could hold him again. Even if I didn't have you."

I put my arms around her again, gazing into her round brown eyes. "You will always have me. That is, if you still want me now that you know."

"Yes," she answered, locking her arms around my neck, "I don't see why you thought any differently, even for a minute. You didn't need to run away from me."

"I was sure you didn't want to be with a criminal."

She let out a breath. "Are you a criminal now?"

241

I shook my head. "No, all that's behind me. I swear it."

She smiled, pulling my face to hers, whispering against my lips. "Then I guess you're not a criminal, are you?"

She kissed me firmly, seductively, powerfully cementing all that she'd said like it was written on stone tablets that could withstand the greatest storm.

An Eric Clapton album played on repeat inside the Bronco, and when "Wonderful Tonight" began I could no longer help myself. She was so damn beautiful.

"Dance with me," I murmured between kisses.

She pulled away, confusion creasing her eyebrows. "Right here? Now?"

"Yes."

I lifted her off the tailgate until she stood, and I put my hands around the small of her back. We danced like that for several moments, gazing into each other's souls, seeing what was beneath for the first time, and accepting what we saw in the other.

But then she stopped dancing, her frame locked, and a worried expression took hold.

"Is there anything else you need to tell me?" she asked in a low whisper.

I'd only temporarily silenced the monsters. They were still there, lurking in the shadowed corners of my brain, cackling like demented villains, parading around their wounded kill.

"No," I said. "You know everything." Then I silenced her with a kiss, her mouth curving into a smile as fireworks whistled and exploded over our heads into magnificent Weeping Willows. We kept our arms around each other as we turned our eyes to the sky, watching a streak of light blaze through the night and burst into a fountain of blue. I used a knuckle under her chin to move her eyes back to mine, taking her face into my hand. Then my mouth was on hers again and within seconds, we were both panting and breathless.

REDEMPTION'S LIST

And when I was an old man, I would never forget the moment I realized I was utterly and irredeemably in love with Rylen Clark, and there wasn't a damn thing I could do while the monsters inside my head celebrated their glorious victory.

Chapter Twenty-Two

Rylen

We danced under the fireworks, still moving in the silence as the song ended, and the colors glittered over our heads. When I shivered, we crawled into the backseat for warmth, agreeing we'd leave and return to the fundraiser as soon as the display ended. But we talked late into the evening, long after the fireworks finished. We shared a blanket, wrapped in each other, while we split a bag of M&M's, throwing them into the air and catching them in our mouths like children.

Except now, we'd touched; some unseen force had changed everything once we'd kissed, a need that drove us half-crazed with the desire to be closer. We couldn't go more than a few seconds without something touching. His knee against mine, his hand resting on my thigh; my hand on his forearm, the heat moving through my palm and radiating into my bones.

And when neither of us could take it any longer, our lips crashed together, each surrendering to the other. He tasted warm and chocolatey, sweet and inviting. I crawled into his lap, my knees straddling his hips, overcome by the hunger for more.

"Your knee," he breathed, a concerned edge in his voice.

"It's fine," I answered, putting my lips on his. It had restrained me long enough, and nothing would keep me from putting my hands all over him.

His hands slipped under the sports coat, peeling it off my arms, and it fell to the floor at his feet. His palms skimmed up my spine while his lips lowered to that spot on my neck that he'd quickly discovered rendered me senseless.

I tugged him closer, opening his vest and starting on the buttons on his shirt. His heart thundered beneath it, matching my own cadence beat for beat. He tangled his fingers in my hair, our lips colliding again. At first, he was frenzied, his tongue slipping between my lips while his hands began to roam my bare shoulders, the swell of my breasts, and the curve of my hips. Then I opened his shirt, and something changed. He slowed our pace, kissing me tenderly, promising without words he'd never leave me again.

This time I broke the kiss, pushing him against the seat as I raked my nails over his bare chest, stroking his skin from his collarbones to his navel, the hair on his chest running downward in my wake. His eyes darkened, and he let out a heavy breath as I explored the muscles that had teased me countless times before. I traced the outline of his sternum, the lines under his pectorals, the valleys between his ribs, and the dips separating his abs. Then I lowered my mouth to kiss all that my hands had touched.

He closed his eyes, his chest expanding, breathing in my scent, and he groaned as I kissed his body. His fingers burrowed into my hips as they had outside the fundraiser, and I knew he was in that place again, teetering on the edges of control and chaos.

I felt that urgency again, fueled by need and something exhilarating I'd never experienced before, rising like a wave about to break at its crest. When I reached for the zipper on my dress, he leaned forward to stop me, encircling his fingers around my wrist. He shook his head, and before I could protest, he brought my lips to his, kissing me with measured movements, deliberately holding back, keeping the wave from breaking against the shoreline.

"If you take that off," he rasped, his lips hovering over mine. "I won't be able to control myself."

"Nobody's asking you to."

He smiled, and I reached for the zipper again, but he held me tight.

"I want to wait, sweetheart. Not here, not like this." His fingers played with a curl hanging over my shoulder. "You deserve better than a post-prom cliché."

"You're driving me crazy!" I declared, but he laughed, his stomach muscles flexing under my hands at the force of it.

He really was the most beautiful man I'd ever seen.

"What do you think you're doing to me?" he asked.

My eyes traveled lower, below his belt buckle, to the place where his jeans were tight, and I was certain he'd felt the urgency too.

"I'll take that as a compliment," I whispered.

"I'm sorry," he breathed. "But I've been trying to keep my hands off you all night and you're making it impossible."

I smirked. "When did you start wanting to put your hands on me?"

"The moment I met you."

My eyes widened. "Really? I wasn't very nice to you the day we met."

"Well, I did bulldoze through that puddle. I don't blame you for being upset."

"If I believed in fate, I'd say you were there that day because of it."

He stiffened. "I saw you fall, and I couldn't just drive off and leave you. Even if it meant risking my life to help you."

I chuckled, wrapping my arms leisurely around his neck. "That day we went to the park, and you bought me a milkshake? I couldn't stop thinking about it."

He grinned, his eyes shining with a newfound brightness.

"I stole your camera out of your bag, so I had an excuse to see you again."

"So soon?"

"Of course, but I needed reassurance, and I always fix what I break. Though I was pretty sure you wanted nothing to do with me that first day."

"I was annoyed about the puddle, but, truthfully, I couldn't stop thinking about you. I also thought you were really hot," I said, suddenly shy, breaking eye contact, "In that scruffy, unkempt cowboy kind of way. So, there's that."

He smirked, a small laugh escaping him. "I thought you were stunning."

"I was covered in mud."

"Doesn't matter. You were more beautiful than anyone I'd ever laid eyes on."

He lifted a hand and found my jaw, his thumb tracing the outline of my lips, his fingers spreading behind my neck. And he brought my lips to his. It wasn't long before his hands started to roam again, and before he could take things further, he pulled away, breaking our connection.

"Do I get a say in this?" I asked, frustration spilling into my words.

"We can't, Rylen," he breathed. "As much as I want to, it wouldn't be fair to you."

"If you're worried about protection, I'm on the pill, and I got checked for everything after I found out Andon cheated on me."

"Good to know, but I wasn't worried about that, sweetheart."

"Andon's the only one I've been with. I never wanted to be with anyone else," I paused, meeting his gray-blue eyes. "Until now."

He ran his hand through my hair again, lazily letting it slip through his fingers.

"I'm clean too, but you should know I've slept with more women than I care to admit." He dropped his hand, breaking eye contact.

I grabbed his jaw and turned his head to face me, "None of that matters to me, but when you're with me, it's only me. I want to be the only one you kiss."

"Only you. And I don't plan on sharing you, either."

"Only you," I agreed, putting my forehead to his. "Always."

He inhaled the air between us, letting it out slowly. "Do you have any idea how many times I wanted to kiss you?"

"What took you so long?" I whispered.

"Fear," he said boldly. "I wasn't sure how you'd react. I was afraid you'd run."

I shook my head, "Running away is your thing, remember?"

He nodded, pursing his lips. "Fair enough. But now I'm here. And I want to do this right, sweetheart. I want you to feel good, but this isn't the place for our first time."

It was already better than I'd ever had, better than I imagined, and we hadn't even started yet. I was also Andon's first, and we dated for three years, but it was never like this with him. Not even close. Never a fire, an urgency, or a passion that blinded me with desire. He spoke again, pulling me from my thoughts.

"I want to take my time with you, Rylen." A curl bounced into my eyes, but he tucked it behind my ear. "I want to taste every inch of you." He lowered his lips to my neck, trailing hot kisses down to my collarbone. "But I can't properly do that here. Not when I can do a more thorough job if you were in my bed."

My skin pricked with goosebumps, but I wasn't cold.

I was on fire.

"You've given this a lot of thought. What else are you planning?"

He gave me a wolfish grin, and moving aside my curls, he whispered in my ear.

My eyes widened at the description, the graphic scene dancing in my head, sending a lightning bolt of warmth straight to my core. No one had ever described it like that, in such explicit terms, such precise details, and I was going to hold him to his word.

"Is that a promise?" I asked once our eyes met.

Jack's face split into a grin, and he pulled me off his lap, tucking me into the crook of his arm. Then he pulled a blanket over us, and I nestled beside him.

"I promise," Jack said, kissing my hairline. "I'll make love to you, and then I'll do everything else."

His shirt was still open, and I laid my cheek on his bare chest, basking in the warmth of his skin while his hand caressed my shoulder.

"Do you have any crazy exes I should know about?" I asked, feeling him chuckle.

"No, I've never had a girlfriend."

I turned my head to look at him, shock on my face.

"You haven't?"

He shook his head, "I wasn't the girlfriend type. That is," he paused, his fingers trailing down my arm. "Until now."

I smiled at his admission, snuggling into his warmth as he pulled the blanket higher.

"Ten minutes," he replied. "Then we'll get your jacket, and I'll take you home."

"Twenty," I corrected, "I'm not ready for goodnight yet. You'll be back tomorrow, right?"

"I'm not going anywhere."

"It may take some time before I believe you."

"We have time," he whispered, his lips grazing my temple. "We have all the time in the world."

8oc~o8 8oc~o8 8oc~o8

When I opened my eyes, the sun was peeking over the horizon, barely shining into the Bronco's windshield. The windows inside were fogged over, and beads of moisture streaked trails from top to bottom.

I lifted my head from Jack's shoulder, the blankets falling from my chest as my breath clouded the air in front of me. There was a kink in my neck, evidence that I'd slept on Jack's chest. My upper body leaned into him while my legs were bent at the knee on the seat next to us. His arm was around me, his head laying back on the seat, his hat tilted over his eyes. His feet were crossed at the ankles.

An anxious current zapped through me. It was morning, and we'd slept the entire night in the back seat, lying on each other.

I shook his shoulder, "Jack, wake up!"

My mouth tasted like death, and I hoped he didn't try to kiss me. Our relationship was too new to ruin it with dragon breath.

"Hmm," he groaned.

"Wake up," I repeated.

"Uh-huh."

"Yes," I said, taking his hat from his eyes.

"Five minutes," he grumbled.

"It's morning."

His eyes snapped open, and he pulled himself into a sitting position.

"What time is it?" he asked, taking in the daylight. He reached for the sports coat he'd wrapped around himself and pulled his flip phone from the pocket.

"Six twenty-three," he said. "I need to take you home."

In all the years I dated Andon, I never stayed out all night with him. We had been in high school, and my dad had insisted I was home by eleven at the latest, and if I was late, I was required to call.

I should've been calling my mom on Jack's phone. I should've been worried about not being home hours ago.

But I wasn't.

Jack crawled into the space between the seats, waking a snoring Bam Bam with the toe of his boot. He turned the key and adjusted the heater to warm. Then he opened the door and slid to the ground, the dog jumping out behind him.

"I'll be right back."

I put his sports coat around my arms and held it in front as I crawled into the front seat. Moments later, the door opened, and Bam Bam hopped inside. Jack climbed in behind him and reached for the cowboy hat on the dashboard. His vest was open, but he'd buttoned his shirt, leaving the tails hanging against his thighs.

"Do you need me to find you a restroom?" he asked, putting on his hat.

"I'm okay, thanks. I'd better get home."

He nodded, putting the truck in gear.

He handed me half a package of M&M's that lay on the dashboard, and I poured some into my hand, feeding him the yellow ones as he drove. I ate a few, the chocolate flavor more pleasant than dragon death— breakfast of the utmost champions.

I had no desire to turn on the radio or search for the right music. The silence between us felt like something we'd earned. The ability to sit quietly, just enjoying the other person existing in the same space as you without the need to fill it with words.

I spoke first when he turned into my driveway.

"That's Michael's Jeep!"

The green Jeep Wrangler was now parked in front of the garage. The vehicle lived on the edge of the driveway under a vehicle cover. The Jeep that was supposed to be mine once I could drive again. It was a piece of Michael that belonged to me, and it was uncovered and exposed.

My blood began to boil.

But there was another car in the driveway. One I didn't recognize. The plates read that it was from California, making it seem even more out of place.

Jack parked the Bronco and killed the engine as panic sliced through me.

No. She'd never do that! This was my dad's house. No way did she bring her lover home.

I took Jack's hand.

"My mom invited her boyfriend to the fundraiser," I said, trembling.

His eyes widened, "The guy in the blue suit?"

"Yeah, how did you…"

"I saw you talking to him. I didn't know he was your mom's boyfriend."

"Come in with me, please? I don't know what I'm going to find in there. I don't want to be without you."

He nodded. "Okay, lead the way."

The house was quiet when I opened the door. The jacket I'd left at the fundraiser was folded neatly on the bench next to the door.

252

Somebody had figured out I'd disappeared and grabbed my belongings in my irresponsible wake.

Jack stepped in behind me, and I closed the door gently, unsure if the house was awake.

"Come on," I whispered, tiptoeing to the kitchen.

But when I rounded the corner to search the living room, a voice spoke behind me.

"Hello," it said in a low baritone.

I jumped out of my skin, levitating for a moment before falling back into my motionless, statue-like body.

"Holy crap, man!" I cried, a hand on my heaving chest. "You scared the hell out of me!"

It was Adam; he leaned his elbows on the kitchen counter while the coffee pot percolated behind him.

"Sorry," he said, standing straight. "I didn't mean to scare you."

He wore his suit pants from the night before and a wife-beater tank top. His hair was messy, sticking up every which way like he'd awakened and walked to the kitchen for caffeine. His feet were bare.

This man had spent the night in my house.

"Want some coffee?" he asked, selecting a mug.

"No!" I snapped. "Where's my mom?"

"Upstairs. How about you, cowboy? You want some?"

Jack stood a few paces behind me, silently watching the stranger pour coffee into mugs.

"I'd love some," he said, his hand extended.

"Jack!" I growled.

"No," he blurted, retracting his hand. "No, thank you."

My brow furrowed, and Jack shrugged.

I rolled my eyes. Why did men have to be so clueless?

"Suit yourself." Adam chuckled, then he opened the fridge and pulled out the creamer as if he'd been in my kitchen a hundred times before.

He poured a dollop of cream into each mug and stirred with the spoon that was lying on the counter. Then he rubbed his eyes with his thumb and fingertips, squinting his eyes into tiny slits.

"Do either of you happen to have any contact solution?" Adam asked, closing the refrigerator with a swift kick.

Jack shook his head.

"No," I grumbled.

"Damn," he said, bringing his coffee to his lips.

I inhaled slowly, deciding I needed a diplomatic approach, or his head would land on a nearby platter.

"Adam," I began, watching his eyes find me over the brim of his mug, "Why are you in my house?"

He leaned on the counter again; his mouth opened, about to answer when a loud voice boomed from upstairs.

"Rylen! Is that you?"

It was Diana Clark, and from the sound of it, she'd either just found a snake in the drain or discovered that I was home.

There were footsteps descending the stairs, padding into the kitchen.

"Rylen, dear," she said, scanning me head to toe. She took in the dress, the disheveled hair, and Jack's sports coat.

"Are you just getting in?"

Diana was surprised, astonished even. She was only now discovering this, but a faint piece of me wanted the "How dare you stay out all night!" speech or the "I'm glad you're alive so I can kill you," lecture. Either of those speeches would've been typical. Either of them would've shown an ounce of concern.

But Diana Clark wasn't typical.

Diana didn't concern herself with those sorts of things. Her daily checklist never included her daughter's well-being, even when her daughter had vanished without a trace.

I opened my mouth to answer, but Jack spoke, "Please, don't be upset with her, Mrs. Clark. It's my fault."

She cut her eyes to Jack, staring at him the way she stared at Madam Plunkett when a mouse helplessly dangled from her lips.

"What are you doing here?" she snapped.

Jack took off his hat, holding the brim between his fingers.

"I met Rylen outside, and she told me she was hungry. We went to get some food. Then I suggested we watch the fireworks from the football field. I intended to bring her home after, but we fell asleep. It's my fault she was out all night."

She kept her eyes on him, but she spoke to me.

"Rylen, you realize you were supposed to return to the table to relieve Juanita, and you never showed."

Juanita! Oh crap! I forgot about returning to the table. After Andon accosted me, Adam surprised me, and Jack swept me away from it all, I'd forgotten about my commitment.

"I forgot about Juanita," I admitted, my eyes downcast.

"You need to call her and apologize for disappearing, *again*. Juanita stepped in and did you a favor and you took advantage of her. People were counting on you, Rylen."

"I'm sorry," I said sheepishly, though I was annoyed that she cared more about saving face with Juanita than she did about my disappearance. "I'll call her this afternoon and apologize."

She nodded, "Okay. Let's let it go for now."

Maybe it was sleep deprivation, my lack of a wholesome breakfast, or aliens had abducted my mother. And the terrestrial that sounded and looked like Diana Clark had eaten her brain. But as she walked past me into the kitchen to collect the steaming cup of coffee

Adam had poured, I did a double take once I realized what she was wearing.

Sweatpants.

Flawless Diana Clark was wearing gray, frumpy, Nike sweatpants. I should have noticed it sooner, but her hair was pulled into its usual twist, and I was too occupied to see she wore a blue sweatshirt and sweatpants with white socks pulled up her ankles.

I blinked a few times to focus as she brought her coffee to her lips and took a long drink.

"Good coffee, sweetie," she crooned.

Adam, who'd made himself comfortable sitting at the bar, looked up from his newspaper and smiled.

Sweetie? She did not just call him that! Jack, seeming to notice the steam piping out of my ears, walked to me and took my hand.

"Mom?" I started slowly, my voice wavering on the edges of wrath. "What. The hell. Is he doing? In my house?"

She set her coffee on the counter.

"Rylen, you will not speak that way to me that way. This is my house, and you will show respect."

"Respect?" I bellowed. "This is Dad's house, and you brought that thing here." I pointed a finger at Adam, whose eyes widened like saucers.

"That is enough, Rylen! Now, it's time to show Jake the door. The three of us have a few things to discuss."

"It's Jack!" we said simultaneously. Then I added, "Why, so you and California boy can justify your behavior?"

"Um, I'm from Milwaukee," Adam cut in. "The car's a rental."

"Shut up, dude," Jack barked.

"Rylen, there are a few things I need to explain to you," Diana growled. "I can't do that in front of Jack."

"Anything you say to me, you can say in front of him," I said, my eyes traveling to Jack. "He's...he's, my boyfriend."

A small smile teased the edges of Jack's lips, and that was all the reassurance I needed.

Diana sighed, "So, that's why you stayed out all night with him."

"Nothing happened. We fell asleep." I ripped open his shirt and made out with his abs, but she didn't need to know that. "Tell me why he's here," I demanded.

"Fine," she grumbled. "Fine, you want to know why Adam is here? I'll tell you. A blizzard closed the highway last night. I told him he could stay until they opened the road. We started talking; it got late, and he stayed the night."

The chill in the air last night had suggested a weather system was moving right toward us. Only it'd rained in Davenport, which could easily mean a blizzard had hit somewhere east of us, blocking Adam from returning home.

"And," she continued, walking around the bar. "Since we're on the topic, he's also interested in buying your brother's Jeep."

Anger tore through me. "It's mine! No fucking way."

"Language, Rylen!"

"Over my dead fucking corpse!"

"I don't have to buy it," Adam said, sliding off his stool, his hands up defensively.

"Damn right, you don't!"

"Rylen!"

"Dad gave it to me, Mom! It's mine which you would know if you paid attention even for a moment."

"Your dad never said anything about it, and honestly, Rylen, I think we can dispense with the drama. When you decide to drive again, we can buy you something else. It's not doing anyone any good just sitting there."

Tears pricked the corners of my eyes, and I swallowed the lump in my throat.

"It's not doing any harm sitting there, either," Jack retorted. "And don't act like Rylen has a choice about when she starts driving. Trauma doesn't work that way."

A small smile tugged at my lips. Jack had cut her off at the knees.

Her eyes narrowed, and she took a few steps toward him.

"Young man, I don't know you very well, but I suggest you leave my house, or I'll call the police and have you arrested."

Jack smirked. "For what? Calling you on your bullshit?"

"Everybody, just calm down!" Adam interjected. "There's no need to involve the police. Diana, I had no intention of upsetting Rylen. If she wants the Jeep, she can have it."

"How noble of you," Jack deadpanned.

Diana walked to her coffee and brought the mug to her lips.

"I think it might be best if I leave," Adam replied.

"Yes!" I blurted while my mother simultaneously said no. "Let me be very clear," I started, pointing a finger at him again. "If he stays, I'm gone."

"Rylen, the highway is still closed. Don't be ridiculous."

"I'm not. I will not be here if he's here. It's him, or it's me."

"You're being childish," she growled.

But I straightened, gripping Jack's hand tighter, hoping to channel some of his inward strength down his arm, through my palm, into my chest. But her mouth remained in a straight line, glaring me down like a puppy who'd pissed on the floor.

"You made your choice," I said evenly. "Come on, Jack. I need to change. Then we're leaving."

Jack held my hand as I turned my back on her. I walked to the front door, hoping to forget it all. Jack walked beside me, tucking me under his arm, shielding me from the sting of her rejection. She

258

called after me, reciting my name like a commandment that would stop me. She promised we could discuss this, saying she had more to explain and that I didn't understand the whole picture. But what I understood was that she'd chosen him, and it was too late. And there wasn't a day I'd be alive where I would be all right with that.

Chapter Twenty-Three

JACK

We sat in a booth at Sally's Diner when Rylen smacked her hand on the table between us.

"Can you believe her?"

I shook my head.

"My mom picked her boyfriend over me! I'm her flesh and blood, and she still chose him. What the hell?"

"Calm down," I said, placing my hand over hers. "You need to eat something before you pass out."

Shortly after we were seated, Sally took our orders, but Rylen refused food. I pushed my burger towards her, but she scrunched her nose and pushed it away.

"I'm not hungry," she grumbled, crossing her arms. "I'm too pissed off to eat."

"Take a couple of bites. Being angry takes energy, too. And if Gran has taught me anything, it's to never trifle with a woman who's hungry, so please." She relaxed a bit, and I pushed the plate in front of her. "Eat. You'll feel better afterward, and I won't fear for my life."

That made her laugh, but her eyes still held a mixture of mirth and annoyance. She picked up an onion ring and nibbled the golden breading. Meanwhile, my thoughts drifted back to the hour before.

We stood in the driveway at her house. Rylen took my hand and led me to the small studio apartment. She lifted the rug in front of the door and bent to pick up the key. The lock clicked, and the door creaked open.

"How long have you been staying out here?" I asked.

"I've slowly been moving in," she answered. "I haven't actually slept out here yet."

I stepped inside as she closed the door.

The bottom level was a music studio with a recording room behind a glass window. The floor was carpeted, and shabby furniture that looked like it belonged in a college dormitory was pushed back against the white walls. Much like Michael's bedroom, posters of musical artists decorated the living space, and a small kitchenette with a round table and four chairs took up the entirety of one corner. An open door behind the table revealed a bathroom vanity on tiled flooring. There were stacks of banker's boxes piled high to the ceiling, the name of the rightful owner written in black Sharpie.

"Up here," Rylen said, facing me on the bottom stair.

I followed her up the staircase, my arms positioned to catch her if she tripped while she climbed. She held the railing for support while she pulled herself up. Her knee brace clicked with every step, and she straightened at the top.

A four-poster queen-size bed was the centerpiece of the room. The bed was made with a royal purple comforter pulled up under lavender pillowcases. Clothing was strewn about the floor, spewing out the tops of boxes, suspended on hangers hooked to door frames, or lined up on a wheeled clothing rack. Her name labeled other boxes, and some said "music," "photography supplies," "clothes," and "shoes"—the stacks in piles of three against the short wall by the stairs.

"Excuse the mess," she said, swiftly kicking a lacy bra under the bed. "I haven't finished moving in yet."

I bit back a chuckle. "It's no problem."

The dressers were matching mahogany. A lamp with a purple shade, a remote, and an alarm clock sat on the nightstand in the corner. Atop a dresser was a TV, the screen angled towards her bed.

I watched her open a drawer and dig out jeans, socks, and underwear. Then she pulled a shirt off a nearby hanger that hung from a clothing rack.

I sat on the edge of the bed. "Is this the staircase you wiped out on and sprained your ankle?"

"Yep. I was trying to put some distance between my mother and me. Then I fell. Worst six weeks of my life."

"Not true, or we never would have met."

But even as I said it, I knew that wasn't true. I would have found her whether she was in the chair or not.

Rylen thought momentarily, "Hmm, I guess you're right. I never thought of it that way."

She walked into an open door behind the stairs— the bathroom. She flipped on a light, and the mirror over the sink reflected an exhausted Rylen. She closed the door, and I heard the water run in the sink. I stood and busied myself, admiring the photos that lined the wall. Pictures of orange sunsets and landscapes with red barns and purple flowers. Sailboats in blue water with golden suns. Waterfalls with whitecaps against mossy green rocks. A man in a cowboy hat throwing a frisbee into the air for an exuberant canine.

The man was me.

Behind me, the bathroom door opened.

"I like this one," I noted, glancing over my shoulder; she'd washed the smeared makeup off her face and pulled her hair into a claw clip. "When did you take this?

"When we were at the park," she said, leaning on the door frame. "You and Bam were the perfect models."

"You took all of these, right?" I asked, remembering the photo in Michael's room with her arms around him.

"I did," she said. "I was going to go to photography school."

"They're incredible. I knew you were good, but…" I trailed off. "These are amazing."

"Thanks." She pushed off the wall and walked toward me. "I had them displayed at House of Brew, but my dad walked in and bought them all."

"He did?"

She rolled her eyes, "Yeah. He was trying to be supportive. I can't decide if he bought them because he thought they were terrible or because he thought they were great."

"Isn't it obvious?"

"He said he wanted them to decorate his office, but then Michael died and…" She shrugged. "Everything just kind of stopped after that." She turned to one side, gesturing to her back, "Can you unzip this, please?"

"Sure," I said softly.

I slid the zipper down, opening her back to me, and she lifted her arms, the dress pooling around her feet.

I felt myself take a breath in, but I wasn't breathing.

There was no air left.

Her bra was black – strapless and silky.

Her panties were purple, high-cut, and lacy.

Oh God, I loved purple.

Her shoulder blades were peaked, defined beneath smooth skin; the bumps of her vertebrae were visible, tapering to a trim waist and curved hips.

My mouth went dry, and I bit my lip as I balled my hands into fists so I wouldn't touch her. I never knew shoulder blades could be so sexy, and I wanted to know what they felt like under my fingertips. What would she do if I put my lips between them? We would never get out of here.

She bent to pick up the gown, and I turned my back before I did something I'd regret.

I heard her hang up the dress, then she seemed to notice I'd turned my back, and she let out a breath.

"You don't have to turn around if you don't want to."

"Yes, I do. I'm really trying to be a gentleman here."

"There's no need for chivalry."

"Rylen, you're making this impossible."

I heard her take a step forward.

"It's no different than a swimming suit."

"Trust me, sweetheart; it's different."

"How?" she asked, a challenge in her voice. "It's exactly the same."

I chuckled humorlessly. "Women only say that because they have no idea how a man's mind works. Because it has nothing to do with what you are or aren't wearing and everything to do with the beauty wearing it."

She was quiet, contemplative, then said, "I don't understand."

"Because it's you, Rylen. You could wear a snowsuit, and I'd want to rip it off you. Not because the snowsuit is sexy, but because you are."

"No one's stopping you," she breathed.

"I know that. But I won't, because right now you're upset. You're not thinking clearly. I won't take advantage of you." I heard her exhale, seeming to accept my answer.

"So please," I continued, my voice wavering. "Get dressed so we can get the hell out of here."

She moved swiftly about the room. Drawers opened and closed. There was a zip and a snap, the sounds of material against her skin. She said nothing until she was fully clothed, and I turned to see her wearing jeans and a gray sweatshirt, kneeling to tie her shoe.

Rylen's voice snapped me back to Sally's Diner, back to the girl who was squirting ketchup on the edge of a plate.

"What are you thinking about?" she asked.

You. Wearing nothing but your underwear.

"Something doesn't add up." I decided to tell her what else churned in the back of my mind.

She picked up the burger, waiting for me to continue.

"I think your mom is telling the truth about Adam. I don't think it was planned for him to stay the night."

"I disagree," she said, a cheek full of food. She chewed a few more times and swallowed. "He was at the fundraiser. Why else would he drive all this way if he didn't plan on hooking up and staying over?"

"Maybe he was being supportive. And we know the road did close."

"A convenient excuse," she grumbled.

"I don't think so. He also asked for contact solution. If he drove here intending to stay over, wouldn't he have brought it with him?"

She set the burger down, pushed the plate away. "Or he was in such a rush to get laid, he completely forgot."

I shook my head. "No, think about it. Usually, people having affairs are calculated and secretive. Your mom wouldn't bring him to the house if she were trying to hide a relationship. They'd go to a hotel."

"Or she's done hiding it and wants to be with her lover out in the open."

"They didn't act like lovers, Rylen."

"She wouldn't be all over him in front of me."

"No, but still," I picked up my Coke, and slurped the icy remains.

"She called him sweetie. She used to call my dad sweetie."

"That doesn't mean anything. We can't assume they're having an affair until your mom admits it."

"We can't assume they're not, either. All of the pieces fit, Jack. What else is it?"

I leaned forward. "You won't know until you ask her."

She sighed, defeated, and I pushed the burger in front of her again.

"I don't want to know where they met or hear how in love they are. What if she and my dad are getting a divorce?"

I took her hand, running my thumb over her knuckles.

"I know you're scared, but until you know you can't assume. It's not fair."

I paused, and she wiped a tear that slipped from the corner of her eye.

"I'm not ruling out the possibility they're together, but you won't know until you talk to her, sweetheart."

She met my eyes, smiling weakly, "I will, but I'm not ready yet. I want to be with you."

"Why don't we go to Gran's? There'll be a pot roast." I gave her my best grin, wide and toothy. "And when you're ready to talk to your mom, I'll go with you if you want."

She smiled softly. "I'm not sure my mom will ever let you in the house again."

She picked up the burger and took a small bite, but I was satisfied that she was pleased with my attempts to defend her.

"She deserved it. If defending you puts me on her hit list," I shrugged. "Oh well."

The bells over the door frame chimed, signaling customers had arrived. Behind the counter, Wendy's voice sounded a greeting and invited them to sit anywhere. I'd never seen the couple before. He was much older than her, with salt-and-pepper hair and a white beard. She was likely in her early twenties, with long auburn hair and bold red lipstick.

"What's their story?" I asked, gesturing over Rylen's shoulder.

She pivoted in her seat and watched as the couple scooted into a booth in the corner. The redhead pulled her purse off her shoulder; the white beard perused a menu while reading glasses balanced on the end of his nose.

"I'm not really in the mood for this," Rylen grumbled

"Then sit back and watch how it's done."

She rolled her eyes, keeping them on me as she picked up her glass and slurped from the straw.

"Let's see," I thought, tapping my chin. "Father and daughter?"

"No," she replied. "They're not related."

"I thought you weren't interested?" I retorted.

She smirked, putting her chin into her hands while her elbows rested on the table. "I'll let you know when you get it right."

"Professor and student?" I offered.

"Scandalous, but something tells me no."

"Hmm. Part of a cult group? Looking for their next virgin to sacrifice to the Goddess of Desire."

"What?" she said through a laugh.

"Never mind," I chortled, "I'm at a loss. They're going to bigger and better places; I know that much."

"Well, of course. She wants to be a model," Rylen added.

"Ah, and he's, her photographer."

"Agent. The blizzard made them take an alternate route."

"They were driving and decided they were hungry. Sally's was a logical option."

"Hungry enough to abandon their vegan ways."

"There's no way in hell he's vegan!" I declared.

"Nope, but she is," Rylen countered.

"Oh, definitely. Once they get to California, they will open their own clothing line."

Rylen grinned, then she added: "For poodles."

I laughed at that, hoping our banter had lifted her spirits, and before I could offer any more ideas, my phone buzzed on the table between us. It was Scott. I punched the ignore button, but seconds later it buzzed again.

I sighed. "Hold on, Rylen. I'll be right back."

I could feel her eyes on me as I stood, walked to the hallway that led to the restrooms, and accepted the call.

"Scott, what is it?" I said, facing the wall.

"Jack! Hudson's in the hospital."

My chest tightened. "What?"

"He was stabbed in the chest in a prison fight. The ambulance just left."

"Jesus," I breathed. "Is he going to…"

"It's too soon to tell. It's Cora you should worry about. She's looking for you and she's pissed."

The rumble of an engine caught my attention, and I turned to see an El Camino tearing into the parking lot. The driver slammed the brakes, the tires squealing to an abrupt halt.

"She found me," I said. "I'm at Sally's. Get here now!"

I ended the call and charged out the front door, but Rylen watched my every move. I'd have to think of an excuse later.

In the parking lot, the driver's door was open, and Cora was climbing out of the vehicle. I had to get to her first before she ruined everything. Before she let out my secret.

"Cora," I said.

She whipped her head around, her eyes flashing with anger, and she slammed the door so hard the car rocked side to side.

"You bastard!" She stumbled when she stepped towards me, and her breath was thick with whiskey.

"Calm down." I lifted my hands to steady her, but she smacked them away.

"This is your fucking fault!"

I grabbed her arm, but she'd stopped moving, her eyes wide with shock. I followed her gaze to the window behind me, where Rylen was watching, her hand pressed up against the glass.

She yanked her arm away. "You haven't told her yet." The statement was humorless and laced with surprise.

"I *am* telling her, now back the hell off." I reached for her keys, but she jerked them away.

"Why didn't you tell her already?"

I didn't answer. I was overwhelmed with the compelling need to run from her, to conceal my truth, but it was no use.

Cora already knew.

"You're in *love* with her," she breathed. "That's why you haven't told her. You love her."

"Time to go, Cora," I said, as Scott's cruiser pulled into the driveway, red and blue lights whirling. He pulled up beside us and opened the door.

"You're being selfish, Jack!" she snarled. "The moment you touch anything it breaks, and that's what you're doing to her." She pointed to the window where Rylen was watching. "You're a fuck-up!

269

And you're going to ruin her life the same way you ruined mine. So, stop being a scared little boy, and own your truth."

She lunged for me, but Scott grabbed her arms from behind and held her tight.

"Enough, Cora!" he barked. He opened the back door and pushed her inside. She flopped on the seat like a beached seal.

"I'll take her home, Jack," Scott said.

"Thanks, man. I appreciate it."

He closed the door, but the window was half down. I could see Cora covering her face, her shoulders shaking with wretched sobs.

"So, you told her the truth, right?" he asked. His eyes had floated to the window where Rylen sat.

I hesitated and bit my lower lip.

"Christ, Jack!"

A retching sound came from the backseat, and we turned to see my sister holding her stomach as vomit pooled onto the floor.

He grimaced, shaking his head.

"Look, Hudson's been taken to Bismarck. He needs surgery, and they'll have to keep him for a few days."

"Is he going to make it?"

"I don't know. Cora's leaving tomorrow to be with him."

"Good. It'll relieve the pain in my ass."

"But I suggest that whatever *this* is." He pointed between me and Rylen. "You end it before Cora gets back."

"Don't pressure me, Scott."

"I'm not. I'm warning you. Because if you don't, I'm pretty sure Cora will."

She lifted her head at the sound of her name, and she met my eyes. They were narrow and sharp, puffy yet blood-shot, and I felt daggers slicing into me, only confirming that Scott was right.

REDEMPTION'S LIST

It was only a matter of time before Cora told Rylen everything.

"Get her out of here," I demanded.

He opened the driver's door but paused to look back at me, resting his elbows on the door frame. "Don't be a dumbass, Jack."

Scott peeled out of the parking lot, the lights still rolling as he sped onto the highway. All I could do was watch them go, knowing deep within myself that Cora was right, I was being unfair. I needed to end it, and with every passing minute, I was running out of time.

§o૮৩o§ §o૮৩o§ §o૮৩o§

Sally was still standing by Rylen's table when I walked back inside. She wore her waitress uniform and reading glasses hung on a gold chain around her neck. Her hair was bundled in a net, and she held a coffee pot in one hand.

"Everything okay out there, Jack?" Sally asked.

"Yeah, Cora's just upset," I said, sliding into the booth. "She drank too much. She does that sometimes." I lifted my glass and tipped back the ice.

"Was it about her fiancé?" Rylen chimed.

I inhaled and sucked an ice cube straight down my throat, the pointy peaks stabbing me from within. Rylen's eyes widened as I coughed violently, and Sally clapped me on the back.

"How do you know about him?" I choked out.

"She mentioned him at the fundraiser."

I tipped my glass back again, but the ice was gone. I scooted my mug towards Sally.

"Coffee, please," I managed.

"Sure, honey." She poured the steaming liquid into my mug. "Rest assured Rylen, whatever's going on with Cora, Scott will take good care of her."

I nodded. Yeah, what she said.

"It's so nice to see you two. Speaking of the fundraiser, I noticed you weren't there last night, Jack and I thought, 'Oh no, he's going to break that poor girl's heart.'"

Rylen smiled, "He didn't."

"I was late," I added, shrugging, then my eyes traveled to Rylen. "And no, I'd never break her heart." Her face broke into a grin.

"That's so good to hear, hon," Sally gushed, padding me on the shoulder. She looked out the window, her eyes turning wistful and nostalgic. "Bill and I have been married forty-three years on Monday."

"Congrats," Rylen said.

"Thanks, honey. Hasn't always been easy, but the Lord's been good to us." She set her coffee pot on the table and placed a hand on her hip. "You know, sometimes you meet someone, and you just know your heart was made to love only them. And if, for some reason, those hearts get separated, you know you'd spend the rest of your days searching for them."

I adjusted in my seat; pulled at my shirt collar. Was I that obvious? Did Sally know how I felt about Rylen?

"Hey Sally!" a voice boomed from behind the bar.

Sally turned, glancing over her shoulder at Wendy. "What is it, Wendy?"

"That fryer is acting up again. It'll turn on for a few minutes, then turn off before the cycle is through."

Sally swore under her breath, ripping our ticket from her pad. "Not again. Sorry, kids, but I've got to go. Come back soon, though, okay."

I stood, reaching for Sally's elbow. "Wait, Sally, let me have a look at it again."

"Oh, I don't want to bother you with it."

"It's no bother."

"Would you, Jack? I'd sure appreciate it," she beamed. "The last time I called a repair man, he said he couldn't get here until sometime next week."

"Let me see if I can fix it. If Rylen doesn't mind waiting for me," I said, turning my eyes to her.

"Go ahead," she replied, waving a hand. "I can wait a bit."

I gave Rylen a thank-you smile. Knowing she knew why I had to help Sally took tremendous pressure off of me.

I sat my keys on the edge of the table. "Rylen, will you let Bam out in a bit?" I asked.

"Sure."

"Thank you so much, Jack. You're an angel. Rylen, honey, help yourself to coffee; it's on the house," Sally added, stepping beside me.

"Oh, thanks."

I followed Sally to the kitchen, and out of the corner of my eye, I saw Rylen dig out her phone from her pocket. She frowned at the screen, swiping her thumb across it. A piece of me hoped she'd call Diana, even though I wasn't ready to take her home, but there was only one way to solve the mystery of Adam, and I hoped the answer didn't tear her apart, because I wouldn't be able to watch it.

Chapter Twenty-Four

Rylen

Hey Kiddo,
Your mom called. I guess you've met Adam. I was as surprised as you. Now, you know why I left. It hasn't been easy. I haven't been able to forgive her. She also told me you're off the crutch. I'm glad to hear it. I'm in Dallas for another week but call me anytime if you need to talk. We're in this together, kid. You and me.
Love you.
-Dad.

"Everything okay?" Jack asked, noticing I hadn't taken my eyes off my phone.

We were waiting at a stop light when my cell phone chimed that I had a new email. I'd read my dad's words three times, stuck on the line that said, "I haven't been able to bring myself to forgive her." It answered so many questions and left a dozen more in its wake.

"Yeah," I said, pocketing my phone. "Just an email from my dad. My mom called him."

"Oh, maybe he can solve the mystery," he offered.

"I'll call him later. I don't want to deal with it right now."

A light over the porch illuminated the front of the house as Jack pulled into the driveway. The sun was a golden sliver over the horizon, and puffy gray clouds began to roll over the sky. Another storm was forming, and it would hit at any moment.

The farmhouse was painted baby yellow with white trim, and patches of lilies framed the porch. They'd endured their first frost; as ice crystals caught the porch light, the edges of each petal twinkled like glitter.

Jack cut the engine, turning to look at me.

"Why are the police here?" I asked, unbuckling.

He snapped his eyes to the cruiser and groaned.

"It's Scott."

"O-kay," I said, biting back a laugh.

"He's, my cousin. Gran feeds him on weekends."

"You guys are lucky. My last grandparent died when I was eight."

He straightened and stared at the steering wheel while he spoke. "I don't think I would've called it luck when I went to live with Gran."

"I meant that she was in your life, and you got to know her as an adult."

"I know what you meant." He took in a deep breath, and I could tell his mind had traveled somewhere else.

"Do you want to talk about it?"

275

"About what?"

"Whatever it is that's got you all tied up in there." I pointed from his head to his toes, and he smiled weakly.

"I was just thinking, I used to sit up at night and watch for my father, hoping he'd gotten sober and come back." He paused, shaking his head, "But he never did." He lifted a finger and traced the letters of FORD etched into the steering wheel. "All he ever did was disappoint me, even after he left."

"You had Gran," I said. "Frank *never* deserved you."

"Maybe. I was angry for a long time. I drank a lot, got involved with some bad people, but now I realize how fortunate I was to have Gran even if Frank didn't want us."

I nodded. "Is this where you grew up?" I asked, taking in the house, the barn, the property.

"Partly. I lived in the house down the street until I was nine. Then Gran came and got me, and I never went back."

Bam jumped between the seats and whined, nudging my knee with the end of his snout. I patted his head, his puppy eyes asking for me to set him free.

I gestured to the door. "He looks like he's going to burst."

"Come on, boy," Jack said, reaching for the handle, but as soon as he opened the door, Bam ran under his legs and jumped into the grass.

"Hey, wait!" Jack bellowed, leaping out after him, and the door slammed closed.

I opened my door and walked around the front of the truck just in time to see Bam squatting in the lily patch.

"Not there!" Jack yelled, but it was too late; sweet relief washed over the dog's face. "Stupid animal," he growled.

I stifled a laugh as Jack took off his hat and threw it on the ground. Bam scratched at the dirt, burying the evidence, then barked a few times for good measure as he ran into the yard, a new spring in his step.

I chuckled, trailing my fingers down his sleeve to his hand, interlacing our fingers.

"Come on, worry about him later. I'm starving."

Jack kept his hand in mine and bent to pick up his hat. I leaned on him for support while we walked up the stairs to the porch, the wooden decking creaking under our weight. The light above the screen door illuminated an outside table and chairs under a covered deck.

As Jack reached for the handle, the door opened, and the woman I'd later learn was Margaret Young stood in front of us.

"Jacky!" she chimed. "I've been expecting you. Supper's almost on the table."

Grandma was thinly built, barely a few hairs over five feet tall, her gray hair pulled back into a French braid, a red scrunchy holding the end.

"Sorry we're late, Gran. Sally needed a hand with her fryer," Jack explained.

"That's good of you, dear. The potatoes needed a couple more minutes anyways."

Gran's eyes traveled to me, scanning me head to toe, then she smiled warmly. "Now, who might this be?"

"Gran, this is Rylen."

"I know who it is!"

Jack rolled his eyes, sighing, and I giggled.

"Welcome, Miss Rylen," Grandma cooed, extending her hand. "I've heard so much about you."

"It's nice to meet you…" I trailed off.

"Margaret, but please call me Gran." She put her other hand on top so both hands held mine. Her thin skin was soft, but her palms were calloused, having known the meaning of hard work.

"Now, come on inside before you both catch a cold." She dropped her hands, and turned to enter the house, shouting into the living room, "Scott, turn that down! We have company."

"The Vikings are playing, Gran," a voice said in protest.

I followed Jack through the doorway and removed my jacket. He hung it on a peg behind the door, then he pulled out a chair at the table and gestured for me to sit.

"Can I help with anything?"

"No. I'll take care of it," Jack said, "I'll bring you something to drink."

"Okay," I answered, watching as Gran stuck a thermometer into the roast on the stove.

The farmhouse was small, yet perfect for a woman all on her own. The kitchen was open, with the table and chairs pushed to one corner by the front door – a tablecloth with white lilies under the place settings. A tall bookshelf sat in the opposite corner by the TV; pink paperback Harlequins were lined up in neat rows, three layers deep. Knick knacks decorated coffee tables, a porcelain boy and girl in front of a well was my favorite, the boy pulling up the pail for the girl to fill her bucket. A crocheted Afghan was lying against the back of a pink floral print sofa, and matching easy chairs were angled toward the T.V. Portraits of people I didn't know, except for a younger Jack and Cora I recognized, were displayed in wooden frames on the white wall behind the couch. The living room was tidy; the latest playoff game blared on the T.V., knee-deep into the third quarter.

Scott sat on the couch staring at the screen, an opened beer can on the table next to him. He wore a tan deputy's uniform, but his shirt hung unbuttoned, revealing the white t-shirt beneath. His feet were crossed at the ankles, his hands behind his head.

"Go, go!" he shouted as a player in purple caught the ball and started running.

"Ignore him," Jack said, setting down two cans of Coke and two cups of ice. "I do."

He sat in the chair next to me, opened a Coke, poured it into a glass, and slid it in front of me. He did the same with the other Coke, lifting the glass to sip the foam.

"Okay," I replied, smiling. "I don't think he knows I'm here."

Then his voice dropped, and he was inches from my face. "We can leave if you want."

I chuckled. "He's not that bad."

There was a belch from the living room, the sound of a beer can crinkling in a fist.

Jack grimaced. "You're too nice."

I laughed again, "What would you rather be doing?"

He smiled coyly, bringing his lips to my ear. "I can think of a few things," he whispered huskily. "And all of them include you. Completely naked."

I felt his breath against my neck, my skin pricking with goosebumps. I adjusted my weight in my chair, hoping to hide my flushed face. I lifted my drink to my lips as his hand slid down my thigh to rest on my knee.

"I'll take another beer, Jack," Scott announced.

"Get it yourself, Scott!"

"Fine, it's a commercial anyway."

He got to his feet and pulled up his pants while he lumbered to the kitchen, but then he saw me and stopped short.

His eyes darted between us, before locking with Jack's.

"What's she doing here? You didn't tell me she was coming," Scott grumbled, suddenly aware that his shirt was unbuttoned and his pants were unsnapped. He fastened them and began tucking in his shirttails.

"I don't need your damn permission," Jack snapped.

Scott shook his head. And for some strange reason, I felt like his disgust was aimed at me. Dumbass."

"Freeloader."

"Stop it, you two!" Gran interjected, setting a platter of carved meat on the table. "Jackson Timothy, you will not use that language in my house!" She turned to Scott. "And you! If you'd taken your eyes off the dumb-dumb box, you'd have seen Miss Rylen walk in. Now, no more fighting. Turn that off and come eat."

Scott reached for the remote but stopped once an urgent weather warning filled the screen. A newscaster held a microphone under his mouth while standing on a street corner. He wore a rain jacket with the hood pulled over his head. Buckets of rain poured down on top of him while he spoke.

"A cold front is moving in over the greater Davenport circle. Thunderstorms and heavy rainfall are expected to...."

"Turn that up, please, Scott?" Gran asked. She set a bowl of mashed potatoes on the table and turned to see the screen.

The newscaster's voice grew louder. All eyes were on the T.V. "...it is advised that all travel between seven p.m. and ten a.m. cease until the storm lifts. For hourly updates, please visit our website or find us on Facebook. This is Howie Henderson with all things weather. Back to you, Tom."

Scott clicked the remote, and the screen went black.

"Jack, after supper, I want you to go and get Maverick and put him in the barn," Gran asked, pulling out a chair for herself. She sat down and began filling plates with sliced meat, mountains of potatoes, and piles of salad.

"Sure, Gran," Jack said, passing his plate.

"Who's Maverick?" I asked, placing my hand on his thigh. He handed me a filled plate, the meaty gravy dripping over the side.

"Gran 's horse."

"It's going to be a long night," Scott grumbled, collapsing into a chair. "My shift doesn't even start until six. I bet, I get called in before the night is through."

"There's no need to worry. The storm will blow over, and we'll be just fine." Gran said, smacking Scott's hand when he dipped a finger into the Jello.

"Rylen, would you like some Jello?" Scott asked with a smug grin stretched across his face. "It's sensationally good."

"No thanks," I answered, giving him my best you're-an-asshole smile.

"Good, now there's more for me," he said.

"Leave her alone, Scott," Jack warned, clutching his butter knife like a murder weapon.

"What? I believe in the importance of honesty, Jack. Better she finds out the truth now than…."

Jack's leg moved from under my palm and the sound of Jack's boot colliding with Scott's shin silenced him like a mute button. He quit talking; his mouth opened like a cavern in shocked silence. Then he let out a howl that sounded like a hound on a coon chase. Jack smiled wickedly, and I bit my lip, my shoulders shaking with inaudible laughter.

Scott bent to rub his leg, smiling at Gran, who held her fork up in mid-bite, assuring her he was alright.

We resumed eating, and Jack scraped his salad onto my plate. I stabbed a few slices of meat and slid it onto his. Across the table, I caught Gran's eye. She'd seen the exchange, and I assumed, her amusement was a sign of approval.

"You know, Gran," Scott began, his cheek full of food, "If traveling is prohibited. I don't see how I'll make it home tonight." He barely swallowed before he stuck another forkful in.

"I got some Duct tape," Jack deadpanned. "We'll manage."

Scott's eyes narrowed, and Gran chuckled before lifting her hands to calm the storm around the table.

"Everybody can just stay here. There's plenty of room. No need for tape, Jacky."

Jack nodded, but I felt his eyes travel over to me, and for a moment, we were frozen in time, and no one was around but the two of us. We stared at each other, reading the other's thoughts like they were bubbling over our heads. And as the first crash of thunder rumbled over the sky, shaking the house like a freight train through the living room, I realized that I'd been given a free pass to stay, and I intended to use it.

§oc∽o§ §oc∽o§ §oc∽o§

I couldn't eat another bite if I tried. I pushed my plate away, leaving a few bites of potatoes uneaten.

Jack stood, taking our dishes; they clattered into the sink.

"It was delicious, Gran," I offered, finishing the last of my Coke.

"I'm glad you liked it, sweetie."

Gran sat at the table, her back turned, but she lifted a finger into the air. "Jack, just leave that."

"It's a lot of dishes, Gran."

The kitchen was small, and whoever designed it had overlooked the need for a dishwasher.

Scott, who'd finished his entire plate in under five minutes, had retired to the couch where he lay, asleep, snoring like a buzzing bumblebee.

"I can help." I got to my feet, but as I rose from my chair, the thunder crashed, the lights flickered, and then it all went black.

"Get some candles!" Gran demanded, the sound of her chair scooting back.

I dug my phone from my pocket, the screen dimly shining over me.

A snort. Movement from the couch.

"What happened?" Scott's voice. *Thud.* "Ouch!" *Crash.* "Shit, sorry, Gran."

Footsteps. Jack approached me in the dark. His hand found mine.

He clicked on a flashlight.

A match struck, the flame dancing across Gran's face as she lit a candle.

A horse whinnied. A flash of lightning broke the sky – a rattle of thunder rumbled.

"Gran, I need to get Maverick!" Jack said, reaching for the handle. Bam, who'd been yipping at the door, ran inside and bolted under the table.

"Go!" Gran shouted over the storm's noise. "Scott, help me with the generator."

Jack led me outside, and seconds later, we were soaked, our wet clothing sticking to us like we'd submerged ourselves. The storm raged all around us, with rain falling so fiercely that the drops hit the ground and bounced, filling puddles until they were lakes. Lightning sliced the sky, the fierce thunder answering, roaring through the clouds like a battlefield.

Jack pocketed his light, released my hand, and ran into the pen. The black stallion bucked and reared up on his hind legs, mud and manure flinging into the air, as he released a drawn-out, high-pitched whinny.

"Open the doors!" Jack yelled, pointing to the barn as rain pelted his face.

I pushed open the barn doors as Jack slapped Maverick's backside, and the horse ran. I jumped out of the way as the animal trotted into the barn, Jack sprinting behind it.

I followed them inside.

"Doors," he said, and I helped him close the gates with a loud slam.

He clicked on his flashlight. "Are you alright?" he asked, reaching a hand to touch my arm.

"Yeah, I'm fine."

"Good," he answered. "Hold on. Let me get him situated."

I clicked on my phone light. The barn had a dirt floor, and housed a tractor, combine, and a rusty Chevy truck. To one side sat unoccupied gated pens, but piles of manure and half-empty watering basins showed Maverick often used them. On the other side, there was a place to milk cows or shear sheep. The high ceiling featured lofts on each side, one with a wall and the other open with a ladder leading up to it. I could see stacks of yellow hay piled to the roof.

Jack walked into a pen, and I watched him fill a trough with water, fill a bucket with oats, and spread fresh hay. Then he went to the horse and made a clicking noise, taking hold of his mane and leading him into a wooden pen. Jack closed the gate, his eyes traveling to me, the flashlight shining in the space between us. With his mouth slightly opened and his chest heaving, we took in the drenched sight of each other.

Our wet clothing clung to us.

His shirt—white and translucent— I could see his chest beneath it.

My jeans were as stiff as raw noodles. My shoes—cold and squishy.

His boots—caked in manure—mud traveling up the legs of his Levi's.

He exhaled, closing his mouth, and I watched raindrops run off the ends of his hair, then trail a path from his cheek to his jaw and disappear below his shirt.

I shivered. "I'm freezing."

"Okay," he said, a few tones above a whisper. "Come with me."

I took his hand, and he led me up a staircase in the back corner of the barn, the flashlight illuminating our path. Then he opened the door to his bedroom. I quickly realized that this was where he lived.

He released my hand and knelt in front of the fireplace. "I'll build a fire," he said.

I dug my phone out, the bright screen lighting my surroundings.

The loft was simply made with wooden floors and wide beams that held up a vaulted ceiling. The area was small, big enough for a bed and a shaggy couch. He used a short bookcase as a nightstand. An alarm clock, a woven basket, and a lamp sat on top of it. A dresser with a small TV was angled toward the sofa. An opened door behind the stairs revealed a stand-up shower with a black curtain. A pair of horseshoes hung on the wall, a poster of a man riding a bull next to them. The only window was above the bed, the pane speckled in raindrops.

As the yellow flames crackled and shadows danced around us, Jack stood and clicked off the flashlight. He flicked on a lantern, placed it on the nightstand, then walked past me into the bathroom.

"Be right back," he said.

The thunder boomed again, and I sat on the couch in front of the fire, elevating my knee. I'd gone the entire day without the brace, and I was at my limit. I rubbed my fingertips over my knee, massaging the sore tendons beneath.

Jack returned, two towels stacked in his hands.

"Do you want dry clothes?" he asked, setting the towels on the couch beside me.

"Sure."

He opened a drawer and retrieved a black t-shirt and gray sweats, and I bent to work on my shoelaces. It wasn't long before I had a relentless muddy knot.

"Dammit," I growled.

"Let me."

I looked up to see Jack watching me, holding the clothing in one hand. He tossed it on the couch and knelt before me, taking my heel into his hands. He picked at the knot until it loosened and slipped the shoe off my foot. He copied his movement with the other shoe. Then, running his fingers up my ankle, he found the hem of my sock and pulled it down until my feet were bare. He ran his hands over the arch of my foot, up my ankle bone, and down the top of my foot to my toes. He did the same to the other foot, the friction under his palms warming them, melting away the cold.

"Thanks," I said, realizing I was breathless.

He smiled, reaching past me for the towel he'd laid on the couch. He opened it, swung it around my shoulders like a cape, and held the corners in front of me. Our eyes locked, and I reached for his shirt, pulling him so our foreheads pressed together.

"Jack," I breathed his name, but it was a plea.

His eyes closed. His throat bobbed. I didn't need to say more. He already knew.

"We can still wait. It doesn't have to be tonight."

"I can't wait any longer," I whispered, my lips hovering over his jaw.

He opened his eyes, peering into me. "I don't want you to think I only brought you here to get you naked."

"Do you want me naked?"

There was a dash of lightning, and I felt him take a breath and pause before he admitted the truth. "Yes."

"Well," I said in a throaty whisper, "No one's stopping you." I lifted my arms above my head, the towel slipping behind me, and his face registered what I was asking of him. Slowly, he reached for the hem of my sweatshirt and pulled the material over my head, taking my T-shirt with it and throwing it on the floor. He was still as a statue, admiring my upper body, my breasts covered by a black bra.

Reaching for the buttons on his shirt, I whispered the truth that for weeks had burned inside me, "I want you naked, too."

He smiled as my fingers worked the buttons. But my hands shook, and I became impatient, so I grabbed the two ends and yanked, the buttons popping, scattering to the floor.

His face morphed into surprise, and he let out a husky laugh as he slipped his arms out of the sleeves, letting his shirt land in a heap behind him.

"Do you have any idea how long I wanted to do that?" I asked, gripping his biceps.

He stood and reached for me, hauling me against his chest, and his mouth was on mine as he spoke. "I hated that shirt."

Then Jack kissed me, drinking me in like I was oxygen, and he'd newly discovered what it meant to breathe. We came together and pulled apart, switching rhythms, kissing slowly and then wildly, carefully and then amorously, each of us taking the lead. Playfully, I sank my teeth into his bottom lip, softly biting. He groaned quietly into my mouth, the sound of it like a gentle hum, and then did the same to me.

I wrapped my arms around his back, grazing my nails against the cold on his skin, the sharp crests of his shoulder blades, the taut muscles under his flesh, and still, I needed more. I moved my hands further down, leaving goosebumps as I passed his narrow hips, slipping beneath his jeans, and I filled my hands with what I've always wanted to grab – his ass. It was tight and sculpted, and he smiled against my lips before breaking our kiss.

"Hold on," he said gruffly, stepping back to remove his boots.

Thunder still drummed outside, but nothing matched my heart slamming against my chest, beating with a tempo made for him. I barely had time to catch my breath before his mouth was on me.

And it was everywhere. All at once.

Within seconds, I was in that place again. Where only Jack could take me. Where the wave was rushing to the shoreline. Where the crushing demand for more pulsed through me, warming my center. Yet this time, it was fueled with something stronger than need, more potent than desire; it was carnal and innate, sensual and rousing, and I quivered with growing anticipation.

I tangled my hands in his hair and sighed his name as he planted worshipful kisses down the curve of my neck, across the tops of my breasts, and down the plane of my stomach. He followed the same trail back up, his mouth lingering wherever he tasted, his hands skimming my sides and around my back to my bra strap.

"I need to look at you, baby," he rasped, kissing my lips again. "I need to see all of you."

I nodded and he took my bra clasp between his fingers. "Is this, okay?"

"Yes," I said as the clasp popped open, and the straps slid off my arms, freeing my breasts. He threw my bra on the floor, then unsnapped my jeans, peeling wet denim down my legs. He hooked his thumbs in the elastic of my panties, guiding them down, and then I heard his breath catch.

He stepped back, taking in the sight of me bared to him. His lips parted, his chest expanding as his darkened eyes traveled over me, my nipples hardening from the exposure. And I was grateful the room was dimly lit, with only the crackling fireplace cascading our silhouettes onto the walls around us.

"My God," he whispered under his breath as thunder clapped. "Unbelievable."

A curl bounced into my eyes, and he stepped closer to me and brushed the curl off my forehead. "I've never seen anyone more breathtaking."

I fought the urge to cover myself. I'd never been admired so honestly before, and it made me feel beautiful and terrified at the same time. So, I decided to even the score.

"I need to look at all of you, too," I told him boldly, as lightning broke the sky.

A knowing smile spread across his beautiful face, and he nodded, unbuckling his belt. He slid his pants down and kicked them away. Underneath, he wore boxer briefs—black and tight—tented in the front. When he pulled them down, he sprang free, and he shamelessly stood in the firelight.

I copied his movements, stepping back to let my eyes trace him from head to toe—his bare feet and hairy legs, his impressive erection, his defined abs, and wide shoulders. His handsome face. Damn, that face. There were nights I went to bed dreaming about it.

He was gorgeous, and he was mine—all of him.

"You're perfect," I declared.

He grinned again, then scooped me up, catching my lips in a kiss as he took me to his bed. He placed me on top of the comforter and tugged it from beneath me, and, resting his weight on his elbows, he covered me with his body.

He started with my lips, kissing, sucking, nibbling. Then he moved to my breasts, teasing with this stubble, licking my nipples, spending ample time on each one, pulling them into his mouth with careful teeth. A clamorous moan escaped me as he suckled, the sensations intoxicating, clouding my vision as they pulsated through me, and I dug my nails into his back, pressing him for more.

"Easy, baby," he breathed, his breath warm on my skin. "I want this to last a while."

"If you do that again, I won't be able to last at all," I said through uneven breaths.

He chuckled, a low hum in his throat. "You have a perfect body." He ran his hands over me. "Perfect breasts. It was hard for me not to stare at them when you fell into that puddle."

My mouth dropped open. "You noticed?"

His face broke into a wolfish grin. "Yeah, it was hard not to. I couldn't take my eyes off you."

"Don't look too closely. I'd hate to disappoint you," I said, suddenly shy, but he shook his head like the notion was preposterous.

"Nothing about you would ever disappoint me."

Then he was gone again, running his tongue between my breasts, kissing my hip bones, down my thigh to my injured knee. He kissed each scar, lingering on the longest, the most jagged. It was why we met, and he kissed every inch of it.

He moved to interlace our fingers and positioned his face between my legs, and I stiffened. I tried to remain calm, though I was keenly aware my inexperience could ruin this for both of us.

"Relax, baby," he cooed. "I'm going to give you pleasure."

"W-wait, nobody's ever…" But all coherent thoughts evaded me, and my head spun as Jack's gray-blue eyes bored into me, a shocked expression on his face.

"He didn't?"

I shook my head, a nervous whimper slipping out of me.

"Figures. Selfish bastard," he scoffed. "Okay, baby, just try to relax."

Before I could respond, his mouth made contact, and I gasped sharply, my head rolling back into the pillows as he tasted me.

I released his hands and grabbed his hair, twirling the ends around my fingers and lightly tugging as his mouth consumed me—teasing, darting, circling me. Deeply he groaned, the vibrations bringing every inch of me alive and electric as the most magnificent pressure grew low in my belly.

It wasn't long before my hips lifted off the mattress and my back arched, but he grabbed my waist, pulling me closer, his hand traveling up my stomach to pin me down. That wave built again, forming its crest, charging to the shoreline with such intensity there'd be no stopping it; it'd rip me in two. And with every taste, he only brought me higher, spooled me tighter, until I was teetering on the unbearable edge.

"It's okay, baby," he said, pulling away to speak. "Let go."

And then the wave broke, and an eager noise rushed out of him as I unraveled, flying and falling simultaneously. Soaring and crying out in unfamiliar sounds as my body quaked and ripples of pleasure tore through me, inebriating all my senses.

When I floated back to earth, like a sheet of paper fluttering to the ground, Jack was waiting for me. He lay on a pillow beside me, leaning on an elbow, a smug grin plastered across his face.

I exhaled and reached for him, pulling him on top of me.

"Do you want to do it again?" he asked, grazing my lips with his.

"I want you," I whispered. "Right now." I never wanted anyone more in my life.

He hesitated, but I wiggled my hips beneath him, lining us up. "I want you inside of me."

He nodded, reaching for a basket on his nightstand, but I stopped him.

"You don't need that. I don't want anything between us. I want to feel you, baby."

He drew his arm back. "Are you sure?"

"I am sure. I've never been more sure of anything."

The thunder had ceased, diminishing only to the sound of a gentle rain sprinkling the metal roof above us.

"Make love to me, Jack," I whispered against his lips. "Then, when you're done, do it again."

His throat bobbed, and his eyes darkened with something I recognized, and it made me feel desired as he began pressing into me. He started slowly, hissing in a breath as he filled me, then pushed in further until his body was flush with mine. And then something else overtook him, and his movements became deliberate, like an artist who'd spent a lifetime painting. Like we'd made love a hundred times before. His mouth came crashing down on mine, murmuring something I didn't understand. I was too overwhelmed by what I felt—where he was taking me. The pressure returned, and having been over the edge mere minutes earlier, I couldn't take much more. I would snap at any moment.

"Oh God," he growled. "You feel so damn good."

His thrusts grew stronger, faster, pushing me across the mattress until my head hit the wall. I clutched his back and screamed into his shoulder, the tension snapping like a slingshot, and my body writhed beneath him as I ricocheted into the air above us.

Then at that moment, I wanted to admit another great truth; it started the minute I fell into that puddle. I wanted to tell him I was in love with him. And while his face was in my hair, and my name spilled from his lips, he let himself go.

Chapter Twenty-Five

JACK

Sent Saturday 11:35 PM
Cora: Hudson has an infection. If he dies, I'll tell Rylen everything.

Sent Sunday 6:08 AM
Jack: We can dispense with the threats. I already told her.

Sent 6:10 AM
Cora: Liar! Naked ass on fire. I heard about your little sleep over. 🥒

I snapped my phone shut and tossed it on the bookcase by the bed. I wasn't going to be controlled by anyone else. I would tell Rylen when I was ready.

Sliding under the blankets, I reached for Rylen, drawing her closer. She stirred, lifting her head, then moved against me, draping an arm around my torso.

"What time is it?" she muttered sleepily, laying her cheek on my chest.

"Almost six thirty," I answered, kissing her head.

"I was planning to sneak into your shower."

"Without me?" I asked in mock defense.

"You were snoring like a monster."

I felt her smile. I'd been accused of snoring before, but I wasn't going to tell her that.

"You're mistaken. Those horrific noises weren't coming from me."

She shifted her head to look at my face. "I've heard chainsaws that were quieter."

I laughed, her head slightly jumping while it rested on my chest. "I don't think so, sweetheart, and you slept longer than I did. I know what I heard."

"I require my beauty sleep." She stretched like a cat in the sun, deeply yawning.

I laughed and planted a kiss above her eyebrow. The power had returned sometime in the night, but the rain continued to fall in a steady trickle, the sound like small pebbles on the metal roof above us. We'd made love three times in the night until both of us were too exhausted to continue, and the rain lulled us into a slumber. As we drifted in and out of sleep, I reached for her, needing to know she was still there. I feared it'd been a dream, and I'd wake up cold and alone.

Rylen drew tiny circles across my abdomen with her fingertips. I lazily ran my hand through her hair, letting her curls slip through my fingers, the afterglow of lovemaking still prevalent between us.

She was the first to speak. "Tell me something I don't know about you."

"Where did that come from?" I asked.

"Just thinking. I want to know everything about you."

She turned to look up at me, her round brown eyes big and searching.

"My middle name is Timothy," I said, but she shook her head.

"Nope, I already knew that. Gran said it at dinner last night."

"Hmm, of course," I said thoughtfully. "What's your middle name?"

"Don't try to change the subject."

"I'm curious," I pressed, "especially since you're avoiding the question."

"Who's avoiding?"

I sighed, shrugging, "What do you want to know, baby?"

"I don't know..." she paused, turning on her stomach to gaze up at me.

"Ask me something. Whatever pops into your head."

She thought for a moment, then grinned wickedly. "Who was your first kiss?"

"I don't kiss and tell."

"Tell me!"

"Sarah Miller."

"Like a real kiss?" she clarified.

"Like she could tell I'd eaten sour cream and onion potato chips."

"Ewww," Rylen giggled. "Were you scared to kiss her?"

"She kissed me. I was innocent."

She lifted a brow. "I have a hard time believing that."

"It's true. I was twelve, and Gran dragged me to a church picnic. She got me all dressed up in a stupid bow tie. I had to carry this big ass watermelon up a hill. Sarah kept following me around like a dog in heat."

She laughed, crawling up to the pillow beside me and leaning on her elbow. "It must've been the bow tie."

"Maybe. She had a big gap in her front teeth, and sometimes she'd whistle when she spoke."

Rylen snorted, "Like a gopher? Poor girl."

"Yeah. Finally, I turned around and shouted at her, 'What do you want?' and she grabbed my face and kissed me in front of the whole church."

"Wow. Can't blame a girl for knowing what she wants."

"I guess." I turned on my side, facing her. "But I must've been bad at it because she never spoke to me again."

"Well, I can attest you've greatly improved."

"Yeah?"

She nodded. "I mean, I don't have much to compare you to, but I never wanted to rip off Andon's clothes the way I do yours."

I chuckled. "I should start buying shirts in bulk then?"

"Shirts, jeans, boxers – they're all endangered species."

I laughed again, planting a kiss on her lips, "Now, who was your first kiss?"

She rolled her eyes, groaning, "Andon," she admitted. "I was fifteen. I had a huge crush on him, and he invited me to a movie. We sat in the back and made out."

"At least you didn't kiss a gopher."

She whistled. "True. At one point, I thought he was it. Marriage, kids – the whole white picket fence. I was a fool for being so wrapped up in him."

"It's natural to want commitment, Rylen."

"I suppose. He was my first *everything*...." She trailed off, breaking eye contact. "Except for that one thing." She looked at me again, and I felt a grin spread across my face. "You were the first to do that."

"So, you liked that then?"

She kept her eyes downcast, tracing a crease in the sheet with her finger. "Wasn't it obvious?" she asked shyly.

"Yes," I said. "I just like watching you squirm while you admit it."

She punched my arm, and I yelped, rubbing my palm against the blow.

"If you must know, it was the best I've ever had. Three years of mediocre sex, and that's what I was missing? I didn't know it could feel that good."

"I'm glad, baby. I wanted it to be good for you."

"It was, and I'd return the favor," she began, twirling a thread on a blanket around her finger. "But the truth is, I've never done that before either, and I'm afraid I'd do it wrong."

"Hey, look at me." I used a knuckle and moved her chin to meet my eyes. "There's no pressure. I didn't do that because it was a *favor*. I don't expect anything in return. Okay?"

She nodded. "Okay." Then she kissed my lips again, seeming more relaxed.

"Now, tell me your middle name," I pressed.

She groaned, shaking her head and closing her eyes, "Marie."

"Marie," I repeated. "What's so bad about that?"

"Nothing, that's why it's everyone's middle name. It lacks originality."

"Could be worse. I thought you were going to say... Iphigenia or something like that."

She chuckled, "No, thank God."

I tucked a curl behind her ear. "What should we do for your birthday? I need some ideas."

"My birthday isn't until next month." She began moving, uninterested in my question. She crawled up the length of my body, her hips straddling mine, her arms flanking my head.

"So." I said, but she shifted her weight, and I could barely speak. "I like... planning ...ahead." I had more to say, but her naked breasts hung in the space below my chin, and my gaze dipped to gawk at them.

"Do you believe in love at first sight?" she asked thoughtfully.

"I do now," I said, blatantly staring.

She giggled and took my jaw into her hand, lifting my eyes. "I'm up here. Now answer the question."

"I'll need coffee before I solve that mystery."

"It's not a mystery; it's your opinion."

Her eyes brightened, and she grinned wickedly, lowering her mouth to mine and speaking, "Try not to move." She grazed my lips, barely touching, almost kissing. Then her lips moved on my jaw, trailing kisses down my neck to my chest, down my sternum,

"I'm not sure," I managed, unable to focus. "I suppose it's possible. What do you think?"

She kept kissing downward, between my ribs, past my navel, before she paused to speak. "Oh, it's definitely possible," she breathed.

She worked her mouth over my skin as I shuddered beneath her, watching her dark curls disappear under the blankets. When I couldn't take it anymore, and before she could go further, I grabbed her arm and hauled her up, capturing her open mouth in a breathless kiss.

"Don't rush it, baby. We have time." I turned us so her back hit the mattress and buried my lips in her neck. Her mouth spread into a grin when she felt the effect she had on me against her thigh.

"You smell so damn good." I nibbled her collarbone and nuzzled her skin. "Like sex and traces of cherry vanilla shampoo."

She giggled and took my face into her hands, taking in a breath like she'd had a random thought.

"Yesterday at dinner, why did Scott say he believed in the importance of honesty? What was he talking about?"

That got my attention, and I pulled back to speak to her. "When Scott's not working, he's continually inebriated. So, who knows?"

"He didn't seem drunk," she countered. "It was like he already knew who I was."

"He's a deputy. He's met everyone at least once."

She shook her head. "No, I don't drive, so he wouldn't have pulled me over."

She had me there, and I felt myself grasping at threads. "He was at the fundraiser," I blurted. "He stood beside me when I saw you across the gym."

"Oh," she said, considering. "So, he wasn't referring to something specific then?"

I shrugged. "He's pea-brain-Scott. I don't pretend to understand him. But I'm sorry he was an ass to you."

"It's okay." She smiled, seeming satisfied. For now.

I made a mental note to punch Scott in the nose the first chance I got.

"I need to take a shower," she said. "Can I borrow those clothes now?"

"Sure." I hooked a finger over the edge of the sheet. "Or you could just stay naked forever."

"I'm pretty sure there are laws against such practices."

"Do you see a cop?"

Slowly, I inched the sheet down, but she grabbed the seam and yanked it up, her eyes flashing a don't-you-dare at me.

"And there are safety concerns. I like bacon too much," she added.

"Hmm, naked bacon makin'. I could get into that," I said, speaking against her jaw.

She giggled again; then I bolted to my feet. Her eyes took in the nude sight of me, I was already hard, but I wasn't shy. I swiftly yanked the sheet off of her like a cloth on a set table. She shrieked at the sudden unveiling as if I hadn't memorized every naked inch of her last night. Rylen leaned over the bedside, hugging her breasts, searching for a nearby blanket, but I gathered her into my arms.

She laughed as I lifted her, wrapping her arms around my neck and tucking her forehead under my chin while I carried her across the floor. I flipped on the light inside the bathroom and set Rylen haphazardly on her feet. She reached out a hand to the wall to steady herself. I turned the shower on warm and tugged the curtain closed.

Then she was against the wall, clutching my back, while my mouth moved over hers in reverent kisses. I lifted her, and she wrapped her legs around my hips until the mirror fogged, and the steam seeped beneath the curtain. I turned, walking us into the shower, her lips never leaving mine as we slipped under the spray. And then I finished what she'd started.

§oc∾o§ §oc∾o§ §oc∾o§

After our shower, I quietly tiptoed inside the house and threw our clothing into the dryer. She wore my sweatpants and a T-shirt while we waited, and we played cards on my bed.

When the dryer finished, I retrieved our clothes – returning to the loft to see Rylen bending at the waist, examining the comic books on the bookshelf by the bed.

"I never got a chance to snoop," she said giddily.

I laid her clothing on the comforter, the fabric still warm from the tumbling dryer.

"At least you're admitting it."

She chuckled, taking the top booklet from the stack. She turned it over in her hands, reading the back. "*The Return of Superman.* I didn't know you were such a comic book fan."

"Ah, I'm not," I answered. "They *sort* of belong to Cora."

The truth was they belonged to Hudson.

"Oh. Why do you have them?"

"She had to move out of her apartment. She doesn't have room for them."

I walked to the couch and flopped into the seat, but she was right behind me.

"I was thinking about that. It wasn't even your fault. She can't be mad at you forever."

"You don't know what Cora's capable of."

"Okay. Is there something else she's *lording* over you?"

You. There's you.

I needed to tell her the rest of the truth. The guilt was suffocating me. I pulled at my shirt collar. Gran was right; it was going to blow up in my face.

Cora would make sure of it.

"She's being unfair. I should talk to her."

"No!" I snapped, and her eyes widened. "Look, Rylen, I know you're trying to help, but…" I trailed off, chewing my bottom lip. "But that would just piss her off."

And make things more difficult for me. Cora never gave empty threats. She could return at any moment.

301

The clock was ticking.

"So, butt out!" I blurted.

She took a step back, and her eyes held traces of hurt and surprise. My tone had been sharper than I'd meant, but with Cora's recent threats, I couldn't have Rylen anywhere near here.

It would end me.

"Sorry," I said gruffly. "I didn't mean to bark at you."

She sat on the sofa beside me and pulled her legs into her chest. "I shouldn't have pushed you," she said. "It's my fault."

"Why do you always assume it's your fault?" I was snapping again, but her willingness to take the blame only twisted the knife.

"Because you're right, it's none of my business." She put her hand on my forearm. "But I can tell when something is bothering you."

It was the perfect opportunity to come clean, but not now. I wasn't ready to say goodbye. I wasn't ready to give her up. I'd only gotten one night, and it wasn't enough. The withdrawal had already started.

"Tell me what's bothering you," she pressed.

"Nope."

"It might make you feel better if you tell me."

"It won't."

"If I guess, will you tell me?"

"Nope."

She sighed and hurt filled her eyes again. If I told her, it'd be over, and I needed more. A lifetime would never be enough.

I reached for her and pulled her into my lap, so her knees straddled my hips.

"No more talking," I whispered.

I lowered my lips to her neck, tasting her skin. She hesitated at first, the pain I'd caused still lingering. But I'd win her over. I knew where to touch her. And within moments she relented and captured my lips in hers.

"Jack?" The voice came from below the loft. It was Gran, likely wondering why we hadn't appeared in the kitchen for food. "Jack!" she said again.

I broke our kiss, shouting through the floorboards. "Yeah, Gran?" But that didn't stop Rylen. She kept kissing everything near her.

"Come on inside. Breakfast is gettin' cold."

"O-okay. We'll be right there." There were footsteps below us as Gran left the barn, and I turned my attention back to Rylen. "Hold that thought. We gotta go."

§ос∾о§ §ос∾о§ §ос∾о§

I opened the front door, and the smells of bacon and biscuits enveloped me.

"Mornin' Gran," I said, watching as Rylen stepped in behind me.

The morning news blared on the TV, and a newspaper lay open on the table. A half-empty cup of coffee sat next to it.

"There you two are. I'm just making a fresh pot," Gran said, pouring water into a coffee pot. "I was wondering if I'd have to eat alone."

She winked at me, and I pulled on my shirt collar. When your grandma knows that you've been up all-night having sex, yeah, that's not awkward at all.

"I'll set the table."

"I'll help," Rylen chimed, following me into the kitchen. I opened a cabinet and reached for plates.

303

"Thank you, dears. Just three of us. Scott got called out early this morning. Sun wasn't even up yet. Poor thing."

"Poor baby." I deadpanned, and Rylen giggled.

Gran turned on the faucet and ran water through the coffee filter.

"You need to be nicer to him, Jacky. He *is* your family," she scolded.

I sighed, opening a drawer to gather forks.

"How are they related?" Rylen asked as she dealt out plates on the table.

"My two daughters. Their mothers were sisters." Gran answered, pressing a button on the coffee maker. She put the coffee canister in the cupboard and walked to the stove.

"I don't have to claim him as anything," I grumbled. I was still pissed from last night.

Gran carried a pan of scrambled eggs to the table and set it in the middle. "Scott is your family, Jacky, and unless things change with Cora, he's all you have, and I'm not getting any younger."

I sighed. "I know, Gran."

"Oh, I heard on the news this morning that one hundred and fifty houses lost power last night. Can you believe that? It was the worst storm Davenport has seen since 1976."

We pulled out chairs and sat down as Gran began filling plates, and I passed the first one to Rylen.

"I just want you to know I really appreciate all your help around here, Jack. It's a good thing you put Maverick away. There were so many lightning strikes last night, Lord knows if he would've made it."

As I stabbed my fork into fluffy eggs, the door swung open, and Ned popped into the entryway.

"Top of the mornin' to ya, Margaret," he cooed.

"Nedford, how are you?" she said, scooting back her chair. She got to her feet and threw her arms around Ned in a tight embrace.

Pete peeked around the corner, shaking his head. "I told him to call first, Margaret, but he doesn't listen to me."

"Nonsense, you're both welcome!" Gran declared, wrapping Pete in the same affectionate hug. "Won't you stay for breakfast? Jacky, please get them some coffee."

I stood as Ned removed his hat and jacket and pulled out a chair.

But Pete hesitated, "Oh, we couldn't impose, Margaret. We didn't even…"

"Sit down, Pete," Ned interjected and yanked his arm. Pete plopped into a chair with a resounding thud, looking stunned.

"I'll just throw a bit more on," Gran said with a laugh. "Now, you boys, sit and enjoy yourself." She cracked eggs into a frying pan and laid out strips of bacon.

Rylen looked up from her plate, catching Ned's attention.

"Miss Rylen, so lovely to see you," he said. "I'm assuming you and Jack worked everything out?"

"We sure did," she answered warmly.

"Good, I thought for sure he wasn't dumb enough to let you get away. But sometimes he surprises me."

"I'm standing right here, Ned," I piped, opening the mug cabinet, and Pete choked back a laugh.

"I should've known things were better," Ned added, "You're just glowing."

"Thank you," Rylen said, breaking eye contact. "How have you been?"

"I'm good, honey. I'm serious, though; something's different about you. Is it the hair?"

A mug slipped from my fingers, crashing to the counter, the handle busting into two pieces.

"Be more careful, Jacky," Gran scolded, stirring milk into the eggs.

"Sorry." I offered, clearing my throat. I discarded the pieces in the trash, catching Rylen's eye, and she bit her lower lip, laughter brewing in her eyes.

She shrugged. "Nope, same ol' me."

Ned thoughtfully stroked his bristly chin, "Nah, something's different. I'm going to figure it out."

"Mind your own business, Nedford," Pete chimed in, taking off his ball cap and hanging it on his knee. "He's always putting his nose where it doesn't belong."

I decided Ned needed a different topic. "That was a hell of a storm last night, wasn't it?" I asked, carrying two mugs of coffee to the table. Pete nodded thanks when I placed it in front of him.

"Sure was!" Ned said, as Gran set their plates piled with food in front of them. "I haven't seen one like it in forty-five years."

"It was a mean one," Pete commented. "Thank you, Margaret."

"Yes, thank you. Ol' Jacky here wasn't hiding under the bed, was he?" Ned asked, and Rylen chortled.

"I don't think so," she replied.

She'd know too.

"Here we go," I sighed, burying my face in my hands, knowing what story Ned was about to tell.

Ned chuckled, "I tell you, this boy was scared of his own shadow. Nine years old. There's a huge thunderstorm outside, and I get a call from Gran. She can't find Jacky anywhere. I come over and find him under the bed, scared out of his wits."

Pete chuckled and elbowed Ned, "Poor boy probably pissed himself once you showed up and drugged him out."

"I had no choice. I tried everything I could to coax him out of there," Ned said. "But the stubborn ass wouldn't budge."

"Some things never change," Gran commented.

Traitor.

"Should've tried M&Ms," Rylen added, lifting her coffee, and I winked at her.

"He did," Gran said.

"Yep, he grabbed the package and darted back under. Plastered himself to the wall," Ned finished.

I stared at my plate, my ears turning red as Rylen's gaze traveled to me.

"Finally, I just grabbed his ankles and yanked as hard as I could. You would've thought he was a cat headed for a bathtub. I've never seen a kid claw the carpet like that."

Rylen laughed, lifting a hand to cover her mouth as her shoulders shook. Even Gran let out a howl, the sound coming from deep in her belly.

"I've gotten better," I interjected, lifting a biscuit, but Pete slapped me on the back so hard I coughed and dropped it.

"Not true! When you took off last year, we figured something spooked ya," Pete chimed.

"Took off?" Rylen asked.

"Yep. Didn't say a word to anyone."

Shut up, Pete. My palms were growing sticky.

"Just poof. Vanished," Pete said, snapping his fingers.

"You better watch him, Miss Rylen," Ned added. "The moment something scares this boy, he'll run and hide like a fox to its den. But maybe now that you're here, he's come to his senses."

"I hope so," Rylen murmured, peering at me, her round eyes hopeful. Under the table, her foot found my shin, and she rested it there. I stared back, a slight smile on my lips.

Ned's eyes danced between our faces, hearing the things we'd left unspoken, seeing the irrevocable force connecting us, and his face broke into a grin. "So, that's what's different."

"Who needs more bacon?" I asked, lifting the plate.

The phone rang, and Gran rose from her chair to answer it.

Confusion perched over Pete's eyebrows. "What's different?" he asked Ned, who brushed him off and lifted his mug to his lips.

"Rylen," Ned started, ignoring Pete. "You never told me what happened to your knee. Is it feeling better?"

"Yeah," she answered. "A little over a year ago, I was in a gas station robbery and…."

Ned listened intently, but Pete slowly turned to look at me, his eyes like laser beams. I shakily lifted my coffee.

A hand landed on my shoulder, and I saw Gran standing above me, her face white as a sheet.

"Jacky," she said weakly. "It's Scott."

"Gran, you don't look so good." I took the phone from her fingers, but they were cold and clammy.

She was panting, and I heard her let out a breath, saw the sweat drip from her ashen face, and then her eyes closed; she clutched her chest and collapsed to the floor, hitting her head on the table's edge.

"Gran!" I cried, getting to my feet. Rylen stood, and Ned and Pete were instantly beside Gran—holding her hands and patting her face.

I put the phone to my ear, "Scott! I gotta call you back."

"No, Jack! Don't hang up!" he bellowed. "Last night, Sally's Diner burnt to the ground."

Chapter Twenty-Six

Rylen

There were paramedics everywhere. I kept my distance, watching as they shuffled Gran out the door. Jack fell in step beside the gurney as the medics wheeled Gran down the driveway, and I was a few paces behind them. Ned said that they'd meet us at the hospital, and they drove off in his pickup.

I watched Gran reach for Jack, her shaky wrinkled hands grabbing him and squeezing until her knobby knuckles turned white. When a paramedic tried to take her wrist to start an IV, she refused to let go of him, squeezing tighter and Jack stiffened.

"Let them, Gran," he said hoarsely, but she shook her head.

She tried to speak, but the words wouldn't come, and she threw her head back in frustration. She tried again, muttering and murmuring; the mask humming and fogging with attempted words, but she couldn't form them. She raised a hand to lift the mask away, but Jack stopped her.

"Don't speak," he pleaded, but she shook her head and pulled the mask down.

"Tell C-orah," she croaked, "It was me." She flopped back onto the pad, her strength depleted.

Jack nodded, shifting his eyes to me and then back to Gran.

He brought her hand up to his lips and kissed her fingers. "Okay, don't worry about that right now." Her eyes closed, and she slightly nodded, neither convincing him nor me that she'd make it through.

Then he pleaded with her. "I still need you. You can't die."

"On three, lift," a medic said.

They loaded her into the ambulance, and Jack was forced to let her go.

Hours later, at the hospital, Ned, Pete, Jack, and I were still in the waiting room. There'd been no update on Gran, though the doctor said they suspected a heart attack and would know more after the test results came in. Jack asked to use my phone because he'd forgotten his. I unlocked it, handed it to him, and he walked toward the restroom. When he returned, Ned and Pete announced they needed to go home, so I promised to call them when I knew more.

"Thanks, honey," Ned said, "Call me anytime."

I sat in a chair in the waiting room by the fireplace, watching as Jack paced the floor, clutching his arms behind his back, blazing the same trail into the carpet. He'd hardly spoken a word to me; if he did, he responded curtly with one-syllable, annoyed answers.

"Jack," I said carefully. "Please, sit down."

He ignored me and continued to pace, his boots softly tapping on the carpeted floor.

"Jack," I tried again, "This isn't helping you. Sit."

He stopped a few steps before me, and his eyes met mine; they were glassy and tired, but they were traces of something else I'd never seen in him before.

Fear.

"It's my fault, Rylen," he said gruffly.

"What is?"

"All of it," he answered. "Gran. Sally's Diner. They're both my fault." He plopped into the chair beside me, burying his face in his hands.

"Wait," I replied, shifting towards him. I put a hand on his shoulder, but he shrugged it off. "Neither of them is your fault. Don't be ridiculous."

But he shook his head, his words muffled by his hands. "It was that fryer. I never should have touched the damned thing."

"The fryer?" I repeated. "At Sally's?"

He nodded tightly. "I must've made a mistake in the wiring. One spark and the whole place burnt to the ground."

He lifted his face, balled his hands into fists, and sank his teeth into the knuckles on his right hand.

"Jack, you don't know if that was the cause. There was a lightning storm last night. Buildings burn down from lightning strikes all the time."

"There'd be no way to prove that," he growled, cutting his eyes to me.

"There'd be no way to prove it was the fryer either," I countered. "Not if there's nothing left. You're beating yourself up over a possibility."

He stood facing me, exhaling, scoffing at my attempt to alleviate his guilt.

"You don't understand. I *needed* to fix this for her. I owed it to her. That diner belonged to Sally's mother; without it, she'll be destitute."

"You don't know that either. She probably has fire insurance," I offered. "A lot of restaurant owners do."

311

"Stop trying to fix it, Rylen!" he snapped, and my eyes widened at the sharpness in his tone. He noticed my surprise, then spoke again, softer this time. "Bill told me when I was in the back, he had to drop the insurance because they couldn't afford it anymore."

"They did what?" I gasped, getting to my feet.

And Sally told me they donated all of their savings to my brother's charity because that's the sort of people they were – kindly putting their desires aside to help others, even if it meant never remodeling.

Jack spread his fingers out against his hip bones, his feet shoulder-width apart. "It was only supposed to be temporary," he explained. "They have nothing, and it's my fault, because why wouldn't it be? I fuck things up. It's what I do."

"Hey," I said, reaching for him, but he stepped back. "Don't say things like that."

He glanced away, speaking above my head to no one in particular. "No matter what I do, my existence fucks with people's lives."

A tear slipped out the corner of his eye, and he swiped at it with his sleeve.

"That's not true," I declared, and before he could back away further, I grabbed the lapel of his jacket and pulled him against me. "I refuse to believe that. You have no proof."

"It is true, Rylen," he blinked, and another tear spilled out. "I have all the proof I need."

"What do you mean?"

I watched him swallow, his throat bobbing, forcing himself to say aloud whatever else tormented him.

"Gran fainted the night of the fundraiser. I found her inside the house on the floor. She's been having dizzy spells. I should've made her go to the doctor, but..." he trailed off.

"You can't make Gran do anything," I said pointedly. "Even I know that."

"No, but I could've called an ambulance. She could've been checked out. Instead, I went to the fundraiser."

That was a step too far. That was a gut punch. The fundraiser was where he went to get me, and I couldn't help but feel that maybe he regretted that decision.

That he regretted *me*, if this was the alternative.

I released his jacket, his words like an arrow piercing my chest, but only grazing my heart. Yet blood had started to seep from the wound, filling in the cracks.

"Jack, I understand you're upset about Gran but *think* about what you're saying."

"I know what I'm saying."

I felt the arrow plunge further in, the tip piercing my heart, shattering me into tiny pieces. I was going to lose him. He was going to walk away from me again.

His throat bobbed, "No matter what I do for people, I'll always make the wrong choice, and somebody I care about will pay for it, and I can't fix it."

I was powerless to stop it now, and my eyes filled with tears as blood gushed down my chest, soaking my gray sweatshirt into a light amber. Whatever flesh wound I'd started with had turned into a kill shot because, with every phrase, Jack only pounded the arrow in until it knocked me to the ground. I was slowly dying.

Clearly, he'd lost his mind.

"So," I started, my voice wavering as fresh tears spilled. "What about us? Was I the wrong choice then?"

His eyes flashed with the sudden understanding of his words, and he exhaled, his face reflecting deep regret.

"You went to the fundraiser to get me," I began, "And now you regret that? I don't want to be with someone who regrets me."

He shook his head and tried to grab my arm, but I swung it away.

"Don't touch me!" I snapped.

"No! I-I didn't say that!" he stammered. "That's not what I meant!"

"I thought you knew what you were saying," I retorted, turning my back on him. I'd already given him a chance to take it back, and the stupid ass dug his heels in.

I heard him step forward, and he grabbed the back of my arm and spun me around.

"No! Don't walk away from me!" he growled, gripping my shoulders.

"Why? You think you're the only one that gets to walk away?"

"Stop!" Then his tone softened, and he loosened his hold on me. "Jesus, Rylen, I could never regret you. Not in a million lifetimes. Don't you know that?"

I shrugged. "I guess, I don't."

He exhaled and lowered his hands from my shoulders.

"I wasn't saying I regret you, sweetheart. That's not it. It's—there's something else."

He cupped my face, gazing into me. I'd seen that look in his eyes before; it was the same one he had when he left me on the porch the morning after we'd visited The Captain. It was a strongly mixed cocktail of pain and regret, but it was infused with so much fear, I shuddered as to why. It had to be about Gran, but I had a sinking feeling there was something more that had Jack terrified.

My heart began to race, and Ned's words came back to me, "You'd better watch out, Miss Rylen. The moment something scares this boy, he'll run like a fox to its den."

314

"There's something else you need to know," he began, his voice breaking, and I felt my stomach twist into a knot. He bit his lower lip. "Oh God, how do I tell you this?"

He shakily lifted my hand, kissed between my knuckles, and spoke again. "I don't know how to say this, and when I'm done, you might never…" He trailed off, his chest heaving as his eyes glazed over.

"Rylen," he pleaded. "I…" But he stopped again, his gaze traveling over my head, his eyes the size of dinner plates. I turned my head to find my mother approaching us, and my jaw hit the ground.

She was in a fine suit again, with polished heels and a long black coat. Her hair was pulled back in a clip, and she wore full makeup with a string of pearls and matching earrings. This was the Diana Clark I'd always known. Poised and perfect, returning as if she could plead temporary insanity when I'd seen her wearing frumpy sweatpants. But now that was beneath her.

"Hi Jack," she said. "Is everything okay?"

My brow creased.

What. The. Hell?

"Mom, what are you doing here?" I asked.

She scanned me head to toe, and I was suddenly conscious of my Walk-of-Shame attire. She lifted a brow, scrutinizing me. But I pushed all forms of judgment away, forcing indifference. She had no room to speak. God knows what she'd done with Adam.

"Jack called me an hour ago," she said, her hands in the pockets of her long coat. "He said you needed a ride home." She shrugged. "So here I am."

"He did what?" I slid my eyes to Jack. "Is this true?" He nodded and my broken heart sank.

So, when he'd asked to use my phone, that's what he was up to. He'd been plotting to get rid of me, and he'd called the one person

I wasn't ready to confront. He could've asked Ned or Pete to take me back to Gran's, but no.

He'd called her.

Betrayal surged through me, and red seeped into the edges of my vision. I was going to tear his head from his shoulders.

"Why would you do that?" I growled, my eyes filling with tears.

"There are some things I need to sort through," he explained. "And it would be better if you went with her."

"No!" I hissed.

"Rylen let's not make a scene, please," my mother interjected. "You've been gone for almost two days; it's time to come home."

I shook my head. "You had no right to do that, Jack!"

I blinked, but devastated tears blinded me, and it only hurt more when he nodded, agreeing with me. He knew this would hurt me, but he'd chosen it. That hadn't stopped him.

"I'm sorry, but there wasn't any other way. You need to go with her."

"Come on," my mother said softly, wrapping an arm around my shoulder.

"Go," Jack said, and a kick to the stomach would have hurt less.

I wanted to kill him, but he was already killing me. My body turned on autopilot, my legs wobbling like they didn't belong to me, as she pivoted us towards the sliding doors. I wanted to protest, but I wasn't in charge of myself anymore; my brain had turned off. I wanted to stomp and scream like a bratty child, but neither of those options changed the cold hard truth that I wasn't wanted.

In the parking lot, Cora was walking into the hospital as my mother, and I were leaving. Her eyes caught mine and she stopped to watch us go. Then she charged forward, her steps deliberate and purposeful.

My mother opened the car door for me, and I slid into the front seat, my tears diminishing into small hiccups. I looked out my window to see Jack in the waiting room, standing in the same area and watching us through the large windowpane, his hand flat against the glass. Cora approached him and she said something to him, but he shook his head. Instantly she was angry, flailing her arms, her face morphing into a snarl. He tried to walk away from her, but she punched his shoulder and stabbed a finger into his chest.

She must've been upset about Gran.

I stroked my window where he stood, wishing I could take back the piece of myself I'd left with him, the part I'd freely given, or maybe he'd taken it, and I'd willingly let him.

My mom turned the key and looked away. This wasn't happening. I had to be dreaming. At any moment, I'd wake up in Jack's bed and be curled around him. And I'd never have to survive in a world where I wasn't wanted.

§oc∽o§ §oc∽o§ §oc∽o§

Neither of us dared to speak on the ride home, and I preferred it that way. The last thing I wanted was to explain to her the previous twenty-four hours and crumble into an ugly cry in front of her. I'd watch her face change with mock concern, and then she'd turn the conversation back to herself, and I'd pretend to care, but I wasn't as good of an actress as her. She'd see through it, become angry, and we'd be back to the safety of forced silence. So, I was grateful for the quiet, it was far less excruciating, and there was no risk of saying something I'd later regret.

I leaned my head against the window as my mother pulled her Mercedes into the driveway. I was overwhelmed with the need to know why Jack had pushed me away again.

317

My brother's Jeep – my Jeep – sat to the right in front of the studio. It had been washed and polished, and the tires changed and inflated. It was likely the work of Adam, paying penance, trying to make up for his transgressions, but it would take more than a few good deeds to pay for being a homewrecker. He wasn't going to get off that easy.

I unbuckled and reached for the door handle, but my mom spoke first, stopping me.

"Hold on, Rylen," she began, lifting a hand in a halt motion. "Don't run off yet."

I felt myself deflate, and I sighed. Did we have to do this right now?

"Mom, I'm exhausted. I want to go in and crash."

She killed the engine and unbuckled, shifting in her seat to face me. "I understand, but I've been trying to talk to you for days. Can I please have a few minutes of your time?"

Her tone was sharp, and I watched a yellow leaf skitter across the windshield until it fell to the ground. It couldn't avoid the light breeze that had kicked up since we'd left the hospital. Like me. I could no longer avoid her, and even if I ran inside and closed three doors between us, she'd beat them all down until I faced her.

I sighed, my stomach twisting itself into one giant knot. "Okay, what do you want to talk about?" She opened her mouth to speak, but I cut her off. "I don't want to talk about Adam, Mom." Her mouth closed, and her jaw tensed. "Please? It's the one thing I can't handle right now."

She sighed. "Fine. But at some point, we do have to talk about him. It's important."

Jack's words ran through my head. I would never learn the truth if I didn't hear her out, but I was too emotional right now. Too tired and spent to give her the attention she demanded.

"Agreed," I admitted. "But not right now."

318

She sucked her teeth. "Okay, consider it off the table. But there's something else I need to tell you; the DA's office emailed me. The man who robbed the gas station pleaded guilty. The case isn't going to trial."

I blinked at her. "It's not?"

She shook her head. "No, and really dear, it's better this way." She dug out her phone and opened her email.

"Look," she said, showing me her phone. "Hudson Bauer gave up the other men involved for a lighter sentence. He'll be sentenced next week."

Hudson – the name of the man who shot me. I felt the knot in my stomach tighten, then it loosened and pulled again. Like a boat tied to a dock, the rope jerking and tugging every which way as the waves rolled and thrashed beneath it.

It couldn't be the same Hudson.

"W-who else was involved?" I asked.

"I don't know, dear. You'd have to ask the DA. Though, I think it might be better to put this incident behind us and move on with our lives."

"Yeah," I said dully, my eyes dropping to my knee. "Easier said than done."

"Well, I've been thinking about that too." She slid her phone into her purse.

I rolled my eyes, watching as she fiddled with her visor mirror. She checked her lipstick, then grinned big to inspect her teeth for residue. Of course, she'd been thinking of another way to control my life.

"I think it would be good for you to start working at my office part-time. Gainful employment always helps people's mental health, especially after an accident."

I gaped at her, waiting for her to tell me she was joking, but all she did was blink at me, waiting for my reply.

"You're serious?"

"Of course I'm serious. You could answer calls, take messages, and file paperwork. Nothing too difficult, but you can't keep wasting your days flitting around with Jack. I don't care how handsome he is."

"I'm not wasting my days. I…."

"I could really use the help. I'll pay you a decent wage, of course."

"Mom, I don't…"

"Adam got your Jeep running, by the way. But I'll take you to work until you decide to…"

"Mom!" I bellowed, and she jumped at the sound of it. "Will you please just stop?"

She exhaled, her nostrils flaring. "I was only trying to help."

"I don't want your help," I grumbled. "And I don't want to talk about Adam….at all." I turned my head to look out my window, though I knew her retaliation was imminent.

"What the hell is your problem?" she growled. "I thought sleeping with your cowboy would've removed the stick that was permanently shoved up your ass."

I snapped my head towards her. Out of everything she could have said, I hadn't expected her to say that.

"Please," she added, staring me down. "I was nineteen once, too, you know? It was written all over your face when I saw you this afternoon."

I sighed, but there was no sense in denying it. She'd called me out. It was better to admit it than hide from it. "I knew you could tell," I said, not meeting her eyes.

"Were you safe?"

Jack told me he was clean, and I'd popped my birth control that day around noon, so it was close enough.

"Yes," I answered sheepishly.

She considered this and bit her bottom lip before she spoke again, "Are you in love with Jack?" But it sounded more like an accusation than a question.

"I don't know," I muttered, but I did know. "Why are you asking me? You've spent the last three years not asking me about anything. Why start now?"

Maybe it was the stress of the hours before or the exhaustion that laid on top of me like a wet blanket, but the words were out of my mouth before I could think better of it.

Her eyes narrowed, her brow furrowed, and she scoffed.

"Well, that's the biggest load of bullshit I've ever heard," she shot. "Why the hell would you say something like that?"

"Because it's true. You've never asked before," I answered.

"That doesn't mean I didn't care," she countered, raising in volume. "And for the record, I didn't need to ask. I already knew you and Andon were…" She trailed off, and I nodded.

"I figured you knew about that too," I replied, fidgeting with a thread on the end of my sweatshirt.

"Of course, I knew. And I didn't want you to end up like…" but she stopped, exhaling a long breath, shaking her head. "So, I called Juanita and asked her to take you to the clinic for me."

That caught me off guard, and I threw my eyes to her. "You did?"

"How else would my insurance cover your birth control if I didn't authorize it?"

I blinked at her, stupefied by what I was hearing. "Why didn't you say something? Why did you ask Juanita?"

"Believe it or not, Rylen, I actually do give a damn about you. And I thought if I told you something was purple, you'd scream at me that it was blue."

"What the hell is that supposed to mean?" I snapped. "I don't do that. I…"

"You're doing it right now," she said pointedly. There was laughter in her voice, but it was humorless and filled with a crushing irony that blindsided me. "I figured you'd listen to Juanita, okay?" she said, frustration seeping into her words. "You weren't going to listen to me, but you needed to listen to someone, and I figured it would be her."

"Wasn't going to listen to you?" I bellowed, "You didn't even try. Would it have killed you to give me the benefit of the doubt?"

"It wouldn't have made a shit of a difference," she growled, speaking to the steering wheel. "You just would have pushed me away. So, I handled it. I wouldn't let some dumbass boyfriend jeopardize your whole future."

"No, I wouldn't have," I countered, but my voice quivered, and I didn't sound as confident as I wanted to. "I wouldn't have pushed you away, Mom. And I didn't want Juanita. Hell, half the time, I didn't even want Andon." And then I heard myself say, "I wanted you."

Sometimes great truths slip out of you without your permission, and you don't realize it was a great truth until you hear yourself say it aloud, and it echoes in your ears.

Her eyes pooled with unshed tears, and she sniffled. Pulling a tissue from her jacket pocket, she dabbed at them.

"You're impossible," she whispered. "I can't win with you." She blinked, and another round of mascara tears streaked her cheeks. "Because I would like to believe that, but I don't." She paused. Sometime during our conversation I'd started crying too, but I was just now aware of my tears. "I tried to give you the space you needed to mourn your brother's death, and you believe I didn't care. But when I get too close? When I ask for help? Or I ask how you are when Andon gets engaged? You're contemptuous, and you push me away. So, which is it, Rylen? What do you want from me?"

"Mom," I whimpered, but she lifted a hand to stop me.

"That's not even the worst part. The worst part was you believed I didn't care. And you couldn't even imagine a possibility where you were wrong."

She exhaled, a shocked expression on her face as she spoke again. "What sort of a monster does that make me? I know you think I've been a shitty parent, and you'll get no objection from me. I could've done about a million things differently. But I never stopped caring about you, not even for a second, so don't you dare believe otherwise."

She opened her door and planted her heels on the ground. I lunged for her arm, but she slipped away – she'd never been further. I wanted to call for her, but all words froze in my throat as the shock of her last phrases cut through me like sharpened ice.

Despite the streaked mascara and puffy eyes, Diana stood and straightened her suit. She tucked a strand of loose hair behind her ear and instantly returned to her usually poised countenance. Then she leaned down and spoke through the opened door to me.

"I don't think it would have killed you to give me the benefit of the doubt either."

Her gaze traveled to the Jeep, then back to me, telling me more than words could ever articulate.

"Mom," I croaked. "Wait."

But the car door slammed, and I watched her climb the steps and enter the empty house.

Chapter Twenty-Seven

Rylen

Sent Monday 7:34 PM
Rylen: Why the hell would you call my mom?! We need to talk.

Sent 11:17 PM
Rylen: I still haven't heard from you. I saw Cora screaming at you at the hospital. Call me.

Sent Tuesday 2:35 AM
Rylen: I miss you. I can't sleep. I'm getting worried.

Sent 2:54 AM
Buzzzzzzzzzzzzzz
You can text back anytime, you know. The suspense is killer.

Sent 3:03 AM
I want you in my bed even though you snore like a bear in its den. I miss you beside me. I like the way your skin feels against me.

Sent 8:36 AM
Rylen: What the heck, Jack? I had to call the hospital to check on Gran. Why haven't you texted me?

Sent 10:54 AM
Rylen: Jack, come on. Don't do this! I'm not mad anymore. You said if I asked, you'd always come. I'm asking.

Sent 3:36 PM
Rylen: I'm past the point of looking desperate. Please, talk to me. I feel like you're slipping away again. You said you weren't going anywhere. So where are you?

Sent 4:27 PM
Rylen: Don't run away from me. I won't be able to take it.

⁂

Dr. Sullivan sat across from me in her high-back chair, her legs crossed at the knees. She listened intently as I recapped every detail from last week. I started at the beginning, explaining the dress, Andon's engagement, and the fundraiser, which she was pleased to hear I'd attended. I told her about Jack finding me outside, sweeping me away, and kissing me while fireworks exploded over our heads. A small smile tugged at the corners of her mouth like she knew all along Jack would return.

Then I told her about Adam in my kitchen, that he'd spent the night because of the blizzard, and my mom called him sweetie. It made my skin crawl and worse when my dad's email confirmed my suspicions about his absence, but I lacked the courage to ask my mother myself. I told her about Gran's heart attack, the vicious fight I'd had with my mom, and that she'd revealed a few things I never knew.

The last thing I told her was that I'd slept with Jack during the lightning storm, and she nodded as if she expected that, too.

"I don't know what to do," I said, adjusting my weight on her shiny green leather sofa. It reminded me of a giant raincoat with big brass buttons. "Jack won't answer my texts or my calls. I had to call the hospital to check on Gran. I'm afraid he will run again, but this time he won't come back."

"What makes you say that?" she asked, tapping the pen on the notepad in her lap.

"Something Ned said, and I've witnessed it myself. He'll have these freakouts and run away. He did it to me right after I met The Captain." I stared at my hand and fidgeted with the bracelet on my wrist. "I really thought we were past all that."

"Did Ned say why?"

I sighed, shrugging. "He said fear. But he was talking about when Jack was a kid, but…"

"But we see the same behavior patterns now," she finished.

I nodded, pursing my lips. "That's what I'm worried about."

She clicked her pen and jotted notes in loopy handwriting on the pad in front of her. "I can see why that would worry you, especially since your relationship has become more intimate."

"I don't understand why he can't just face whatever it is that's bugging him. I can't do this back and forth. It's exhausting."

"I don't think Jack pushed you away because he didn't want you," she said reassuringly. She pushed her glasses higher on her nose and cleared her throat. "My guess is, Jack pushed you away because he was afraid of something."

"I know he was upset about Gran, but it hurt like hell," I said.

"Maybe more than just Gran's health has got him scared. Fear generally elicits three different reactions from people. It's that flight, fight, or freeze response, and they can be learned behaviors from childhood. Didn't Ned say that Jack's been doing this run and hide and thing since he was a kid?"

I nodded.

"So, Jack's learned response to fear started in childhood. Now in adulthood, when he feels afraid his natural response is to run because it's what he's been doing all his life." She uncrossed her legs and shifted in her chair. "It's kind of like tying your shoes. When you were a kid, you had to learn it. When we learn, we create memory paths so that when we return to tie shoes, we remember how until," she snapped her fingers, "we don't have to think about it. It becomes automatic."

The last time I tried to drive flashed through my mind. I'd peed myself, then threw up, plastering the steering console in vomit. I'd cried hysterically because I couldn't make my hands stop shaking. And every time I tried to drive, it happened again, paralyzing all future attempts.

"Does it work that way with trauma, too?" I asked.

"It does. Trauma *blazes* brain pathways, so instead of learning something over time with practice, it's forced, and the brain is taken to places it doesn't want to go. So, when we have an experience, a time of day, a smell, our brains go back to the memory and the feelings associated with it, regardless of whether it's good or bad."

"That happens to me," I admitted, staring at the orange and blue whirly patterns on the carpeting. "When I try to drive, I panic. I feel powerless to stop it." My hands began to shake, my breaths escaping me in small puffs. "I'm afraid I might kill someone else."

"Take a deep breath, Rylen."

I did as she asked, inflating my lungs to fullest capacity.

"Good, now do it again," she said soothingly.

I exhaled and I felt my heart rate settling. I felt the carpet beneath my shoes. "I want to drive again. I *need* to go to Jack and help him, but I can't stop the fear."

"It's not about stopping the fear. It's about working through it and creating an alternate path."

"How do I do that?" I asked. "Not just for myself, but for Jack, too?"

She exhaled, her lips puffing up while she released air. "Well, the only person that can help Jack is himself, but we could work on creating new brain patterns, working through your feelings, so that your response to getting behind the wheel is different. It will take some time, but we can get there."

"What about Jack? I don't want him to run away from me anymore."

She thought for a moment, and I could see the wheels of her mind turning. "I suppose you could try and discover what it is that's making him afraid. Maybe it is just Gran, and maybe there's more. I'm not saying that will change his behavior, but it might help you better understand things."

I exhaled. "I think he's hiding something. He tried to tell me something at the hospital, but my mom showed up, and he made me go with her."

Her brows rose. "That was bold of him."

"Now he's ghosting me again which makes me more suspicious."

"And if he is? Where does that leave you?" she asked.

My stomach churned like I'd ingested sour milk; I needed honesty the way I needed oxygen, if he'd lied…it'd be over.

"I can't bear to think that way about him," I admitted.

She nodded, taking off her glasses. "Understandable, but I think the only way to remove all doubt is to speak to a reputable source. Who's going to tell you what you want to know?"

I sighed. "Jack won't tell me anything."

"I wasn't suggesting, Jack."

I cut my eyes to her as if the idea of speaking to someone else would break some unspoken rule.

But Dr. Sullivan's eyes assured me it wouldn't.

I deserved to know the truth, and maybe the person who entered my mind would feel a sense of loyalty to her grandson and not tell me anything at all. But asking Gran face-to-face was worth a shot, and I couldn't wait any longer.

ᨵᨶᨾ ᨵᨶᨾ ᨵᨶᨾ

I'd walked to therapy that afternoon and planned to walk home. But when I opened the door to the parking lot, the last person I expected to see was Scott. He sat in his police cruiser, the engine running, the passenger window down. He watched me as I approached his vehicle. It had started snowing, and a light sprinkling of flakes dusted the ground and melted against the hood of his car.

"Need a lift?" he asked, as I leaned into the window.

"I'd rather walk."

"It's snowing. Get in."

He wore his deputy uniform. He'd showed up to give me a ride while he was on duty.

I sighed, reached for the door handle, and plopped into the front seat. The heater was warm, and my jacket was thin, so I'd made the right choice.

"Thanks," I murmured as he pulled onto the highway.

He nodded to me and adjusted the radio's volume, clearing his throat before speaking.

"Have you heard from Jack?" he asked.

"Nope."

I hoped this was something we shared, and I wouldn't feel Jack's silence was only directed at me.

"He texted me and asked me to pick you up. He's been at the hospital every day."

So, Jack could text Scott, but it was too difficult to send me a two-second text? Way to twist the knife, Jack.

"This thing with Gran's really got him worried."

"I've noticed," I said, digging my phone out of my pocket.

There was still no reply from Jack, and disappointment filled every cell within me.

Where was he?

I ran my thumb over the home screen. I'd taken the picture of Jack standing next to Maverick in the corral. I'd asked him to pose next to the stallion, but I'd wanted the photo to seem candid.

But the cowboy on my screen was perfect. His hat was black, his jeans were fitted, his boots were caked in mud, and his shirt was partially unbuttoned, exposing the V of his chest and the gold chain on his neck. His eyes were steel blue, and his hair was the color of nightfall, slightly curling around his ears and above his collar. His jaw was squared and coated in dark whiskers that filled the space above his upper lip, wrapped around his mouth, and met the hairs on his cheeks and chin.

He was my Jack – the one who rescued me from myself.

The simple act of staring at his photo took my breath away. I couldn't bear the thought of losing him again.

"Just be patient with him," Scott said, as my screen went black.

"I'm running out of patience," I said coolly.

The light turned red, and he slowed the cruiser to a stop.

"Look, Rylen, I know I'm not your favorite person, but there are a few things you need to realize about Jack."

"Like what?"

Scott hesitated, seeming to debate whether to finish what he'd started. He drummed his hands on the steering wheel, and then I heard him take in a breath before he spoke.

"If you tell Jack I told you this, I'll lie like a dog."

A chuckle bubbled in my throat, but I nodded.

"Did Jack ever tell you about Frank?" he asked.

Frank – Jack's father – the one he'd spoken of during Slugger Therapy. The person he'd called a drunk bastard and who'd abandoned his family when Jack was a kid.

"A bit. Why?"

"Well, Jack didn't tell you the whole story."

I started to fear that Jack never told me the whole story about anything. The light turned green, and Scott stepped on the gas.

"Okay. Let's just say there are bad fathers, and then there's Frank Wylder. After his wife died, Frank became the most condescending, nastiest son-of-a-bitch you ever met. He'd drink until he'd black out, then wake up covered in piss and vomit."

This wasn't going to be a good story, and my stomach started to flip-flop like the car was being tossed in the ocean, and the relentless ping-ponging had me nauseated.

"Frank and my dad were brothers-in-law. My dad was Chief of Police. When Jack was seven, Frank was tryin' to teach him how to milk a cow. Well, Frank had had a couple, and Jack missed the pail, and Frank gave him a black eye. Jack said he was sorry, but it didn't matter; Frank made him earn his forgiveness."

"How?" I asked, but I regretted the question.

Scott swallowed, and I saw the lump move down his throat.

"He stripped Jack naked and threw him in the barn with the cows. Didn't feed him for three days. Jack told me later he drank milk to stay alive."

"Oh my God," I cried, burying my face in my hands. "That's terrible."

"Frank could be a sick son-of-a-bitch. But not always, though. Something snapped in him when his wife died, and he turned into a mean, drunken bastard. He was always torturing Jack. Always telling him he'd never amount to anything. Making him pay, making him earn his forgiveness, and Jack just stood there and took it. He told me later he was trying to keep Frank off of Cora. Tryin' to protect her."

He signaled to turn left, the steady click of the blinker filling the silence between us. I remembered how Jack described Frank, but he'd downplayed it.

This was so much worse.

"One day," Scott continued. "I rode my bike to his house to see if Jack wanted to ride to the river. Jack had made some mistake, so Frank had tied his wrists together and made him run behind the pickup. But Jack stumbled, and Frank dragged him behind that fuckin' truck for miles."

"How did he end up at Gran's?" I asked, my voice wavering under the threat of tears.

"I rode back to my house and got my dad. He arrested Frank, and Jack was taken to the hospital. His ribs were broken, and Gran told Frank she was taking Jack to live with her, and if he ever harmed a hair on Jack's head again, she'd kill him."

The thought gave me goosebumps, but I had no doubt that Gran would've done exactly as she said and gotten away with it, too.

"Frank went to jail. When he got let out, he was never heard from again."

"Why are you telling me this?" I asked as Scott pulled into my driveway.

"Because it doesn't matter how many ways you explain to Jack something's not his fault, he'll always believe otherwise. The best thing you can do is be patient."

"I have been patient, but I need honesty, Scott," I reiterated. "There's something he's not telling me, and I can't be lied to."

"I'm not telling you all this because it excuses him. I told Jack to…" he trailed off, letting out a puff of air before starting again. "He's a stubborn ass. He's that scared little boy again, and he doesn't know what to do. But Jack will tell you. Just give him time."

I stood in the driveway and waved as Scott drove away. To my surprise, my mother's Mercedes was parked in the driveway in front of the garage. I didn't expect she'd be home. Since our fight, we'd effectively been avoiding each other.

I felt helpless. I wanted to say something, and 'I'm sorry' wasn't good enough, so I said nothing. I also feared we'd fight again, and more things would come to the surface, and we'd drown in them, the hurt holding us under. So, I hoped that she would find me and break the ice between us, and everything under the surface would disappear. She was better at finding the words when all I could do was stare at her car and wish for the bravery I didn't possess.

I pulled out my phone to see if there was a reply.

Still silence.

I couldn't take much more.

I pocketed the phone and looked up at the sky. I watched as peaceful, silent snowflakes fell from the clouds, dusting the top of my head. I wondered if somewhere nearby, Jack was looking at them too.

Chapter Twenty-Eight

Rylen

I tried to sleep in the studio that night, but my conversation with Scott had sent my mind reeling. Scott's words echoed in my ears, and I twisted in the blankets until I drowned in a whirlpool of knotted, sweaty sheets.

The clock on the nightstand said 2:26 a.m., and I was wide awake. I sat up and switched on the lamp. I was tired of fighting it. I grabbed my phone and unlocked the screen.

Still no reply from Jack. My heart sank lower, plunging through the floorboards.

Sent 2:28 AM
Rylen: Come back to me. We don't have to talk. Just let me exist in the same space as you.

I waited a few moments, hoping my phone would buzz in reply.

It didn't.

My last threads of hope vanished. Maybe I *was* unwanted?

I was about to switch off the lamp when I thought I heard a dog bark outside. I turned my head and listened, and there it was again. I threw back the blankets and tiptoed downstairs. Flipping on a light, I heard a dog bark outside my door, whining to be let in.

I reached for the handle, slightly cracking it to see a Rottweiler covered in flecks of snow.

"Bam!" I declared, opening the door wider. "What are you doing here, boy?"

I bent to pet him, and he woofed and scurried past me, shaking the snowflakes from his fur. The darkness moved, and a figure in a cowboy hat emerged from the shadows, the snow crunching under his boots, and my breath caught when I saw him. The light behind me shone on him, cascading his long shadow into the crystal snow, and I was frozen in place as the speech I'd rehearsed evaded me.

His lip was swollen and bruised. His nose bled, and his eye was swollen, turning various shades of purple. The open gash over his eyebrow spewed blood, and it had streaked down his cheek.

"Jack," I breathed, watching as he stumbled into the doorway. "What the hell happened?"

He didn't answer, and I closed the door as he peeled off his jacket. He flung it over a nearby chair and plucked the hat from his head. Then he reached for me, molding me against the chill on his clothing, sliding his lips to mine in a firm kiss. I quickly broke away.

"You've been drinking," I stated, mystified. "Did you drive here?" He neither confirmed nor denied my questions, but he didn't have to – he tasted like it. He took my face into his hands and used his thumb to trace my lips and jaw. He moved to my cheeks and the bridge of my nose, delicately touching them. Then, using only his fingertips, he lightly touched the outline of my ears, the bone of my forehead, the creases of my eyebrows, and the soft skin of my eyelids.

"What are you doing?" I asked, reaching for his hands.

"Memorizing you," he murmured.

"You could've called."

"I broke my phone." He kept one arm wrapped around me and dug into his pocket, retrieving what was left of it. "I got angry and threw it. Shattered the screen."

He tossed it on top of his jacket, but it bounced to the floor.

"Jack," I said, breaking his embrace. "You can't keep doing this. I have so many questions. I need you to…"

He stepped forward and closed the space between us, cutting off my words with another kiss. I stiffened, breaking away.

"You can't just kiss me and…"

But he did just that, kissing deeper this time, beckoning my cooperation. I was made a liar right before him as my body began to awaken, and his hands began to wander.

He could indeed just kiss me.

"Your lip?" I managed between bated breaths.

"I don't care," he rasped. "I want you in bed."

I reached up and touched the gash over his eye, then his swollen lip. I kissed him gently, careful not to hurt him. And when I tried to pull away, he held me tighter, leaning into me, his mouth devouring mine. I threw my arms around him, gripping his shirt in my fist like I'd been deprived of oxygen and holding my breath for hours. His tongue tasted like beer and cigarettes, but I could no longer deny him or myself what I desperately wanted.

Never breaking our kiss, he lifted me, grabbing my ass, and I wrapped my legs around his waist as he climbed the stairs to the loft.

He set me on my feet and yanked my T-shirt over my head. I was naked beneath it, and he filled his hands with my breasts, my nipples between two fingers on each hand. He applied gentle pressure, and I hissed in a breath as my head rolled back. He gathered my nipple between his lips while I unbuckled his belt and slid my hand into his boxers. He growled against my flesh, the sound beautiful and barbaric, and my breast fell from his mouth while my hand moved up his length.

Jack tugged down my shorts. I ripped open his shirt. We kept going like that—frantically undressing, clutching, and clawing until nothing separated us. I gripped his shoulders and pulled him over me, landing chest-to-chest in the middle of the bed.

He leaned his weight on his hands, his drunken haze long gone as he lowered his lips to mine. He kissed me the way a man kisses a woman when words can't begin to convey all he intends, and his kiss was so fervent it left me ravished and spellbound.

He clasped my wrists above my head and whispered against my lips. "Don't move, baby. I'm going to make you come."

Then he lowered himself, and his face was between my legs. I gasped as I was sent whirling, seeing a blur of colors, gripping the headboard above me as if my bones had detached, and I was left as drunk and euphoric. And when I couldn't take it any longer, I grabbed him, practically hauling him up by his ears to my lips, and I tasted where his tongue had been.

He rolled us until I was on top of him, and he groaned low in his throat when I took him inside, my breath hitching at the full sensation. He dug his fingers into my sides, moving me back and forth until I took over, pumping my hips. Within seconds, and before I knew it was happening, I was falling out of the sky as an orgasm blazed through me, tearing me apart so fiercely I threw one hand out to the headboard so I wouldn't collapse on top of him. Before I returned to earth, he rolled us again, withdrew himself, and tilted my hips further up.

"I need you, baby," he rasped, hovering over my entrance. "I've never needed anyone the way I need you." He pressed our foreheads together, his eyes glowing with something sensual, and I knew what it meant to be alive—to be loved. "I need to hear you say it. Tell me that you're mine."

"I'm yours," I breathed.

"Swear it!" he pressed, entering me in one fluid movement, and I gasped.

"I swear, baby," I managed. "Only you. Always."

He rewarded me with a boyish grin that touched his ears. And he began moving inside me, pushing, and pulling, forcing himself to love me slowly and dream-like for as long as he could. Until he could no longer hold back, and his thrusts became relentless.

I had that burning need to tell him the truth again – that it was more than needing him, but my brain had disconnected itself, and I no longer possessed the ability to speak. The thought of losing chilled my soul until I shuddered, so I refused to believe that he was guilty of anything or that he'd lied or kept part of the truth from me. He wouldn't do that.

He'd never lie to me.

He was my Jack; we belonged together, and as he emptied his soul into me, every muscle in his body quivered in ecstasy, and his eyes closed while my name fell from his lips – it was all the reassurance I needed.

I was a damn fool for thinking otherwise, even for a moment.

§o℃ঽo§ §o℃ঽo§ §o℃ঽo§

I lay my head on Jack's chest while we watched the snowflakes fall outside my window. We'd made love until neither of us could move, and our bodies demanded sleep. Then, sometime just before dawn, he reached for me again. Now, the clock on the nightstand said it was approaching six, and if I'd slept, I'd only catnapped, waking every hour to see if Jack was still there.

He lay on his back, lazily running one hand through my hair, letting the curls slip through his fingers. There was silence between us, but it wasn't like the morning I'd awakened in his bed, where the quiet was peaceful. This silence demanded to be heard, to be filled with an explanation.

I felt his chest expand under my cheek, and I thought he'd break the silence and tell me what happened to him, but he didn't. I wanted to believe that the sex would fix what was wrong between us, and we'd have an unspoken agreement that everything before now would never be spoken of again, and we'd go back to being us. Yet now that it was over, I had to push away my compelling need to find answers because it didn't evaporate like I believed it would.

"What happened to your face?" I said softly against his skin.

I had to start somewhere, and that seemed like the least dangerous question to ask.

"I was in a fight," he replied. "I met Scott down at Drake's for a beer."

I looked up at him, doing nothing to conceal my shock.

"You were in a bar fight?"

He nodded, smirking. "Technically, I was outside the bar."

"Why were you fighting?"

"A bunch of guys wanted my lunch money." He laughed at his attempt at humor, but I sat up, switched on the lamp, and faced him.

"Jack, be serious. They kicked your ass."

He sighed. "Yeah, three against one usually turns out that way." He threw back the blankets and bent to pick up his underwear. He pulled them on and reached for his jeans.

His answer wasn't good enough. I needed more.

"Why did they jump you?"

"We were playing darts," he said, buckling his belt. "Some asshole accused me of cheating. Which I wasn't. Drake threw him out. When I went out for a smoke, his asshole pack jumped me."

"Cheating?" I asked, drawing my knees into my chest.

He sat on the edge of the bed and pulled on his socks, his boots on the floor next to him.

"We were taking bets," he answered, stepping into his boot.

I felt the crease between my eyes deepen. "You were gambling?"

"No," he snapped, looking at me over his shoulder. "Just a little friendly wager."

He stood, wearing only boots and jeans, the gold chain around his neck, and I felt my breath catch. I wondered if I possessed the same powers as him – if I kissed him the way he kissed me, could I convince him to stay?

He slipped his shirt on.

"Since when do friendly wagers include getting an ass beating?"

"Look, Rylen," he grumbled, frustration seeping into his words. "I don't have time to talk, okay? It was a wager gone wrong. That's it."

I watched his fingers fasten the snaps on his shirt, and then he unzipped his jeans to tuck in his shirttails.

"We can talk later," he added. "Maybe tonight? Right now, I need to go to the hospital and check on Gran."

I tried not to be wounded by his frankness, but he had shown up on my doorstep and taken me to bed. He'd made himself familiar with my body, and I'd let him. He'd been rough yet soft, wild, and then gentle, and I thought our undeniable connection counted for something. But he was cold and distant again.

"I'll come with you." I tossed back the blankets and got to my feet, but he was already reaching out to stop me.

"No," he said forcefully, resting his hands on my shoulders. "It's better if you stay here. Gran's pretty tired." He pressed a kiss to my forehead like that was supposed to console me, but it only made me feel worse.

Hadn't he said he never wanted to miss me again? Hadn't he made me swear that I belonged to him? And now, he was pushing me away again, putting me in a box to be played with later.

He took a step back, and I reached for my t-shirt on the floor and pulled it over my head.

"Call me?" I asked, flipping my hair out of the collar. "As soon as you get another phone."

"I will," he said reassuringly. "I'm going to pick one up today. Now get some sleep."

"Stay," I said, wrapping my arms around his neck. "Or take me with you."

He beamed at me, the kind of smile that made his eyes twinkle.

"No can do, sweetheart."

He helped me under the blankets and tucked me in like a child ready for bed. He turned out the lamp and kissed my cheek. He was halfway to the stairwell when I spoke again.

"Jack?"

His darkened silhouette turned to face me.

"You know you can tell me anything, right?"

He was quiet for a beat, and I heard my heart pounding in my ears. Did I make him feel like he couldn't be honest?

"Of course I do," he said, a chuckle in his voice. "Now go to sleep, baby."

His boots tapped on the steps as he descended the staircase. He whistled for the dog, who'd made his bed on the shabby couch downstairs. The door opened, the hinges squeaking, and right before the door closed again, I heard Jack say, "Goodbye, Rylen."

Chapter Twenty-Nine

Rylen

I heard Ned's engine rumbling down my street before he pulled into my driveway. I'd waited until the sun was up a little further before I called him that morning, and without hesitation, he arrived in my driveway to pick me up. As I climbed into his rusty pickup, I wondered if the bumper would fall off somewhere along the road.

"I sure appreciate the ride, Ned," I said, buckling my seatbelt.

"I'm happy to help, Miss Rylen. Now, did Jack say where he was going?"

"To the hospital. He said he wanted to check on Gran."

"Okay, we'll go over there and see if we can find him."

"I'm afraid he's going to run away, Ned."

"Yeah, he does that sometimes. But we'll see if we can intercept him."

"Thanks. Where's Pete?" I asked.

"Oh, he said he had to milk the cow. I said he shouldn't talk about his wife that way."

I laughed low in my belly. "You're evil, Nedford Hampton," I chortled.

But all he could do was laugh. "Pete said he would pick up Sally and meet us over there. Sally made Gran a fresh peach pie."

"That was kind of her."

In all my confusion and chaos, I'd forgotten to call Sally and ask how she was doing since the diner had burned down. I shouldn't have been surprised that Sally was being kind to others when she was in the middle of a crisis.

"Come on, ol' Prissy," he said, patting the steering wheel like she was a faithful companion. Ned lifted a booted foot and stomped on the clutch. The gears ground together as he shifted into first. The truck lunged forward with a jolt, my neck snapping. Then the engine backfired, and the truck rumbled onto the highway.

"Sorry, Miss Rylen," he offered, using both hands to wrestle the steering wheel.

I giggled. "It's okay. Everyone should know we're on our way."

His whiskery face broke into a grin. "That's right. Going out with a bang."

Ned rolled onto the freeway, the gears grinding with every shift. The motor rumbled like it was about to take flight, and we'd either be airborne or broken down alongside the road, leaving pieces of ol' Prissy in our wake.

"I need to replace the clutch," Ned said, digging a toothpick from his shirt pocket. He put it in his mouth and went to work on the spaces between his teeth. "First gear's been giving me trouble."

My phone vibrated in my jacket, and I ran my thumb over the screen to find a text from my mom asking where I'd gone.

Disappointment filled every inch of me. Jack likely hadn't gotten a new phone yet, but I'd hoped it was him, setting my mind at ease.

If Diana Clark communicated with me, it was best to be cordial. I texted my mom that I was going to the hospital to visit Jack's Gran and wouldn't be long. She wrote back with a simple OK, and I decided to take it for all it was worth.

"Have you heard from Jack yet?" Ned said.

Yeah, a few hours ago. He showed up drunk on my doorstep. We had hot sex, and then he got distant and weird and promptly left. Thanks for asking.

"Yeah," I answered. "I saw him last night, but he left again."

"He'll come around," he said reassuringly.

The light turned red, Ned stepped on the brake, and the truck came to a squeaky halt.

"Should probably replace those brakes, too." Ned pulled off his cap and ran a hand through his salt-and-pepper hair. "Jack offered last week, and I should've let him, but enough's enough, you know?"

That got my attention, and I threw my eyes to him. "You knew?" I asked, not hiding the astonishment in my voice.

"Of course, I knew! But you know how Jack is – taking the blame upon himself and fixin' things for people. It wasn't his fault, and all that was taken has been paid back in full. He can let it go."

The light turned green, and Ned shifted into first, the gears grumbling as the truck chugged forward.

"So, all along, you knew Jack was helping you because of..."

"Yep, I caught that sneaky summabitch in the act, but I figured he needed it more than me, so I gave it to him. I never liked that kid, but you can't help who people bring around."

"Are you the only one who knows?" I asked.

"Nope. After Jack fixed the fryer a second time, Sally figured it out too."

"What about Pete?" I managed.

346

He sighed. "He was the first to figure it out. He may not be much to look at, but Pete's pretty smart."

I watched as large snowflakes peppered the windshield, trying to make sense of it all. Ned clicked the wipers on, but only the wiper in front of him swished back and forth. The wiper in front of me vibrated against the windshield like a rattlesnake, but didn't otherwise move.

"And what about Cora?"

Ned tapped the steering wheel and let out a long breath. "Cora remains loyal to a fault. But none of us knows why. It was an awful thing that Hudson did, and if I'd known that Jack was going to try to work off Hudson's debt, I'd have done things differently."

I sucked in a sharp breath as my head started to spin. My ears rang as that name clanged in my head like church bells.

"Wait, *who* did you say?"

Ned glanced at me. "Hudson? Hudson Bauer. His family lives off of Silver Maple Road. Went to school with his mama. She'd be so disappointed to see what's become of him."

The sharp sting of betrayal fired within me, but this was worse than Ali and Andon. It was worse than my mother sleeping with Adam. The debt Jack was paying off was for Hudson Bauer. The same man who'd pulled the trigger that fateful evening and destroyed my life.

I felt lightheaded. I was going to pass out. I forced myself to breathe, long and slow, as all the pieces began to fit together. Falling into that mud puddle, and how Jack insisted on giving me a ride home. Drinking milkshakes in the sun while we spent the day in the park. Showing up in front of House of Brew, where I fell into his arms, and he took me to the river. Smashing the windshield on that old Chevy while I revealed my secrets to him.

None of it was a coincidence.

Then he'd stare at me, and I felt like he was holding my heart in his hands, and no matter what I did, I couldn't take it back. He'd already made me willingly give it to him. It all made sense now, why he'd been so quick to help me. So quick to be my friend, to give me gifts, and to come get me at a moment's notice. Why he'd hesitated to kiss me and ran instead. But he'd chosen to return, and kissed me while his hands roamed my skin, and his lips tasted every inch of me.

But it was all part of a greater plan, and every moment I'd spent with him had been a lie. I was no better than a checkmark—another name on a list of people he owed – no more significant than a fryer, a rain gutter, or an ancient truck.

But there'd be no way to fix me.

"I hate to say it, ol' Prissy," Ned said apologetically, patting the dashboard. "But it might be time to say goodbye. I can't afford you anymore." The toothpick fell from his lips into his lap, and he grabbed it, and put it back in his mouth.

His eyes drifted over to me, noticing my silence.

"You okay, honey?" he asked. "You look a little pale."

"Ned," I croaked, "I need to ask you something."

"Sure, honey, anything."

He'd inadvertently filled in the blank spaces in my mind. There was one more thing I needed to verify, though.

Why would Jack pay off Hudson's debt? How were they connected?

"Jack ran an underground poker game. I need to know if Hudson ever played poker for Jack."

Ned rubbed a hand over his whiskery chin as he thought. Then he nodded his head, and something inside of me ached.

"As a matter of fact, I think he did. You'd have to ask Jack to be certain."

My voice cracked, the sting of tears threatening me. "That's why I'm asking you. Jack won't tell me who Hudson is."

Jack did nothing but lie to me.

"Rylen," Ned began, and I turned to meet his eyes. "Hudson's Cora's fiancé."

§၀c~ɔ၀§   §၀c~ɔ၀§   §၀c~ɔ၀§

I felt numb as I walked into the hospital foyer. My numbness turned into nausea, and a tear spilled down my cheek. I quickly wiped it away, refusing to cry. As I approached the information desk, there was a voice behind me.

"Hello, Rylen."

I turned to see Sally holding a fresh peach pie in her hands.

"Sally," I breathed, collecting myself. "What are – what are you doing here?"

Hopefully my makeup hadn't smeared.

"Came to visit Margaret, just like you. I brought her a pie."

She held up the pastry. The top of it was golden brown, with perfectly pinched edges, and it smelled sweet and fruity.

"That's nice of you," I managed, but Sally gave me a look that said she could sense my distress.

"Are you okay, dear?"

I only found out my boyfriend is a liar, and his relationship with me was so he could assuage his guilt.

"I–I don't know what I am right now."

I needed to distract her with a different topic. The moment she brought up Jack, I'd crumble into a puddle of tears.

"I'm so sorry about the diner," I blurted. "I meant to call you last week."

"Oh, that's very sweet, dear." She patted my shoulder. "But don't you worry about that, okay? Everything's going to be alright."

"I feel badly," I told her. "That place was your mother's."

She nodded somberly. "Yes, it was, and Lord knows she'd be devastated." She set her pie on a small table next to a stack of magazines. Then she took my hand in both hers, "But you know what, I'm grateful it wasn't worse. Bill had just closed up the place when he smelled smoke. He got out just in time."

"Bill was inside?" I asked, astonished.

"He sure was. He said the smoke was coming from the restrooms. When he went to investigate, the flames were so big there was nothing he could do but let it burn."

"You mean it wasn't the fryer?" I tried to hide the delight in my voice.

"The fryer? Oh goodness, no. The fire marshal said lightning struck the roof above the bathrooms."

Another tear slipped out, and I tried to wipe it away before she noticed, but she pulled me into a hug, and I'd lost the ability to do anything but let her hold me.

"Oh, sweetie. It's going to be alright," she murmured, and I rested my cheek on her shoulder. "It's just a building. I'd have been beside myself if I'd lost Bill. We'll rebuild soon."

I pulled back to look at her, using my sleeve to wipe my eyes.

"I thought you couldn't? I thought it wasn't insured."

She chuckled. "Well, I overheard Jack and Bill discussing that. I told Bill that he'll be looking for a new wife if he touches that insurance. It was a good thing, too. It's going to be cheaper to rebuild than it would've been to remodel."

She took my face into her hands, gazing into my eyes, and I felt another round of tears forming. "And just so you know, even if it were the fryer, I never would've blamed Jack."

I sniffled, "Jack blames himself."

"I know he does."

She hugged me tighter as I cried, but my tears weren't only for the diner, but also for me, and all I'd discovered in the last few hours. Maybe I was a fool for believing there was still a chance for Jack to explain himself, but I wanted to hear the whole truth from him. I prayed there was some misunderstanding.

The ding of an elevator drew my eyes to nurses running through the lobby. It was Sheila and Renee – The Captain's nurses – and two others I'd never seen, briskly running through the foyer and out the main entrance. Scott followed them with two hospital security guards a few steps behind him.

"Come on," Sally said. "Let's see what's going on."

We followed them outside, and when the doors opened and I walked under the awning in front of the loading area all I heard was shouting.

"Take your hands off me! I have a right to see my son!" Cora stood in front of the hospital entrance, her body sluggish.

Scott stood behind her, trying to restrain her from entering the building, but she smacked his hands away.

"Don't touch me!" she snarled.

Jack stood in front of her, his back to us, blocking her path to the doors. He hadn't noticed that Sally and I were right behind him.

Parked in front of us was his Bronco, but the door was open, and Gran sat in the front seat, an oxygen mask covering her nose and mouth. Pete stood next to the hood watching as the scene unfolded before us. It looked as if Jack had been in the middle of taking Gran home and had to stop because of Cora's commotion.

Sheila and her nurses stood a few paces behind Scott. All of us were circled around Cora, our eyes glued to her like she was a gladiator in an arena.

"Move!" Cora spat again, bringing her eyes to Jack's. "I haven't signed anything that says the baby's not mine. So, get the fuck out of my way!"

351

"You're not going near him," Jack snapped. "Not until you're sober."

My eyes darted to Sheila, to Cora, and then to Jack.

She was demanding to see a baby?

"The Captain!" I said, speaking to Cora, "He's your son?"

Jack spun on his heels, facing me. His face was a mixture of surprise and worry. He hadn't expected that I'd take matters into my own hands and show up unannounced.

Cora's face broke into a smile, and she cackled wickedly.

"Well, well, look who's here," she crooned.

"Rylen," Jack croaked, reaching for my hand. "You shouldn't be here."

But my brow furrowed, and I backed away.

"Let her stay, Jack," Cora snapped. "She deserves to know the truth. To answer your question, yes, The Captain is my son. Although, I think we can dispense with the cute nickname. Now move!"

Sheila stepped forward. "Hospital rules, Cora. You can't go in if you're intoxicated."

"Fuck your rules, Sheila!" she spat. Her movements were jerky as she turned to face the nurses. "You're just punishing me because your son is in jail, and you think it's my fault." She lifted a finger and pointed it at Jack. "Well, he's the one you should crucify."

She spun around, tears spilling from her eyes, and spoke to Jack as more people gathered to see the commotion.

"Tell her, brother. Tell everyone here how it was your fault Hudson robbed the gas station. How you threatened him, then he took the fall, and you got off scot-free."

I sucked in a sharp breath.

"What's this?" Cora chuckled, hearing the sound that had escaped me. "Looks like my twin *didn't* tell the truth?"

Twins? They were twins?

"Jack?" I croaked.

I wanted him to deny it, but he kept his eyes on Cora, and all reasoning with her had vaporized.

"Shut the hell up, Cora," he snapped.

"What, are you too chicken shit to tell the truth, Jack?" Cora snarled, then she turned and spoke to the crowd. "He's got you all fucking fooled. Especially you." She nodded towards me, her words drenched in disgust. "You all think he's a saint, fixin' shit, driving you around, putting himself in your good graces. But what he did was unforgivable."

"I didn't know Hudson was going to…" Jack cut in.

"Carry out your plan?" Cora finished. "Because the robbery was your idea. You put it in his head, then you bailed, and you ran like the scared little coward I always knew you were."

I'd heard her words, but for a split second, my brain refused to comprehend.

The robbery was Jack's idea? I turned to meet his eyes, and he held my gaze for a heartbeat before dropping his eyes to the pavement. He hadn't denied it, and my heart sank and drowned within me.

Deny it. Please, deny it. Call her a liar. Anything. But don't just stand there!

Cora wiped her nose with her hand. "You may not think you did anything illegal," she paused, and more tears spilled. "But what you did was wrong, and you're guilty as hell."

"I can't change what happened, Cora," Jack said evenly. "And nobody will be more sorry than me, but what the hell else do you want from me?"

"I want Hudson!" she screamed, slamming her fists into Jack's chest. "I fucking hate you! Hudson got sentenced to ten years! He will never meet his baby outside of prison, and I will spend the rest of my days hating you."

353

She collapsed into him, and Jack put his arms out to catch her, but she slid to his feet. She knelt and pounded the ground, her fist imprinting into the snowy earth. Her shoulders shook as she wept. Releasing sobs so wretched and tragic, her soul opened and shattered before us.

Sheila was the first to move, and she walked up behind her and put a hand on Cora's shoulder.

"Get the wheelchair, Rene. Jamie, call Dr. Grayson. We're going to take her to the ER." Then, to the crowd gathered, Sheila spoke in a voice edged with authority. "All of you, go about your business."

The nurses moved quickly, gathering Cora into the chair and wheeling her inside.

The crowd slowly dispersed; Pete and Sally announced they were leaving. Scott helped Gran into his police cruiser, saying her would take her home. Ned said he would wait for me in the truck if I wanted, and I nodded.

Then Jack and I were alone, staring at each other like neither of us had seen another human. He opened his mouth to speak, but I shook my head. The damage was already done, and there was nothing he could say to change it.

"The comic books in your bedroom. They belong to Hudson."

It was a statement rather than a question, but he nodded slowly.

"And the Captain? He's your nephew?"

"Yes," he answered. "She worked the late shift at a bar. Holding him was the least I could do."

"Did you owe her money? Or was that a lie too?"

"It was a gift. I was trying to help her."

My stomach twisted into itself. Cora was out of her mind, drunk and hysterical, and still he admitted it. So much for plausible deniability.

"So, everything Cora said is true, then?" I breathed, biting my underlip.

"Most of it," he said, keeping his voice even.

"You know what?" I growled. "It doesn't matter."

"Yes, it does," he shot. "When I confronted Hudson, I was pissed as hell. He kept making excuses and blaming other people. I told him I didn't care if he robbed a gas station, he was going to repay what he'd taken from my friends. And if he didn't, I'd tell Cora he was cheating on her." He took off his hat and raked his fingers through his hair. "I was drunk. I didn't think he'd take me seriously."

I crossed my arms. "And I suppose you think that clears your name?"

He shook his head. "I never said that, Rylen. Cora holds me responsible, and I only halfway disagree with her. If I hadn't threatened Hudson, maybe..." he trailed off. "I was a different person then."

I exhaled, fighting the sting of tears. I refused to cry again.

"That's no excuse, Jack. Why didn't you tell me the whole story if you weren't guilty? Why ghost me and then show up on my doorstep? Were you going to run?"

"No." He stepped forward like he wanted to touch me, but my eyes narrowed, and he stopped. "That's not why I was there."

"So, what was last night then? If it wasn't some sort of fucked up goodbye."

"Cora was going to tell you. She'd been threatening me for days. Then she saw you leaving the hospital, and it was only a matter of time."

"So, you showed up for one more romp in the sheets before the gig was up?"

I turned my back on him, briskly walking along the sidewalk, but he ran after me, stepping in my path.

"Rylen, listen to me!" he begged, gripping my shoulders.

"Don't touch me!" I snarled, pushing him away, and he dropped his arms.

"Listen!" he said between gritted teeth. "I came there to tell you the truth before she could." He shrugged, "Then when I got there…" he paused, and my mind filled in the banks.

He'd made love to me, but that wasn't the truth. The truth was he'd manipulated me. He'd used it as a ploy to avoid telling me the whole story.

I watched his throat bob and his bottom lip quivered. "I couldn't do it."

"You were different," I said, my lips trembling. "You weren't *my* Jack."

"I know. I couldn't bear the thought of you hating me too."

I was helpless to stop the stream of tears dripping off the edges of my jaw, and another round spilled in their wake.

"Anything would have been better than this," I said weakly.

"I'm sorry," he offered. "I was afraid to tell you that…"

"That I'm no different than Pete or Sally," I cut in. "That you felt *obligated* to spend time with me."

His eyes closed like it was too painful to hear said aloud. "It wasn't like that…"

"Yes, it was, Jack," I said. "I don't think you'd know the truth if it bit you in the ass. When you told me the whole story, you purposely left that you *owed* me too. From the moment you showed up, I was just another name on your list, but you were only with me to make up for what Hudson did."

He sighed. "It started that way, but then it got real. The more time we spent together, I just…" I shook my head, and it silenced him.

356

"That doesn't make it any better, Jack," I stated in a low whisper. "You lied to me."

The anger I'd fought to hold at bay began seeping out of me, and I felt it rising inside like a storm brewing in the darkest clouds. "Then you kept lying to me. Right to my face. And like a damned fool, I believed every word."

I shook my head, reality hitting me like a strike of lightning. This was the end. There'd be no hope for our relationship.

"How am I ever supposed to believe a word you say?" I asked.

"Because," he breathed. "I'm in love with you."

A truck must've rolled by the vibrations rattling my bones, thundering in my soul, but all was quiet. We were alone, and the thundering sound, I realized, had come from within me.

He loved me, and I wanted his words to matter. The way they would've if he'd told me at any moment before now.

"Rylen," he said again, reaching for my hands. "I love you. And I don't know when it started, but it was easy. It's like I've spent my whole life loving you, and I can't remember a day when I didn't. I'm so sorry for everything, but I *need* to know if you love me too."

His words broke me; slashed me into pieces. I did love him back. I had for a while, and I'd been aching to tell him, but it didn't matter. It wasn't that simple. He was no better than Andon – no better than my mother. I'd never be able to trust him again.

I pulled my hands back. "You're trying to manipulate me," I whispered. "Did you think I was going to fall into your arms? You can't use your feelings for me to get what you want."

His brow furrowed, the crease between his eyes deepening.

"Jesus, Rylen." He laughed humorlessly. "I just told you I'm in love with you, and you accuse me of manipulating you." He put his hands on his hips and let out a breath, his nostrils flaring at the force of it. "And you think I'm the one that's fucked up?"

"We're done," I hissed.

"Yeah," he said. "I guess we are. Oh, I'm sorry. Am I manipulating you again?"

"You're an asshole," I spat.

"Yeah, I am, but I'm not your mother, Rylen, or your piece-of-shit ex."

"You're right," I snarled. "You're a liar."

It was a terrible truth. But I had all the evidence I needed, and he had no argument, no other objection to my candid honesty. His mouth closed, and his shoulders lowered like a puppy who'd been backed into a corner and there was no way out.

"You're not who I thought you were, Jack, and I don't know how I possibly confused you with somebody else."

I stepped around him, marching in the direction of Ned's truck.

"Don't come after me," I declared. "It won't work this time."

I was climbing into Miss Prissy before Jack spoke again.

"Don't worry, sweetheart. I wouldn't dream of it."

Chapter Thirty

JACK

When I cracked my eyes open, everything hurt – every part of me felt as if I'd been ripped open like a fish and left for dead. I don't know how I got home, but I vaguely remembered Scott finding me at Drake's. I was only three beers in. He tried to get me to leave, but I wasn't done erasing it all. I started taking shots; I only remember snippets after that.

I lifted my head off the pillow, and that's when I smelled cherry vanilla.

She was everywhere. I hadn't erased anything. I dreamt of Rylen. We were in the park by the river. She wore a yellow sundress, and her dark locks cascaded down her back in a waterfall of curls. I stood behind her, pushing her on the swing. Her flowing curls danced around me, and I breathed her in, feeling alive and renewed.

I reached for her in my sleep, but the place where she belonged was cold and empty. Disappointment filled every cell within me, but it was better this way. Cora was right. No matter what I did, I always screwed up people's lives, and those I loved suffered. It was the side effect of being me. I couldn't fix what I'd broken, and when I tried, it'd blown up in my face. I only had myself to blame, but if I was alone, I could never destroy another life again.

You're an asshole.

The memories came flooding back. I'd drowned them at the bar until they were silent, but now they were back. I threw back the covers and got to my feet.

She was all around me, inside my head and in my dreams. She was twisted in my sheets and tangled in my blankets – on the jacket I'd wrapped her in. She was on my couch and in my shower, the droplets from her body trickling through the cracks in the floorboards. Her shadow had crept over my walls, her naked silhouette projected by the fireplace. Her scent was on my skin; it seeped from my pores. There was no escaping her.

You're a liar.

I lowered to my knees and opened my trunk. Inside was a bottle of whiskey. I pulled the cork off with my teeth and spat it across the room. I took a long drink, knowing all too well the amber liquid would deliver on its promise and drown the memories. It would erase them if only for a few hours, but then I'd do it again. I slammed the bottle down and wiped my mouth on my sleeve.

The small black box got my attention. I'd forgotten I hid her birthday present here. The box stared at me. I lifted it and turned it over in my hands. The hinge creaked as I opened it. I'd had the pendant made. It was round with a red and golden sunset and pink puffy clouds over rolling hills. It hung on a silver chain. It would have been perfect for her.

You're not who I thought you were, Jack.

I snapped the box closed and tossed it in the trunk. I slammed the lid closed and pushed it away. Tipping the bottle back, I took another long drink and got to my feet.

REDEMPTION'S LIST

This ends now.

I ripped the sheets from the bed, tearing them down the middle and wadding them into a ball; I opened the window and threw them outside. I gathered the blankets, the pillows still wearing their cases, and threw them on top of the sheets. The clothing was next; I went to my drawers and dug out the sweats and the t-shirt she wore; any shirt of mine that smelled like cherry vanilla went out the window. I threw out the jacket, the towels, the couch cushions, the shower curtain – anything that had a trace of her would disappear.

I don't know how I possibly confused you with someone else.

I took another gulp, whiskey dripping down my chin, and went downstairs to erase it once and for all. Outside, I stacked the pile in the middle of the corral with the rest of the horse shit. I dumped the Whiskey, soaking it yet saving a few drinks for myself, and then I lit a match. The wind bent the flame like fate, asking me if I wanted to go through with it.

And with a flick of the wrist, the flames engulfed her.

Don't come after me. It won't work this time.

I took another drink, wishing the memories would vanish as fast, but the night was still young. I had another bottle somewhere. I'd drown her out until I couldn't remember her name. A smile pulled at the corner of my lips as I watched the fire swirl a few feet above me. She would no longer haunt my dreams or have any place in the web of my mind. I'd no longer feel like I was dying of internal bleeding or wish the pressure in my chest would implode and my heart would suddenly stop.

All traces of her would disappear; I'd see to it. Then I'd pack up and leave and that would be the end. We'd close the chapter, and I'd be remembered as the one who screwed up her life because that was all I was good at. I would forever be a fuck-up – just like Frank.

I'd always ruin what I touched.

361

I swallowed the last mouthful and then threw the bottle into the fire. The glass shattered as the flames danced higher.

Don't worry, sweetheart. I wouldn't dream of it.

Chapter Thirty-One

Rylen

Dr. Sullivan sat in her high-back chair facing me. Her legs were crossed at the knee, and a notebook was open on her lap, but she hadn't written anything down. She only listened as I spoke. I filled her in on everything I'd been through, everything that had happened days earlier at the hospital, and Sullivan hadn't said anything. She nodded when appropriate and gave me ample time to collect my thoughts between bouts of tears.

"I'm sorry for calling you on your day off." I sniffled, using my sleeve to wipe my face. She wore jeans today and a purple and gold sweatshirt with VIKINGS across the front.

"Don't be," she said gently. "I'm glad you called."

It was Saturday. She wore no makeup, and her hair was pulled into a bun on the back of her head. When I called her crying, she asked if I wanted to meet. Ned gave me a ride to her office.

She passed me the tissues from the table next to her. I took the whole box, pulling one to wipe my face.

"You've been through hell," she added. "Nobody can go through that alone."

"Am I crazy for feeling this way? Am I being ridiculous?"

"No, but that doesn't matter. It doesn't make the feelings any less valid."

I sniffled. Maybe I hadn't lost my mind.

"If I found out someone only wanted to be my friend because of ulterior motives, I'd be hurt too."

"So, I'm not crazy?" I laughed, but there was no trace of humor.

"No," she answered reassuringly. "Not in the least bit."

"It was real for me," I whispered, and she nodded, unsurprised. "I don't know what to call it, but my feelings were real."

I would have called it love at one point, but I wasn't sure anymore and didn't dare say it aloud. It was too painful, and I feared if I released the words into the air between us, it might just be true, and I'd end up at her feet a sobbing, hyperventilating mess.

She inhaled and uncrossed her legs. "Let me ask you this: when you were with Jack, how did it make you feel?"

"Good," I answered.

She eyed me over her glasses. "Only good? You spent all that time with him, and good is the best you can do?"

"Great," I admitted.

"Better."

"Fantastic. Amazing. Super-duper." I gave her two thumbs up.

She chuckled. "Okay. My point is that friendships are built when two people stand together to gain something from the relationship. You chose to be with Jack because of how he made you feel. He was your friend when you didn't have any. And in the same way, Jack chose to be with you because it alleviated his guilt."

"But I wasn't trying to make up for something," I said pointedly. "He never wanted to be with me. He did it because he had to."

"No, you didn't befriend him because you owed it to him, but you did befriend him because you needed him. See, human's base behaviors on rewards. When Jack was with you, he was rewarded with feeling less guilty and with the pleasure of your company. One ride, one good deed would've been plenty, but he continued because he wanted to. It's flattering, really."

"I never thought of it that way before," I admitted, staring at the carpet.

"And likewise, for you," she continued. "You were rewarded with his time, his friendship. At its core, your motivations for being together were not so different from each other."

My mind drifted back to the first time Jack showed up unannounced at my doorstep. From that day on, I'd had everything to gain. I'd lost count of how often he'd bought me dinner, brought me coffee, and shared his candy. How many rides had he given me to therapy? How many ice creams did we share with disgusting cold M&Ms? How many nights did I walk into my house in the hours beyond midnight?

In the months I'd known him, Jack had been the best friend I'd ever had, yet it had still been for the wrong reasons and knowing that stung like vinegar on an open wound.

"Please, don't defend him. I can't take it."

"I'm not defending him," she said gently, shaking her head. "I apologize if it sounds that way. I'm *explaining* his behavior, and there is no defense for lying. Not in my book."

JEANA R LAWRENCE

I wiped my face again and blew my nose. All I had done in the past three days was cry. I didn't know the human body could produce so many tears.

Sullivan shifted in her chair, the wood creaking under her weight.

"Tell me this. Was Jack a punctual person?" she asked.

"Yes. Freakishly so."

"Was he reliable? Did he show if he said he was going to be somewhere?"

"Yes," I said again. "I could always count on him."

She lifted a brow. "Except when?"

I thought for a moment. "Well, after we saw the Captain, he freaked and wouldn't talk to me."

"And," Sullivan said, "There was one more."

"Gran's heart attack," I replied, the answer glaringly obvious. "He did the same thing."

She nodded. "Right, now what do those things have in common?"

"That's too much thinking, Doc."

She chuckled, "Okay, both of those instances are when Jack felt out of control. He couldn't help how he felt about you. So, he left you on the porch and ran. Gran had a heart attack, so he ghosted you for days. Jack is a calculated person. He doesn't respond well to feeling out of control."

Flashes of Jack showing up at the studio flooded my mind. He'd been drinking after he'd sworn sobriety. Slipping back into old habits had been a reaction to stress, only I didn't recognize it then.

Then there was the sex. Jack was a selfless lover, the kind that women dreamed about. I'd wanted him fiercely, but something was unmistakably wrong that night.

I should've stopped him. We should have talked things through, but if I dug deep, maybe a piece of me didn't want to know,

366

and it was easier to avoid the heartache. I couldn't say I didn't equally share the blame because I'd wanted him as badly.

Sullivan's voice snapped me back. "Knee-jerk reactions are learned behaviors. It seems to take him a bit before he finds his bearings."

I closed my eyes. Scott's story. Jack's dad.

A lot more things make sense now.

"His dad," I began, opening my eyes. "He was a mean son-of-a-bitch."

She nodded, "That doesn't surprise me."

"What about the lying?" I swallowed the lump in my throat. I was going to cry again. "He lied to me so that he could maintain control. He had to have known I'd eventually find out."

She pushed up her glasses, slightly shaking her head. "I can't answer for him, but I'd assume what started as a way to make amends to you without you knowing became something more, and he panicked."

I blinked, and fresh tears spilled.

She gave me a sympathetic smile. "Has he tried contacting you?"

I shook my head. "No, I wouldn't answer anyway."

"It may be good to take a few days to gather your thoughts."

More tears spilled, and I sniffled, wiping them away with a soft tissue. "He told me he was in love with me," I said. "We were arguing, and he just blurted it out."

"And what did you say?"

"That he was just saying that to manipulate me. That's all he's done this whole time. Why should this be any different?"

She eyed me over her glasses again. "Do you really believe that?"

"I don't know what to believe," I snapped. "How am I supposed to trust anything that comes out of his mouth? How am I supposed to forgive him."

She shrugged. "Actions have consequences. You can forgive him without giving him another chance."

"Forgive him?" I scoffed. "How? How am I supposed to forgive him after everything he's done? After he lied right to my face?"

"Forgiveness isn't solely based on feelings, Rylen. It's a conscious choice. And once you forgive someone, that doesn't mean it'll take all the pain away. Only time can do that."

I crossed my arms and straightened my back. "It's not that easy. I can't make myself forgive him; even if I could, he doesn't deserve it."

"But forgiveness isn't based on a scale of how terrible somebody treated us or how awful they behaved. It's not a judgment that's passed. Nobody deserves to be forgiven, Rylen, but everybody needs it. Forgiveness is based on love."

I sighed, pushing away the aching possibility that I was still in love with Jack. Did she have to bring up the one feeling I was avoiding?

She crossed her legs and set the notebook and pen on the coffee table between us.

"Maybe I can explain it to you this way, and then we have to close for the day. But you can call me early next week if you need to."

"Okay," I murmured. "Thank you."

She smiled. "Sure. Now bear with me for a moment; I promise it will all make sense, but can you choose to be hungry?"

I looked at her blankly. "No."

She nodded. "But you could eat anyway, right?"

"Yes."

"Can you choose to be tired?"

"No."

"But you could go to bed anyway, right?"

"Right," I agreed.

"Can you choose to love someone even when they're unlovable? Even when things about them are imperfect? Even when they break your soul and give you every reason to walk away from them?"

My lips quivered, and my voice disintegrated in my throat. She'd oversimplified it, but it made perfect sense. There were feelings and choices, and we always had the power to choose in spite of what we felt.

She nodded again, realizing I was too emotional to form words, and she pushed her glasses up on her nose.

"Now, I think you understand."

Chapter Thirty-Two

Rylen

Hey Kiddo,

Sorry I missed Thanksgiving. I'm in London, and I couldn't get away. I'm buried in projects from now until the end of the year. I'll video call you on your birthday, but if I miss it, know I'm thinking of ya.

The time change is a real bitch. You should come and spend Christmas with me. I'm heading to Cancun for some much-needed R and R. Something tells me you could use it, too.

You and I should spend some time together. There are a few things we should discuss in person. Let me know, and I'll buy you a ticket.

Love you,
-Dad

He never called me on my birthday. I got a text message at 11:55 that night, and he said, "Happy B-day." I wrote back immediately and asked him to video chat, but he didn't respond, and I fell asleep. I grabbed my phone in the morning to check for a reply, but there wasn't one.

Disappointment overwhelmed me. I'd counted on him to make things better. I wanted to hear his voice and see his face when I asked him to come home. I tried to tell him how shitty everything had been and that I was destined to be alone because I would never trust another soul again.

I wanted to tell him about Jack. I'd ask him why forgiveness seemed impossible. Even if I could find the will to forgive Jack, I'd never be able to take him back, not after knowing what he was capable of. Which meant I would wander this earth alone, looking for somebody else like him, yet I'd never find him.

I was tired of relying on everyone else to make me happy and meet my basic needs. I couldn't even rely on my own father. I'd only be let down in the end, and there wasn't much further I could go.

I threw back my blankets and dressed in yoga pants and a sweatshirt. I stomped into my boots and went downstairs. It was snowing when I opened the door, and the brisk morning air awakened me more than coffee to the bloodstream.

I stood in front of the Jeep. Things were going to change and starting right now. It couldn't be that hard. It was just a Jeep, for

God's sake. I stood with my arms crossed and stared at it like I could intimidate it into submission. I didn't have to like it, but Adam did a good job preparing it for the road. The keys dangled from my hand. I'd remembered to plunk them off the peg.

I couldn't remember the last time I'd tried to drive. It was well over a year, and I'd pissed myself and vomited all over the steering wheel. After that, I gave up, and I had Andon, so it didn't matter.

But now it mattered because I had no one.

Maybe I wouldn't react if I only sat in it?

I eased myself into the seat, and closed the door, my heart thumping like war drums.

Breathe. I told myself. Remember what Sullivan said.

I closed my eyes as I gripped the wheel, the cold almost burning my skin, and my stomach turned. Panic surged through me. I opened the door and bolted out, slamming it behind me before I vomited.

Again. Try again. Just breathe.

I got in and gripped the wheel. My stomach churned. I put the key in the ignition. I coughed violently, but there was nothing to vomit. I got out and closed the door.

Keep going. Keep breathing.

I opened the door and sat in the seat. My hands were shaking and sweat dripped down my brow. My chest heaved with deep breaths, and I tried to slow my breathing, but I thought I'd pass out.

I killed the engine and got out. I leaned my hands on my knees as I took in slow breaths through my nose and out my mouth.

I can do this. I'll never allow myself to need anyone again.

I sat in the seat again, started the engine, and turned on the wipers. Then I closed my eyes and waited, focusing on slow breaths. My hands were clammy. They shook as I turned on the radio. It was an opera. I hated opera, but I didn't bother to change it because I couldn't stop shaking. I gripped the wheel tighter until my knuckles were white. Victory was close, but a wave of nausea rocked me, and I opened the door. I got out and covered the snow again in puke.

The sound of someone clearing their throat caught my attention, and I looked up to see my mother watching me. I hadn't heard her pull up, but she'd been watching me for some time.

Her gym bag was slung over one shoulder, and she wore yoga pants with Nikes. She'd been to the gym and back already, and it was barely six. She eyed me quizzically. I supposed it was a sight – the Jeep running, the wipers swooshing, the opera wailing, and the daughter puking. I bet it seemed like I'd lost my mind, and I was inclined to agree with her.

"Are you okay?" she asked carefully.

"Yeah," I croaked, coughing again. I used my sleeve to wipe my mouth.

"What, exactly, are you doing?"

I bit my lower lip. "Hmm," I started. "Trying to create new brain paths."

My mother nodded stiffly. "Okay." She dug into her bag, pulled out a water bottle, and offered it to me. "Here."

I took it from her. "Thanks." Then I rinsed my mouth and took a long drink. I offered it back to her, but she shook her head.

"Keep it. You might need it again."

"Thanks," I repeated.

Her gaze traveled to the Jeep, then to where I'd retched in the snow, then back to my face.

"Is it working?" she asked.

I sighed, "I don't know yet. This is the first time I've tried it."

"Oh, well. Just keep trying, I suppose."

I nodded. "Dr. Sullivan said I need to create a new brain path that isn't associated with Michael's death." I watched my feet kick at the snow. "Sorry, I'm not explaining it very well."

My mother smiled, seeming pleased I'd given her more than a one-word answer. "I know what you mean," she replied warmly. "Sullivan is good. I was thinking about booking an appointment next week."

"You were?" I gaped at her.

"Yeah," she said gently. "If you don't mind?"

A smile tugged on the edges of my lips. "Not at all."

"Great. Well, I'll let you get back to your brain paths."

She turned to leave, her gym bag swinging with her movements, and I found the words that'd usually be frozen in my throat.

"Mom. Wait."

She pivoted, a surprised look on her face that I'd called out to her.

It wasn't what I'd thought I'd say, yet it was a simple, great truth.

Wait. Don't go.

"Will you stay?" I asked. "And keep me company?"

She arched a brow, considering my request, perhaps perplexed at the oddity of it. Being warm and engaging was new territory, and I didn't want to scare her off.

"I know it's cold, and I'm sure you have better things to do than watch me barf."

That earned me a hearty laugh, and I couldn't remember the last time I heard such a sweet sound bubble out of her.

"Okay," she said, then gestured to her bag. "Let me put this inside."

I watched her climb the steps with the certainty that she'd be back, and I took comfort in knowing she'd be there. Maybe it would only be for a few moments, but I wouldn't have to do this alone, and I realized the lonely ache inside my soul didn't hurt so badly.

§०८⌒ঙ০§ §০८⌒ঙ০§ §০८⌒ঙ০§

My mom stood outside for an hour while I got in and out of the Jeep. Occasionally, she'd clap if I managed to stay inside it long enough to put it in gear and inch it forward. Other times, when I'd throw open the door to dry heave, she'd rub my back while I was hunched over. Finally, she suggested hot cocoa and a shower which I quickly agreed to.

I showered in the studio, and after I dressed, I entered the house to find the living room empty. The Christmas tree was in the corner by the fireplace, and boxes looking like squared airplanes with open wings were scattered like a maze on the floor. It was unlike Diana Clark to decorate, especially for Christmas.

For the past three years, Christmas was something we'd celebrated apart. It wasn't something we'd discussed. It happened naturally, the way a married couple turns into roommates. It was Miachael's favorite holiday, and the pain became too great. The stocking with his name embroidered. The Christmas albums he recorded for Mom as a gift. His cocoa mug featuring a Christmas vampire that said, "Merry and Bite." The memories were all too great and locked away in the depths of a box labeled "do not open."

Over time, we fell into a routine. A few weeks before Christmas, she'd disappear to the spa. I would stay with Jaunita until the holiday rush was over. After Andon and I broke up, my dad and I went to the Bahamas. I was expecting it to be the new normal.

"Mom?" I said, but there was no reply. "Mom."

Her abandoned coffee cup sat on the counter in the kitchen – her cocoa now cold.

375

"I'm up here," she said.

I followed her voice up the stairs, taking two at a time, but I was shocked once I got to the top. What was she doing in there? Light spilled into the hallway because the last door on the right was opened, and my mother was sitting on Michael's bed.

"Mom," I said, approaching, "What are you doing in here?"

She looked down at something in her hands, and it took me a minute to realize what it was. Then I saw Michael's dresser drawer was open.

She'd found my hiding spot.

Stacks of sticky notes – assorted colors, each filled with her handwriting overflowed in her palms. Notes she'd written to me and left on the coffee pot on those mornings when she had chosen to greet me. I'd kept them all as tiny tokens of care, some of which I'd read repeatedly because I'd wanted to feel her near.

She looked up from her hands, her mouth slightly open like she couldn't fathom what she saw.

"You kept them." It was more of a statement than a question.

"Yeah," I whispered.

"But why?"

I swallowed the lump in my throat. "Because I missed you."

Her lips quivered, and she set them on the bed beside her.

"I guess I kind of disappeared, didn't I?"

I nodded again, but the truth was, I didn't blame her. I'd disappeared, too, and only pieces of me could be found in a locked bedroom.

"It's especially hard this time of year," she told me, uncharacteristically honest. "I came in here looking for one of his Christmas singles. I thought it was on a thumb drive in the drawer."

"You wanted to hear him sing?" I asked, astonished.

She nodded. "I come in here when I miss him. Sometimes I lay on his bed, and I play one of his albums. It makes me feel close to him."

How could I have not known that?

"Me too," I admitted.

She patted the mattress beside her. "Come here. I need to tell you something."

Madam Plunkett lay curled in a neat ball, and I gently pushed her aside and sat on the mattress.

My mother cleared her throat. "I need you to promise to listen and try not to hate me when I'm done."

I'd prepared myself for this speech. Here it comes – the talk I'd been avoiding.

"Okay, I promise."

I closed my eyes and drew my knees into my chest, preparing myself for the blow as I heard her say: "Your father and I are getting a divorce."

My eyes snapped open. "What?"

She nodded sadly. That wasn't what I expected.

I sighed. "I guess I'm not surprised." But I needed more. It was time to know the whole truth, no matter how painful. "Is it because of Adam?" I asked carefully, staring at my hands.

"Yes," she whispered, and I felt something inside of me sink. "But not in the way that you probably assume."

That got my attention, and I met her eyes.

She pulled her phone from her pocket, typed on the screen, and handed it to me.

"What's this?" I asked, taking it from her.

"You'll see. Just read."

I scanned the document and reread it, glued to where she had written her name.

"This is a…." I trailed off.

"A birth certificate," she answered.

I cut my eyes to her. "Wait, this means…"

"Yes," she said. "Adam is my son."

There was a ringing in my ears, and my vision blurred.

"Your son," I parroted. "How?"

"What do you mean, 'how?' I'm pretty sure you know how it works."

I bit back a surprised chuckle, and she smirked. I handed back her phone.

"Okay, yes, but you can't just drop that on me and not give me the details, Mom."

She groaned and lowered herself to the floor, leaning up against the foot of the bed. I watched as she buried her face in her hands. I followed her lead and sat cross-legged next to her.

"Mom," I tried again, touching her shoulder. "Please, tell me."

She sighed. "Okay," she relented. "I'm not proud of it, though."

"Trust me, I have no room to speak. My own judgment's been pretty crappy lately."

"Okay," she said again.

Then she told me the story. She was in college, barely eighteen, and her roommate dragged her to a concert. They met up with some guys her roommate knew; among them was Adam's father. He was a grad student at Brown and was as handsome as he was brilliant. She was flattered he was interested. She thought she was in love, but he had a fiancée she knew nothing about. She found out she was pregnant, and he begged her to keep quiet. His family was wealthy, so she was paid for her silence. His aunt had always wanted to have children but couldn't. She agreed to adopt the baby as long as my mother disappeared, and she did, but Adam found her. He'd called her a year ago, and that's how this whole thing started.

378

After she was done explaining, I gaped at her. "Mom," I said slowly. "None of that is your fault. You didn't know…."

"I kept seeing him, Rylen," she said, cutting me off. "I knew he had a fiancée and…" she shrugged. "It was wrong, but I didn't care. I thought I loved him and kept expecting he'd choose me. And when he didn't, my only choice was to take the money. It's how I paid for law school." She broke eye contact and looked at the floor. "I sold my own son."

"You didn't sell him, Mom," I retorted. "You gave him the chance of a better life. Dad wanting a divorce is unfair."

She smiled weakly. "I'm flattered that you're sticking up for me, but I never told your father the whole story. It was a lie of omission."

And there it was again – the virtue of honesty like it was cloaked in gold, but it had to be whole and courageous if it was ever going to be worth anything. Jack's face flashed before my eyes.

"I don't have a good reason for not telling him. I was embarrassed, and I feared his judgment. He can be judgmental sometimes."

That was true, too. My mind wandered to his recent email. Gregory Clark took it upon himself to tell instead of asking, to judge instead of understanding. How often did he pass his judgment upon Michael's desire for a music career?

And now Michael was gone.

"But you didn't mean to lie," I said, my voice quivering. "Can't he understand you were just scared?"

"Honey," she said, reaching out to pat my knee. "It's more complicated than that. We've been having problems for years."

I sighed, a new thought dawning on me. "Why did Adam come to the fundraiser?"

"He did that without me knowing. He wanted to support your brother's death but didn't tell me he was coming."

Oh, that made more sense. When she saw him there, she had a look of genuine surprise. She hadn't expected him.

I sighed, wiping away a tear.

"Why didn't you tell me, though?" I asked, but I already knew the answer. I'd made it impossible for her.

"I tried to," she whispered. "It's hard to open your soul to someone who hates you."

"I don't hate you, Mom," I said. "I've never hated you. I missed you. After Michael died, I think there was a piece of me that felt like you blamed me, or...maybe I just blamed myself."

I had never admitted it aloud before, and the elephant on my chest lifted off of me, and I felt myself breathe again.

Her eyes welled up with tears, and she shook her head.

"I never blamed you, and I am so sorry you felt that way."

Another tear slipped out. We were both crying now.

"I think there was a piece of me that felt like you didn't need me," she said, "You had Andon, and for all of his faults, he took care of you."

I nodded. There was no denying that.

"And you had your dad. You've always favored him. He suffocated your brother, and we lost him. I guess my efforts to give you your space were interpreted as if I didn't care, and I'm sorry for that, too."

Sitting in Michael's bedroom, the pile of sticky notes revealing everything said between us, my mother hugged me, and I sobbed into her shirt while she kissed my forehead. I murmured that I was sorry. I'd misjudged her. I'd misunderstood her. And with her arms around me and her breath in my hair, it was as if she'd reach inside of me and held my aching heart – soothing it, putting it back together, and I finally believed everything would be okay.

I broke the hug, as she spoke again.

"Do you know what I haven't had in a long time?"

"Great sex?"

"No, you weirdo!"

I snickered, and she shook her head.

"What is wrong with you?"

My shoulders shook with an inaudible cackle, and she tried to stop it, but a laugh escaped her, and she slugged my shoulder.

She cleared her throat. "I was going to say pancakes."

"Pancakes," I repeated gleefully. "That sounds great."

"We never did make it to Sally's," my mother said regretfully.

I bit my lip. "Sally's burned down during the lightning storm."

"I know. I was going to see if you wanted to go there when I texted you the other day."

My heart squeezed. My phone buzzed when I was with Ned. My mother had sought me out to spend time with me, but I was unavailable.

She got to her feet, and I followed her lead. Then she was down the hall and, on the stairs, taking them two by two until she got to the kitchen. She reminded me of a child heading to the tree on Christmas morning, eager to see what Santa had left.

I turned on Michael's Christmas single, and her eyes glowed as she cracked eggs into a sizzling skillet. We made enough pancakes to feed the entire county. I made coffee, and she sliced strawberries. I set the table, she whipped some cream, and then we sat across from each other and ate until neither of us could hold another bite.

"Okay, I got one for you," she said, cutting her pancake into a bite-sized square. "What do you call a fish without an eye?"

I thought for a moment. "I don't know."

"A f-sh." She giggled, and I laughed despite the corny joke. My mother had returned, and I wanted to enjoy every second.

"I got one for you. What do you call an octopus that goes into battle?"

"What?" she asked, her eyes glowing.

"Well-armed."

She chuckled. "Who told you that one?"

"Jack," I answered.

Saying his name broke the spell. It muted the light-hearted banter between us. She became serious and crumbled her napkin into a ball.

"You know, it was hard for me when you and Andon broke up. Juanita and I are such good friends, and I thought you two would go to college together."

"I did too," I whispered. "He was everything to me."

"I have no room to judge Ali." She shook her head. "I was no better than her, but what she did was wrong."

"You're nothing like Ali, Mom," I declared. "That's an unfair comparison."

"I was exactly like Ali, Rylen, but not anymore," she amended. "And for what it's worth, I'm sorry she put you through that."

My mind wandered to the past, and I wondered if she was only apologizing to me or also to another woman, from a different life, who'd been engaged to the man my mother loved. She'd willingly slept with that woman's fiancé, and though the blame was only partially hers, maybe an apology to me would float among the stars above us and find its way to her; wherever she was.

"I don't think I believed you and Andon were over it until I caught you upstairs with Jack." Her mouth curved into a grin, and she giggled at the memory. "I thought you'd picked up a hitchhiker."

I laughed at that. "He was a little scruffy, wasn't he?"

"He was," she said. "But he was handsome too. I saw him at the fundraiser chasing after you."

"You did?"

She nodded. "I barely recognized him. You seemed so happy when you were with him. Want to tell me what happened there?"

I sighed. "It's a long story." I fidgeted with a string on the tablecloth.

"I already refilled my coffee." She lifted her mug and took a slow drink. "Tell me what happened, sweetie."

I told her the whole story, starting with the mud puddle and ending with our fight in front of the hospital.

"Then he blurted that he was in love with me," I explained. "But I walked away. I haven't talked to him since."

She looked at me quizzically. "And you don't believe him?"

"Would you? Would you believe anything that came out of this mouth?"

"Yes," she said quickly, and I was taken aback. "It was obvious, Rylen. He would've given you the moon and all the stars had you just asked."

I gave her a shy smile, and she put her hand on mine.

"Honey, I am the last person who should be giving relationship advice, but lately, I've learned that if you expect him to be honest with you, then in return, you need to be honest with him and tell him how you feel."

How did she know what I felt? Could she see what I've tried to keep hidden?

"It doesn't matter how I feel anymore," I countered.

She squeezed my hand. "Of course it does."

"Even if I could forgive Jack, I'd never be able to trust him again. I'd always have doubts."

She pulled her hand back. "Do you have any doubts about me?"

I cut my eyes to her. "You're my mom. You made a mistake."

"So did Jack," she said. "And is his mistake worth throwing away your entire relationship? What if it were you? If you make a mistake in the future, would you want him to walk away?"

My jaw wobbled. "No."

Why would trusting Jack be any different if I could trust her again?

She smiled weakly. "Rylen, I'm not saying it's easy, but loving someone is loving every piece of them – the good with the bad. It's not a question of whether I can live with the bad; it's, can I live without the good? And when you love someone, that doesn't mean they'll never hurt you. We're imperfect people with imperfect love; getting hurt just happens. Then you have to make a choice. Do you forgive him and give him another chance, or do you choose to let him go? But whatever you decide, you have to be all in. To love and forgive means doing it completely."

My mother was no longer a stranger. *This* was the woman I remembered.

Smart, loving, and wise – I knew deep down that this was who she'd always been, and who she'd always be.

The problem was I didn't know if I could do it. Was I strong enough to love someone entirely and accept the unlovable things about them?

"Mom," I said, my voice wavering. "I think I'm in love with Jack."

She nodded, clearly unsurprised by my admission. "Yeah, sweetie, that was obvious, too."

Chapter Thirty-Three

Rylen

When we finished our pancakes, she insisted that I help her decorate the tree. I couldn't help the smile that spread across my face. We'd usually have the housekeeper put up our decorations, but I was more than happy to help. I climbed a ladder, and she handed me ornaments. I spread them out, decorating the front, the back, and the sides. We worked quickly, hanging and stringing, giggling when she found a salt clay angel I'd made when I was four.

Then we popped popcorn and refilled our cocoa, and I couldn't remember the last time I'd spent the entire afternoon with her and thoroughly enjoyed myself.

"I don't think I've done this since I was a kid," I said, reaching for more kernels.

Stringing popcorn was more challenging than it looked. The tree twinkled in the corner of the living room while Mom and I planted ourselves on the sofa. The newest Grinch movie played on the flat screen, but it was muted, and a fire roared in the fireplace across from us. Madam Plunkett was curled in a ball on the other side of my mother.

"I don't know why we quit doing it," my mother said, her eyes on her fingers.

I watched her pick up a piece and wiggle the needle gently into the center until the white puff slid down the line. Meanwhile, I'd managed to crunch the last three puffs into tiny bits that speckled my socks and the carpeting around me.

"I'm glad we put up the tree," I said.

I tied a tiny knot at the end of my string and gathered the line in one hand like a lasso.

She inhaled and took in our surroundings, seeming sad.

"This will be our last Christmas in this house. I wanted to do something we used to do. I wanted to feel normal."

She must've sensed me gaping at her, and she met my eyes.

"Are you selling the house?" I asked quietly.

"Yes," she replied. She tied off her string and set it on the couch beside her. "We don't have any final agreements, but your dad doesn't want it, and I assume you'll go to college next fall. And it's too big for one person. It makes sense."

"It does, but is that what you want?"

She thought momentarily, and I watched her throat bob before answering.

"It is. I could travel more and get a smaller place away from the city. You'd have a room, of course." A smile stretched across my face, and her eyes glowed. "If you want?"

"I'd love that, but I was thinking about getting a dog."

Madam Plunkett lifted her head from between her paws, her whiskers prickling with worry.

"A dog?" My mother parroted. She scrunched up her nose as if I'd said I was getting a poo flinging monkey.

I grinned and scooted closer to her. "Please, you'll need company while I'm in class."

"You aren't leaving for school?"

It was normal for her to assume that. That'd been the plan all along – to live my own life with Andon and to leave all this in the dust. But my plan had changed, and I was all right with that.

I shook my head. "No, I thought I'd enroll at Davenport Community and take you up on the part-time job. If the offer's still on the table?"

She smiled softly and tucked her knees beneath her. "I'd like that, but these are some big decisions. What about photography school?"

I shrugged. "It will always be there." I'd just gotten her back and didn't want to leave so soon. "I thought I could freelance on the side, but I wanted to see what the law world was like. Maybe we could be a team."

She smiled. "Let's not get ahead of yourselves, but if you're sure, I can ask my assistant to email you an application. And I'll think about the dog, okay?"

"Okay."

I watched her as she reached for her coffee mug and brought it to her lips.

I bit the inside of my cheek. There was no easy way to bring up what I had to tell her.

"I should probably mention that Dad asked me to come to Cancun for Christmas."

Her eyes widened, and she swallowed her cocoa.

"Do you want to go?"

"Yes and no. I don't want to leave you, unless you're going to go to the spa until Jan 2nd?"

She arched her brows. "Am I that predictable?"

I shrugged. "Kind of."

She stared at her cocoa and swirled it like it was fine wine. "I let our family fall apart, didn't I?"

"But it wasn't your fault."

"Rylen, please, it *was* my fault. I let grief suffocate me." She paused and put her cocoa on the coffee table. She lifted her knee onto the sofa's seat and turned towards me. "Since Adam has been in my life, I've started reevaluating what's important." She covered my hand with hers, and the warmth I felt wasn't only from the cocoa. "I'm sorry that it's taken him finding me to make me see you. I'm sorry that I abandoned you. I don't want to do that anymore. Adam invited me to come to Milwaukee for Christmas."

"He did?" I didn't even consider that Adam would be involved with our holidays, but I guess it made sense.

She nodded. "But I wasn't going to go. I wanted to spend Christmas with you."

She'd apologized for not being there, for letting her grief get the best of her, and I'd been no better than her. But her son had found her, and though nothing could replace Michael, I wanted her to be happy. I wasn't going to let the past ruin our future.

"Can I go too?" I blurted. "I mean, I owe him a huge apology, and I know it's rude to invite myself, but...I want to be with you." It was another great truth, and her hand squeezed mine.

"He already invited you," she said, unable to hide the glee in her voice.

He'd invited me after I'd been horrible to him. And it dawned on me that while she had a son, I had a brother, and Adam was somebody I needed to get to know – somebody I needed in my life.

"His wife is having a baby sometime in January."

"Wait! He's married?"

She nodded.

"That means you're going to be a granny!"

"Do *not* call me granny?" She grabbed the couch pillow next to her and flung it into my face.

I laughed and smacked it away, about to retaliate with "granny, granny, granny," but her phone buzzed, and she dug into her cardigan pocket.

"Juanita is calling me," she said, staring at the screen. "I'll call her back." She pressed the decline button and stashed her phone.

Then my phone rang, and I lifted the screen to see Andon's picture staring back at me.

"Now Andon's calling me," I said, perplexed.

A concerned look flashed in my mother's eyes, and worry washed over her.

"Answer it," she said quickly.

I took the call on speakerphone.

"Andon…. hi," I said.

"Rylen," he croaked. His voice sounded different, deeper, and desperate. It took me a moment to realize he was crying. "Please, don't hang up. It's Ali. Oh God…." His words came out quickly and jumbled in hysterics.

"Andon, calm down," I said again. "What's going on?"

"It's Ali," he said slowly. "She's…she's bleeding, and I don't know what to do."

"Andon, honey, it's Diana," my mother said. "How many weeks is she?"

"Twelve," he replied. "She's twelve weeks today."

"Okay, where are you right now?" she asked.

He sniffled. "I'm at the hospital. They're going to run a bunch of tests. They won't let me see her." He took in a breath. "There was so much blood. God, I've never seen blood like that."

"Are you alone?" Diana asked.

"Yes, I called my parents, but they're picking up my sister at college," he whimpered.

"We'll be right there," I said, and my mother nodded.

"Thank you," he said, relieved. "I don't know what I'll do if anything happens to them."

I hung up the phone, and my mother was already grabbing her keys.

§oc~ɔo§ §oc~ɔo§ §oc~ɔo§

I'd been spending a lot of time at the hospital lately, and my chest started to ache when my mother pulled into the parking lot. The last time I was here…. I pushed the memory away. Gathering the coffee, I'd picked up at Starbucks, I opened the door and walked inside, my mom by my side.

Inside the lobby, I spotted Andon wearing a white baseball cap, sitting in the corner with his knees up. His head was bowed, and he buried his face in his arms.

"I'll be over here if you need me," my mom whispered. I nodded thanks, and I made my way to him.

"Hey," I said gently.

He lifted his head. His eyes were pink and swollen, and his nose was crusty, and red. Paint was on his cheek and smeared on his forehead.

"Hazelnut, right?" I asked, offering him the latte.

His brows rose, but he smiled weakly and took it from my hand.

"Thanks," he said.

"No problem." I sat on the floor next to him, hugging my knees to my chest. "I'd ask if you were okay," I began. "But it's clear that you're not."

He shook his head. "I feel so helpless. We were in the middle of a project…." He gestured to the paint covering his fingers and the splotches on his wrist. "And then..." he shrugged. "She just started gushing blood...." He stopped again, fresh tears spilling down his cheeks.

"Don't think about it," I told him.

He leaned his head against the wall behind him.

"What if she has a miscarriage? That happened to my mom, you know? After my sister."

"You're not helping yourself by getting all worked up."

He sniffled, nodding weakly.

"Thank you for not hanging up on me," he said. "I didn't have anyone else to call."

It never occurred to me that Andon had experienced loneliness, too. But all of his friends were at college, and he'd taken a job at his father's truck shop. He had Ali, and I had Jack, but that was it. We were more alike than I realized.

"You're a good friend to me, Ry." He patted my knee. "I know, I don't deserve it."

I shrugged. "No one should go through this alone."

"Ali and I broke up," he stated. He lifted his coffee and took a small sip.

"Oh." I tried to sound surprised. "I'm sorry to hear that."

He shrugged. "It was mutual. We're still friends. I'm helping her with the baby's room, and I'll be there when the baby is born." He looked at the carpet between us. "The thing is, she said the same thing you said at the fundraiser. About how I was using you as an excuse."

His gaze traveled to me, and I bit my lower lip. "I was so nasty to you. I'm very sorry."

"Don't apologize. You were right."

I could feel him staring at me, and I looked into his eyes – those dark brown circles I'd met so many years ago. My entire world used to start in those eyes, where I could get lost and be found at the same time.

"I knew we were over the moment Ali, and I got together. I'll never regret anything more, but I knew it was too late for you and me. Then Ali got pregnant, and I've never been more terrified." He paused and sipped his coffee. "I didn't want to be a father," he admitted. "You knew it. Ali knew it. I didn't want any of this. But now, I'm terrified that I'll lose him."

My ears pricked. "Him?" I repeated, and a lump grew in my throat.

Andon tried to smile, his eyes shining with delight. "Him." He said again.

Then it dawned on me: the paint on his face and hands was blue. They'd been painting the baby room.

"We had a blood test to confirm it. I have a son. At least, I think I do." He bowed his head again. "I let myself get excited."

"You do have a son," I insisted, shaking his shoulder. "And he has you as a father. That's something to be excited about."

He scoffed, lifting his head to speak. "Kid better run for the hills if he knows what's good for him."

"That's not true. You aren't defined by bad choices, Andon."

He shrugged, unconvinced.

"Listen to me. After Michael died, you stood by my side and drove me anywhere I wanted. You didn't treat me like the girl with the dead brother; you were my friend, and I loved you for it. Honestly, that was the part that hurt the worst – losing my friends."

He met my eyes again.

"After I cheated on you, my father wouldn't look at me for months. He told me he's never been more ashamed of me."

Harvey was a man of few words, so if he'd told Andon something like that, it meant the shame went deep.

"At first, it didn't bother me. Who gives a shit what he thinks, right? But then, I saw the baby's heartbeat, and something changed; it became real for me." He wiped his face with the back of his hand, and I felt my jaw quiver under the threat of tears. "I wanted to coach Peewee soccer and take off his training wheels. I wanted him to make the honor roll and teach him how to rebuild an engine. I wanted to watch him walk across the stage and graduate, and I'd never be prouder."

He turned to look at me, and his eyes glistened with unshed tears.

"I'm so sorry, Ry," he whispered. "Can you ever forgive me?"

This time, there were no excuses or unwillingness to take the blame. He'd owned his choices and admitted his mistake, and though he'd apologized before, out of them all, this one meant the most.

This one felt real.

My hand found his on the carpet, and I embraced him. He rested his forehead on my shoulder, and I felt him relax as I heard my voice say: "I forgive you, Andon." Though I'd believed I'd forgiven him before now, this time, it was different for me too.

We stayed like that until he laid his temple on my shoulder. Then he fell asleep, and I watched his chest steadily rise and fall, knowing the relief he must've felt. An hour passed before the doctor came out, and I gently shook him awake.

"Are you Andon?" The white coat asked, looking him up and down.

"Yes," he said, getting to his feet. "How is she? How's my son?"

The doctor removed the mask from his face and adjusted his glasses. My mother set aside her magazine, and we stood beside Andon.

"I'm Dr. Chavez. Ali has lost a lot of blood. She'll need a transfusion, and we'll have to keep her overnight to keep an eye on her."

"Okay," Andon said, confusion perched over his eyebrows. "What about the baby?"

"She'll be having an ultrasound soon. If her cervix begins to dilate, unfortunately, a miscarriage is likely. She's not quite out of the woods yet."

"Okay," Andon rasped, and his jaw wobbled. Diana wrapped her arm around his shoulder and hugged him tight.

"She's asking for you. Would you like to see her?" The doctor asked.

He nodded and was about to follow the doctor through the swinging doors when I reached for his hand.

"Can I see her?" I asked hopefully.

"Sure," he said. He settled in a chair next to my mom, and I followed the doctor down the fluorescent-lit hallway, the monitors and machines humming all around me.

The last time I'd spoken to Ali was at the dress shop. I'd been awful to her. I was hurt and angry, but I never wanted this to happen. Even if she had no desire to see me or sent me away the moment I walked in, I at least had to tell her as much.

"Right through here," the doctor said, pointing to a sliding door with a closed curtain.

"Thanks."

I hesitated, my palms growing clammy. I didn't know how to say all she needed to hear, and maybe she'd never believe me, but I opened that door and pulled back that curtain.

I could hear my heart pounding against my ribs when we locked eyes. And her brows rose with genuine surprise. I was the last person she expected to see, but then a slight smile touched her lips, and I let out the breath I'd been holding.

"Hey," I said softly.

"Rylen? What are you doing here?" she asked.

I closed the door and took a few steps towards her. She was dressed in a hospital gown, and her legs were covered with white blankets.

"Andon called me. So, my mom and I came."

Confusion wrinkled her eyebrows. "Why? Why would you come?"

Words evaded me as I searched her face. Dark circles hung beneath her eyes, and they were red and puffy. She'd been crying, and it hit me that while I'd been dealing with my own anger and grief over losing Jack, Ali had been through the same thing with Andon.

Jack was right. Grief was universal and personal at the same time.

"Because I didn't want you to be alone."

I couldn't avoid looking at her any longer, and when I met her gaze, small tears were pooled in the corners of her eyes.

"I hope it's okay that I'm here. I can go if..."

"No!" she snapped. "Stay. I've missed you."

I pulled a stool closer to the bed and sat by her side. "It's going to be okay." I had no idea if that was so, but I would stay as long as she wanted me to.

She nodded, letting out a deep breath. "I'm so scared, Rylen. What if he doesn't have a heartbeat?"

"Don't think about that."

"Or he does have a heartbeat and grows up and realizes how shitty his mother is."

"You're going to be a great mom, Ali. Give yourself some credit."

She pinched the space between her eyes and shook her head. "How can you even say that?"

"Because you had a great mom, and she taught you everything."

She lowered her hand and bit her lower lip. "Oh God, I wish she was here."

My hand found hers on the mattress, and I squeezed tightly.

Sharon.

Beautiful Sharon.

Who got pregnant with Ali at age seventeen but was determined to raise her on her own. Who couldn't cook worth beans but made the best cream cheese brownies you ever tasted.

Sharon.

Who was more of a best friend than a mom and joined our girl's nights wearing hideous flannel pajamas.

Who insisted that orange soda and caramel popcorn belonged together. Ali and I thought it was disgusting, but now I couldn't have one without the other.

Sharon.

Who laughed so hard she was silent. Who loved black-and-white movies, Sean Connery, and Gerber Daisies. Who was never on time for anything but always remembered your birthday.

Who never got angry about anything. Even when we broke her set of crystal candlesticks while playing soccer in the house, even when she caught us sneaking out to meet the boys. She never did tell my mom.

Sharon.

Who told us she had stage four breast cancer and held Ali and me against her bosom while we sobbed. Who battled the illness with more bravery than a gladiator but lost the war.

And took a piece of me with her when she went.

"I miss her too," I said hoarsely.

"You're the one person on this earth who loved her as much as I did," she said.

I couldn't speak, so I nodded. I did love her. She'd called me her second daughter and always referred to me as "Rylen Love."

"Which is why I don't understand why you weren't at the funeral."

My lips quivered, my throat so tight I could barely speak. "Because I'm a coward. I got ready to go, but I couldn't do it. I wasn't brave enough."

She shook her head. "You're the bravest person I know."

"I'm not, though. Your mom deserved better. I should've been there for you. Instead, I was so wrapped up in myself that I became a victim."

Her face fell. "I'm sorry I said that."

"Don't be," I shrugged. "It's true. I let grief suffocate me."

It was no different than spending Christmas at a spa until January 2nd.

"I shouldn't have been angry at you for not coming. I should've been more understanding, but I *needed* you. You always had this way of making things better. You could always make me laugh."

I grinned. "Remember when I told you if you pooped and peed at the same time, you'd die?"

She let out a laugh, and it sounded as if it'd come up from the tips of her toes.

"Oh my God," she said between chuckles. "I'll never forget that. For weeks, I was so careful. Remember when Billy Fleckenstein…"

"Fuckenstein," I amended.

Her eyes gleamed. "…told the whole seventh grade I kissed like a guppy."

I giggled. "You should have gone home after your dentist appointment."

"I couldn't miss your birthday party. Though seven minutes in heaven quickly became seven minutes in hell."

I nodded. "Remember when Andon…." But I stopped, and we met one other's eyes, each of us knowing the reminiscing was over. The merriment was gone because we were still in this place where the past had hindered all hope of a future.

"It's my fault, Rylen. I had feelings for Andon for years, but I pushed them away because he was your boyfriend and…"

"It doesn't matter anymore, Ali."

"It does matter. I was a horrible friend." She dropped her eyes to the bedding before speaking again. "I was a mess after the funeral, and he gave me a ride home, and I kissed him, and…I was angry that you weren't there, but I swear, I didn't do it to punish you. I'm not trying to make excuses, but I couldn't bear to think no one on earth loved me anymore."

Sharon was an only child, and Ali never knew her father or grandparents. So, when her mother left this world for the afterlife, Ali had lost everything.

Including me – the one person who was supposed to withstand it all.

"I'm sorry I wasn't there for you. I've regretted it every day since."

She met my eyes, smiling softly, those deep jade pools full of wonder.

"There aren't enough words in existence to tell you how sorry I am. Nothing was worth losing you."

"Or you," I said.

"I know it's a lot to ask, and I understand if you say no, but do you think we could ever be friends again?"

I chewed my lip. "I don't know, but I'm here now."

Her lower jaw quivered, and she blinked as fresh tears spilled. She squeezed my hand, telling me she couldn't find the words to say, but I got the message. We'd always have a scar, but eventually, it wouldn't hurt anymore. I could choose not to let the past dictate my future.

I put my other hand on top of hers and held on tight because, this time, I wasn't going to let anything rip us apart.

Chapter Thirty-Four

JACK

I walked down the stairs to where my Bronco was parked in the middle of the barn. I was leaving in the morning, though I would've been gone sooner had the fuel pump not gone out a few weeks ago. I laid on my back, the roller beneath me, and pushed myself under. Pieces of rust and dirt from the underside fell into my face. I loosened a bolt to drop the fuel tank.

There were footsteps on the barn floor, and Bam Bam whined, the tags on his collar clinking together as he got to his feet.

"Stay down, boy. Jacky?" It was Gran's voice. I hadn't seen her all day.

I stopped cranking. "Yeah?"

"Come on out. I bought your dinner. Meatloaf."

"Not hungry, Gran," I said, moving to the next bolt. "Just put it on the bench."

"You haven't eaten in three days," she retorted.

I stopped again. So, she'd noticed. Empty M&M bags cluttered the upstairs floor, but I couldn't remember when I'd had real food.

"Gran, I'll eat when I'm hungry. Just leave it there, okay?"

I could see her feet, clad in pink slippers, standing next to the passenger door as if I were in front of her. Her pink bathrobe hung mid-calf; she wore a nightie beneath it.

"Jack, come out here. I want to talk to you."

"I'm busy," I grumbled. "You shouldn't be out here in the cold. Go on inside where it's warm."

I gave the wrench a stiff crank, but it slipped, and I scraped the top of my hand on the underside of the Bronco. Pain radiated up my arm as blood trickled down my sleeve.

"Shit!" I slid out from under it in time to see Gran staring down at me. She put her hands on her hips and shook her head. I got to my feet, cradling my hand.

"Let me see it," she said, grabbing my arm, but I pulled away.

"I got it!" I snapped.

Her eyes widened. "Suit yourself, grumpy ass."

Okay, I deserved that. I didn't mean to be short with her. The only person I was upset with was myself. I grabbed the beer I'd left on the bench and took a long drink.

"I'm sorry," I offered, wiping my mouth on my sleeve. "I haven't slept much."

She'd set the plate on the workbench, and a napkin lay folded under a fork. I took it and pressed it to my wound, wincing at the sting. "You shouldn't be out here. You should be resting."

"Oh, stop fussing over me, Jacky! I'm good as new." She patted the middle of her chest, right over her heart. "Is this what you've been doing out here for three weeks?" She gestured to the Bronco. I'd fixed the broken mirror, and the hood was opened.

"I'm replacing the fuel pump," I said, gathering a first aid kit from the cabinet beneath the workbench.

Gran put her hands behind her back and walked around the vehicle, examining it for further blemishes. "What a convenient distraction for you."

I opened a band-aid with my teeth and stretched it over my hand. "Gran, what do you want?"

She faced me, looking me in the eye, and her stare was so intense I couldn't look away.

"Remember Pop's 35-millimeter camera? The one with the neon green bag?"

I nodded. It happened to be Pop's prized possession; Cora had broken the door that kept the film. She took it to Gran in a panic, afraid that Pop would be angry. Gran gave it to me, and I replaced the spring without him ever knowing Cora had broken it.

"What about it?" I asked.

"You were always good at fixing things."

I ran my fingers over the bandage on my hand. The blood had seeped through.

"I seem to have lost my touch."

She shook her head.

"The dishwasher, the sink, the lawn mower, my sewing machine – there's not much you haven't fixed, Jack."

I finished my beer and tossed the bottle into a nearby trash can; she winced when it hit with a deafening shatter.

"What's your point?" I reached for another.

"How many of those have you had?"

I shrugged, popping the lid.

She snatched the beer from my hand. "This isn't fixing your problem." She slammed it onto the bench, so forcefully the plate jumped. "For someone who knows exactly how to fix everyone else's problems, you're the biggest dumbass when it comes to your own."

"What am I supposed to do?" I barked. "I'm out of ideas here, Gran. So, if you have some crystal ball that tells me how to fix it, I am all ears."

I took the bottle back. To hell with what she thinks.

"Drinking yourself stupid isn't going to magically make it go away, Jack. I certainly won't stand here and watch you destroy yourself!"

She turned to leave, and I should have let her go, but like the dumbass she'd called me, I spoke again.

"Don't worry, you won't have to."

She spun around. Her lips tightened into a straight line, and her eyes took in the Bronco packed with everything I owned; then it dawned on her.

"You're leaving."

I swallowed a gulp of beer, nodding my head.

"Why?" she whispered. "Have you learned nothing?"

I was thirteen when Pop died, but in all of my years of living with her, that was the only time I'd seen her cry. But now, her lips quivered, her jaw wobbled, her face morphing into a look I rarely saw hurt.

"It's better this way," I answered, placing the bottle on the bench.

"Says who?" A tear slipped out.

"There's nothing for me here, Gran."

"I'm here!" She swiped at it. "Does that mean nothing?"

"Of course it does."

"Didn't Sally offer you a job?"

"Gran, I can't stay and watch Rylen move on and forget about me."

Her mouth turned into a weak smile, and a few more tears spilled. "You love her?"

I nodded. "More than anything. I did what you said. I went to the fundraiser. I got the girl. I danced with her. I kissed her; I told her how I felt."

She nodded, her cheeks glistening from spilled tears. "Did you tell her the truth?"

I opened my mouth to say something but closed it, and my defenses slipped away. I bowed my head and leaned against the bench behind me.

"Oh, Jacky," she tsked. She put a wrinkled hand on my shoulder. "None of that matters if you didn't tell her the truth first."

I pinched the bridge of my nose, speaking to the ground. "I was going to tell her. I swear, I was, but it blew up in my face."

"It wasn't an easy thing to say," she acknowledged.

"I should have stayed away. The moment I developed feelings for her."

"You wouldn't have spared her from anything, Jack. Not if she feels the same."

"I guess I'll never know."

I slumped further, and she rubbed my back like I was a kid who'd fallen off a bike.

"Gran, I don't think she'll ever forgive me, and I can't stay here and watch her move on. She's...." I looked around the barn. "Everywhere." Even my attempts to erase her hadn't worked. The memories remained, and I loved and despised them all.

"This is your home, Jack. You can't run away from where you belong."

I scoffed. "I don't know where I belong. My old man always called me a fuck up; maybe he was right."

Suddenly she was moving, standing before me, and she took my face into her hands. Her mystic green eyes bored a hole through me, leaving me open and hollow.

"Don't you ever say that again." She spoke lovingly; her eyes were still warm, but her tone had an edge. "I've given you a lot of slack lately, Jackson Timothy. I know you're processing a lot, but Frank was a sick son of a bitch; I will not stand here and let you believe a lie."

I swallowed the golf ball-sized lump in my throat as her eyes welled with fresh tears.

"We all make choices, and sometimes we don't always get it right, but that has nothing to do with your value, and you're more precious to me than anything."

"Gran." I reached for her hand, but she wasn't finished.

"Some people spend their whole life believing a lie. Your father did, and his father before him. And right now, you have the same choice. You don't have to believe what Frank told you, Jack. You're smarter than that. And if you run away, then you're proving him right. You'll end up just like him. Or you can stay and give yourself the same sort of kindness and forgiveness you'd give to someone else."

She kissed my forehead, and I pulled her tiny frame into my arms. She'd lost weight since the heart attack.

"I can't make any promises," I said hoarsely. "But I'll surely try."

I tried not to hug her too tight. I didn't want to hurt her, but she held onto me fiercely and then announced she was going to bed. She got to the door before she turned and spoke again.

"If you do leave, you'd better not go without saying goodbye. I won't be able to take it this time."

As she opened the door, I could see a streetlight where the road went into a tee. It was between the road to Gran's and the highway. The sky was orange, and the light flicked on and off, unable to decide. It wasn't dark or light; it had no purpose. It had no place to belong.

ౙౘౕఀఄౙ ౙౘౕఀఄౙ ౙౘౕఀఄౙ

It was approaching midnight when I finished repairing the fuel pump. I was putting away my tools when footsteps were outside the barn – the sound of snow crunching under boots. I hadn't heard a vehicle pull in.

Bam Bam sat up, growling low in his throat and padding to the door. I grabbed a pitchfork that leaned up against the wall and crept nearer. I charged around the corner to see a dark hooded figure throwing its hands up in defense.

"Easy! It's me." Cora pulled back the hood on her sweatshirt and stepped into the light. She snorted when she saw the pitchfork. "What were you going to do? Skewer and stack me?"

"You know, sneaking up on people in the dark is a good way to get forked."

She snickered. "Invite me in. It's cold."

I stepped back and stashed the fork. Bam Bam returned to his bed, only interested in our guest if she pulled out a pork chop. Cora walked past me and blew into her hands, rubbing them together. She unzipped her jacket revealing a baby carrier underneath. The Captain lay sleeping on her chest, curled into a tiny ball. She kissed the top of his head and smiled approvingly, then lifted her gaze to me.

"He was discharged yesterday," she said.

"That's great to hear. How is he?"

"He's getting stronger every day."

"I'm glad to hear it."

She tightly nodded and bit her lip uneasily. I wasn't used to seeing a lack of confidence in her, and the silence screamed at me.

"I'd offer you one," I said, lifting my beer. "But I only have one left, and I'm broke."

She smirked. "No, that's okay. I'm sober these days. It's probably best considering…." She trailed off, and a smile tugged at the corner of my lips.

"Yeah, you put on quite a show."

"Really, do you have to say it like that?"

I shrugged. "Calling it the way I see it, sis."

"And how do you see it, little brother?"

I paused and finished the last of the bottle. "You hate me, and not an ounce of me blames you. You're angry, brokenhearted, and devastated, and it's my fault. There's not a damn thing I can do to fix it. Trust me, I tried." She kicked at the dirt floor, and I put the bottle on the bench. "I'd take his place, you know."

"I do know," she whispered, her eyes traveling to my face. "But I don't want that."

"Then what do you want?" I asked.

"Just tell me the truth about something," she said. "Then you never have to see me again."

I nodded. "Lay it on me."

"Sheila told me you held Caleb in the evenings while I worked at the bar."

I couldn't stop the smile that spread across my face. "Caleb?"

Her arms traveled around the baby, and she gazed at him lovingly.

"We always called Pop the Captain, but his first name was Caleb. I guess you inspired me."

I lifted my arm and ran my fingers over the letters of my tattoo. It'd been a memorial to Pop. I had it retouched after I'd held the baby, and the tattoo took on another meaning. Caleb was now the Captain.

"It's a strong name. I've always liked it."

"Me too. Anyways, at first, I didn't believe Sheila. So, I asked Renee, and she said the same thing. Now, I'm asking you. Is it true?"

I shrugged. "He's my nephew, Cora. What do you think?"

She blinked, slightly taken aback by my raw honesty.

"Why would you do that? After the way I treated you?"

"Because I could, and I didn't want him to suffer because you couldn't." The crease between her eyebrows deepened, and I couldn't tell if she was confused or angry. "It was wrong to go behind your back, and I'm sorry, but you already hated me, so what difference does it make?"

I watched Cora exhale, and she took a small step forward. "I don't hate you," she said, a voice wavering. "I thought hating you would make me feel better, but it didn't. I know you've always been there for me, Jack. All those times when Frank would beat on you, I knew you were keeping him away from me."

Shortly after we came to live with Gran, Cora started referring to our father as Frank. He never deserved to be called Dad.

"I didn't want him to hurt you," I said flatly.

"Yeah, but I know you didn't get out unscathed. Then, when Gran demanded that Frank give us to her, and he said he'd only give her one, I know you told Gran to take me."

She'd never told me any of this, and I couldn't deny it. We were ten, and I figured that between the two of us I had a better shot at survival. But it was hell, and Gran managed to save me from Frank's claws anyway.

She looked down at Caleb when she spoke again. "I'm not saying that I forgive you or anything. Losing Hudson still kills me, but I know it wasn't you who turned him in."

I lifted a brow, curious as to how she found out. I hadn't told her what I knew.

"Gran told me she called the police and ratted Hudson out. She was trying to protect me. And you didn't tell me because you were protecting Gran. I'm sorry I blamed you, Jack."

I nodded. "Apology accepted. I know it's not the same, but I'd eat your stew. Even if it tasted like crap, I'd ask for another bowl and tell you how wonderful it was."

She bit back a smile. "People tell me it's delicious. Thank you very much."

"They were lying. You burned the water trying to make pasta."

"I'm working on a veggie recipe."

I grimaced, and she grinned, satisfied that she'd won the exchange.

Cora cleared her throat. "Look, all joking aside. I owe you a lot, and…."

"You don't owe me anything," I said.

"Will you shut up and let me get through this, please?"

"Sorry, continue."

"I think…I could get there if you give me a little more time."

Her eyes were damp, and my throat tightened, so I nodded, but that was all she needed.

"Okay," she breathed.

She walked to the door and pushed it open, but I couldn't let her leave, not yet.

"Hey, do you want to go for a drive?"

She glanced over her shoulder at me, one hand on the handle, surprised at the request.

I put my hand on the hood. "I need to test it anyway. Come with me?"

Her face morphed from shock to delight, and she smiled. "Okay, let me get his car seat."

I slid the barn doors open like a cave into the night and plucked my keys from the workbench.

She climbed inside, strapped in the seat, and then put the baby in the bucket.

"Not too long. I only have a few minutes before the milk monster wakes up," she said, pulling a strap on the buckle.

"Sure," I said, climbing in. "We'll just go to the gas station."

I started the engine and pulled onto the dirt path between Gran's house and the corral. "So, Cora comes back," I said, cruising down the driveway. "She's carrying The Captain. She doesn't drink, and I bet you quit smoking too."

She sighed. "Yeah, I hear they're bad for you."

"Well, so is candy, but that never stopped me."

She chuckled. "Your teeth will rot out of your head, little bother."

"Must I remind you, I'm only younger by three minutes? I suppose there's always a rough draft before perfection."

She feigned surprise. "Is that all? Mom needed all the time she could get before squeezing your big ass head out."

I glared at her, and she stifled a laugh. She looked around the truck in awe.

"How did I not know you had Frank's old Bronco?"

"You were too busy chewin' my ass. You should worry about your own teeth."

She laughed again and slugged me in the shoulder. "You could have mentioned it, you know?"

"I went to see him last year. It's a long story."

I stopped where the road came to a T, waiting for a lone car to pass.

"Well, can you talk and drive?" she asked.

I grinned at her and hit the gas. As I drove down the dirt road back to what I'd run away from, I looked in the rearview mirror to see the streetlight radiantly shining, piercing the night. The darkness seemed to tremble as the light tore through it. And there was no question of where it belonged; no doubt about its purpose.

410

Chapter Thirty-Five

Rylen

"Hi, it's Greg Clark, leave a message after the beep."

I dialed again.

"Hi, it's Greg Clark, leave a message after the beep."

I was determined to talk to him, so I sat on my bed and dialed again, but there was no answer. I sighed; leaving a message would have to do. I stood and walked across the floor.

"Dad, it's Rylen. I've decided I'm staying with Mom for Christmas and umm…." I trailed off, wishing I'd rehearsed something. "I hope you're doing okay." I hung up quickly, but something didn't feel right. I hadn't been honest because there was so much more I had to say – words that ran through my head like breaking news when I should be sleeping. I redialed and waited for the beep.

"Dad, it's me again. I know the real reason why you left, and I think you're being unfair. You're throwing away your marriage

411

because of Mom's mistake. You are all each other has, and Mom's sorry, Dad. You can't just leave when it gets hard. Anything hard is worth fighting for, so fight for what you have. She was afraid to tell you, and you're choosing to punish her, and that's wrong. No one will ever be honest with you if they fear your judgment. No one will ever trust you. And, anyway, I'm staying with her for Christmas, and you should come home. Okay, that's it."

I ended the call and collapsed, spreading out across my bed. My phone vibrated and something within me jumped. I lifted my phone to see a text from Andon saying they'd been discharged. Ali and the baby were going to be fine, and they just had to follow up with the doctor next week.

I let out a long, rejuvenating breath, and texted back that I was glad to hear it, and I would check on them later.

I locked the screen and closed my eyes. Sleep didn't come quickly these days, but I must've dozed off because I dreamed about seeing Jack on the street and running after him. He was leaving the dress shop. I recognized his hat, but I couldn't catch him. There were too many people making their way through the thick crowd. He didn't hear me when I opened my lungs and shouted his name – he only kept walking. Then there were killer bees behind me, chasing me, wickedly laughing that he never loved me; or worse yet, he never knew me.

I jerked myself awake to find my phone buzzing next to my head. I dug through the blankets, searching for it, my mind still hazy with sleep.

"Hello," I said, trying to sound chipper.

"Rylen?" said the voice on the other line, and I was instantly awake.

"Gran?" I said.

"Oh good, it's you. I'm not too sure about these phones without cords."

I chuckled. "Yeah, hi. I was just thinking about you." I sat up and looked around my room – no sign of killer bees.

"I'm sorry to bother you, honey, but I don't know who else to call."

"No, that's okay. What's going on?"

"It's Jack. He's been miserable these past few weeks."

"Yeah," I said, trying to keep my voice even. "It's been rough on me too."

The clock on the nightstand said it was approaching four-thirty. Out the window puffy dark clouds had rolled in, and the sky was gray with the threat of rain. I must've slept longer than I thought.

Gran sighed. "I tried to talk him out of it, but he won't listen. He's too stubborn."

"What are you talking about?" I threw back the blankets and got to my feet.

"I probably shouldn't be telling you this, but his truck was packed last night. I all but got on my knees and begged him to stay. I was hoping you could talk some sense into him."

"He's leaving?" I asked, feeling myself sink.

"He's gone; I can't find him anywhere. He didn't show up at your place, did he?"

"No, he's not here." As the words left my mouth, I realized, despite my anger, that I wanted him to be here. I didn't want him to leave. I didn't want him to disappear and never think about me again.

She sighed again. "Well, you were my first guess, my dear, but there's no telling with Jack. Last time, he disappeared for a year."

"We haven't talked since…." I trailed off. "Since we broke up at the hospital," I admitted.

"Hmm, I've never seen him so upset, but it's not your fault, honey."

"I know, I…."

413

My ears twitched, and I turned my head to the side, lowering the phone.

What was that noise? Something outside?

I raced to the window and threw open the shade.

It was Jack! He was in my driveway.

"Rylen, are you still there, honey?" Gran's voice sounded.

"Gran, I found him. He's in my driveway. I'll call you back."

He was here! He'd come back to me. I ended the call and flew to the stairs, catching a glimpse of myself in the full-length mirror. Was that drool on my cheek? I looked like crap. I darted to the bathroom, stumbling on the jeans I'd shed earlier. I splashed water on my face and pulled my hair up. I tugged on a sweater and stomped into my boots. I flung open the door downstairs, expecting to see Jack waiting for me.

But all I saw was the red taillights of a black Ford leaving my driveway. The snow was dotted with paw prints and boot prints. He'd been a few feet from me only moments ago, but why hadn't he knocked? Why hadn't he barged into my life again?

Something crinkled under my boot, and the corner of a brown wrapper winked at me. I lifted my boot to find a package of M&Ms nestled on the doormat. I went to pick it up, and all I could hear as I held the candy in my hands was a small voice from within my heart revealing a great truth.

Wait. You can't go.

I ran towards the Jeep. I didn't give myself time to think or talk myself out of it. I threw open the door, the hinge groaning from the cold and creaking as it closed. My hands shook as I started the engine. I jammed it into gear and stomped on the gas, but I yelped when the Jeep lurched forward. I hit the brake, trembling as I lifted it into reverse. The tires squealed as I backed out of the driveway and sped onto the road. Maybe he was already miles from here, but I refused to let him slip away. I had to stop him.

Drivers blare their horns and slam their brakes, the tires squealing as I hang a left. I was out of practice, but I didn't dare slow down. I might never see Jack again, and if I got hauled off to prison, I'd plead insanity.

I turned right, banking on my instincts that he'd go to Sally's. Sally's Diner had been running out of a food truck, making to-go orders only. If Jack were leaving, he'd find Sally first and order one last stack of pancakes speckled with M&Ms.

My heart leaped when I saw a black Bronco a few cars in front of me. I changed lanes and laid on the horn, pulling up next to him as the light turned red.

The driver wore a cowboy hat. It was him!

"Jack!" I yelled, opening my passenger window.

I honked again, and he turned his head. His eyebrows curved with surprise as his window slid down.

"Rylen! What are you doing?"

"Wait!" I shouted. "You can't go!"

He was about to answer, but the light turned green, and someone honked behind us. He hit the gas, but I sped in front of him, swerving into his lane. Cranking the wheel, I bounced over a patch of grass, tearing it to muddy shreds, and entered Dr. Sullivan's parking lot. He followed the same path, parking across from me.

I was out of the Jeep and walking toward him before he closed his door.

"Rylen!" he bellowed. He looked above my head to the Jeep. "What the hell are you doing?"

He stood a few paces in front of me. I lifted my eyes to him. There was a light stubble on his face, and his eyes were so steel-blue they were the color of storm clouds. Raindrops trickled off the edges of his hat, and the thrill of seeing him made my heart burst so powerfully that I thought pieces of it might strike him in the chest. And I didn't feel panicky anymore. I was right where I belonged.

415

JEANA R LAWRENCE

"I came all this way, and broke every traffic law imaginable, to tell you that I love you."

A smile pulled at his lips, and those stormy eyes glowed like sunlight behind the clouds.

"I have for a long time, and I know that I was made to love you. If you leave, you have to take me with you because living without you is like living in black and white. You put the color in my world, and I don't want to spend one more second without you."

I dug the M&Ms out of my pocket and opened my hand, holding the package out to him. His smile broadened, affirming he had been on my doorstep.

"I'll never understand your fascination with this candy, but I can't look at them without thinking of you. And no matter what happens to tomorrow, I will always *choose* to love you. Completely. Just as you are."

I waited for him to answer, but sometime in the middle of my speech, his lips thinned, and his smile vanished. I didn't have this part planned out, but wasn't this where he was supposed to scoop me up and start kissing me so uncontrollably the traffic passing by blare their horns?

But he only stood there staring at me in that annoying way of his. His agonizing stillness was harrowing, and it began to gnaw at my resolve.

"Now would be a great time to say something." Thoughts of rejection hit me like a gut punch. I never considered that maybe he didn't want me.

His eyes dropped to the ground. "You're standing in a puddle."

"What? Oh!" I looked at my feet. I was submerged past my ankles, the water sloshing in my boots.

I stepped back, and he followed me, keeping us close.

416

"So, what's their story?" he asked, nodding to his right towards the Jeep parked next to us.

I caught our reflection in the window next to us. He was talking about us. "I bet they met because she was a damsel in distress, and he rescued her," I responded. "From everything."

He smiled so wide it touched his ears.

"His name is Jackson." He cringed. "But he hates being called a last name. So, people call him Jack. For now, he works for his Gran. Her name is Rylen Marie. She hates her common middle name. She's *way* out of his league. He's not sure how he got so fortunate."

I chuckled, smiling shyly as Jack continued. "She's an amazing, witty, talented photographer, and he loves her with everything he's made of."

A warmth washed over me. *This* was our story. When I got to be called Gran, *this* is what we'd tell our grandchildren.

"And she loves him," I said boldly. "More than anything."

His hands traveled around my lower back, drawing me into him. "He knows he messed up."

"She knows too. She chooses to forgive him." My hands slid up his biceps to his shoulders, and my arms wrapped around his neck.

His lips hovered over mine, lightly brushing them while he murmured: "He forgives her."

Then he kissed me, and I knew every ounce of his soul was mine. Drivers of the cars going by honked their horns; they must've known what it looks like to be in love. The way a man kisses a woman when he knows she belongs to him too, and maybe he'll get to kiss her forever; but for this moment, it had to be enough to last a lifetime.

He broke the kiss far too soon and pressed his forehead to mine.

"Who told you I was leaving?" he whispered.

"Gran called me."

"She did?" He pulled his head back.

"Yeah, she said you were packed and leaving town."

He lifted a brow. "Rylen, I told Gran I was going to talk to Sally. She's hiring me to rebuild her diner."

"She is?"

"I just passed the test. You're looking at the new general contractor," he said proudly, eyes beaming.

My gaze traveled to the back window of his truck. It was empty, and Bam Bam was no place to be found.

Gran was sneakier than I ever gave her credit for.

"You mean you're not leaving?"

He shook his head. "I thought about it, but then Sally offered me a job." I nodded, and he shrugged. "I guess...I was holding on to the hope that you could someday forgive me."

"I tried calling you, but I didn't have your new number."

He took my hand and interlaced our fingers. "Well, we can fix that, but you do have to promise me something."

"What's that?"

"Never drive like that again."

I chuckled. "Never leave again, and I won't have to."

He kissed my forehead, hugging me tightly. "Do I dare ask you for a ride? Or am I taking my life into my hands?" he murmured into my hair.

I grinned and nodded towards my ride. "I think I got the hang of it. Get in."

Our doors closed simultaneously, and I cranked the key as he looked about his surroundings.

"Did you get sick while you were driving?" he asked, searching for obvious piles of puke.

"No," I said. "I don't know what happened. I didn't think about it, and even if I did, I didn't want you to leave."

He chuckled. "Gran's very clever."

I nodded. "Yeah. A little too clever."

I put the Jeep in gear and backed out of the parking spot.

"You aren't going to drive into the woods and sacrifice me, are you?" he asked in mock horror.

"Well, we only sacrifice virgins, so…I'm pretty sure you're safe."

"You'd know it, sweetheart," Jack said, his words mixed with laughter.

He reached to adjust the radio, and I dug out my phone and handed it to him.

"Here, you choose the music, but no country."

"No promises." I rolled my eyes as he scrolled through my playlists, nodding approval at rock 'n' roll mixes and oldies.

I stopped where the road came to a T, knowing that this was where it all began, where I began to flourish, and where my world had color again.

"Where do you want to go, Jackson?" I asked, knowing he hated his full name.

His eyes narrowed with playful mirth. "My name's Jack, sweetheart."

I bit my lip to stifle a laugh. "Where do you want to go, *Jack*?"

"I need to find Reynolds and bring him his dinner."

"Let's get him a stack of pancakes at Sally's food truck."

His eyes glowed at my suggestion. "And a milkshake."

"Definitely a milkshake."

As I pulled onto the highway, feeling like I'd driven every day for the last three years, Jack lifted my hand and kissed the back of my knuckles. Then I heard him sing in a low tenor. I'd never heard him sing before, but it crescendoed above the sounds of the radio.

"Do you know what I realized the other day?" I asked.

419

"I haven't seen you in almost a month. I have no idea."

I snickered. "If you and Cora are twins, and you think Cora was an ugly baby. Doesn't that also make you an ugly baby?"

His lips thinned, but his eyes twinkled with amusement. "You're funny, Rylen Clark."

Acknowledgments

They say it takes a village to raise a child—well, I now know it takes a village to write a novel, too. Truly, there isn't enough page space available to fully convey my thanks. To Emily, James, and Andrea, who read and reread and then read again—thank you. I appreciate every moment you spent texting me your thoughts and telling me to write more because you couldn't wait to find out what happens next.

To Veronica, for being the best "everything" editor and cover designer an author could want. You've helped me fulfill a childhood dream, and this book is on the shelf because of your dedication to your clients. You told me I had great potential, and that this book needed to be in the hands of readers. Thank you for loving this story as much as I do. Just so you know, you're stuck with me—this will surely be a lifelong friendship. Besides, you know too much!

To my lovely children: there are pieces of all three of you within these pages. I used your names, your eye colors, your corny jokes. I used the things that made me laugh, and some that made me cry. The character of Jack is a mixture of all your greatest strengths, and I am so proud of the people you are becoming. Thank you for your patience while I made this dream a reality.

And finally, to my mom—the woman who taught me, by example, how to love fiercely yet selflessly. Thank you for teaching me how, and by Whom, we are truly redeemed. And that love is never a question of "can I live with," but rather, "can I live without?"

Please stay tuned for the next installment, where our beloved characters return to face new challenges and discover what fate has in store for them!

www.ingramcontent.com/pod-product-compliance
Lightning Source LLC
Chambersburg PA
CBHW020541120726
47903CB00001B/68